*To Sam, Charissa, and our families,
who make us happy*

Text copyright © 2008 by Mariko Tamaki
Illustrations copyright © 2008 by Jillian Tamaki
Published in Canada and the USA in 2008 by
Groundwood Books
Fourth printing 2009

Groundwood Books / House of Anansi Press
110 Spadina Avenue, Suite 801
Toronto, Ontario M5V 2K4
or c/o Publishers Group West
1700 Fourth Street, Berkeley, CA 94710

We acknowledge for their financial support of our
publishing program the Canada Council for the Arts, the
Government of Canada through the Book Publishing
Industry Development Program (BPIDP) and the Ontario
Arts Council.

ONTARIO ARTS COUNCIL
CONSEIL DES ARTS DE L'ONTARIO

Library and Archives Canada Cataloguing in Publication
Tamaki, Mariko
Skim / by Mariko Tamaki and Jillian Tamaki.
ISBN 978-0-88899-753-1
I. Tamaki, Jillian II. Title.
PN6733.T34S53 2008   741.5'971
C2007-905741-1

Printed on Rolland Opaque, which contains
30% post-consumer waste.
Printed and bound in Canada

SKIM

Mariko Tamaki
AND **Jillian Tamaki**

GROUNDWOOD BOOKS
HOUSE OF ANANSI PRESS
TORONTO BERKELEY

Dear Diary,

Today Lisa said,
"Everyone thinks they are unique."

That is not unique!!

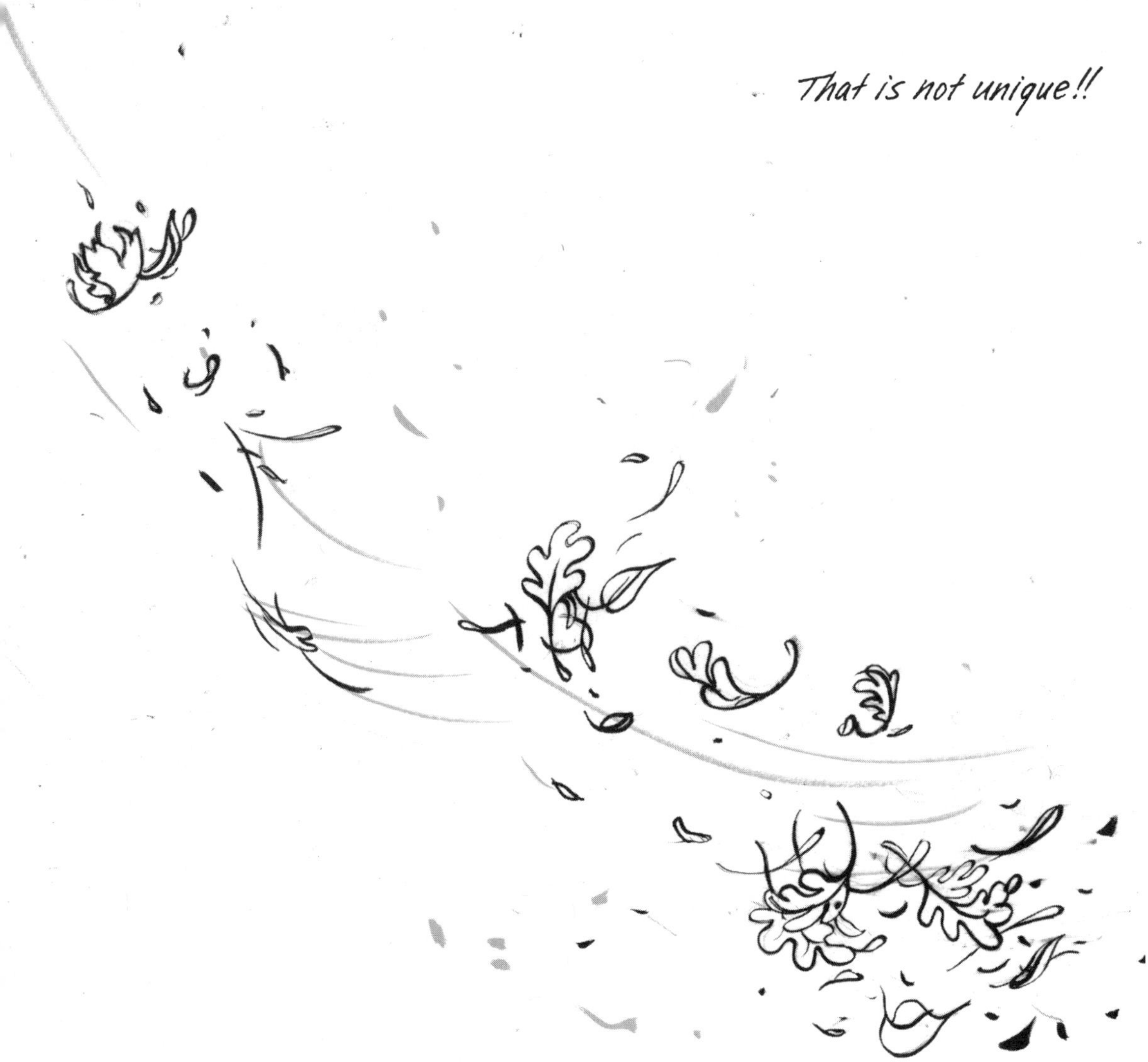

Part I

Fall

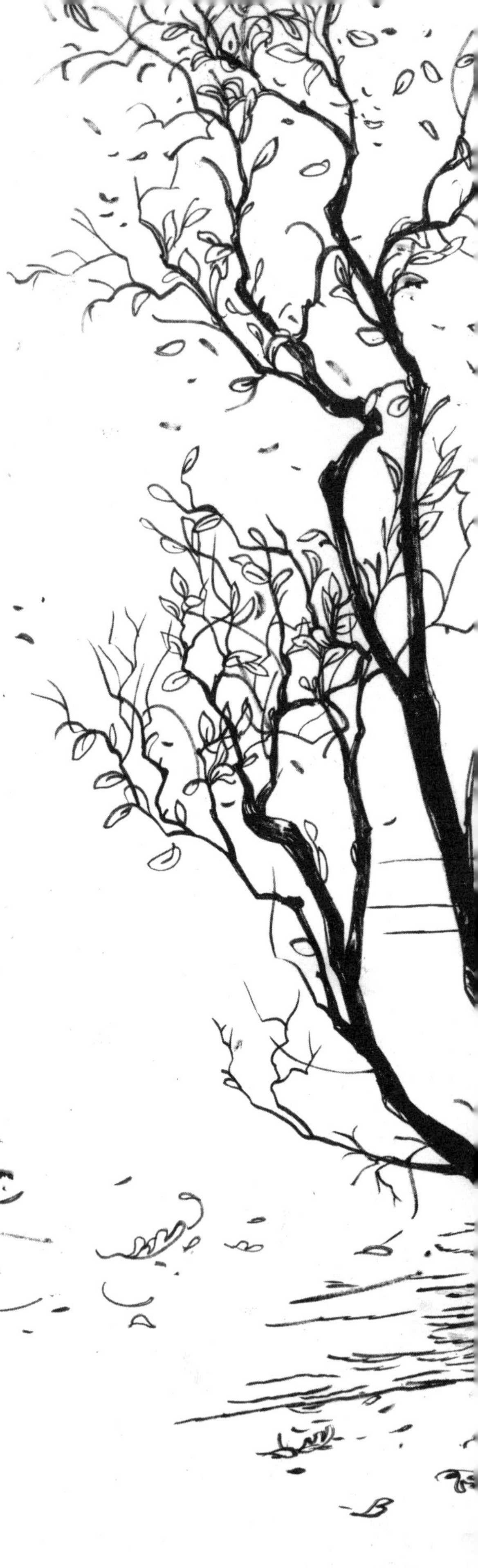

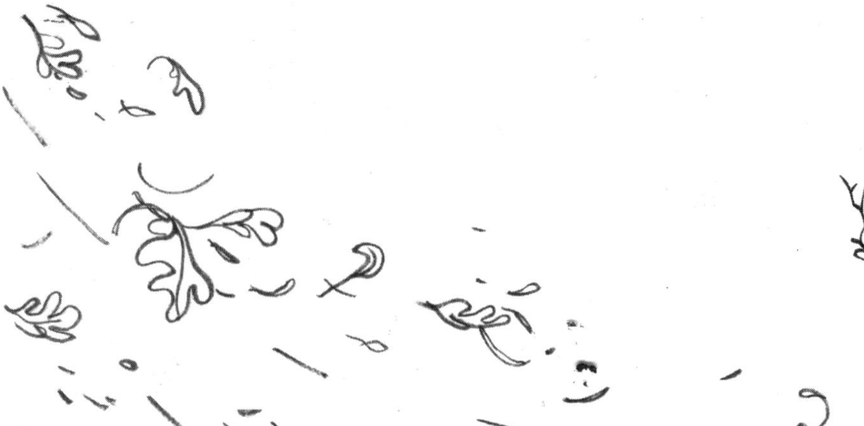

I am: Kimberly Keiko Cameron (aka Skim)

My best friend: Lisa Soor

My cat: Sumo ♡

Interests: Wicca, tarot cards, astrology
(me = Aquarius = very unpredictable), philosophy

Favorite color: ~~black~~ red

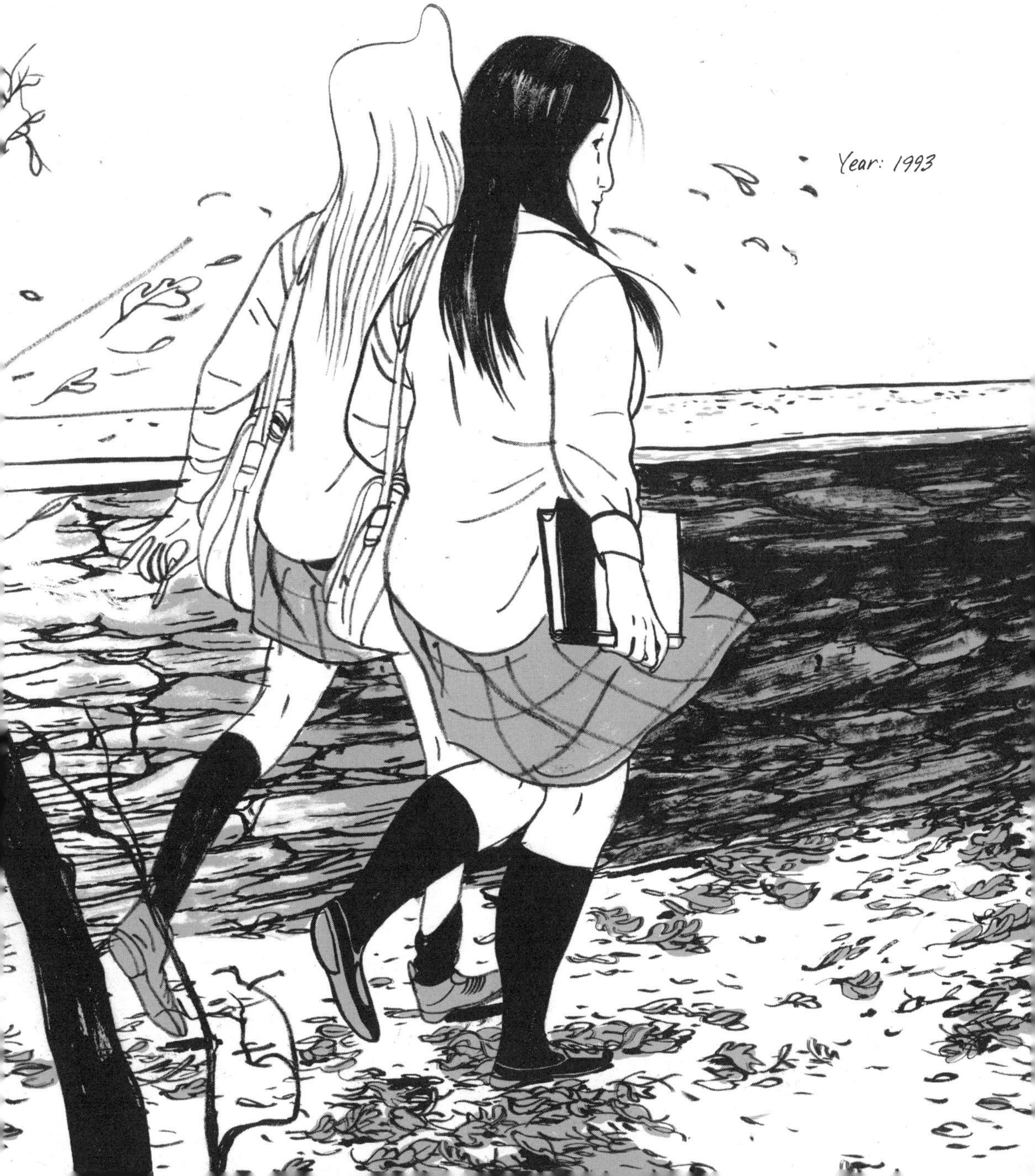
Year: 1993

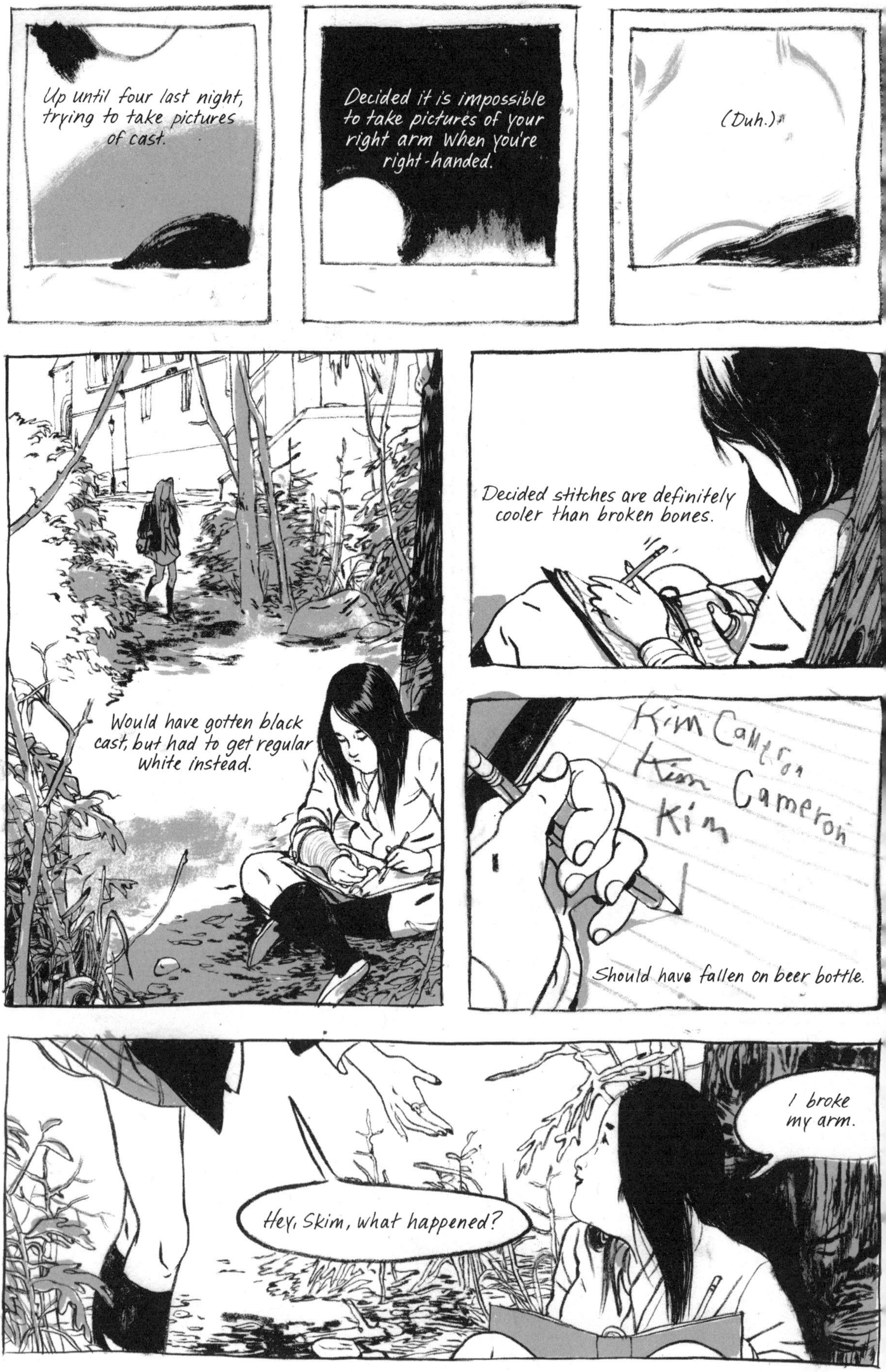

Up until four last night, trying to take pictures of cast.
Decided it is impossible to take pictures of your right arm when you're right-handed.
(Duh.)
Would have gotten black cast, but had to get regular white instead.
Decided stitches are definitely cooler than broken bones.
Kim Cameron
Kim Cameron
Kim
Should have fallen on beer bottle.
Hey, Skim, what happened?
I broke my arm.

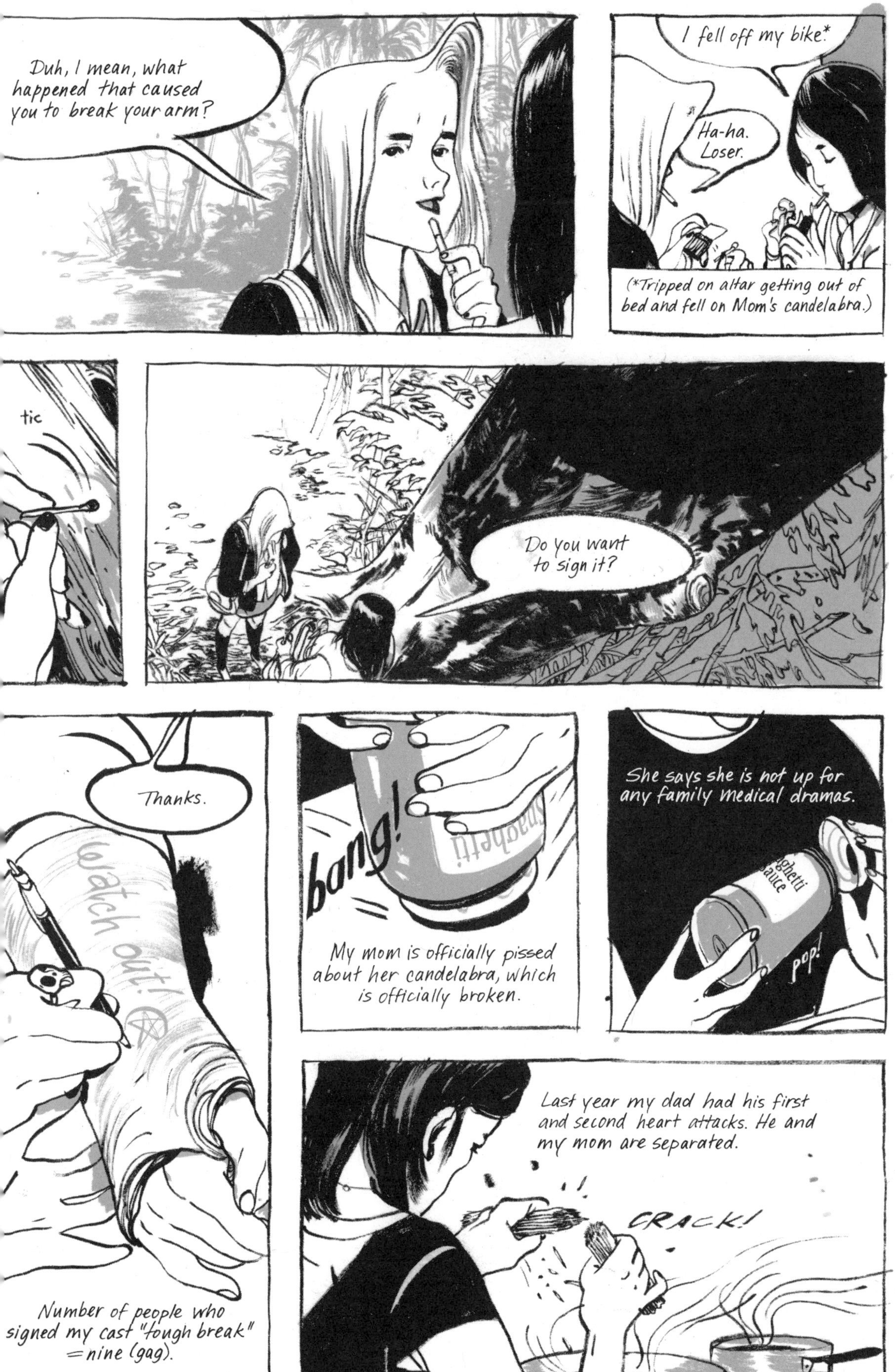
Duh, I mean, what happened that caused you to break your arm?
I fell off my bike*
Ha-ha. Loser.
(*Tripped on altar getting out of bed and fell on Mom's candelabra.)
tic
Do you want to sign it?
Thanks.
Watch out!
Number of people who signed my cast "tough break" = nine (gag).
bang!
Spaghetti
My mom is officially pissed about her candelabra, which is officially broken.
She says she is not up for any family medical dramas.
pop!
Last year my dad had his first and second heart attacks. He and my mom are separated.
CRACK!

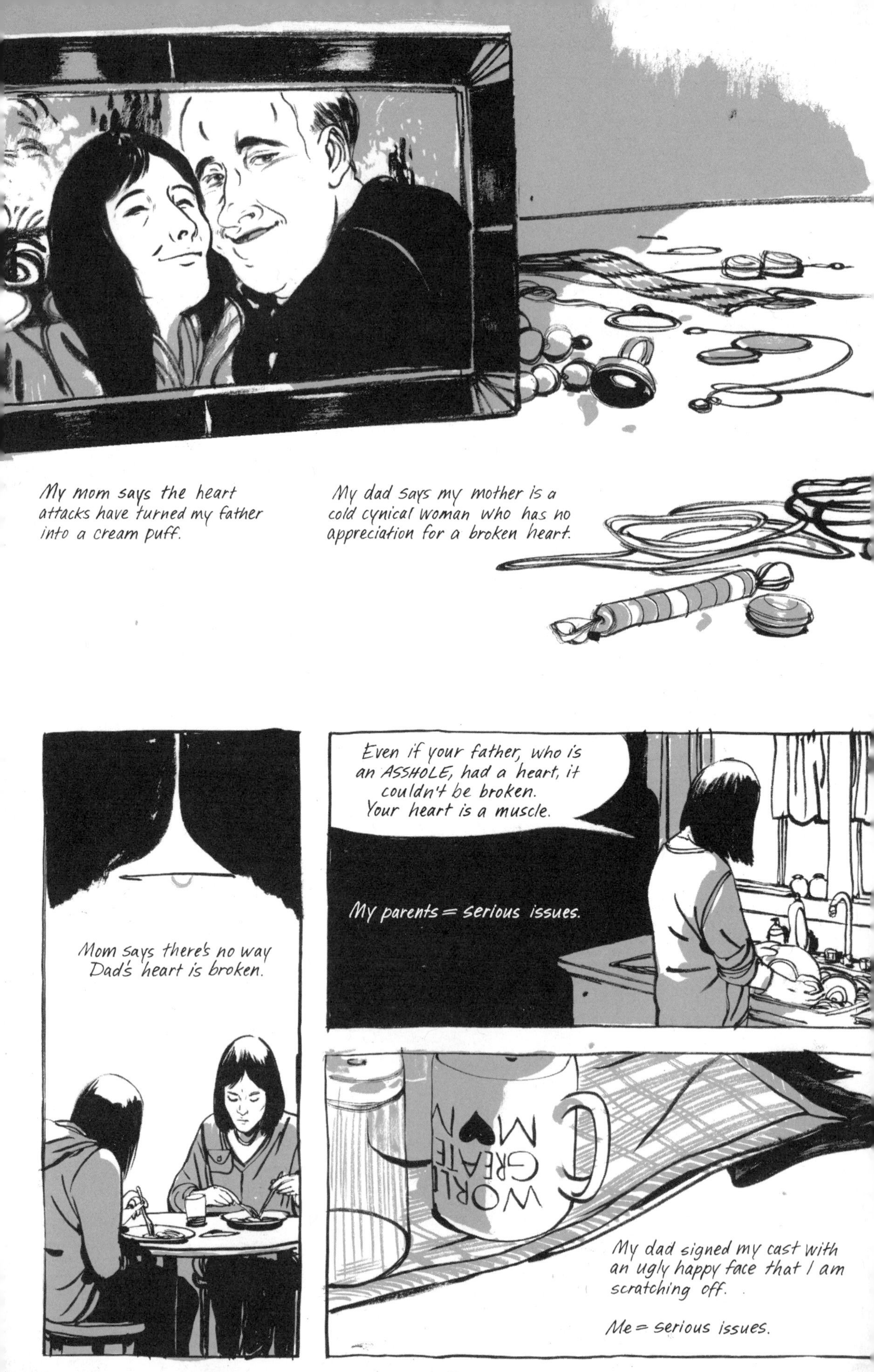
My mom says the heart attacks have turned my father into a cream puff.
My dad says my mother is a cold cynical woman who has no appreciation for a broken heart.
Mom says there's no way Dad's heart is broken.
Even if your father, who is an ASSHOLE, had a heart, it couldn't be broken. Your heart is a muscle.
My parents = serious issues.
My dad signed my cast with an ugly happy face that I am scratching off.
Me = serious issues.

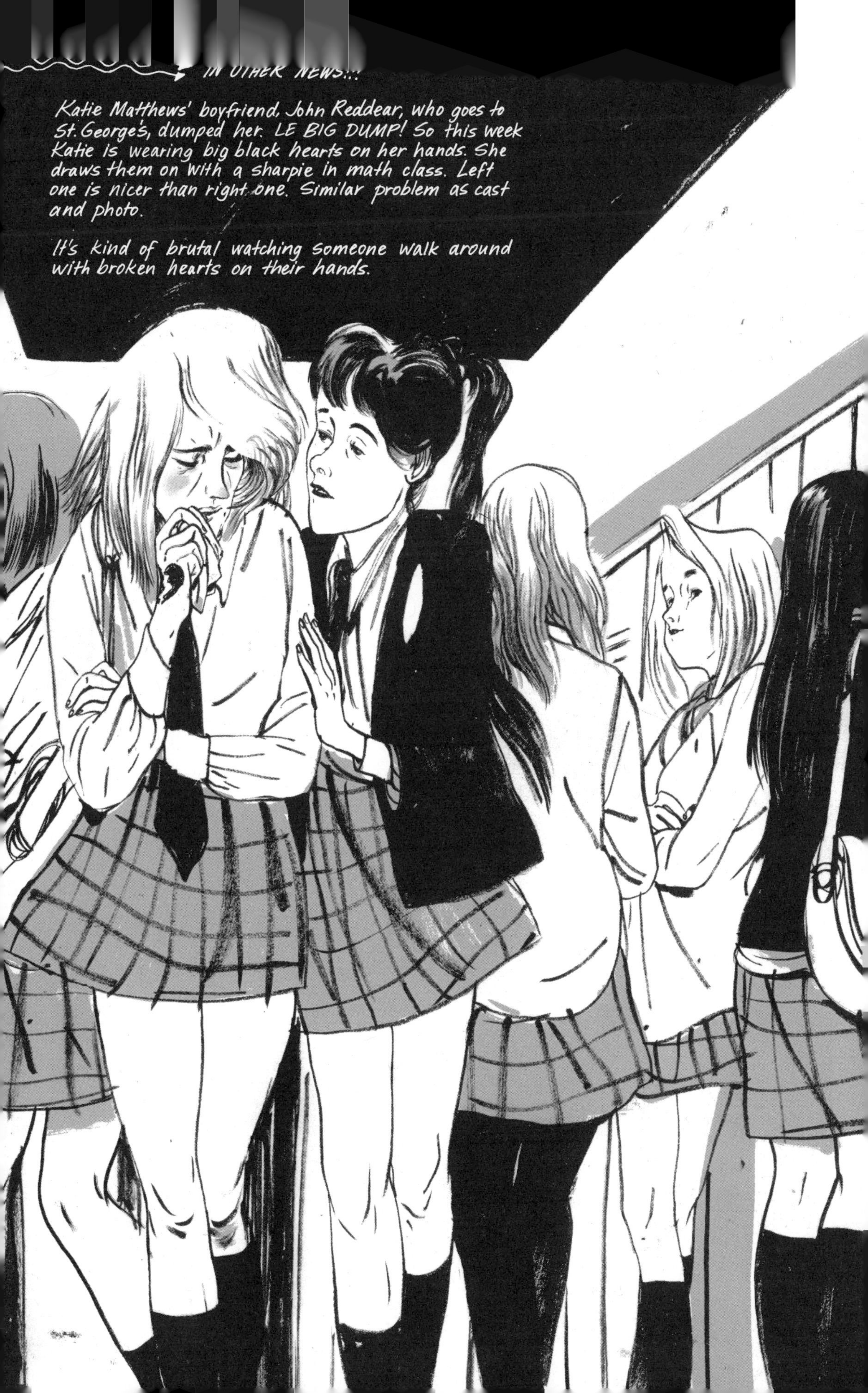
IN OTHER NEWS...!
Katie Matthews' boyfriend, John Reddear, who goes to St. George's, dumped her. LE BIG DUMP! So this week Katie is wearing big black hearts on her hands. She draws them on with a sharpie in math class. Left one is nicer than right one. Similar problem as cast and photo.
It's kind of brutal watching someone walk around with broken hearts on their hands.

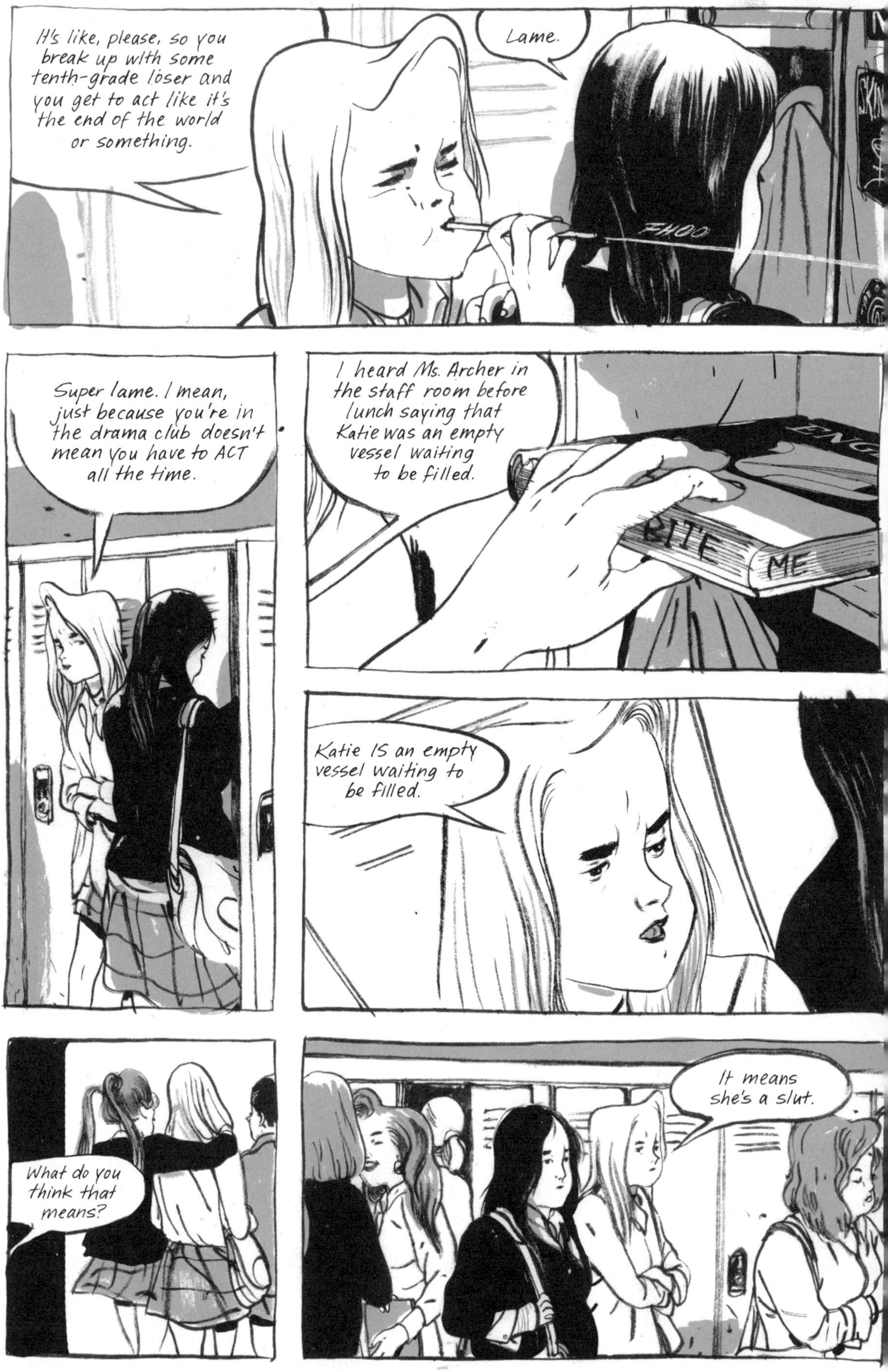

It's like, please, so you break up with some tenth-grade loser and you get to act like it's the end of the world or something.
Lame.
FHOO
Super lame. I mean, just because you're in the drama club doesn't mean you have to ACT all the time.
I heard Ms. Archer in the staff room before lunch saying that Katie was an empty vessel waiting to be filled.
BITE ME
Katie IS an empty vessel waiting to be filled.
What do you think that means?
It means she's a slut.

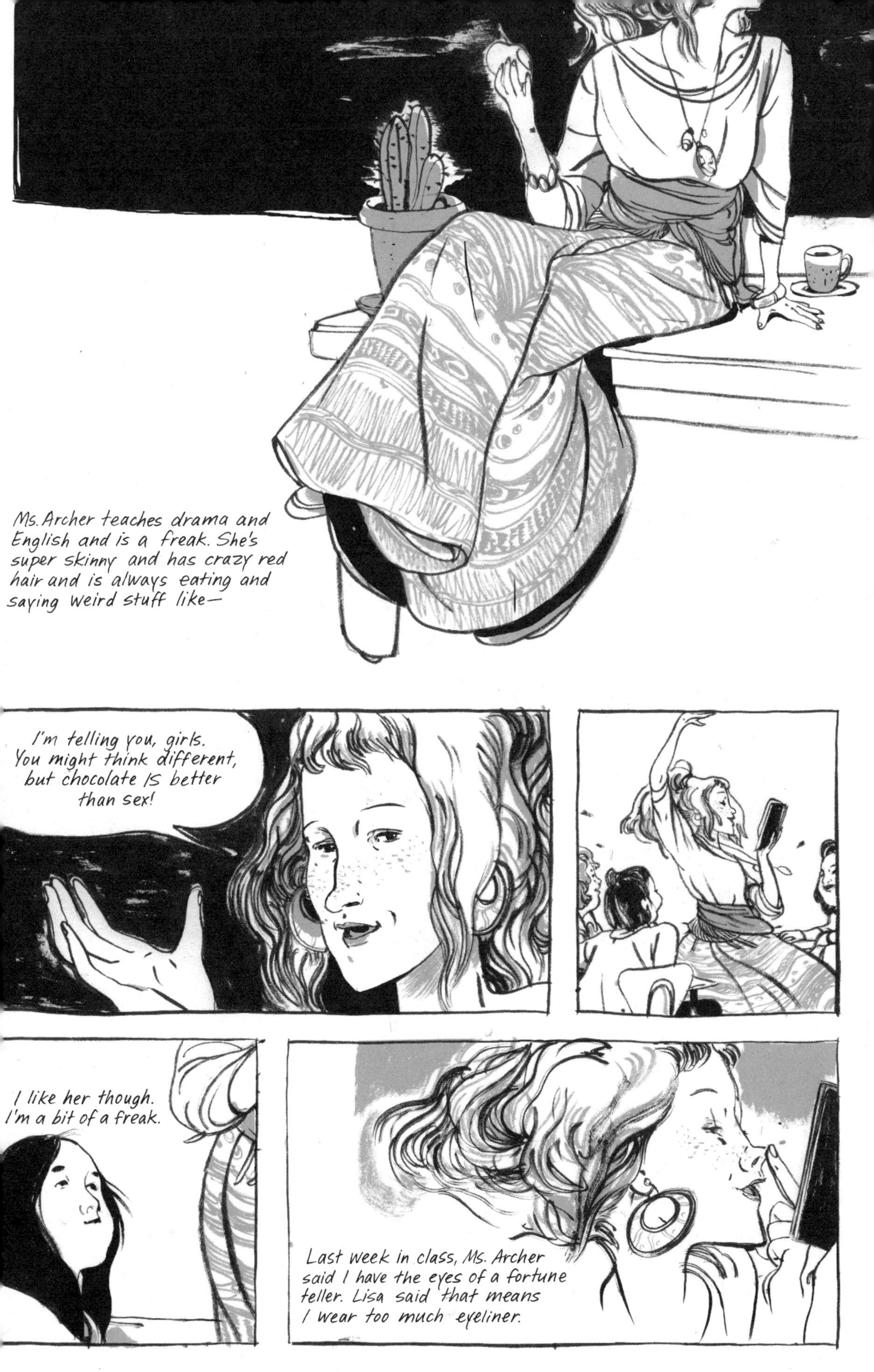
Ms. Archer teaches drama and English and is a freak. She's super skinny and has crazy red hair and is always eating and saying weird stuff like—
I'm telling you, girls. You might think different, but chocolate IS better than sex!
I like her though. I'm a bit of a freak.
Last week in class, Ms. Archer said I have the eyes of a fortune teller. Lisa said that means I wear too much eyeliner.

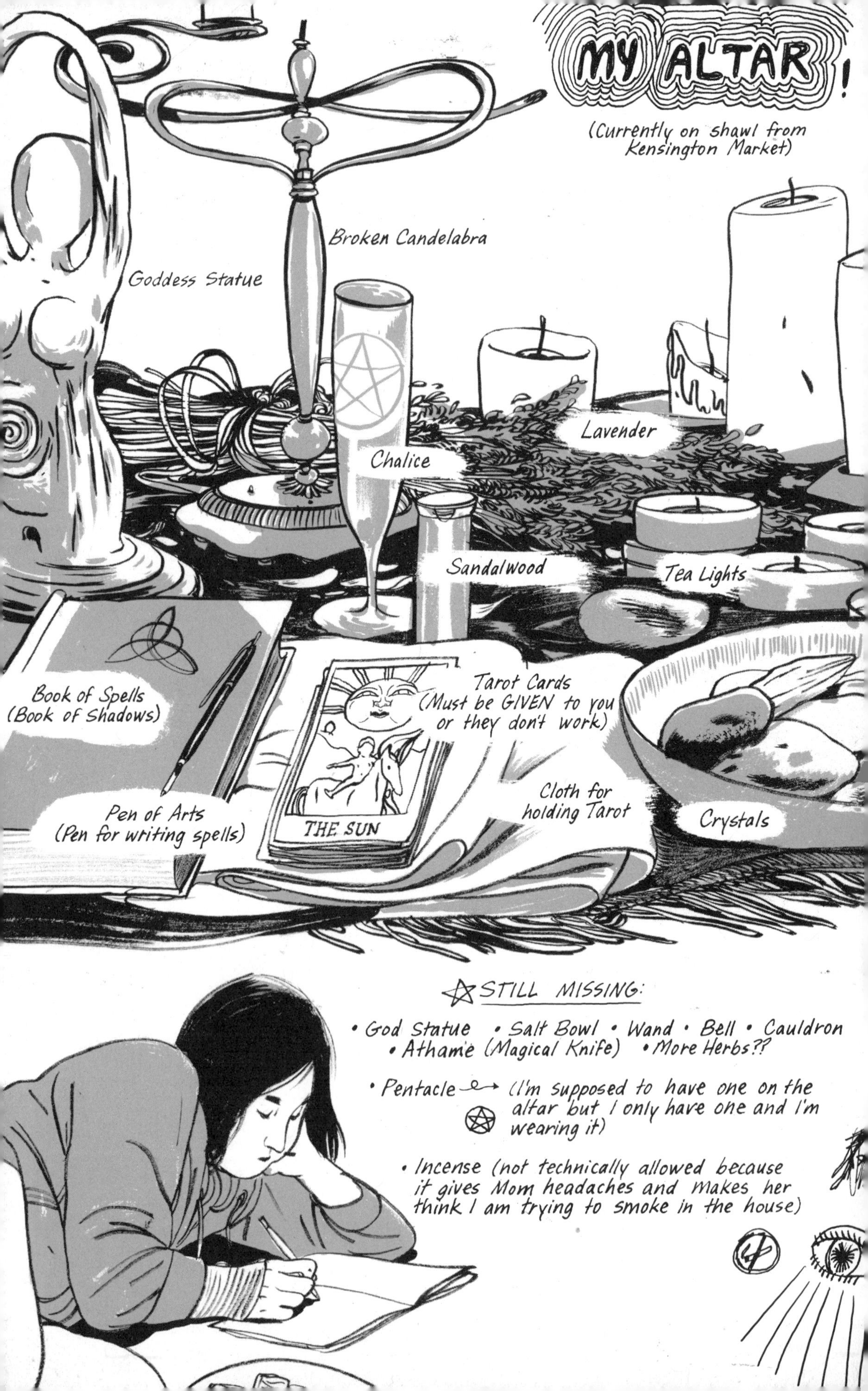
MY ALTAR!
(Currently on shawl from Kensington Market)
Broken Candelabra
Goddess Statue
Lavender
Chalice
Sandalwood
Tea Lights
Book of Spells (Book of Shadows)
Tarot Cards (Must be GIVEN to you or they don't work)
THE SUN
Cloth for holding Tarot
Pen of Arts (Pen for writing spells)
Crystals
STILL MISSING:
• God Statue • Salt Bowl • Wand • Bell • Cauldron • Athame (Magical Knife) • More Herbs??
• Pentacle (I'm supposed to have one on the altar but I only have one and I'm wearing it)
• Incense (not technically allowed because it gives Mom headaches and makes her think I am trying to smoke in the house)

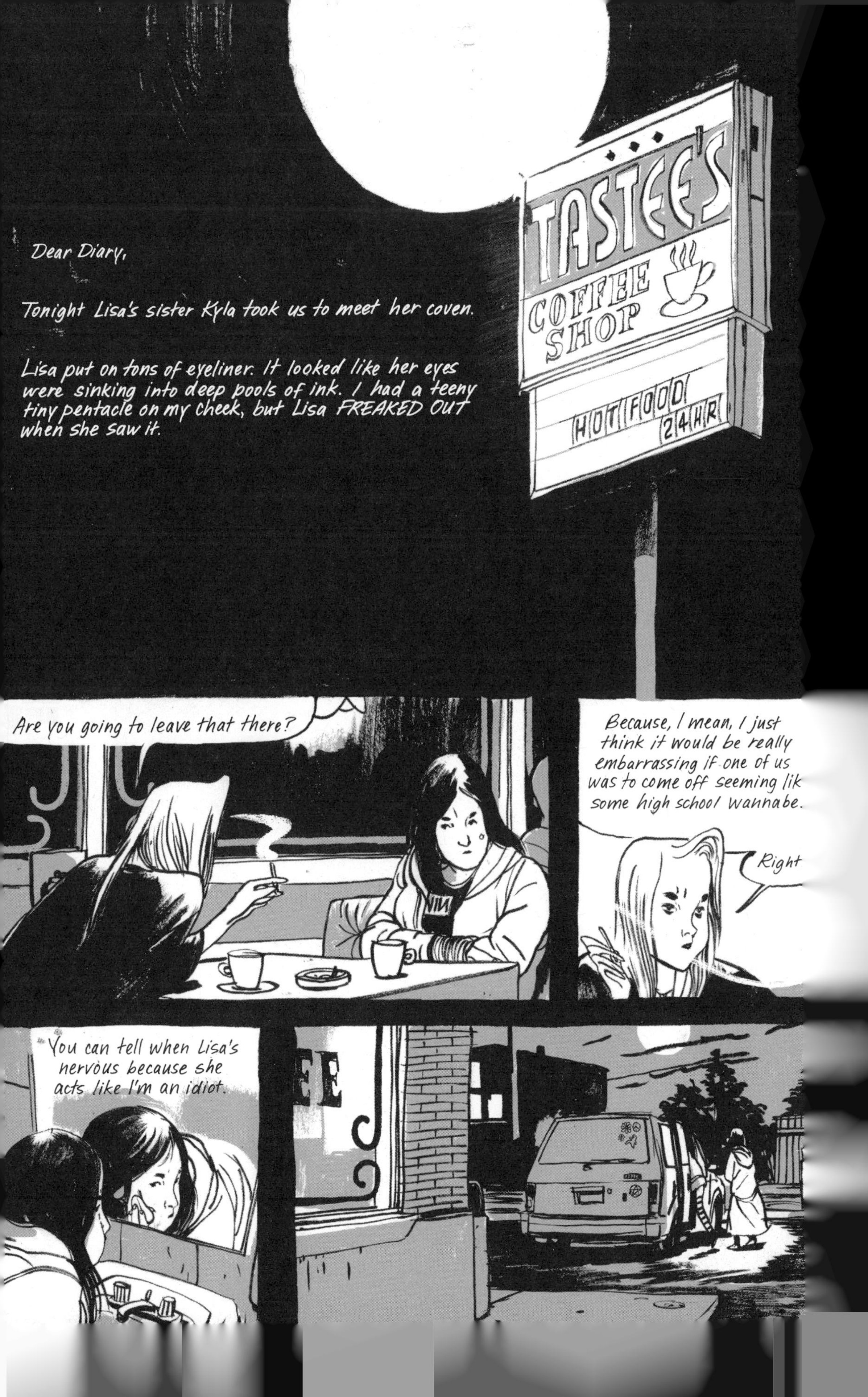
Dear Diary,
Tonight Lisa's sister Kyla took us to meet her coven.
Lisa put on tons of eyeliner. It looked like her eyes were sinking into deep pools of ink. I had a teeny tiny pentacle on my cheek, but Lisa FREAKED OUT when she saw it.
TASTEE'S
COFFEE SHOP
HOT FOOD
24 HR
Are you going to leave that there?
Because, I mean, I just think it would be really embarrassing if one of us was to come off seeming lik some high school wannabe.
Right
You can tell when Lisa's nervous because she acts like I'm an idiot.

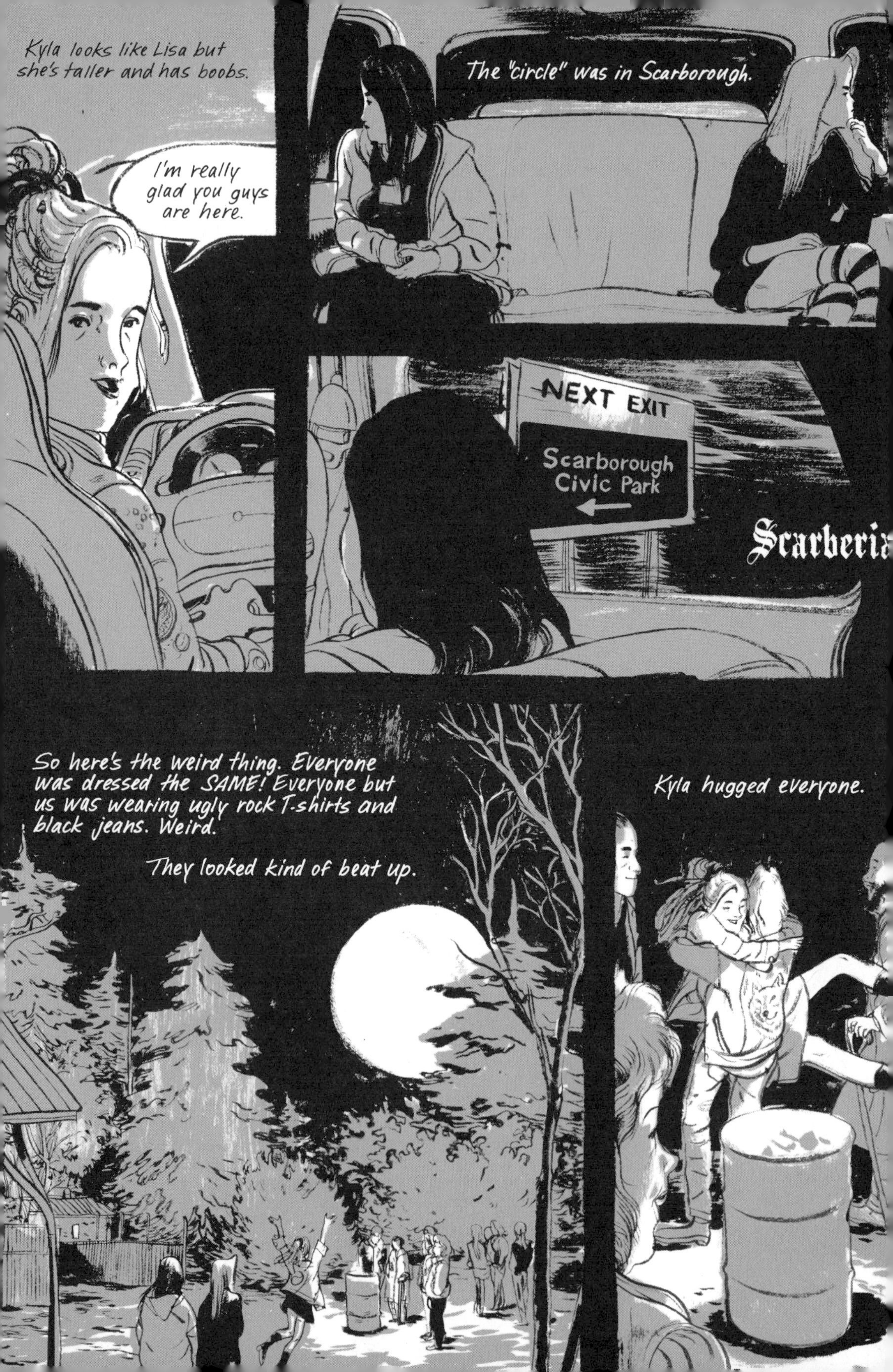
Kyla looks like Lisa but she's taller and has boobs.
I'm really glad you guys are here.
The "circle" was in Scarborough.
NEXT EXIT
Scarborough Civic Park
Scarberia
So here's the weird thing. Everyone was dressed the SAME! Everyone but us was wearing ugly rock T-shirts and black jeans. Weird.
They looked kind of beat up.
Kyla hugged everyone.

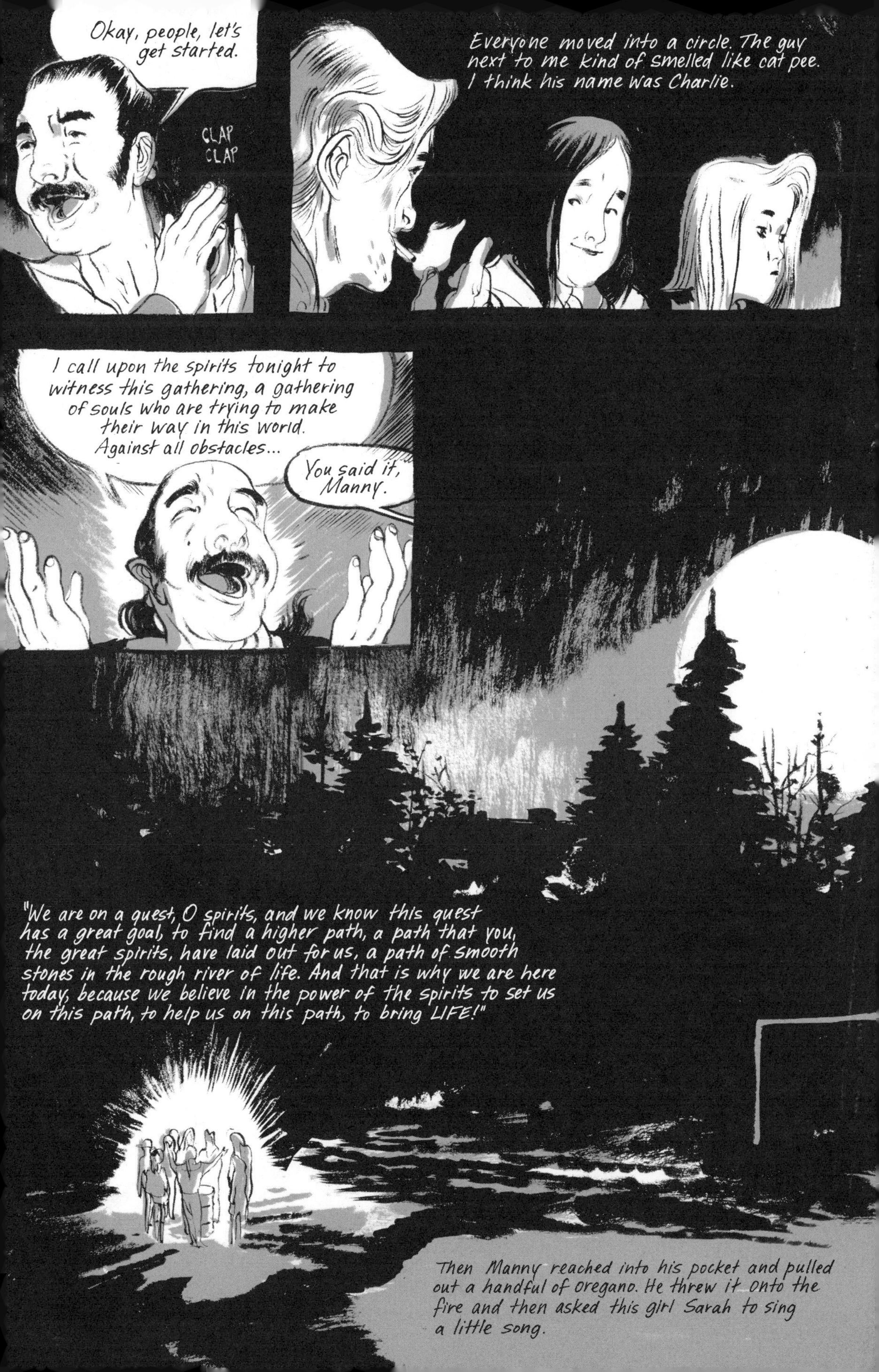
Okay, people, let's get started.
CLAP CLAP
Everyone moved into a circle. The guy next to me kind of smelled like cat pee. I think his name was Charlie.
I call upon the spirits tonight to witness this gathering, a gathering of souls who are trying to make their way in this world. Against all obstacles...
You said it, Manny.
"We are on a quest, O spirits, and we know this quest has a great goal, to find a higher path, a path that you, the great spirits, have laid out for us, a path of smooth stones in the rough river of life. And that is why we are here today, because we believe in the power of the spirits to set us on this path, to help us on this path, to bring LIFE!"
Then Manny reached into his pocket and pulled out a handful of oregano. He threw it onto the fire and then asked this girl Sarah to sing a little song.

Sarah had a little voice, like a kid.

♪♫♪ Earth, Air, Fire and Water ♪ Mother Earth I am your daughter All the world so full of spirit There for us if we choose to hear it ♪♫♪

I don't think Sarah is what most people picture when they talk about witches in the park.

After the song, Manny walked around the circle, touching each of us between the shoulder blades. Then he asked if anyone had anything they wanted to share. And that's when this skinny guy with 80s rocker hair and a turtleneck came forward.

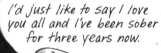

I'd just like to say I love you all and I've been sober for three years now.

Wow.

Amazing.

Blessed be.

Way to go, brother.

It's funny, because I was so nervous before. I thought, like, wow, witches in the park. Isn't that something people warn you about?

I've also been sober for three and a half years. Thanks, everyone.

Altogether six people stepped forward and talked about being sober. Even Kyla.

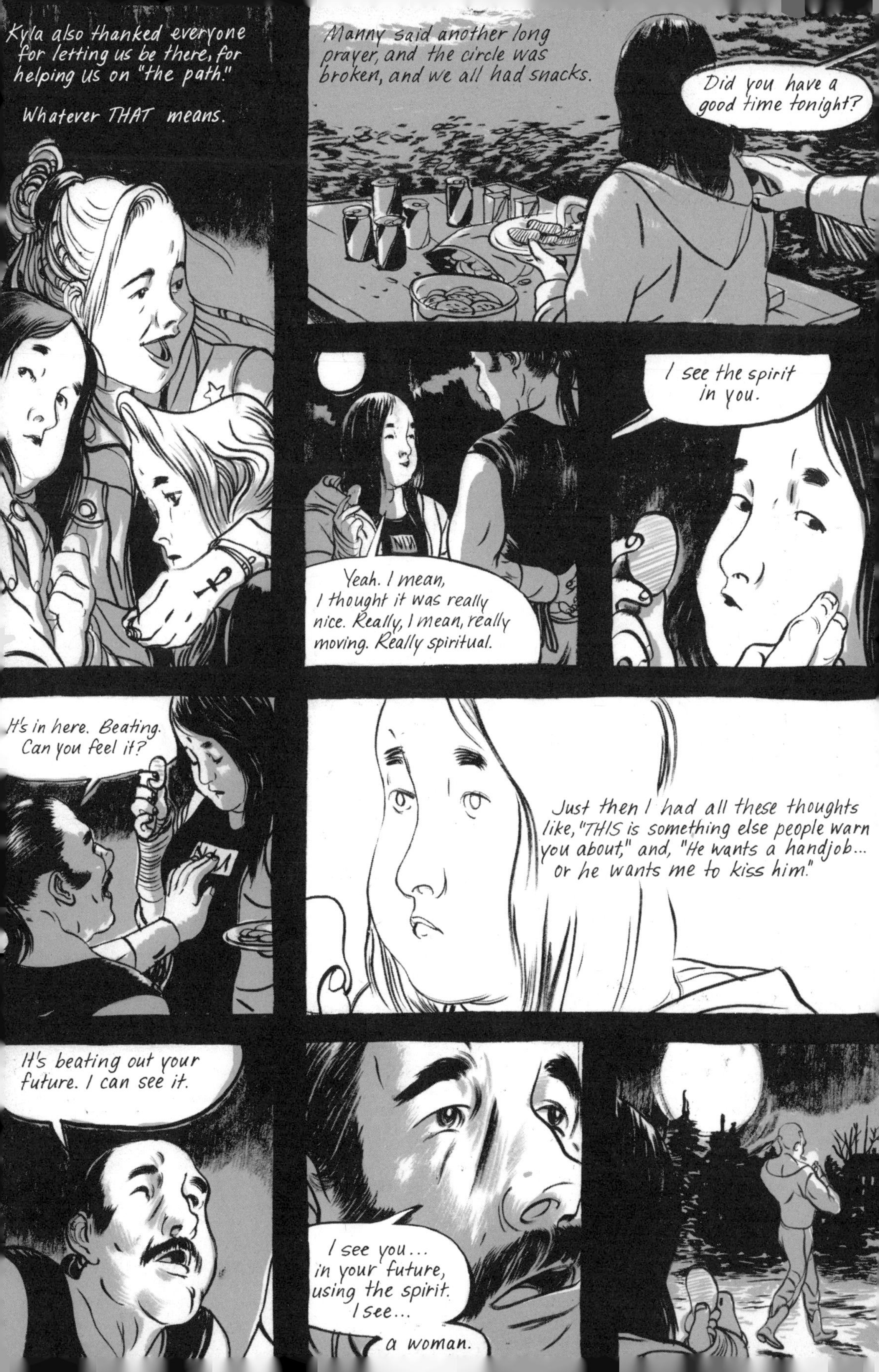

Kyla also thanked everyone for letting us be there, for helping us on "the path."
Whatever THAT means.
Manny said another long prayer, and the circle was broken, and we all had snacks.
Did you have a good time tonight?
Yeah. I mean, I thought it was really nice. Really, I mean, really moving. Really spiritual.
I see the spirit in you.
It's in here. Beating. Can you feel it?
Just then I had all these thoughts like, "THIS is something else people warn you about," and, "He wants a handjob... or he wants me to kiss him."
It's beating out your future. I can see it.
I see you... in your future, using the spirit. I see...
a woman.

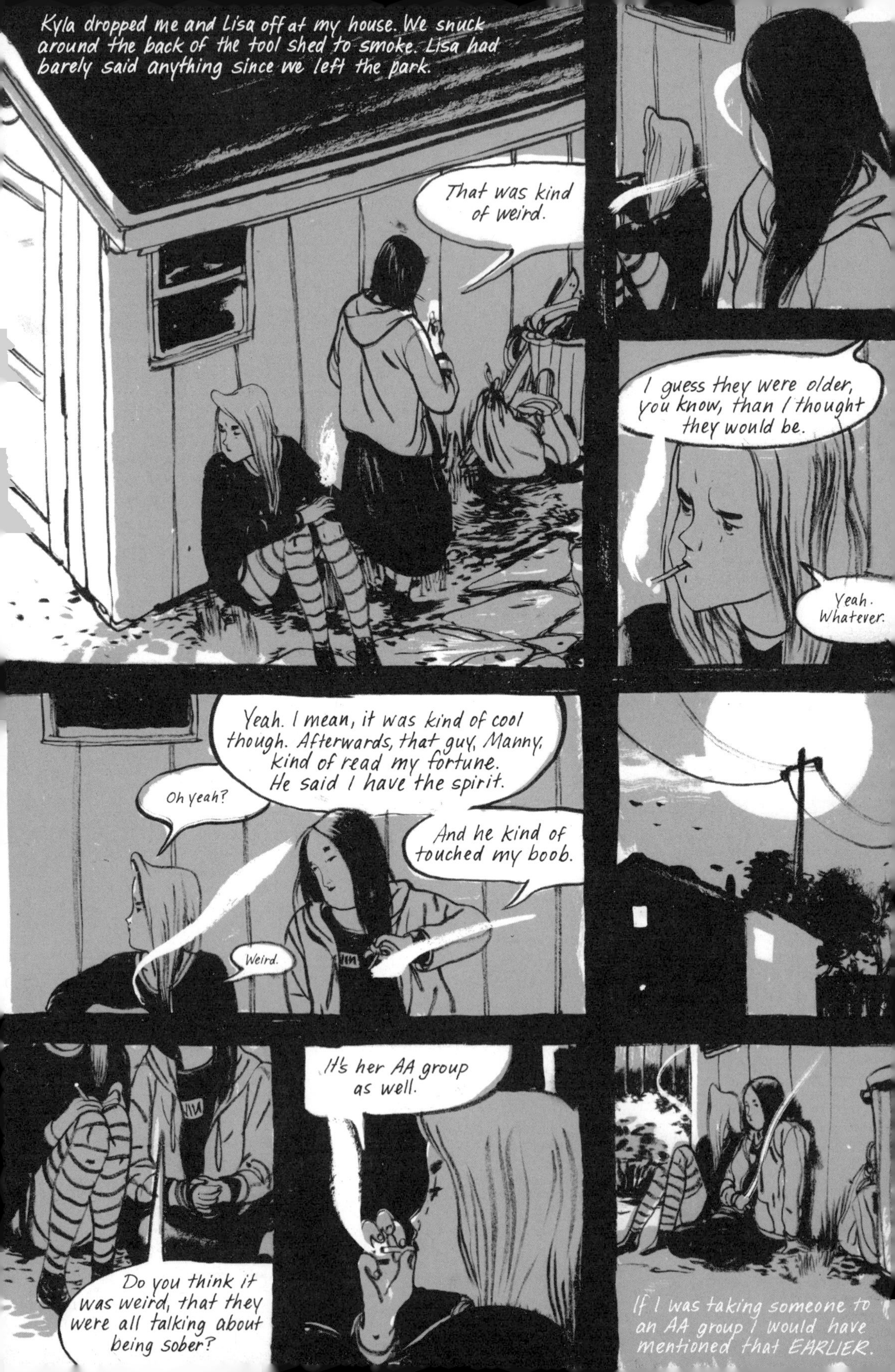
Kyla dropped me and Lisa off at my house. We snuck around the back of the tool shed to smoke. Lisa had barely said anything since we left the park.
That was kind of weird.
I guess they were older, you know, than I thought they would be.
Yeah. Whatever.
Yeah. I mean, it was kind of cool though. Afterwards, that guy, Manny, kind of read my fortune. He said I have the spirit.
Oh yeah?
And he kind of touched my boob.
Weird.
Do you think it was weird, that they were all talking about being sober?
It's her AA group as well.
If I was taking someone to an AA group I would have mentioned that EARLIER.

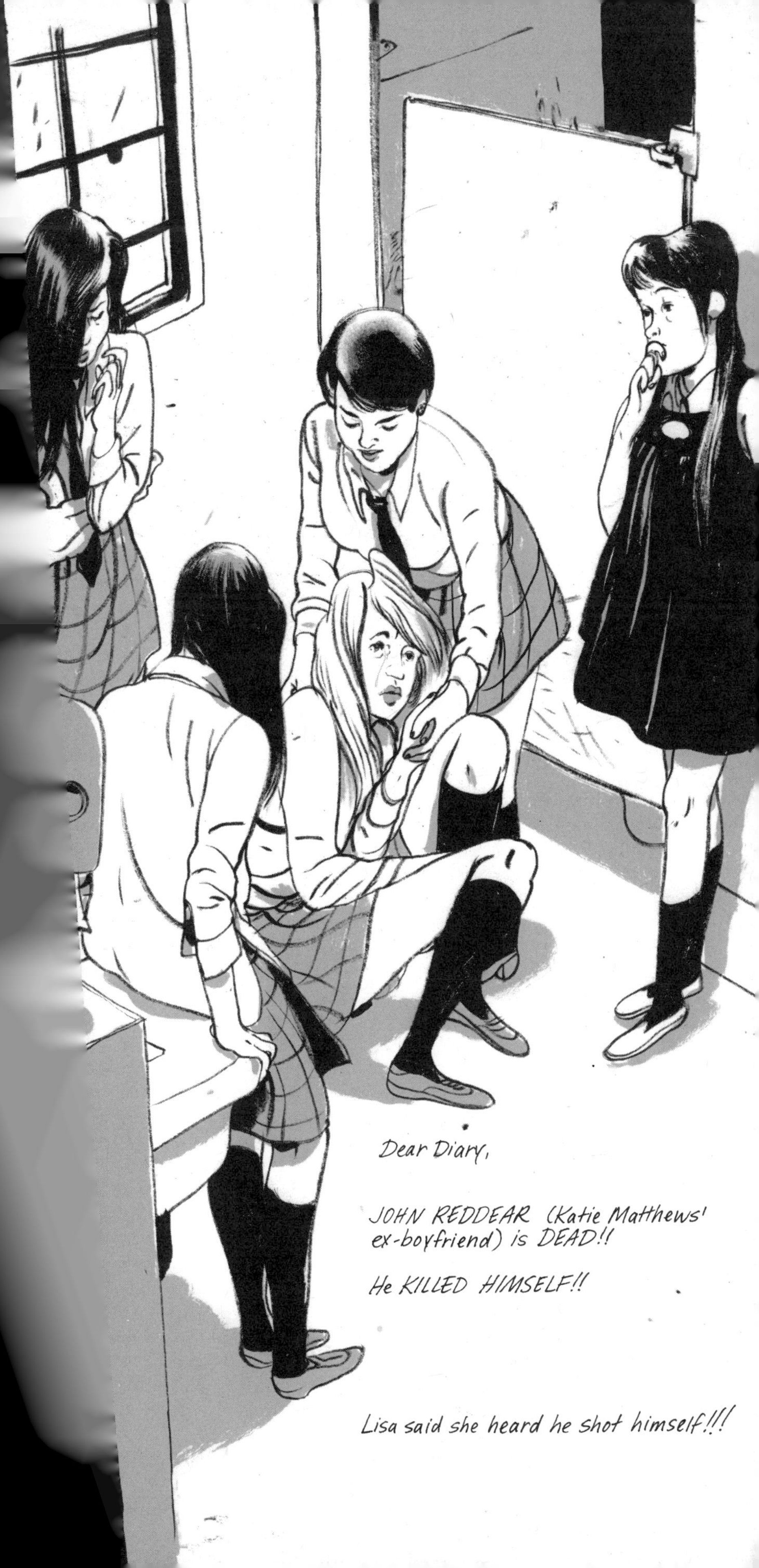
Dear Diary,
JOHN REDDEAR (Katie Matthews' ex-boyfriend) is DEAD!!
He KILLED HIMSELF!!
Lisa said she heard he shot himself!!!

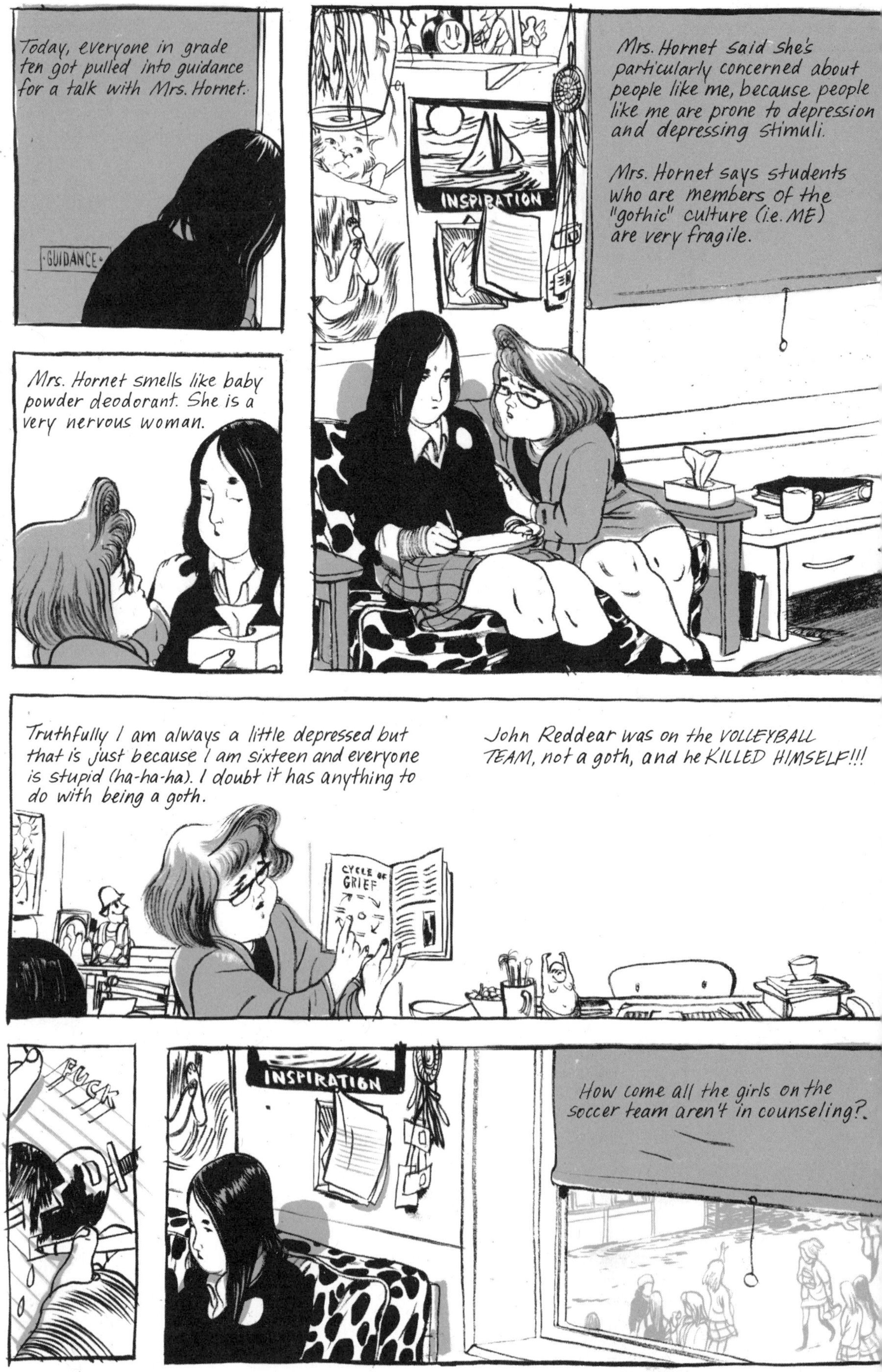
Today, everyone in grade ten got pulled into guidance for a talk with Mrs. Hornet.
GUIDANCE
INSPIRATION
Mrs. Hornet said she's particularly concerned about people like me, because people like me are prone to depression and depressing stimuli.
Mrs. Hornet says students who are members of the "gothic" culture (i.e. ME) are very fragile.
Mrs. Hornet smells like baby powder deodorant. She is a very nervous woman.
Truthfully I am always a little depressed but that is just because I am sixteen and everyone is stupid (ha-ha-ha). I doubt it has anything to do with being a goth.
John Reddear was on the VOLLEYBALL TEAM, not a goth, and he KILLED HIMSELF!!!
CYCLE OF GRIEF
FUCK
INSPIRATION
How come all the girls on the soccer team aren't in counseling?.

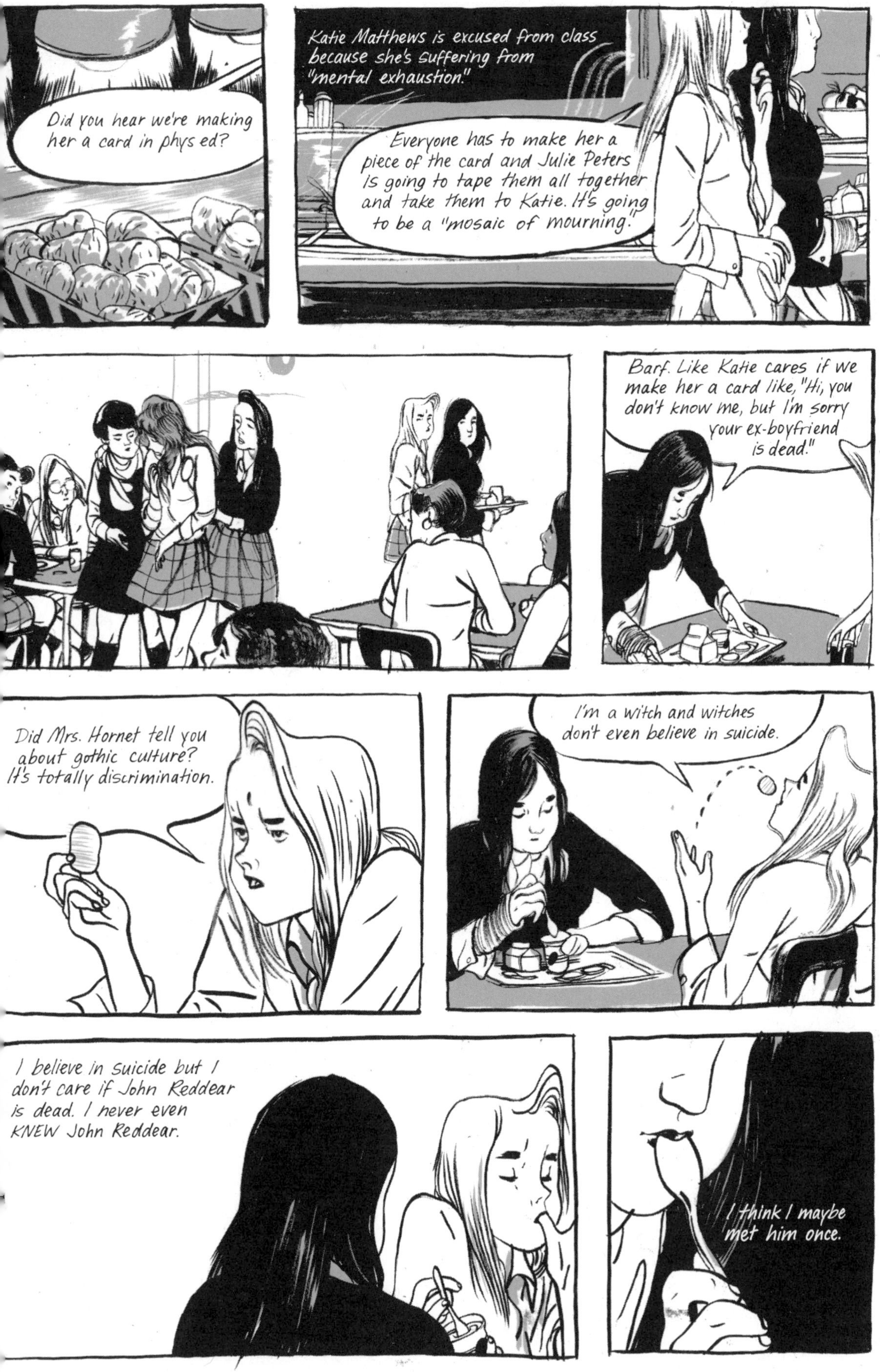
Did you hear we're making her a card in phys ed?
Katie Matthews is excused from class because she's suffering from "mental exhaustion."
Everyone has to make her a piece of the card and Julie Peters is going to tape them all together and take them to Katie. It's going to be a "mosaic of mourning."
Barf. Like Katie cares if we make her a card like, "Hi, you don't know me, but I'm sorry your ex-boyfriend is dead."
Did Mrs. Hornet tell you about gothic culture? It's totally discrimination.
I'm a witch and witches don't even believe in suicide.
I believe in suicide but I don't care if John Reddear is dead. I never even KNEW John Reddear.
I think I maybe met him once.

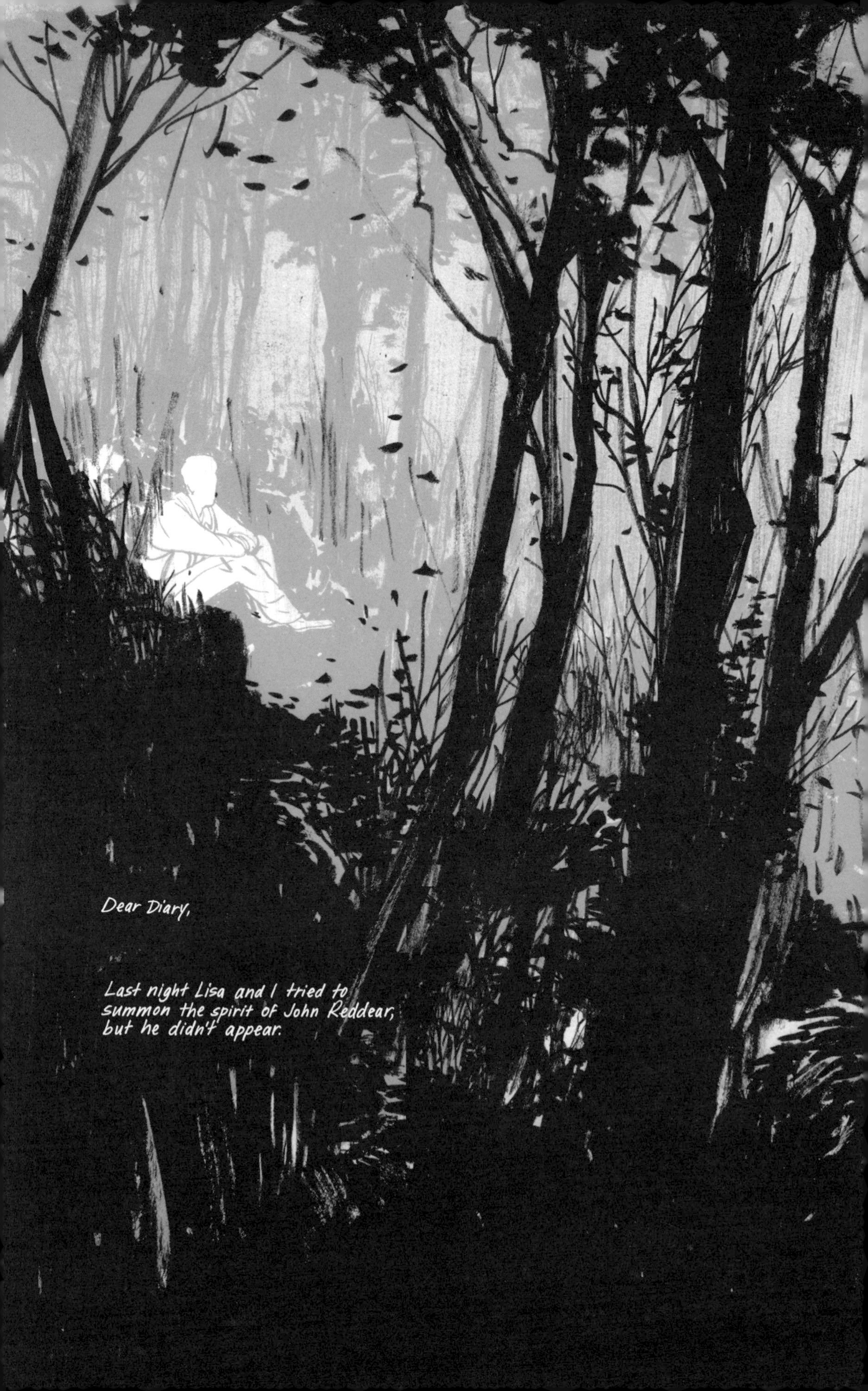
Dear Diary,
Last night Lisa and I tried to summon the spirit of John Reddear, but he didn't appear.

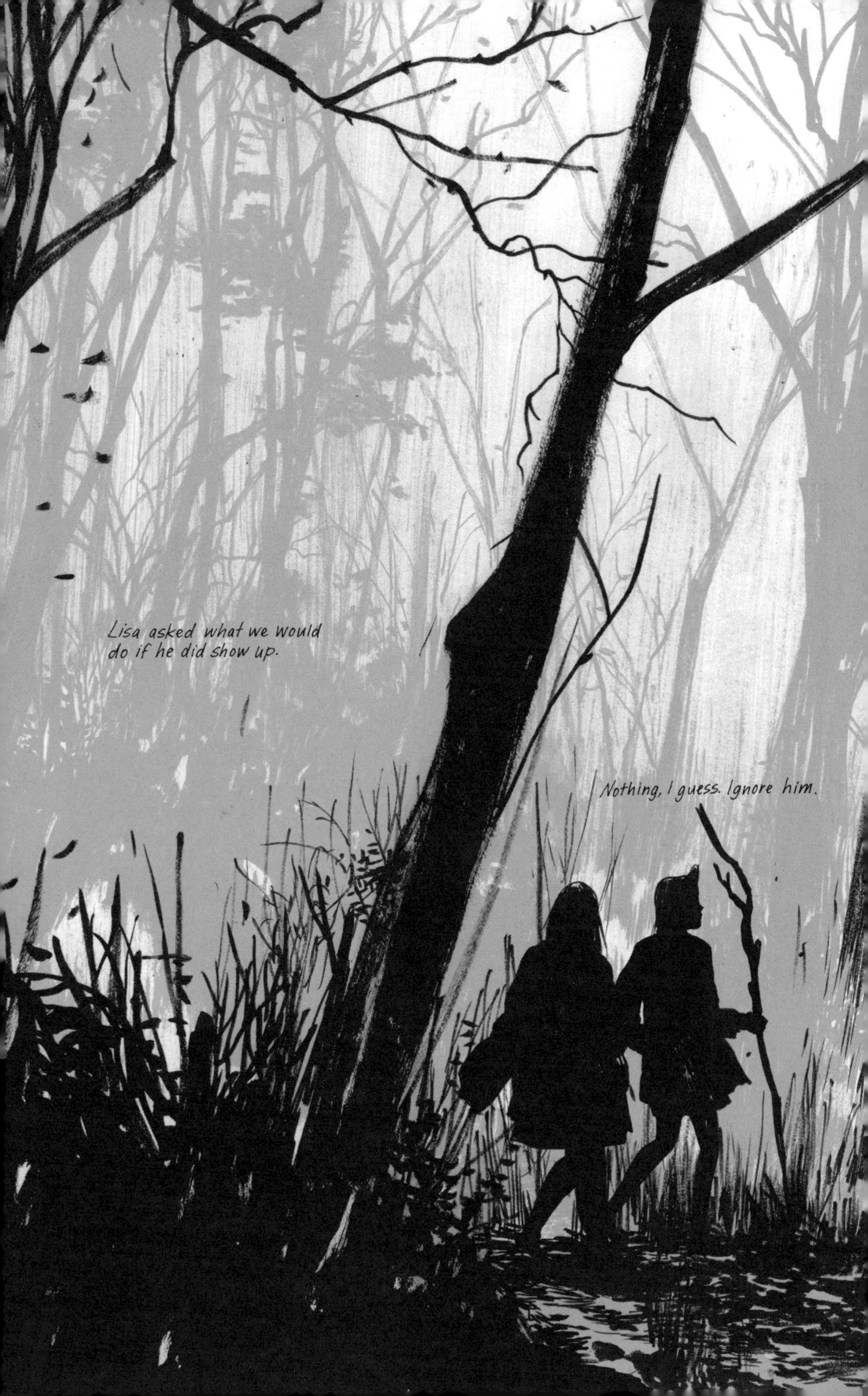
Lisa asked what we would do if he did show up.
Nothing, I guess. Ignore him.

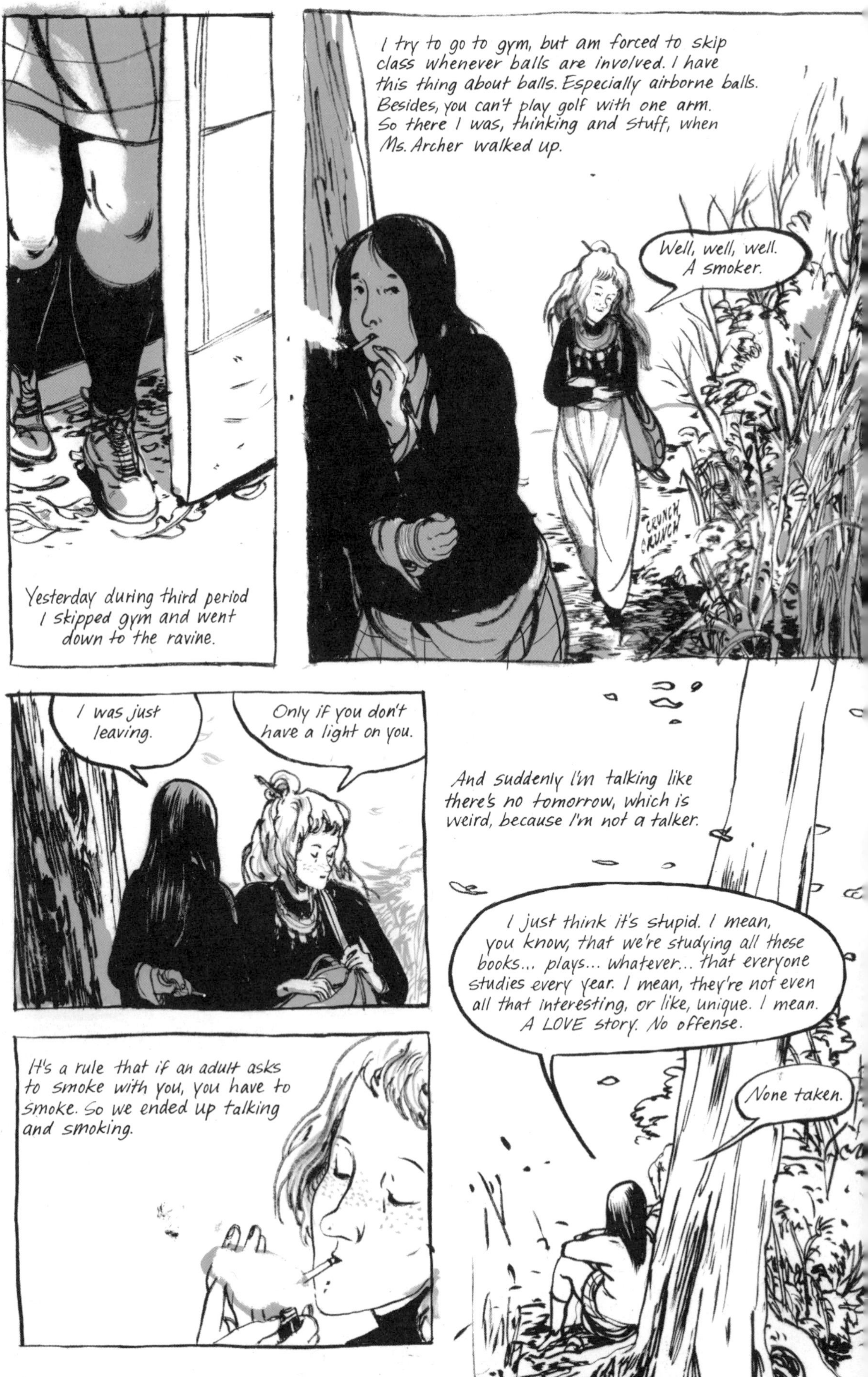
Yesterday during third period I skipped gym and went down to the ravine.
I try to go to gym, but am forced to skip class whenever balls are involved. I have this thing about balls. Especially airborne balls. Besides, you can't play golf with one arm. So there I was, thinking and stuff, when Ms. Archer walked up.
Well, well, well. A smoker.
CRUNCH CRUNCH
I was just leaving.
Only if you don't have a light on you.
It's a rule that if an adult asks to smoke with you, you have to smoke. So we ended up talking and smoking.
And suddenly I'm talking like there's no tomorrow, which is weird, because I'm not a talker.
I just think it's stupid. I mean, you know, that we're studying all these books... plays... whatever... that everyone studies every year. I mean, they're not even all that interesting, or like, unique. I mean. A LOVE story. No offense.
None taken.

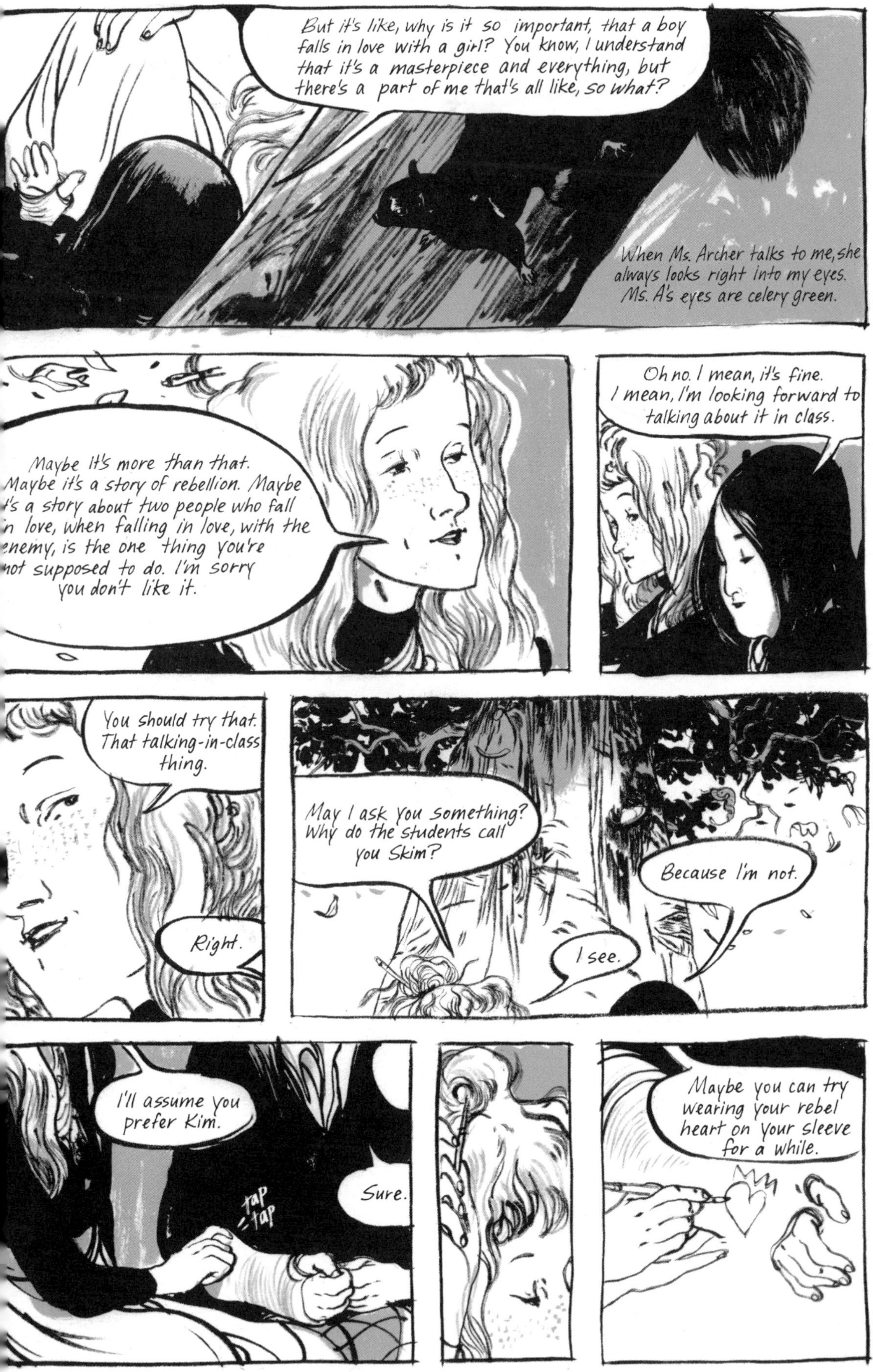
But it's like, why is it so important, that a boy falls in love with a girl? You know, I understand that it's a masterpiece and everything, but there's a part of me that's all like, so what?
When Ms. Archer talks to me, she always looks right into my eyes. Ms. A's eyes are celery green.
Maybe it's more than that. Maybe it's a story of rebellion. Maybe it's a story about two people who fall in love, when falling in love, with the enemy, is the one thing you're not supposed to do. I'm sorry you don't like it.
Oh no. I mean, it's fine. I mean, I'm looking forward to talking about it in class.
You should try that. That talking-in-class thing.
Right.
May I ask you something? Why do the students call you Skim?
Because I'm not.
I see.
I'll assume you prefer Kim.
Sure.
tap tap
Maybe you can try wearing your rebel heart on your sleeve for a while.

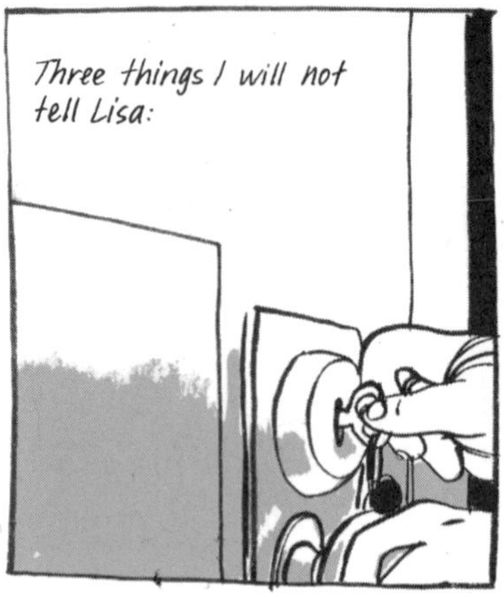
Three things I will not tell Lisa:

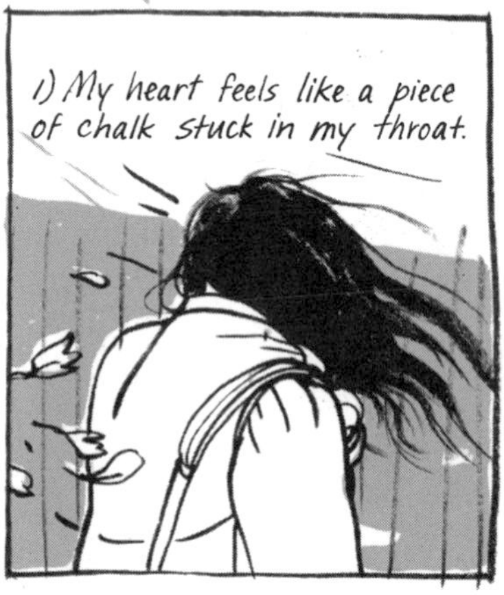
1) My heart feels like a piece of chalk stuck in my throat.

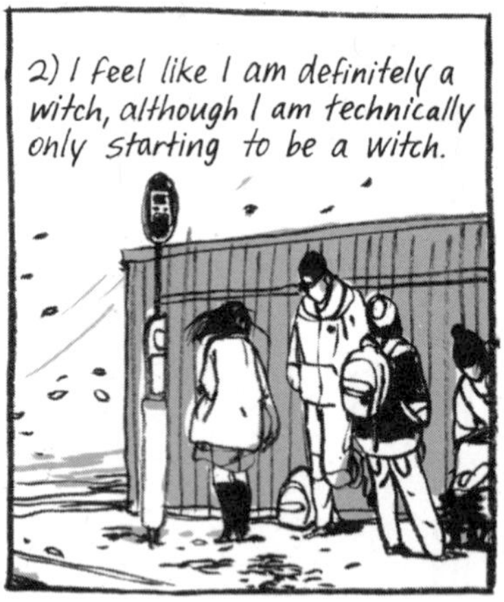
2) I feel like I am definitely a witch, although I am technically only starting to be a witch.

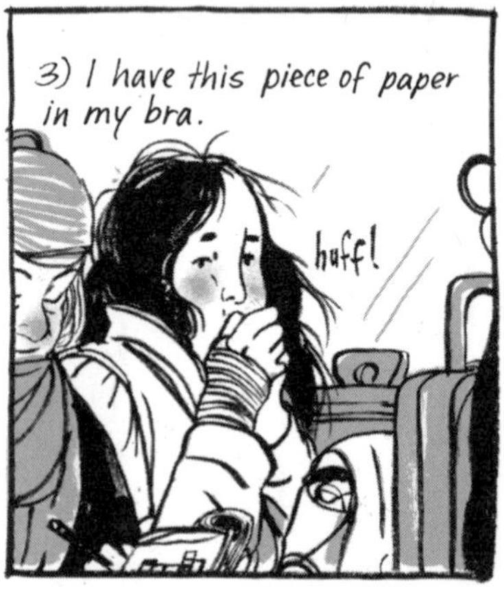
3) I have this piece of paper in my bra.
huff!

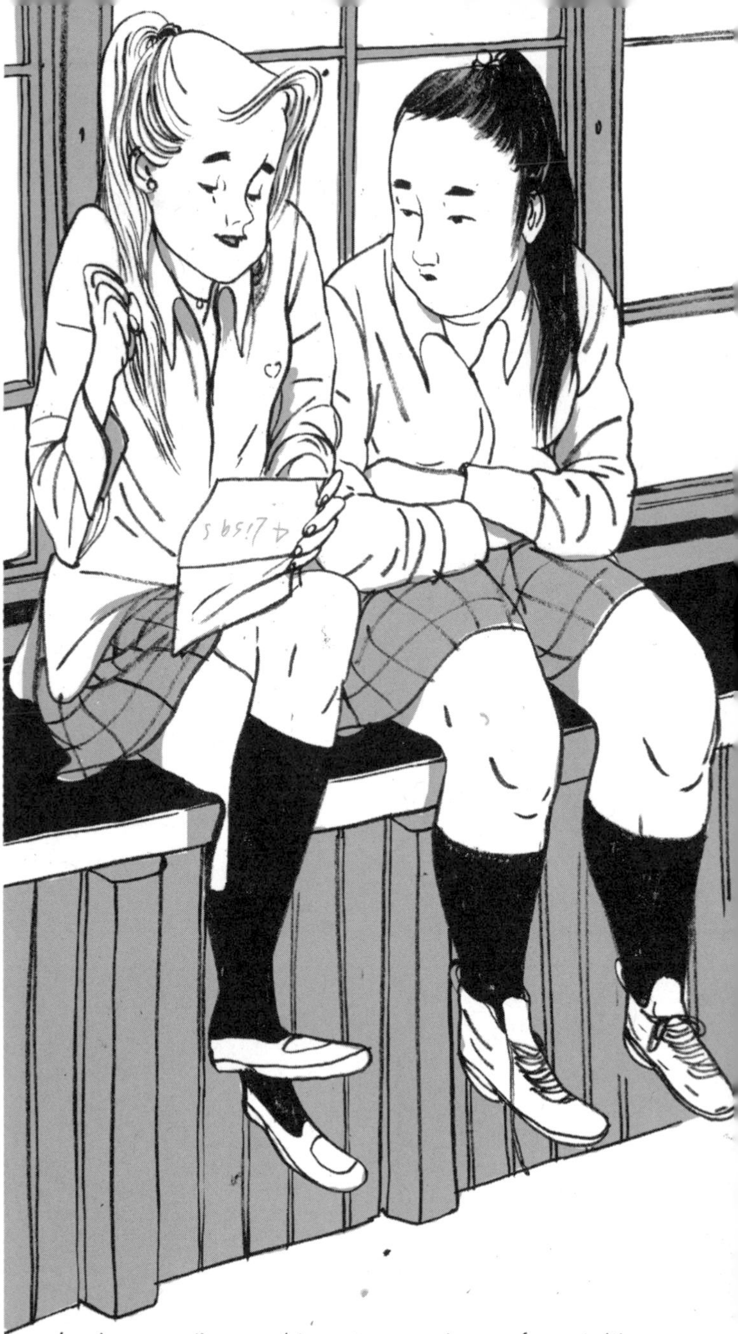

Last year, all year, Lisa wore a stone shaped like a heart in her bra as a love charm. When she wore her school shirt sometimes it looked like an extra really big nipple. Lisa didn't think so. But I did.

A Wicca charm can be a thing or a spell or an incantation. It doesn't have to be a rock.

My Wicca book says one spell you can do is cut a piece of paper into a strip and write on it, "My heart will bring my love to me." Three times you write that. Then you tape the two ends of the paper together so it makes a loop.

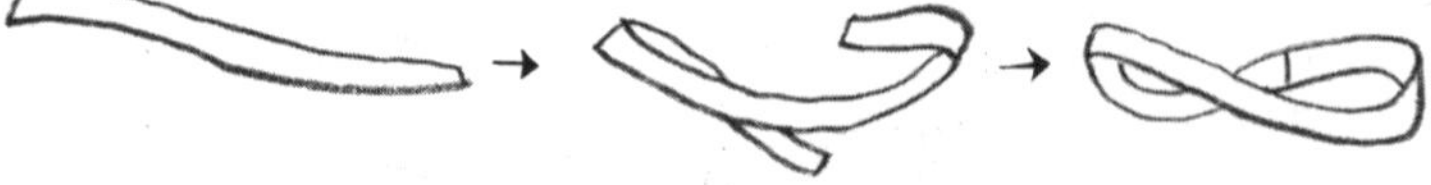

And that's what I'm wearing in my bra now.

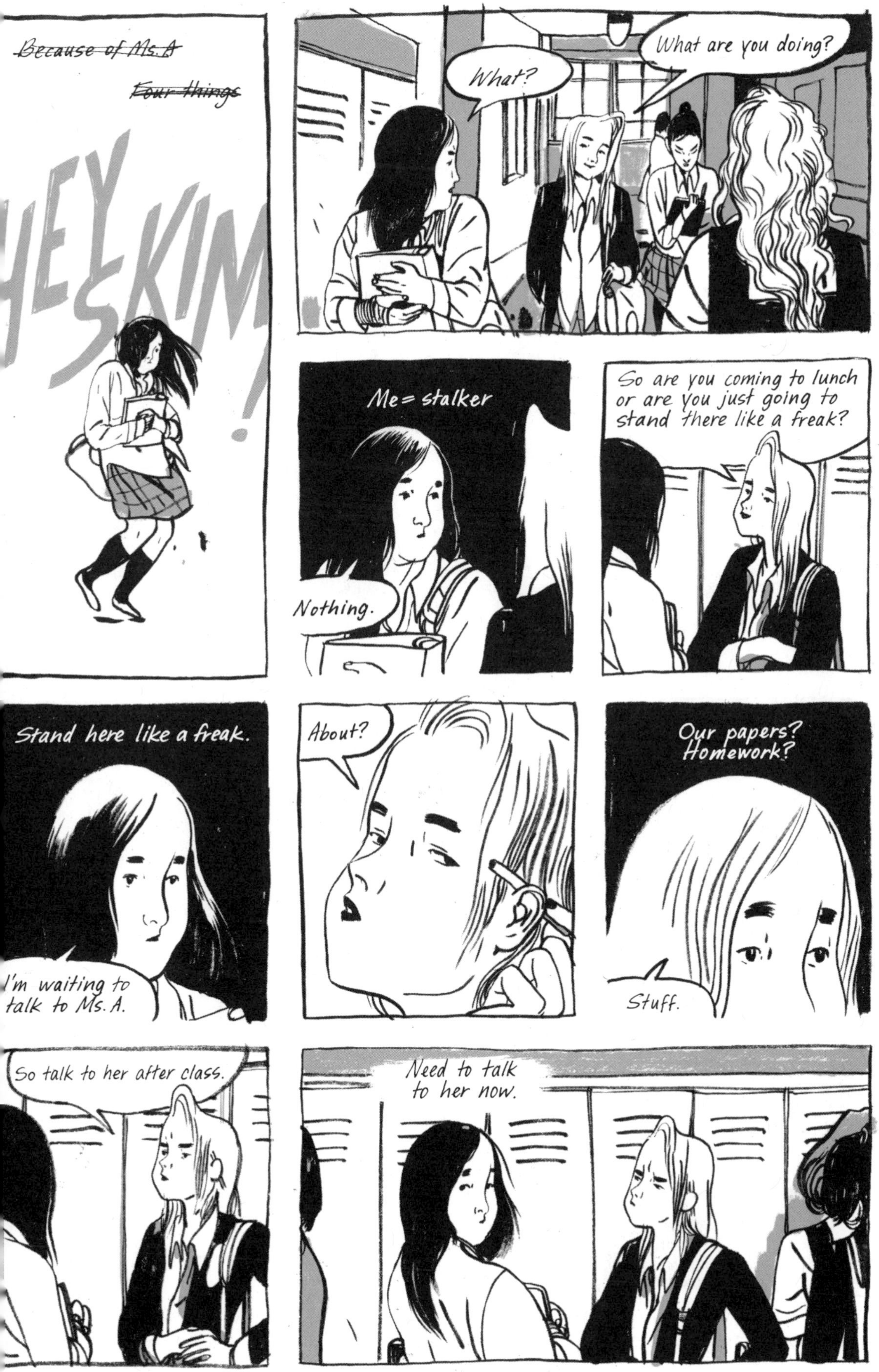

Because of Ms. A
Four things
HEY SKIM!
What?
What are you doing?
Me = stalker
Nothing.
So are you coming to lunch or are you just going to stand there like a freak?
Stand here like a freak.
I'm waiting to talk to Ms. A.
About?
Our papers? Homework?
Stuff.
So talk to her after class.
Need to talk to her now.

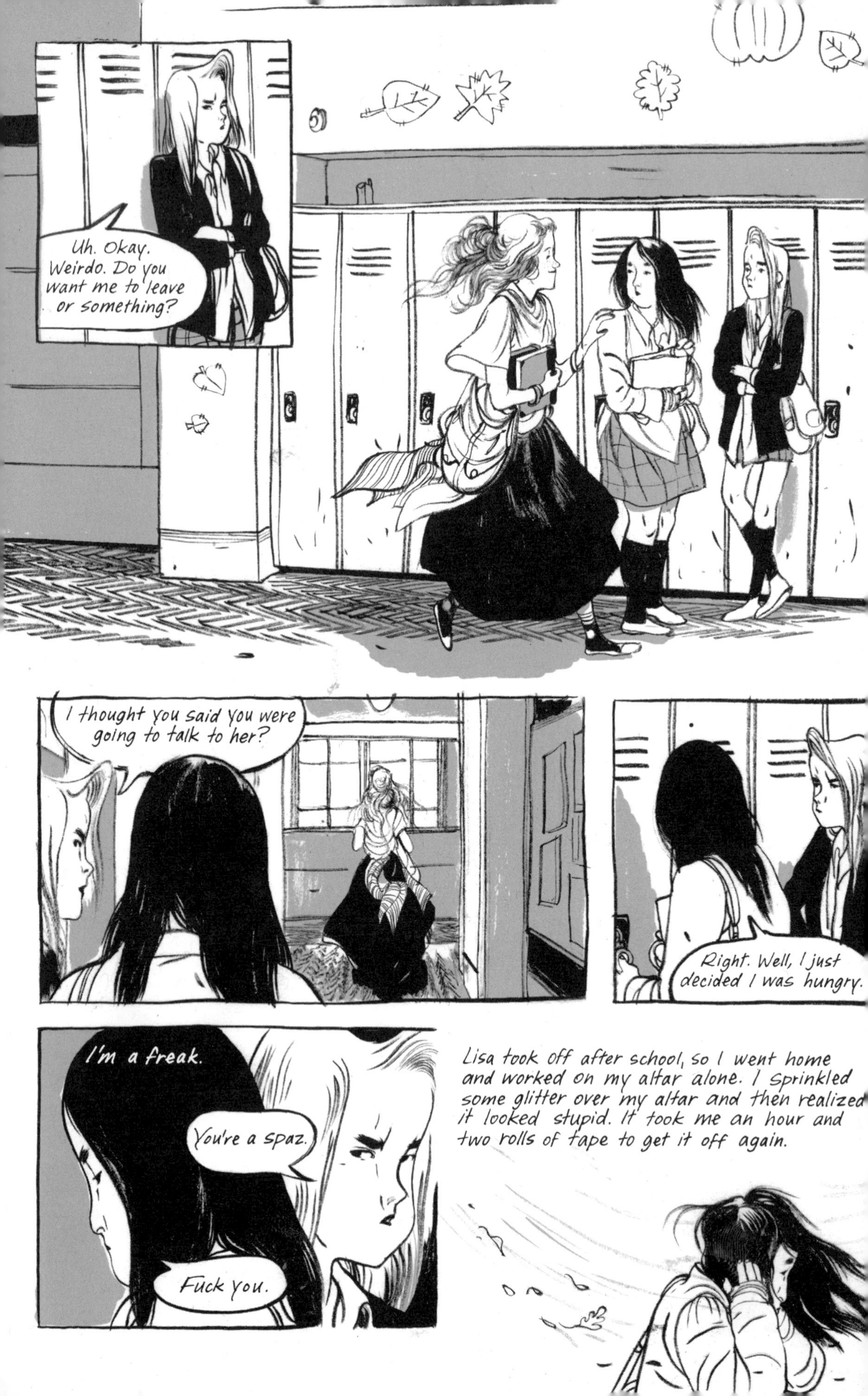
Uh. Okay. Weirdo. Do you want me to leave or something?
I thought you said you were going to talk to her?
Right. Well, I just decided I was hungry.
I'm a freak.
You're a spaz.
Fuck you.
Lisa took off after school, so I went home and worked on my altar alone. I sprinkled some glitter over my altar and then realized it looked stupid. It took me an hour and two rolls of tape to get it off again.

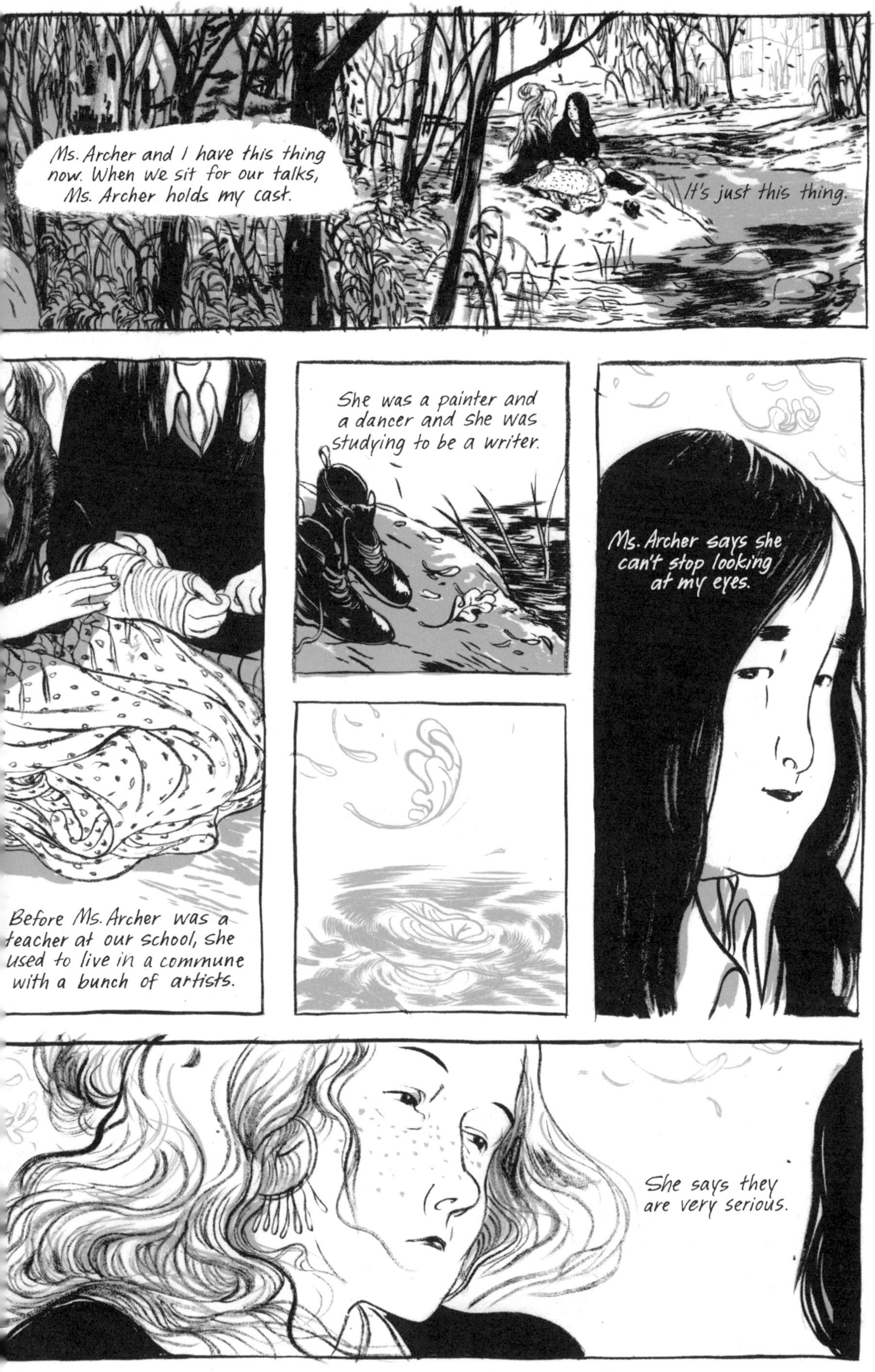

Ms. Archer and I have this thing now. When we sit for our talks, Ms. Archer holds my cast.
It's just this thing.
Before Ms. Archer was a teacher at our school, she used to live in a commune with a bunch of artists.
She was a painter and a dancer and she was studying to be a writer.
Ms. Archer says she can't stop looking at my eyes.
She says they are very serious.

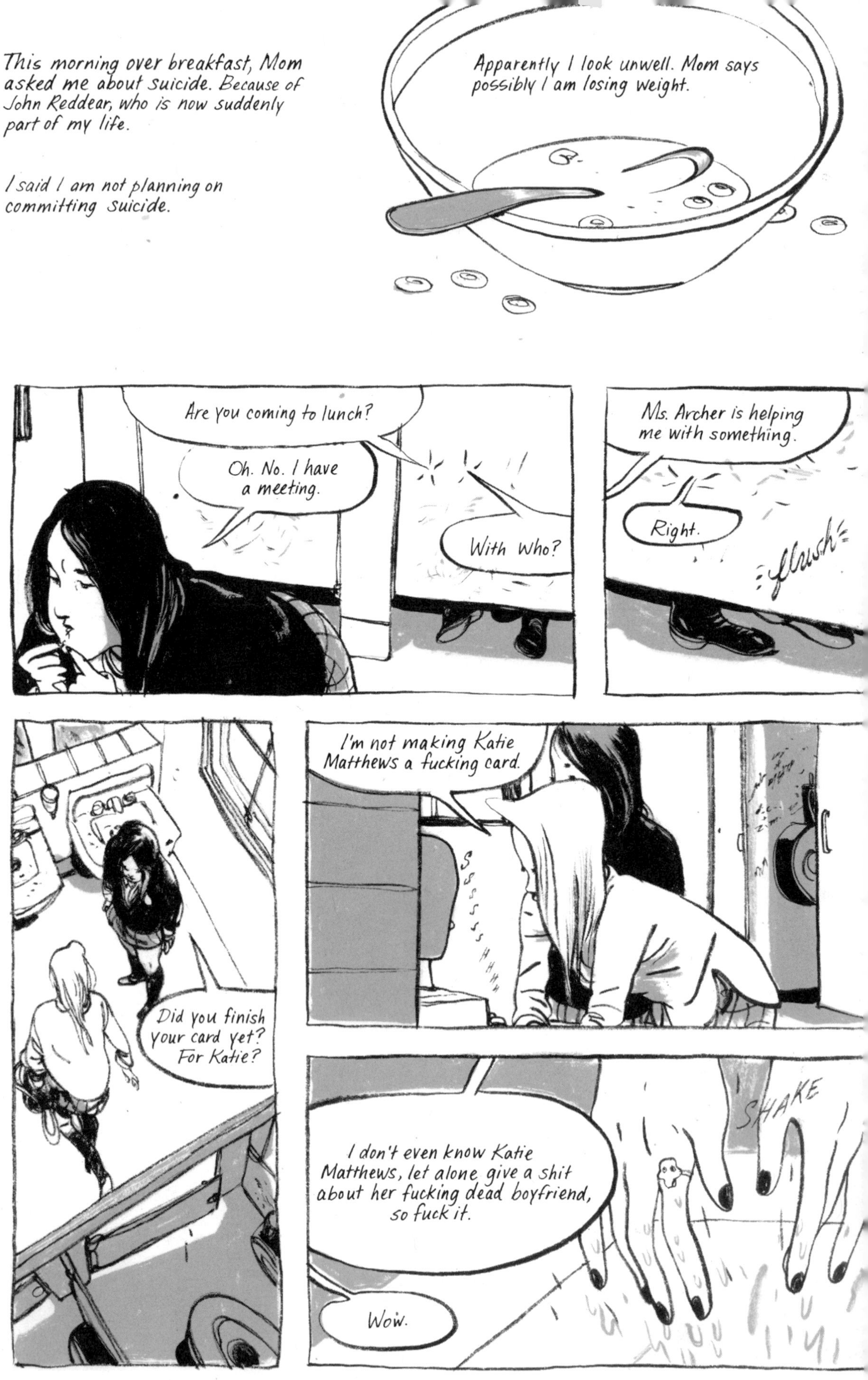
This morning over breakfast, Mom asked me about suicide. Because of John Reddear, who is now suddenly part of my life.
I said I am not planning on committing suicide.
Apparently I look unwell. Mom says possibly I am losing weight.
Are you coming to lunch?
Oh. No. I have a meeting.
With who?
Ms. Archer is helping me with something.
Right.
flush
Did you finish your card yet? For Katie?
I'm not making Katie Matthews a fucking card.
I don't even know Katie Matthews, let alone give a shit about her fucking dead boyfriend, so fuck it.
SHAKE
Wow.

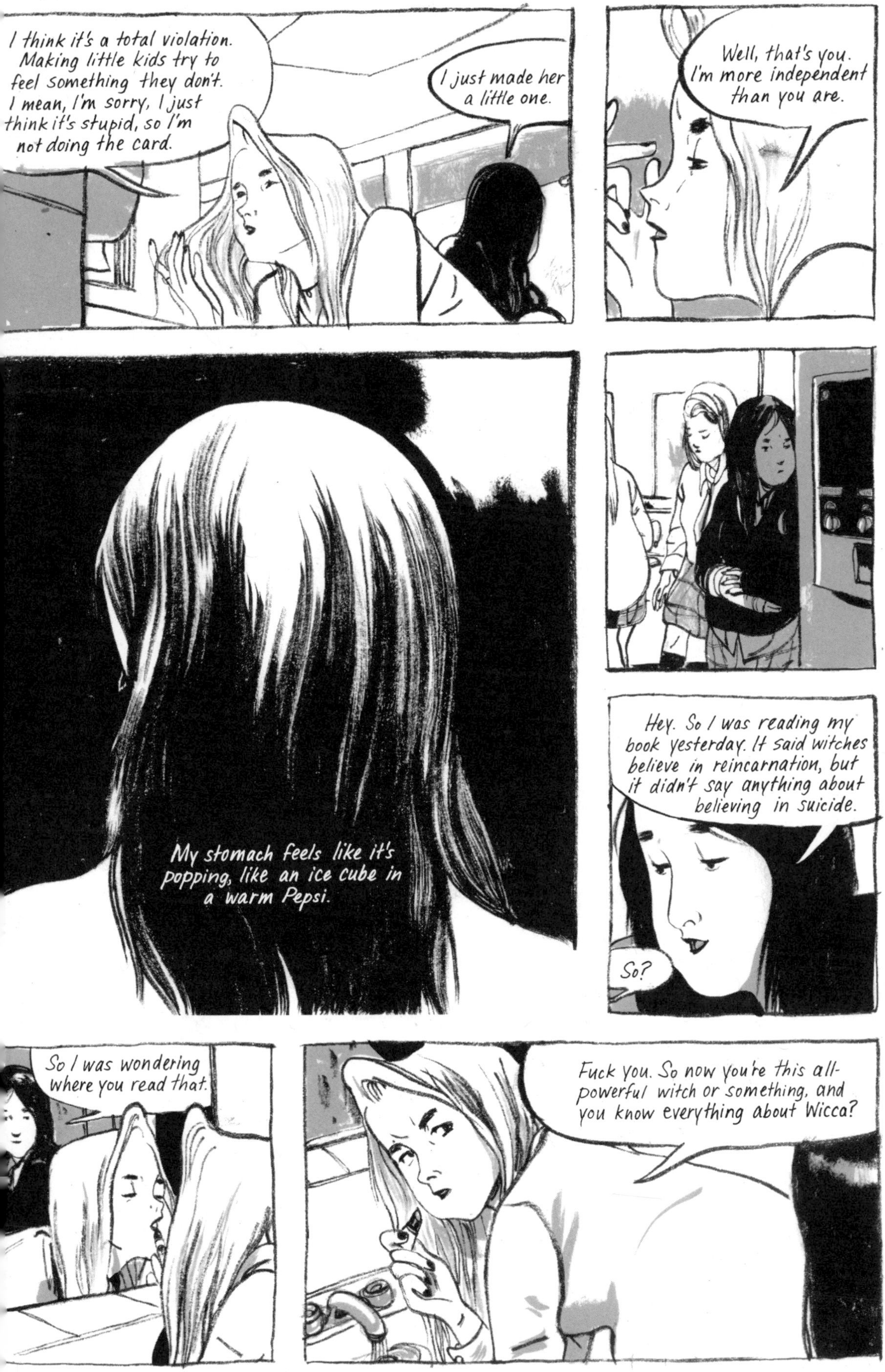
I think it's a total violation. Making little kids try to feel something they don't. I mean, I'm sorry, I just think it's stupid, so I'm not doing the card.
I just made her a little one.
Well, that's you. I'm more independent than you are.
My stomach feels like it's popping, like an ice cube in a warm Pepsi.
Hey. So I was reading my book yesterday. It said witches believe in reincarnation, but it didn't say anything about believing in suicide.
So?
So I was wondering where you read that.
Fuck you. So now you're this all-powerful witch or something, and you know everything about Wicca?

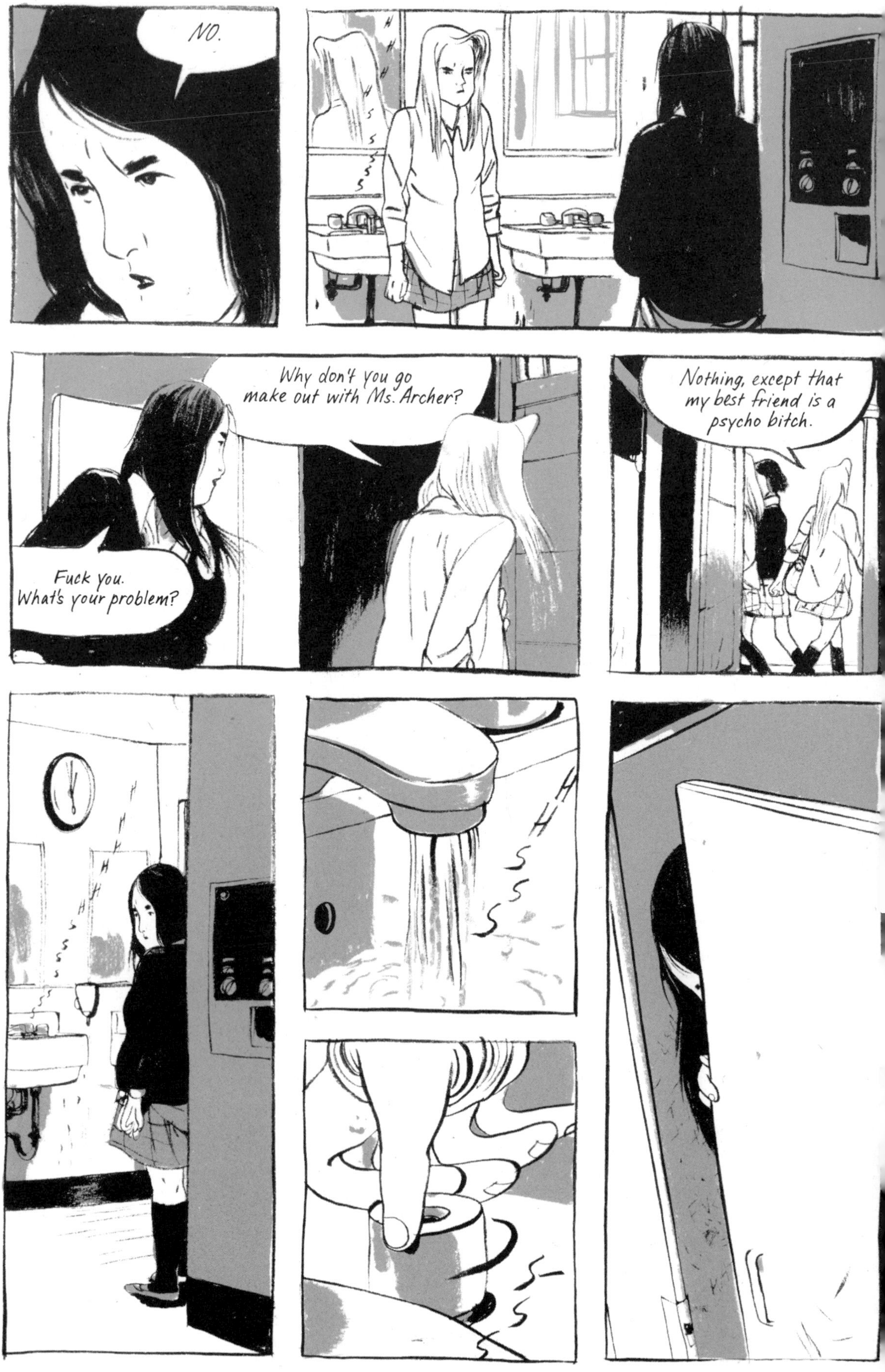
NO.
HHHHHSSSSS
Why don't you go make out with Ms. Archer?
Fuck you. What's your problem?
Nothing, except that my best friend is a psycho bitch.
HHHHHHSSSS
HHHSSS
SSS

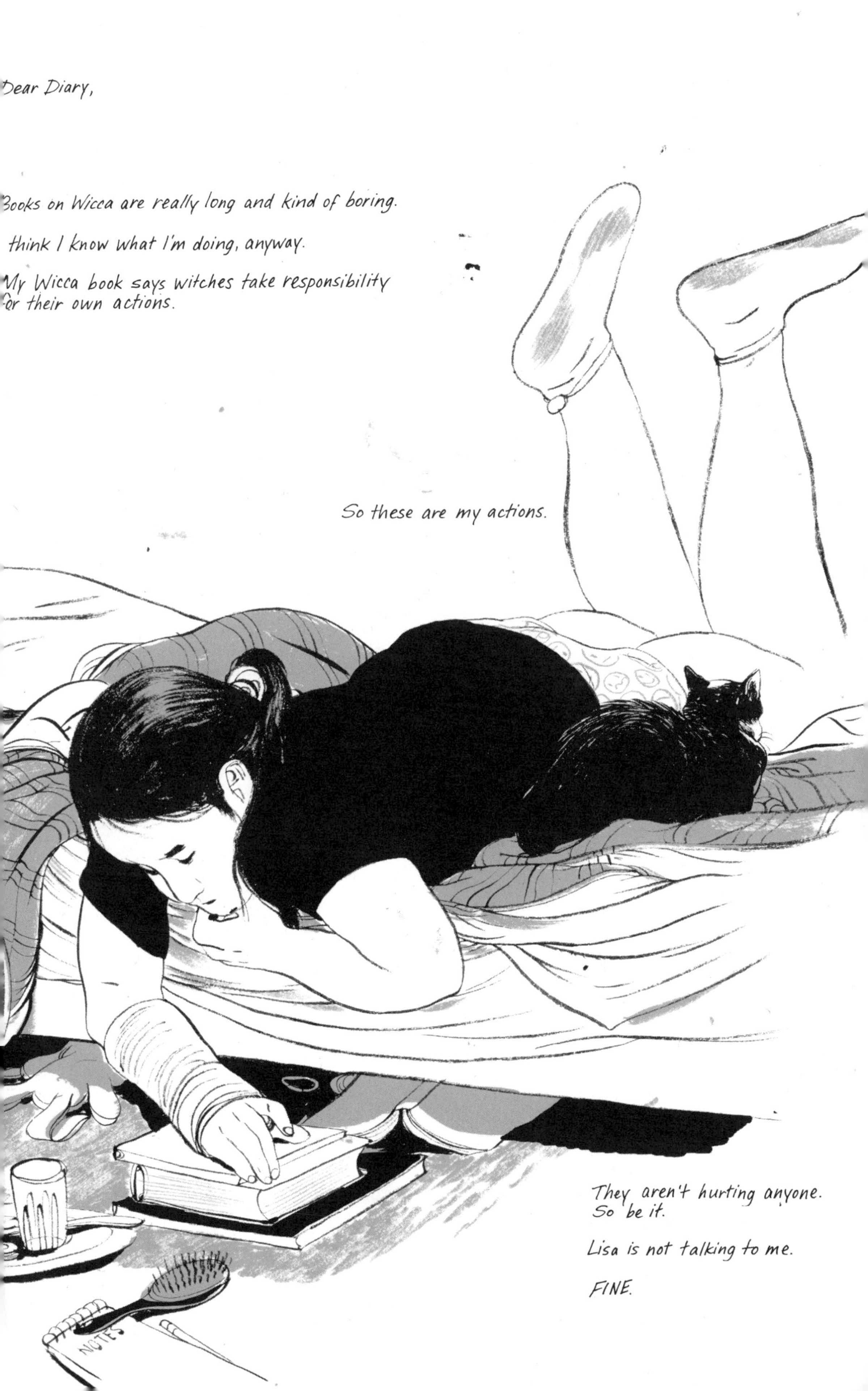

Dear Diary,
Books on Wicca are really long and kind of boring.
think I know what I'm doing, anyway.
My Wicca book says witches take responsibility for their own actions.
So these are my actions.
They aren't hurting anyone. So be it.
Lisa is not talking to me.
FINE.
NOTES

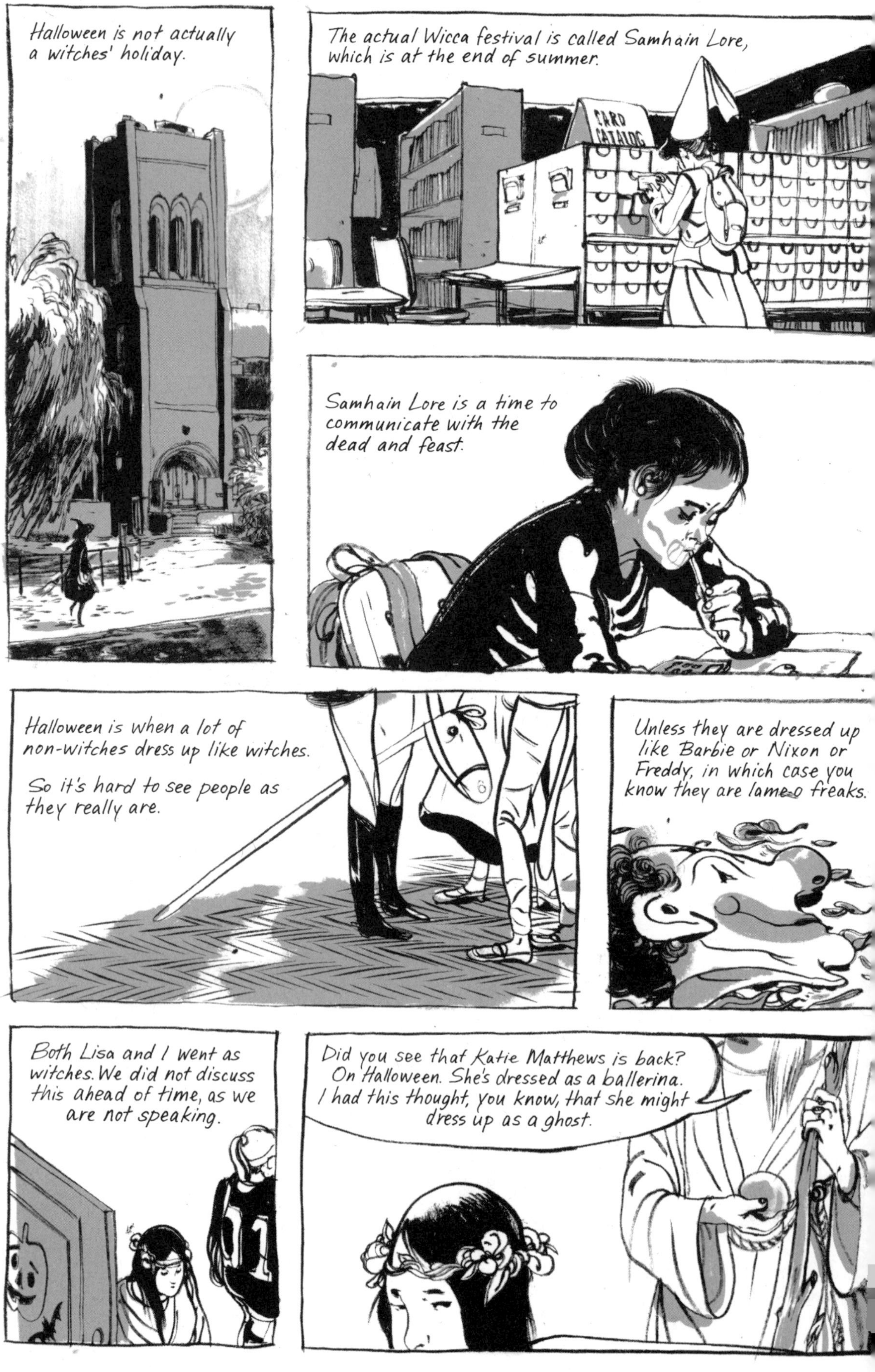
Halloween is not actually a witches' holiday.
The actual Wicca festival is called Samhain Lore, which is at the end of summer.
CARD CATALOG
Samhain Lore is a time to communicate with the dead and feast.
Halloween is when a lot of non-witches dress up like witches.
So it's hard to see people as they really are.
Unless they are dressed up like Barbie or Nixon or Freddy, in which case you know they are lame-o freaks.
Both Lisa and I went as witches. We did not discuss this ahead of time, as we are not speaking.
Did you see that Katie Matthews is back? On Halloween. She's dressed as a ballerina. I had this thought, you know, that she might dress up as a ghost.

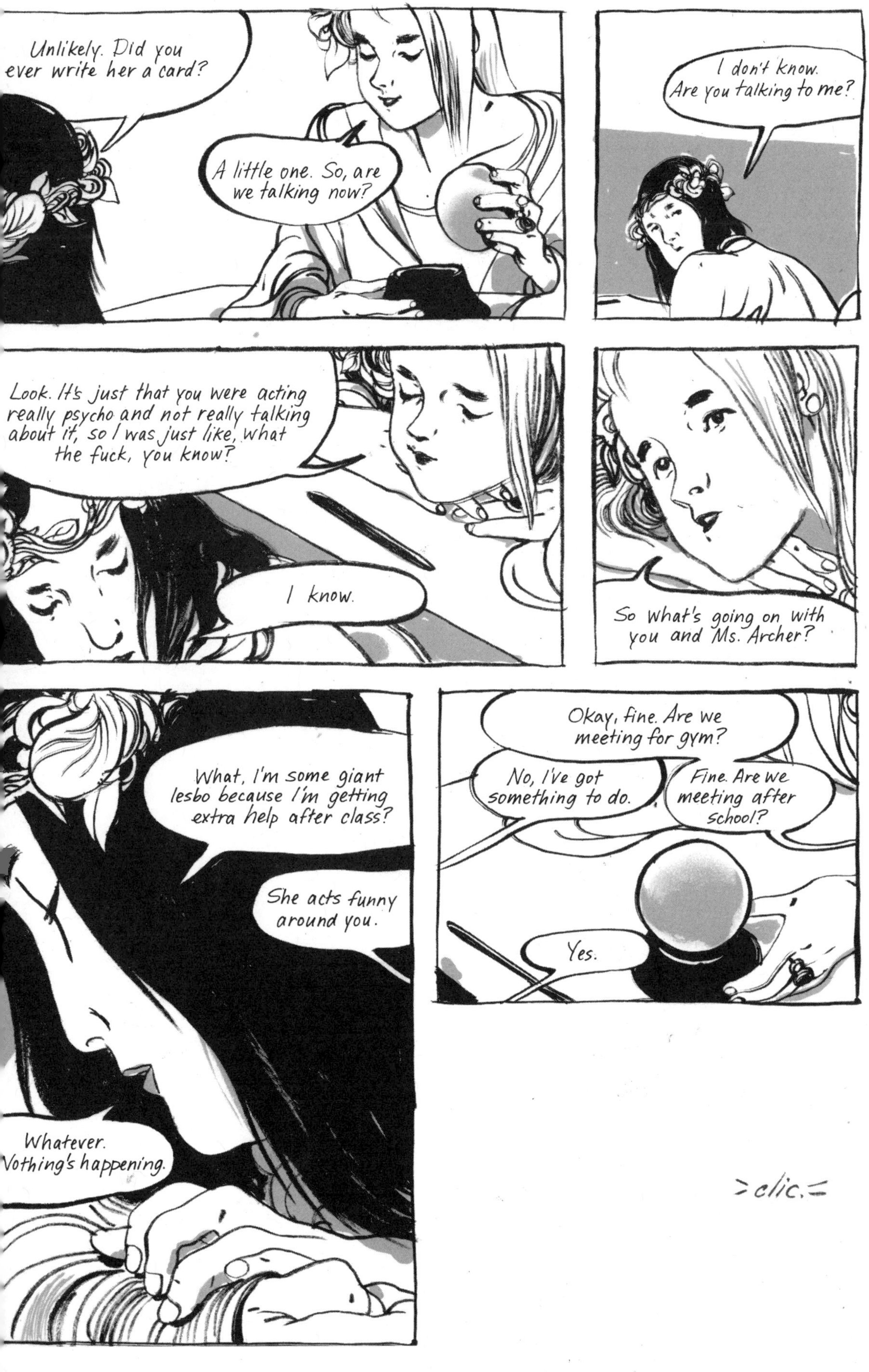

Unlikely. Did you ever write her a card?
A little one. So, are we talking now?
I don't know. Are you talking to me?
Look. It's just that you were acting really psycho and not really talking about it, so I was just like, what the fuck, you know?
I know.
So what's going on with you and Ms. Archer?
What, I'm some giant lesbo because I'm getting extra help after class?
She acts funny around you.
Whatever. Nothing's happening.
Okay, fine. Are we meeting for gym?
No, I've got something to do.
Fine. Are we meeting after school?
Yes.
>clic.=

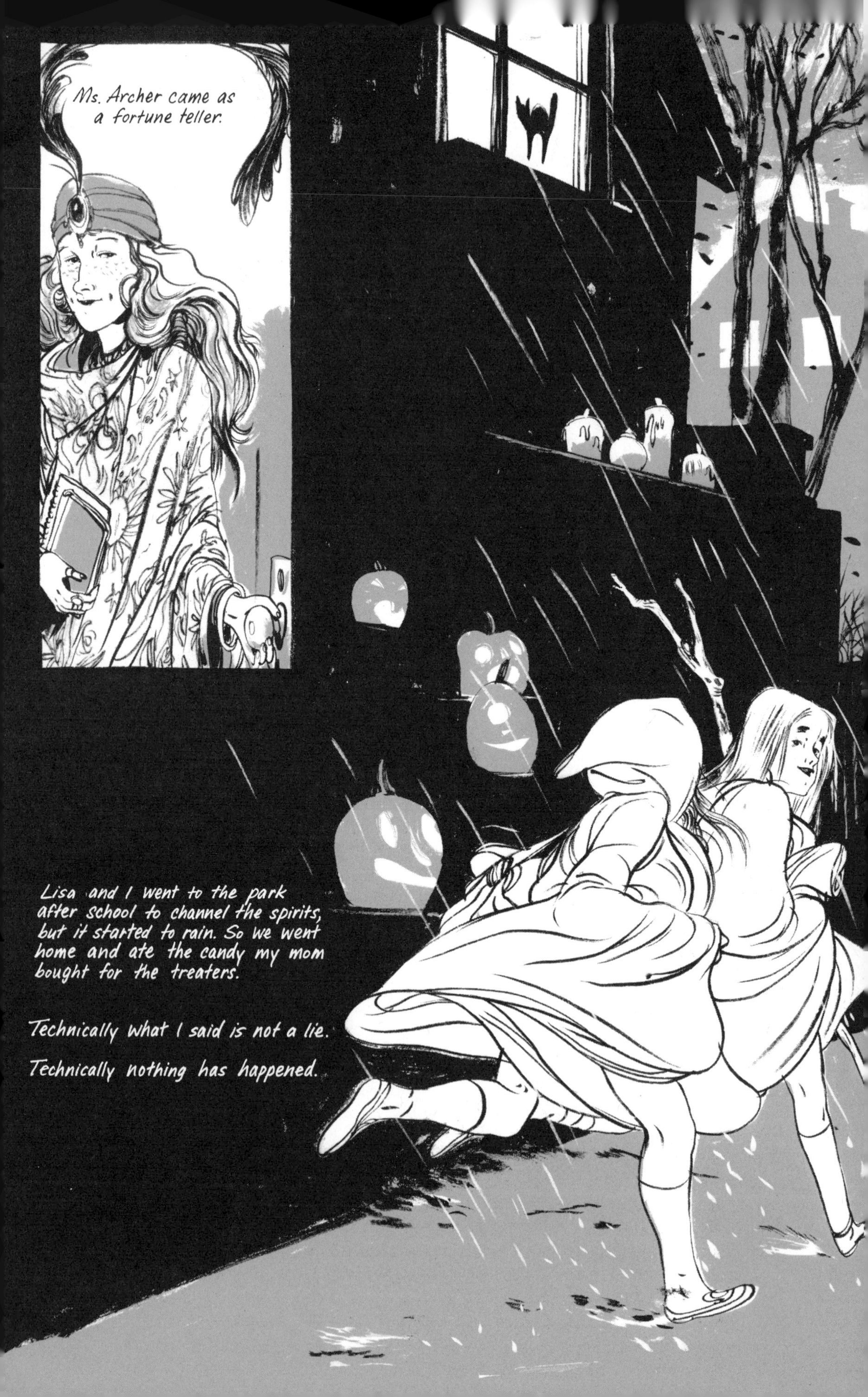
Ms. Archer came as a fortune teller.
Lisa and I went to the park after school to channel the spirits, but it started to rain. So we went home and ate the candy my mom bought for the treaters.
Technically what I said is not a lie.
Technically nothing has happened.

Dear Diary,

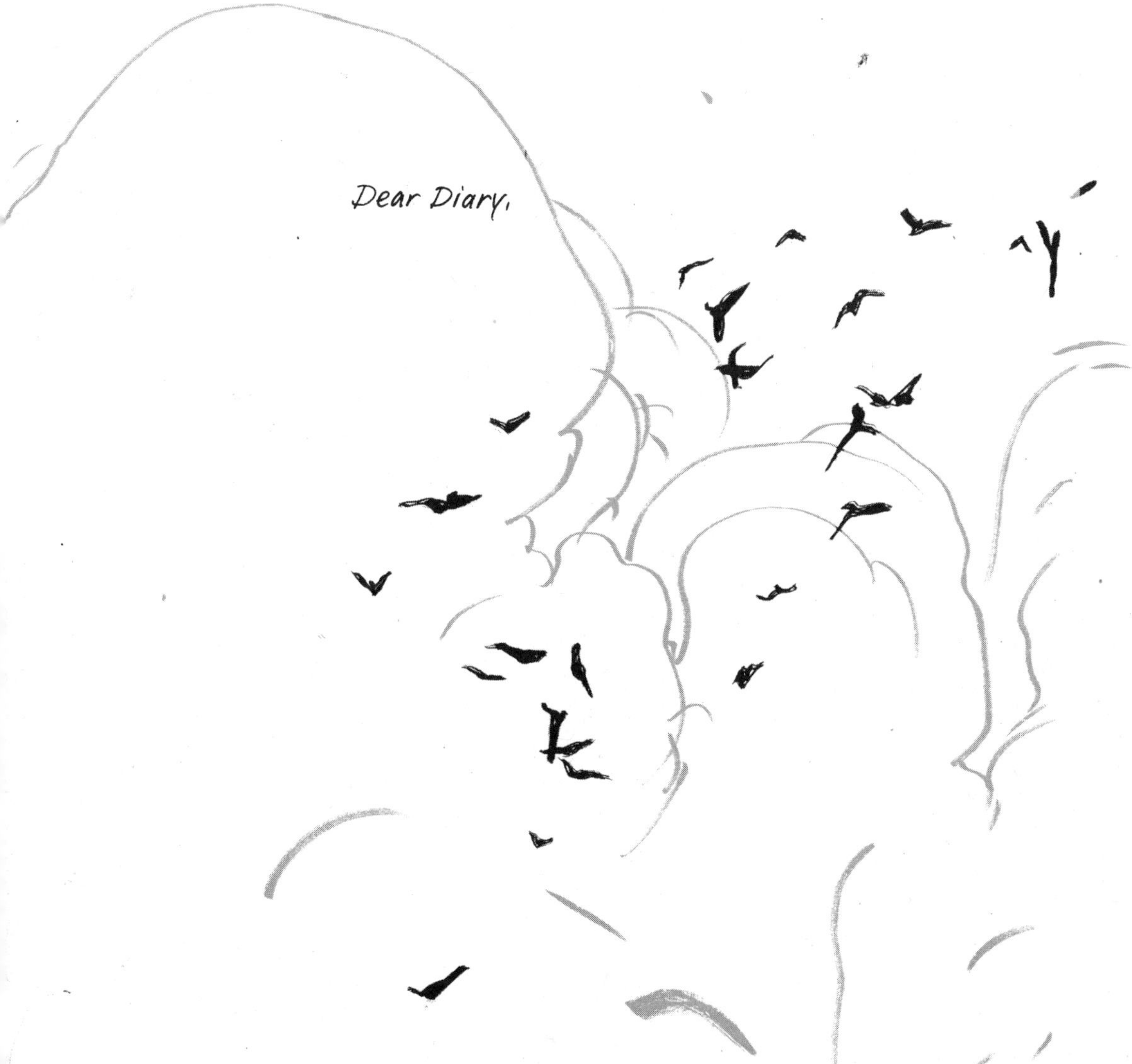

For the record, not all Wicca books are boring.
This is what I found in my new book:

The "Charge" comes to each of us in a different manner. It is that moment in our lives when we feel the Magick of the Universe coursing through us for the very first time, and we know beyond all real and imagined shadows that this calling to the mysteries is indeed there.

Silver RavenWolf, To Ride a Silver Broomstick

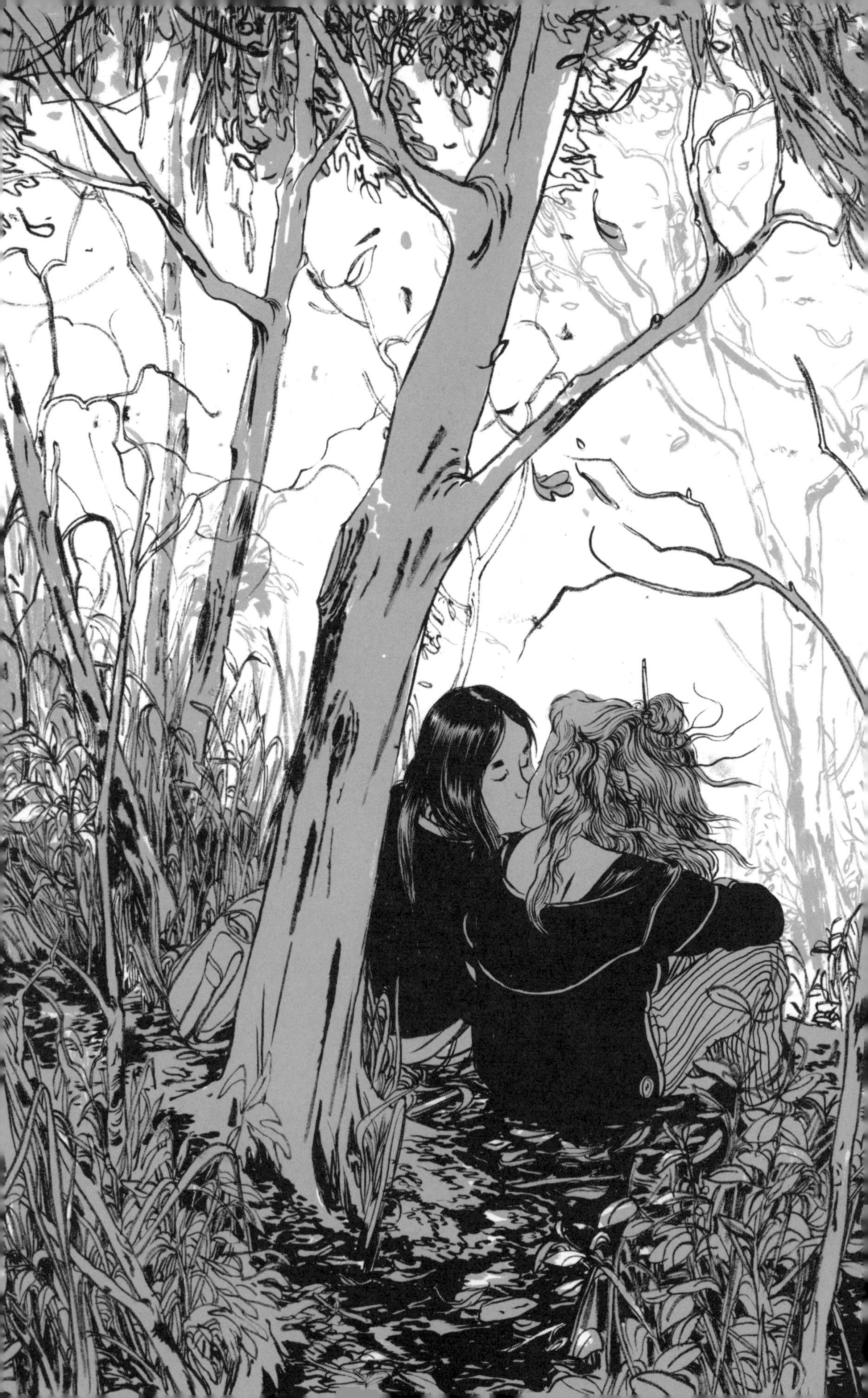

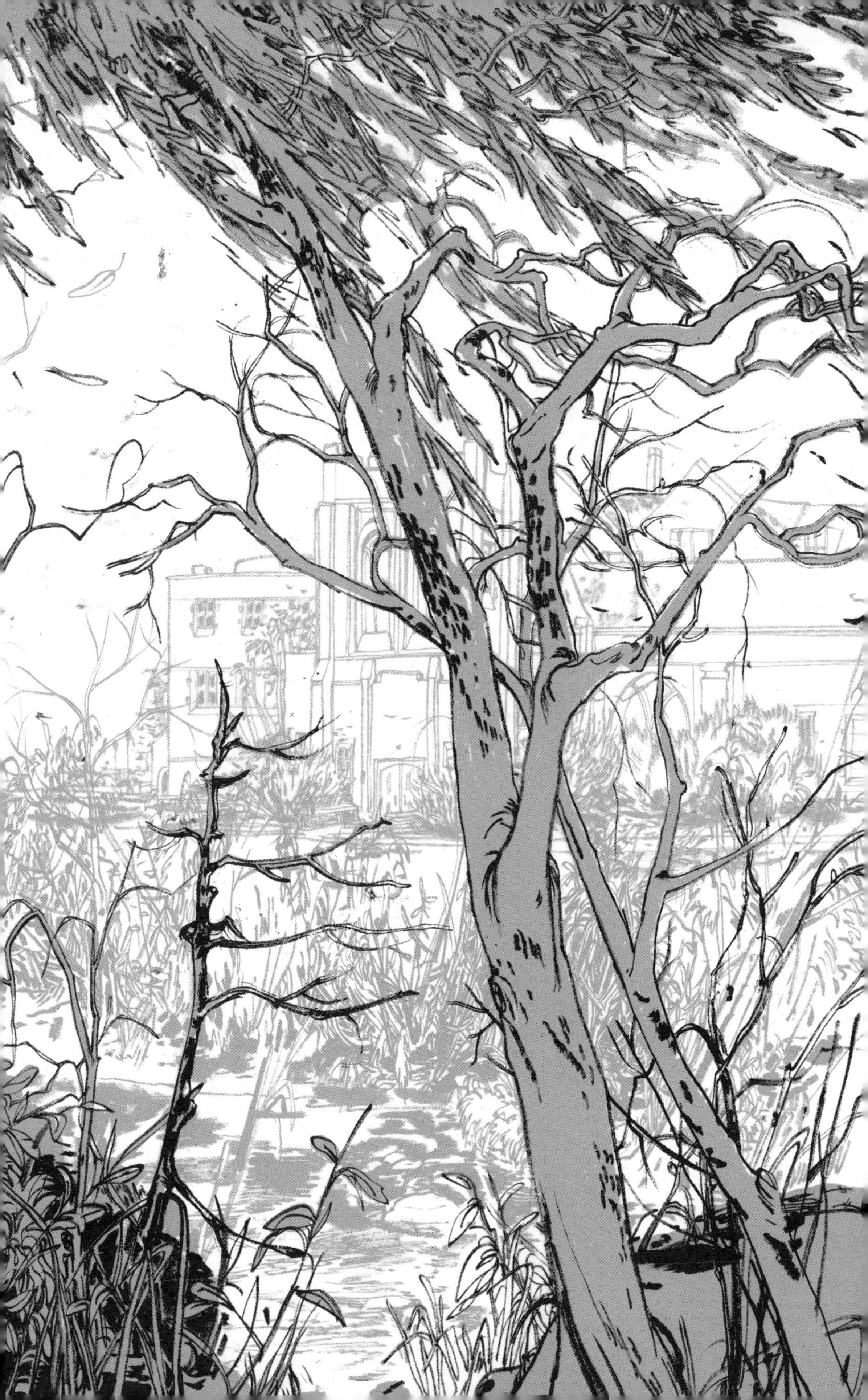

Part II

No Rest for the Wicked

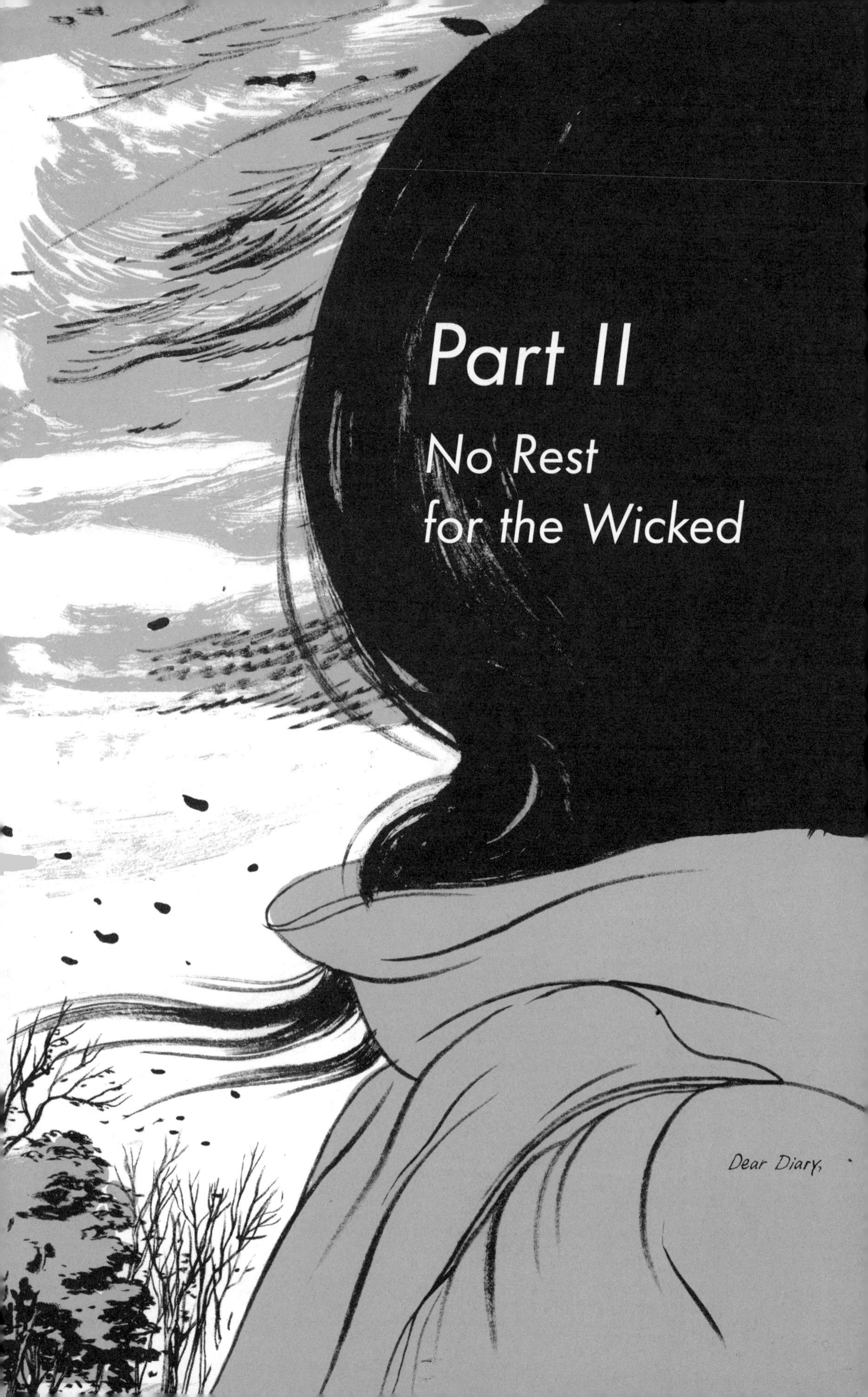
Dear Diary,

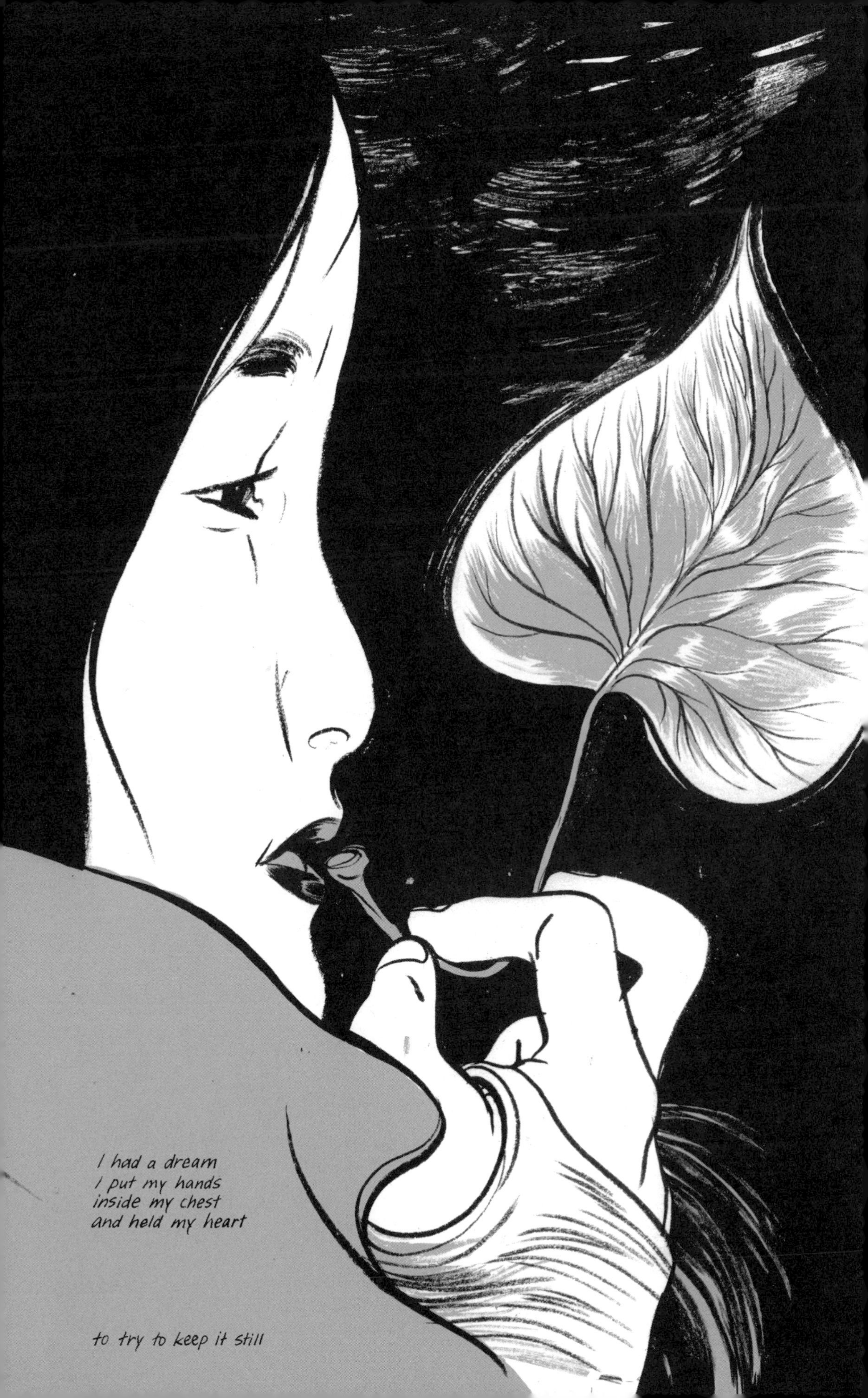
I had a dream
I put my hands
inside my chest
and held my heart
to try to keep it still

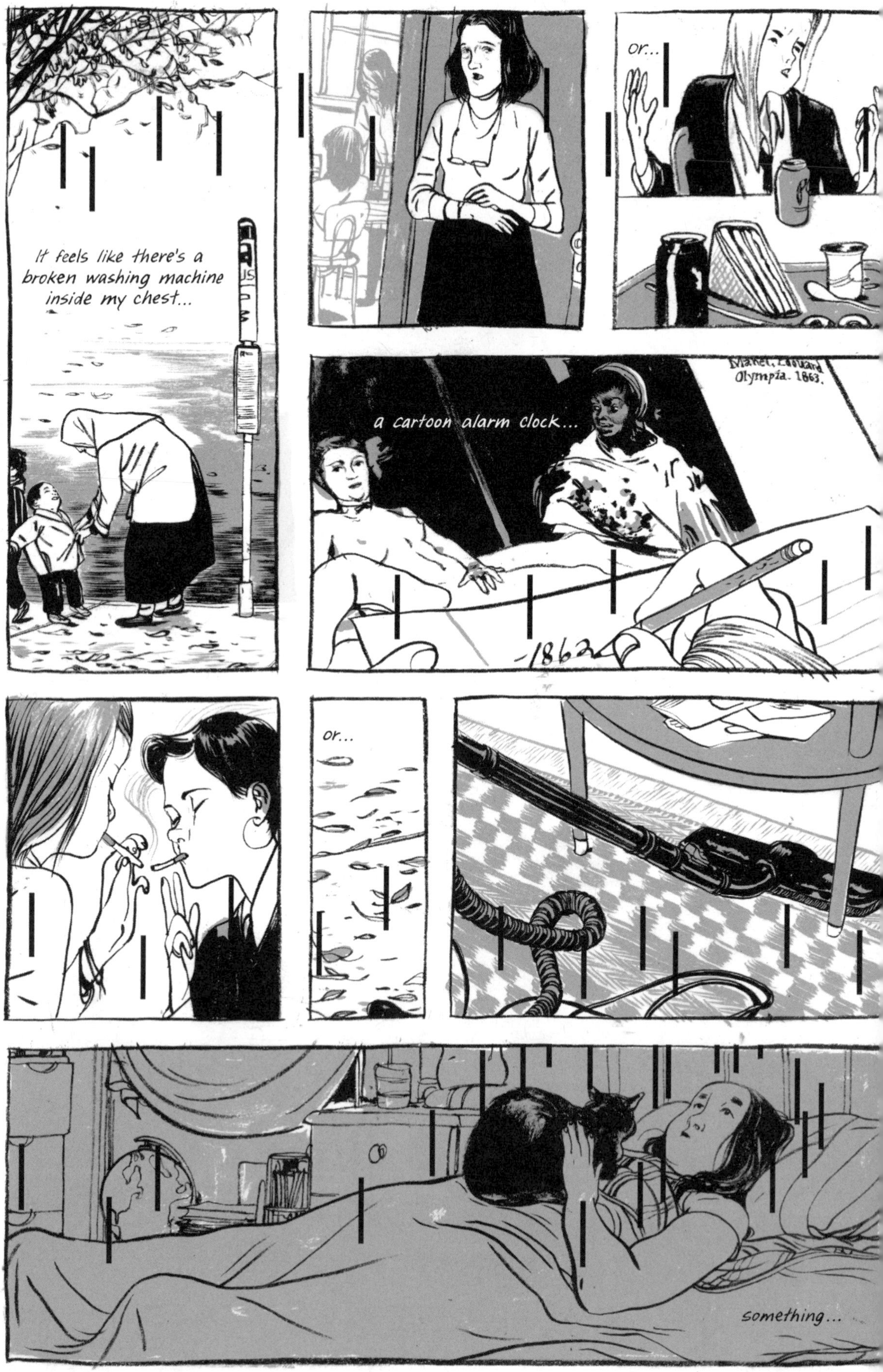
It feels like there's a broken washing machine inside my chest...
or...
Manet, Edouard
Olympia. 1863.
a cartoon alarm clock...
or...
something...

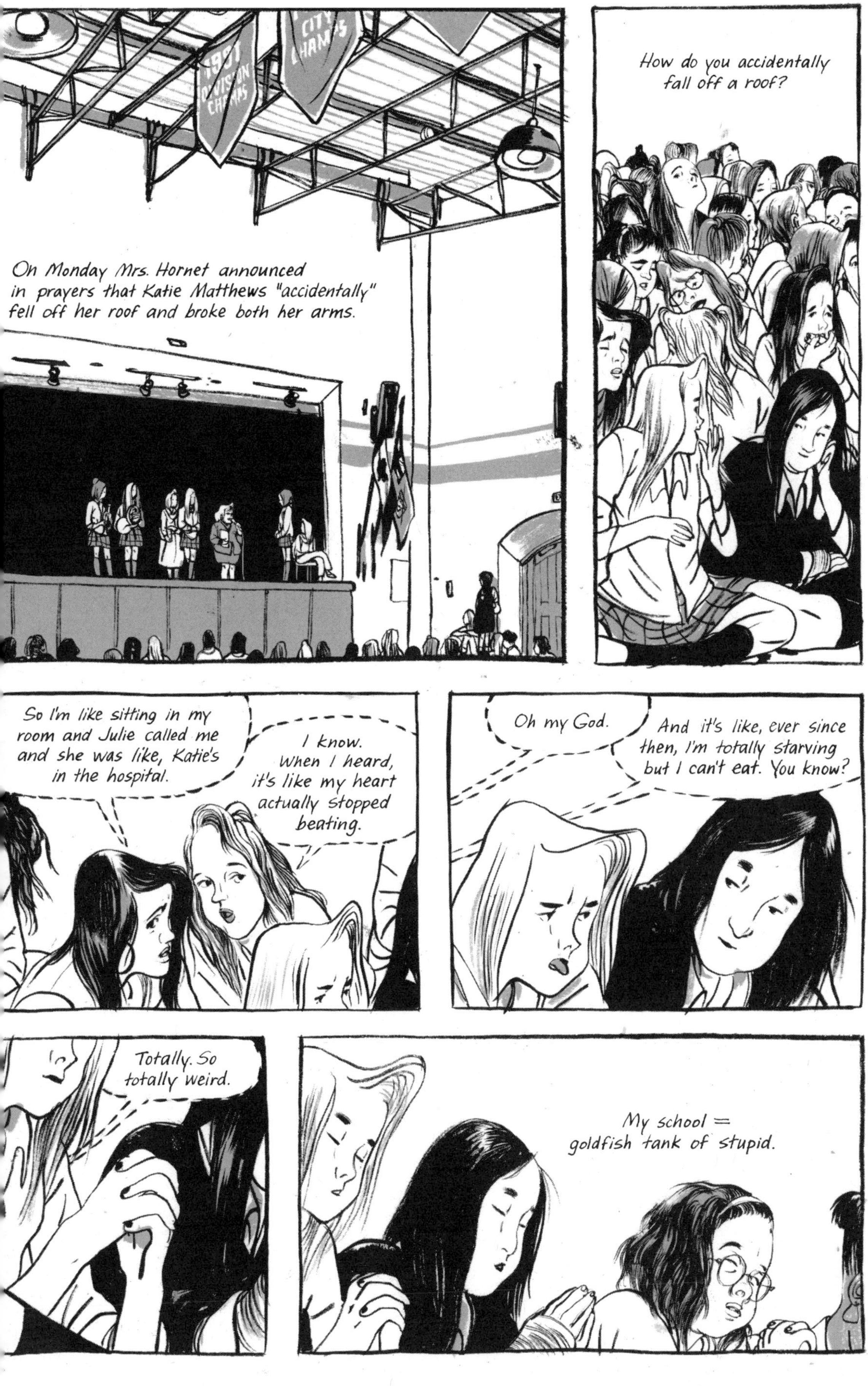
On Monday Mrs. Hornet announced in prayers that Katie Matthews "accidentally" fell off her roof and broke both her arms.
How do you accidentally fall off a roof?
So I'm like sitting in my room and Julie called me and she was like, Katie's in the hospital.
I know. When I heard, it's like my heart actually stopped beating.
Oh my God.
And it's like, ever since then, I'm totally starving but I can't eat. You know?
Totally. So totally weird.
My school = goldfish tank of stupid.

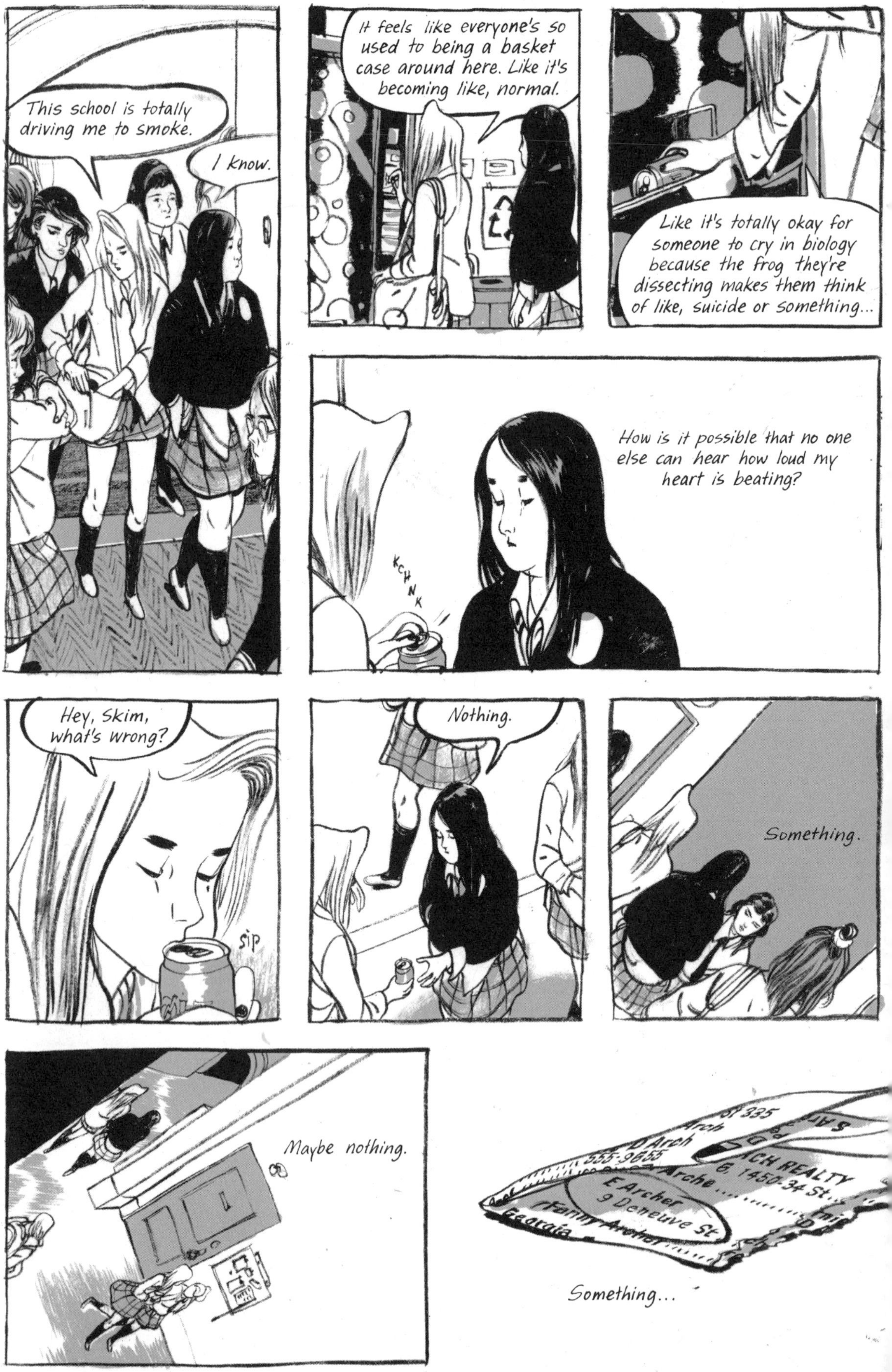

This school is totally driving me to smoke.
I know.
It feels like everyone's so used to being a basket case around here. Like it's becoming like, normal.
Like it's totally okay for someone to cry in biology because the frog they're dissecting makes them think of like, suicide or something...
How is it possible that no one else can hear how loud my heart is beating?
KCHNK
Hey, Skim, what's wrong?
sip
Nothing.
Something.
Maybe nothing.
Something...

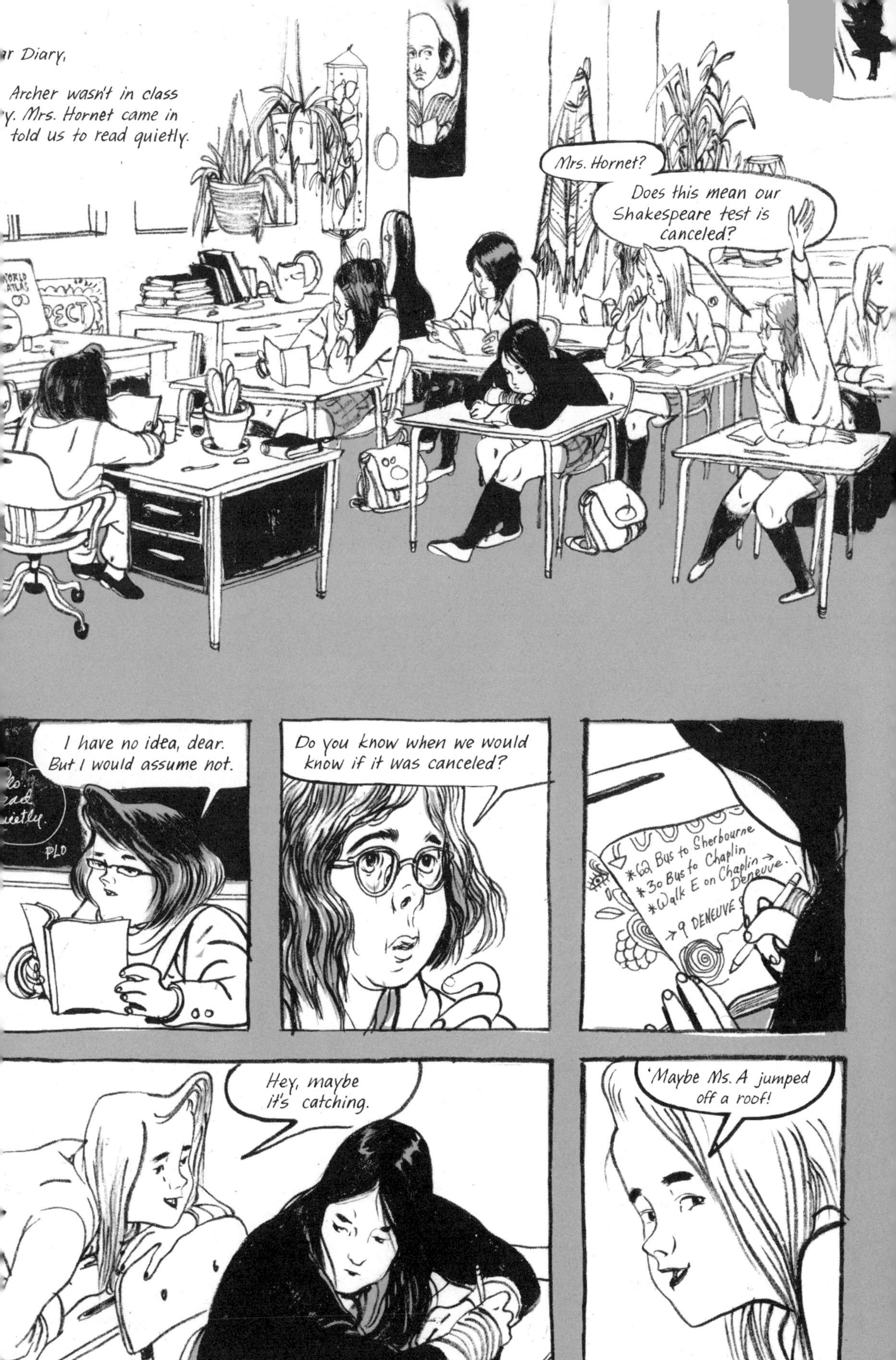
ar Diary,
Archer wasn't in class
y. Mrs. Hornet came in
told us to read quietly.
Mrs. Hornet?
Does this mean our Shakespeare test is canceled?
I have no idea, dear. But I would assume not.
Do you know when we would know if it was canceled?
*62 Bus to Sherbourne
*30 Bus to Chaplin →
*Walk E on Chaplin → Deneuve.
→ 9 DENEUVE S
Hey, maybe it's catching.
'Maybe Ms. A jumped off a roof!

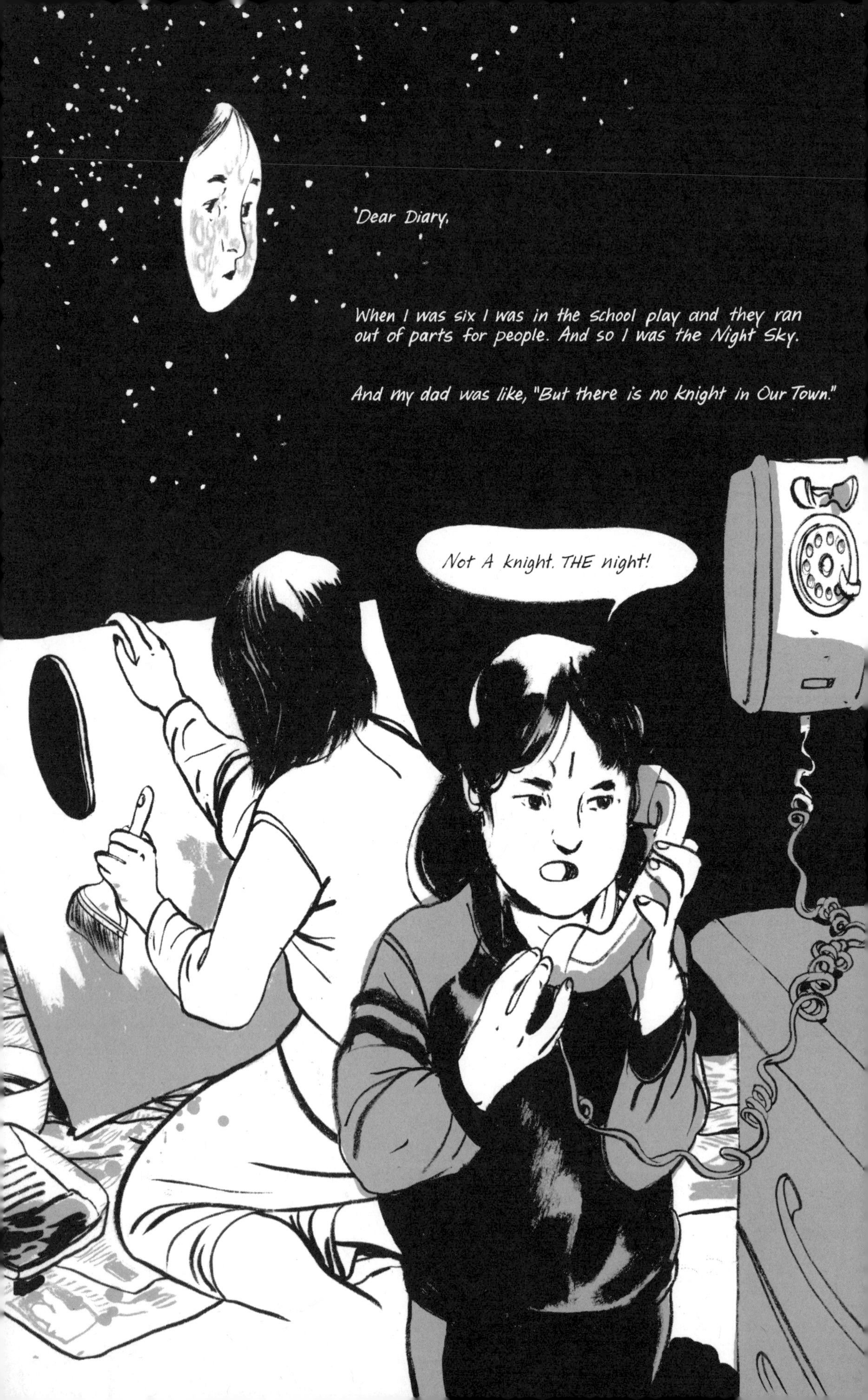
"Dear Diary,
When I was six I was in the school play and they ran out of parts for people. And so I was the Night Sky.
And my dad was like, "But there is no knight in Our Town."
Not A knight. THE night!

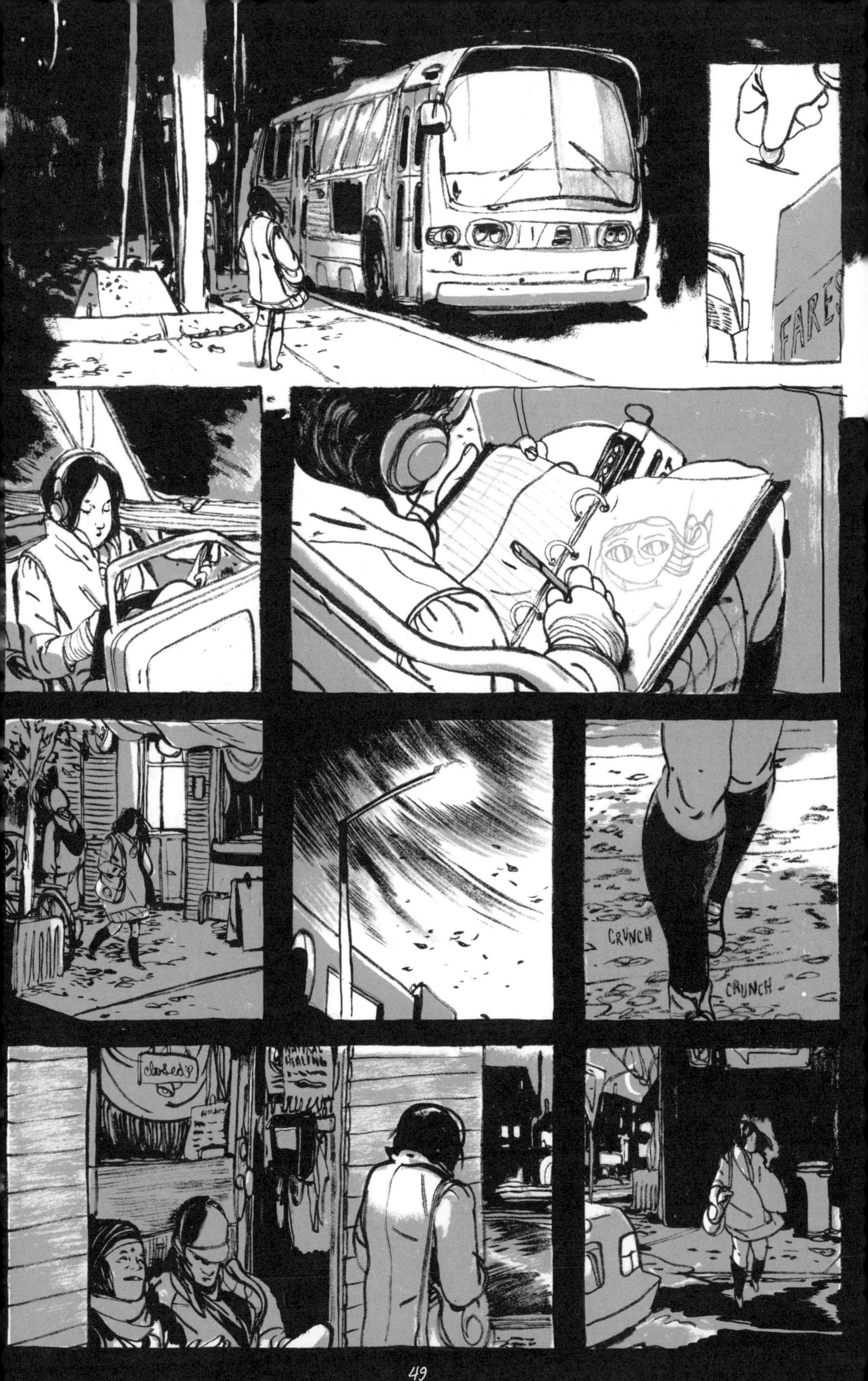
FARES
CRUNCH
CRUNCH
closed

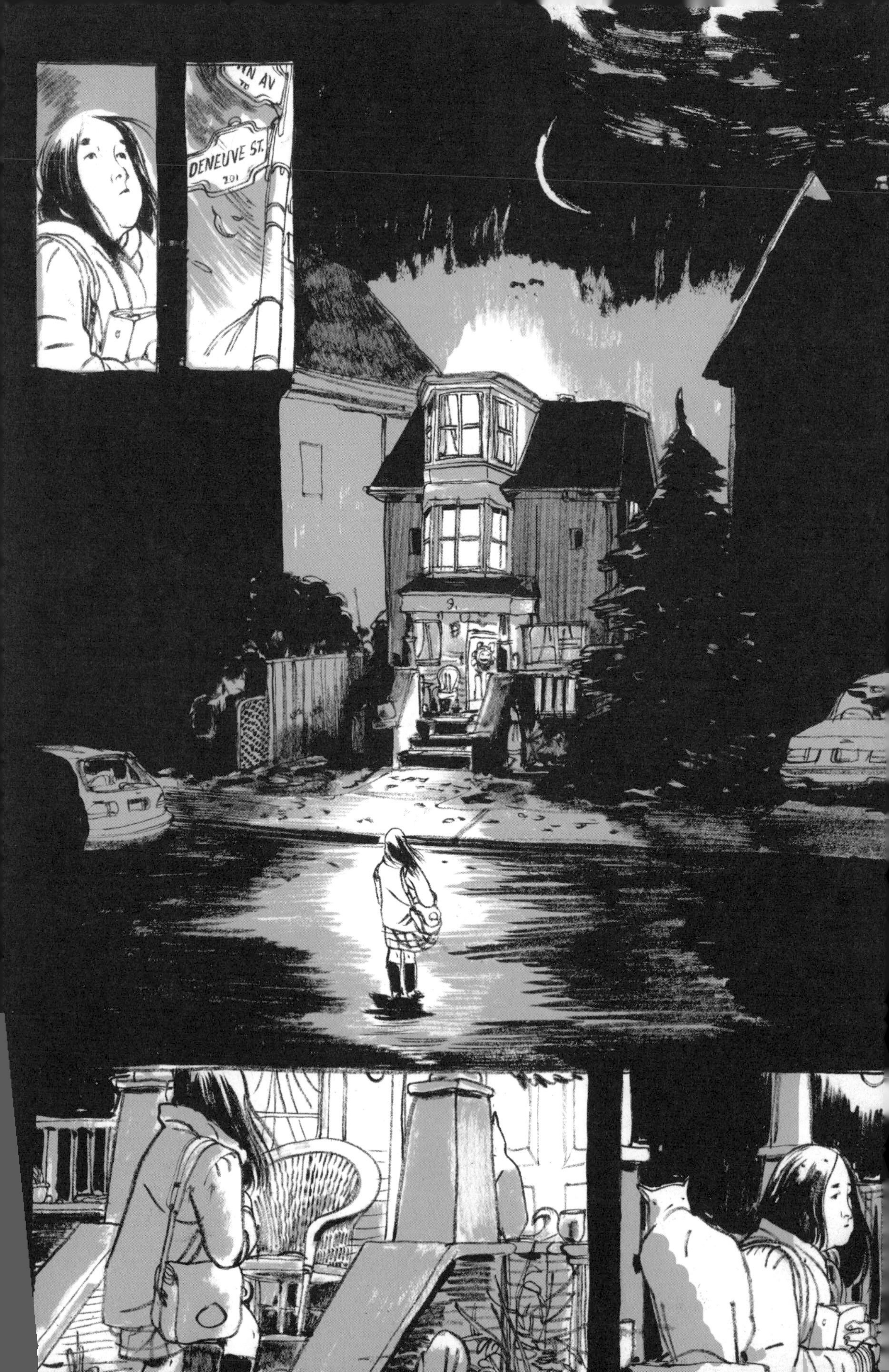
DENEUVE ST.
201

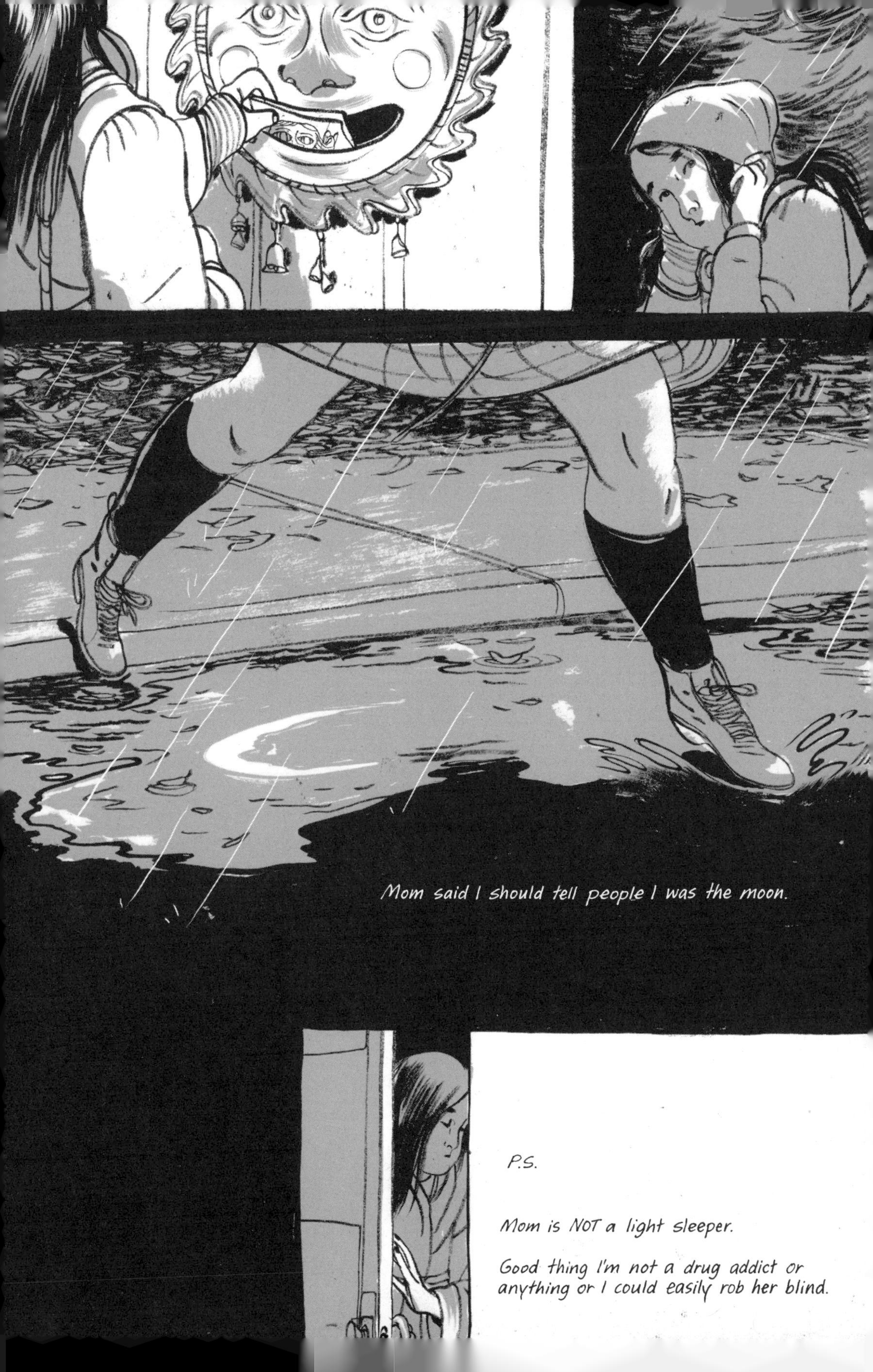
Mom said I should tell people I was the moon.
P.S.
Mom is NOT a light sleeper.
Good thing I'm not a drug addict or anything or I could easily rob her blind.

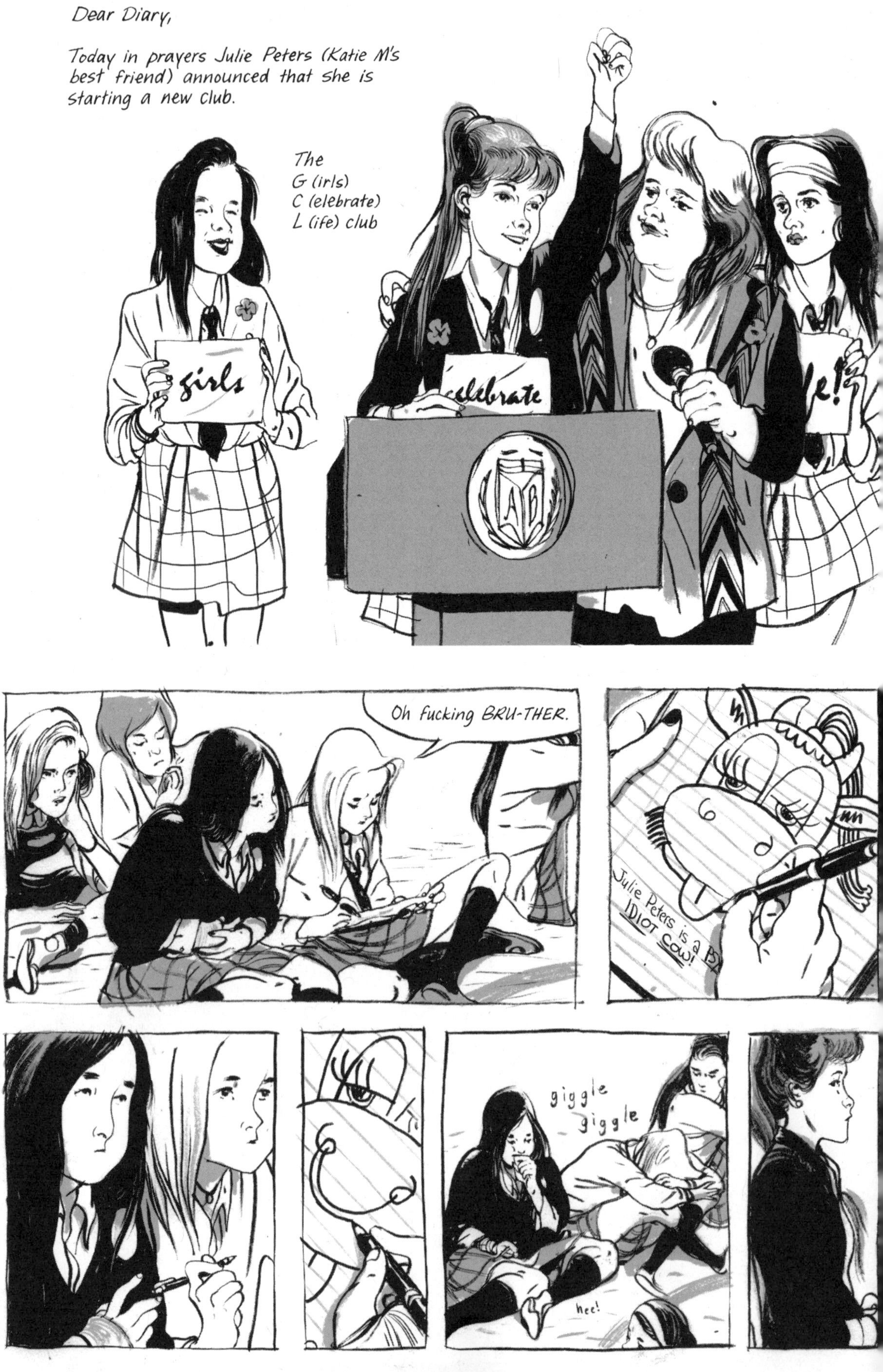
Dear Diary,
Today in prayers Julie Peters (Katie M's best friend) announced that she is starting a new club.
The G (irls) C (elebrate) L (ife) club
girls
celebrate
Oh fucking BRU-THER.
Julie Peters is a
IDIOT COW!
giggle giggle
hee!

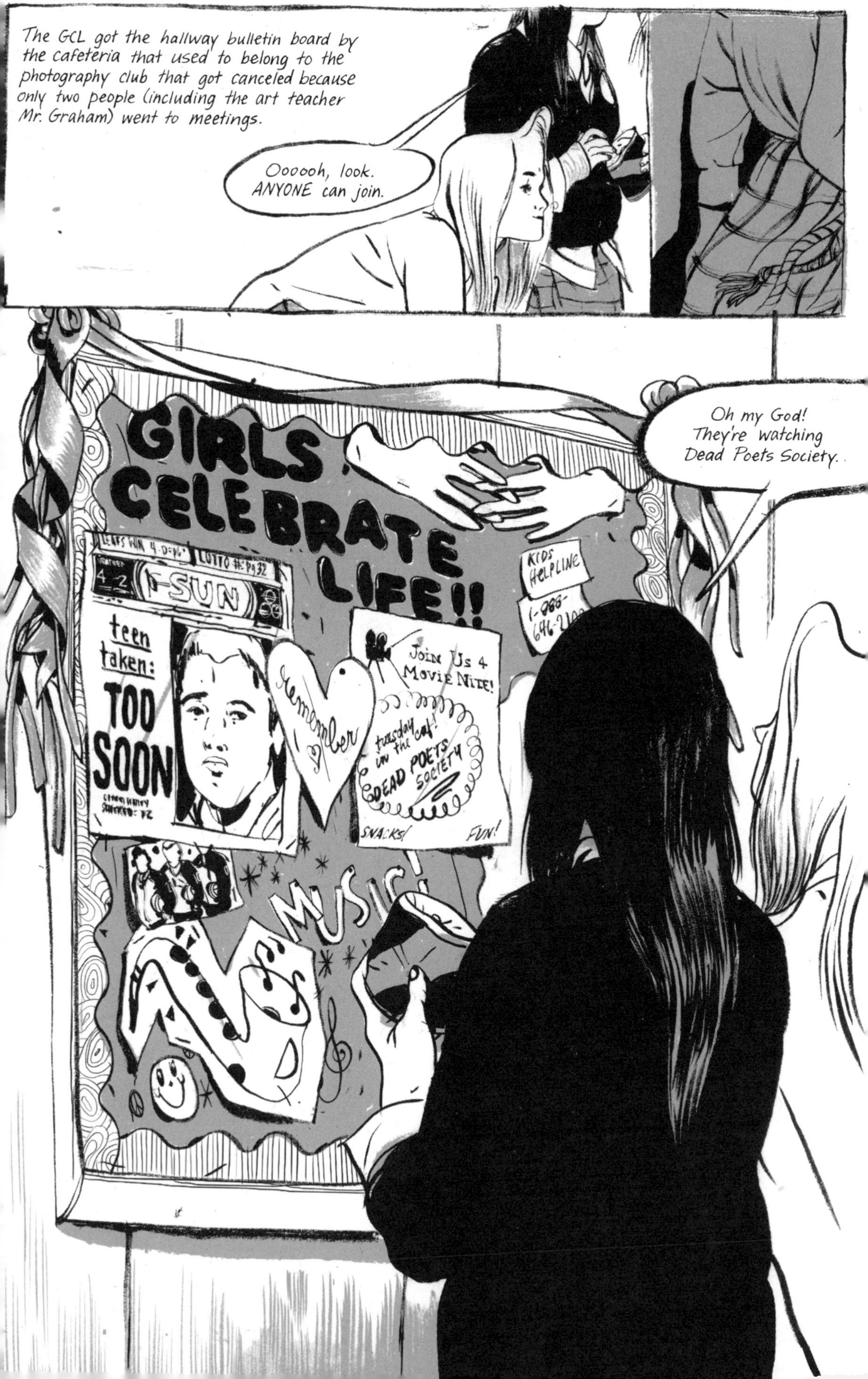

The GCL got the hallway bulletin board by the cafeteria that used to belong to the photography club that got canceled because only two people (including the art teacher Mr. Graham) went to meetings.
Oooooh, look. ANYONE can join.
GIRLS CELEBRATE LIFE!!
teen taken: TOO SOON
remember
Join Us 4 Movie Nite!
tuesday in the caf!
DEAD POETS SOCIETY
SNACKS!
FUN!
KIDS HELPLINE
MUSIC!
Oh my God! They're watching Dead Poets Society.

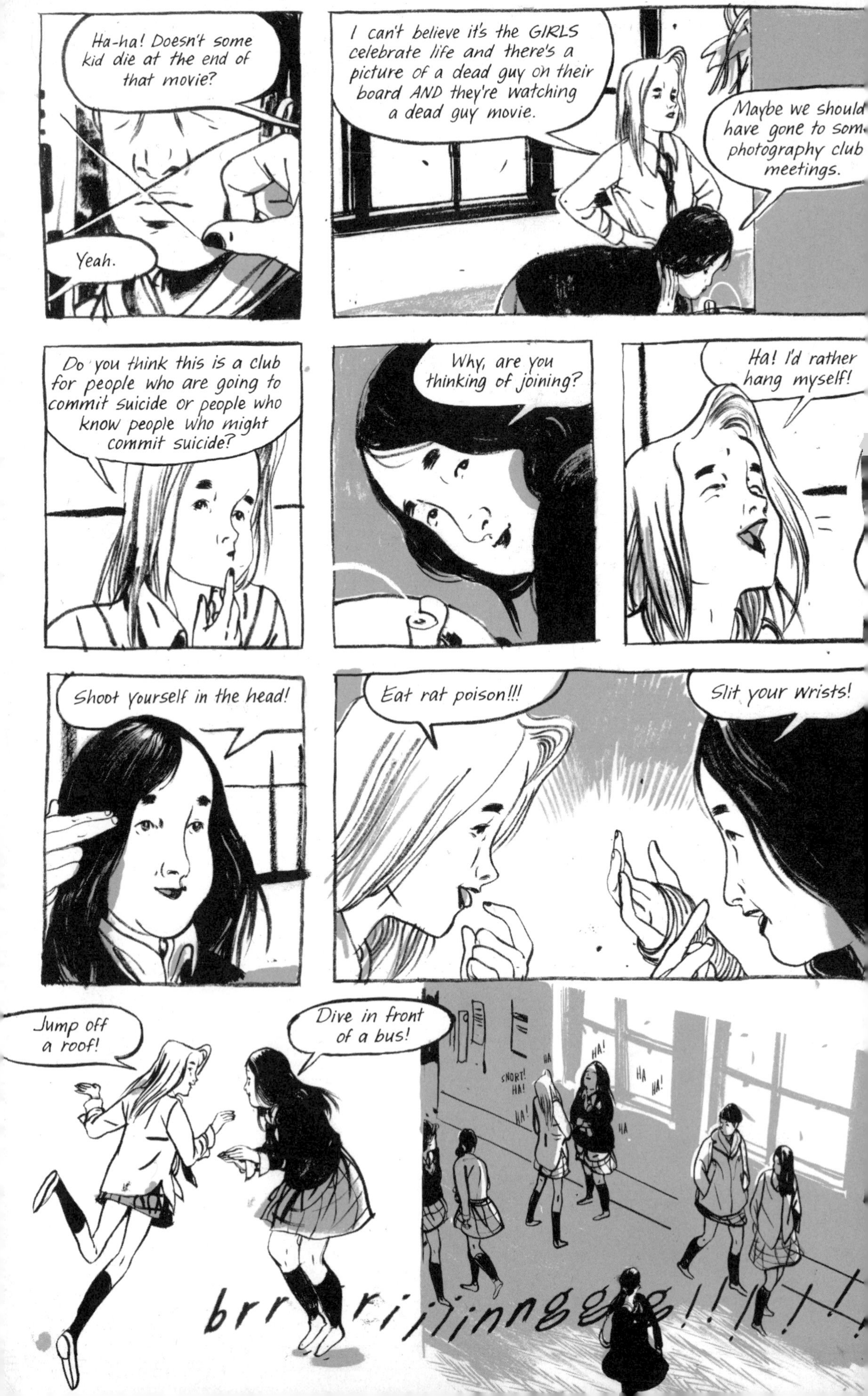

Ha-ha! Doesn't some kid die at the end of that movie?
Yeah.
I can't believe it's the GIRLS celebrate life and there's a picture of a dead guy on their board AND they're watching a dead guy movie.
Maybe we should have gone to som photography club meetings.
Do you think this is a club for people who are going to commit suicide or people who know people who might commit suicide?
Why, are you thinking of joining?
Ha! I'd rather hang myself!
Shoot yourself in the head!
Eat rat poison!!!
Slit your wrists!
Jump off a roof!
Dive in front of a bus!
SNORT!
HA!
HA!
HA
HA!
HA
HA!
HA
brrriiiinngggg!!!!!

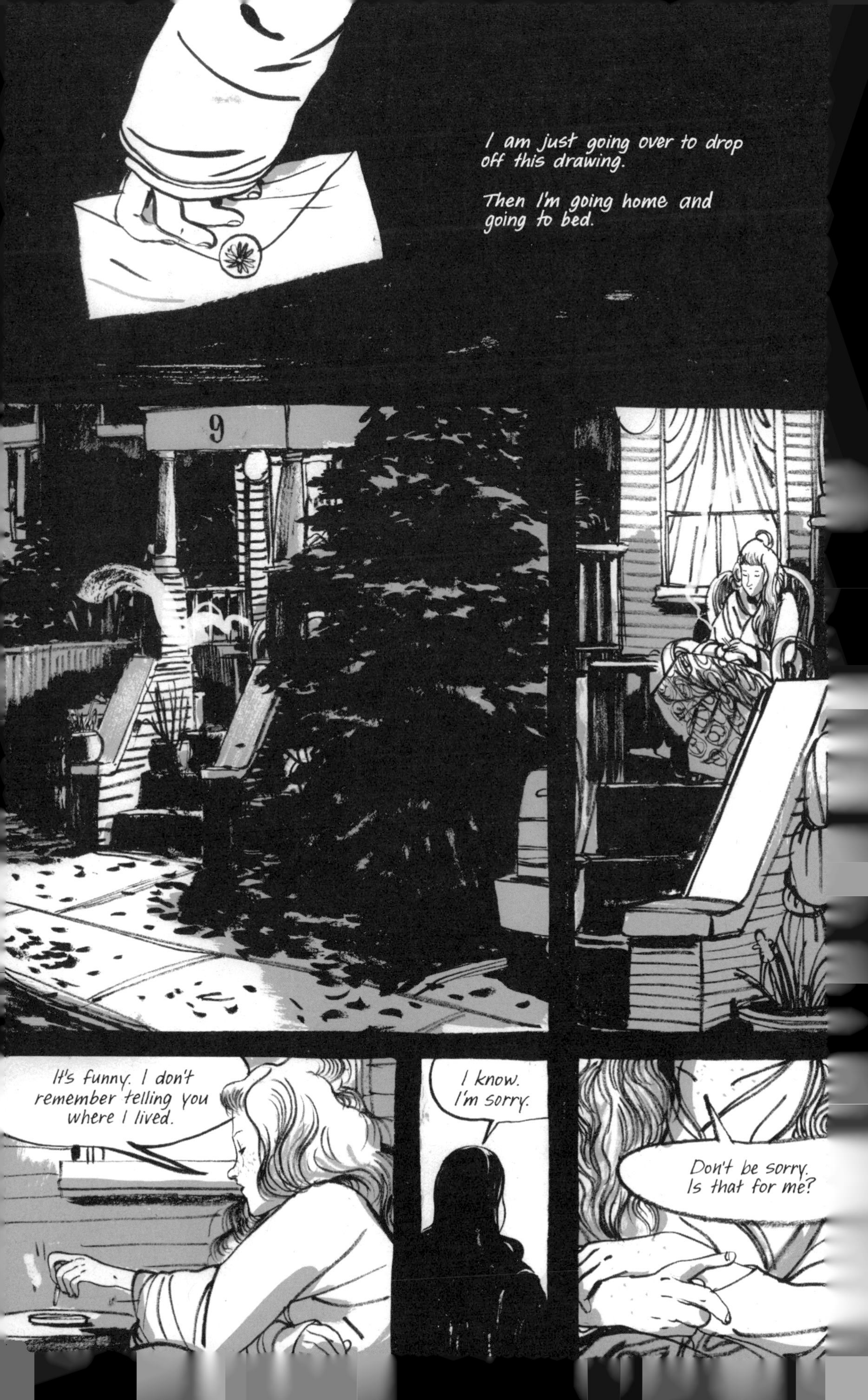
I am just going over to drop off this drawing.
Then I'm going home and going to bed.
It's funny. I don't remember telling you where I lived.
I know. I'm sorry.
Don't be sorry. Is that for me?

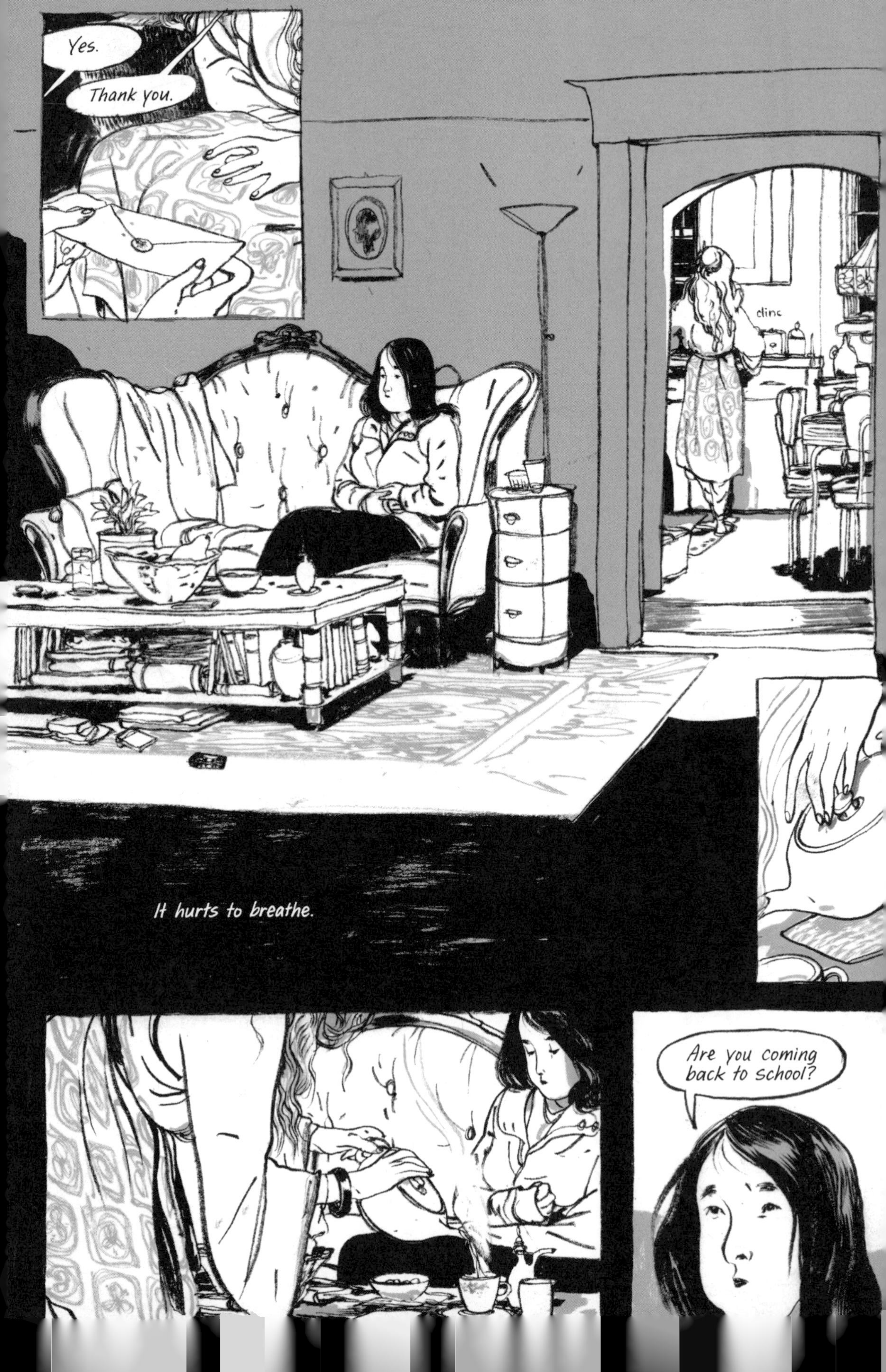
Yes.
Thank you.
clinc
It hurts to breathe.
Are you coming back to school?

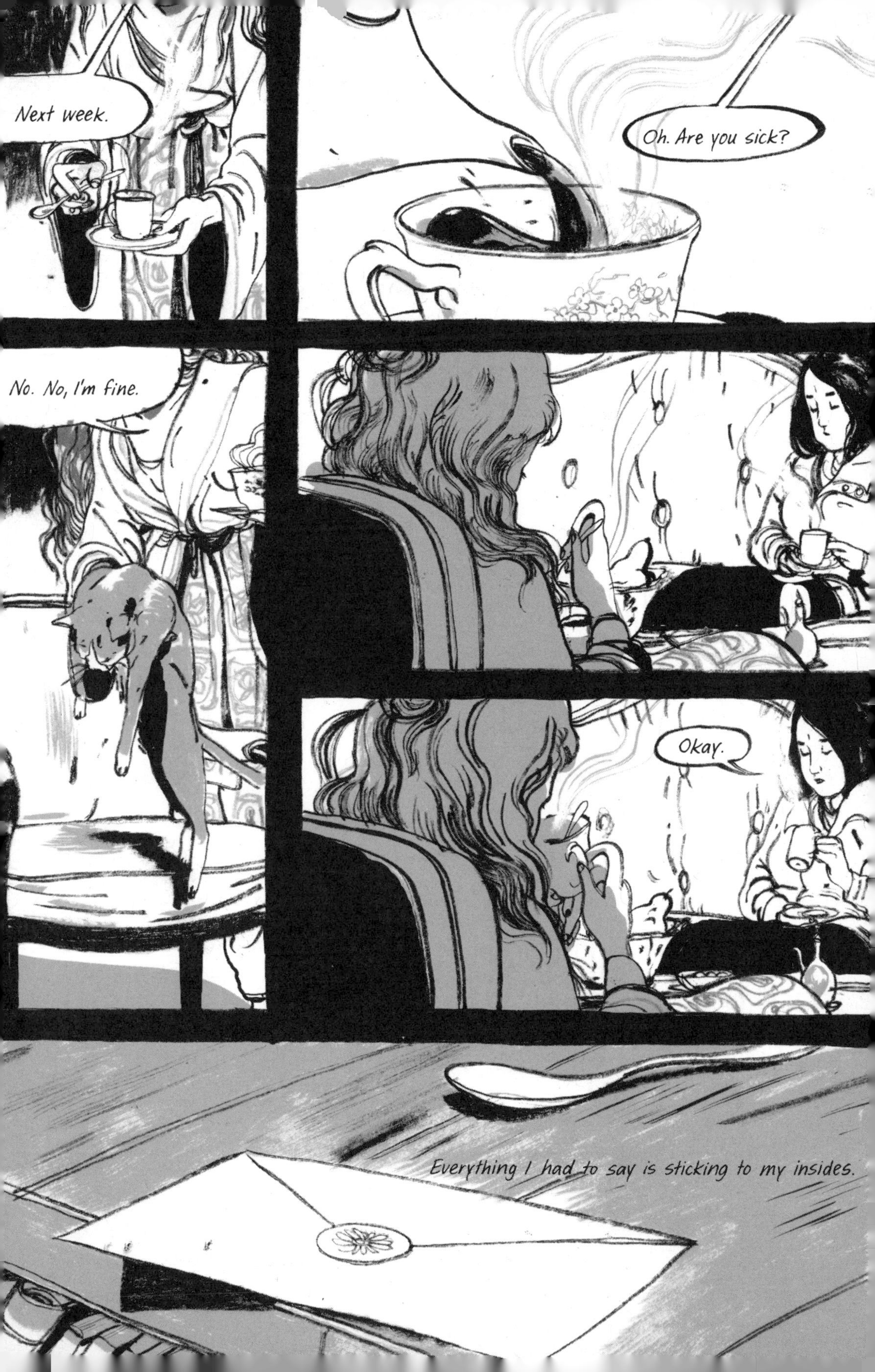
Next week.
Oh. Are you sick?
No. No, I'm fine.
Okay.
Everything I had to say is sticking to my insides.

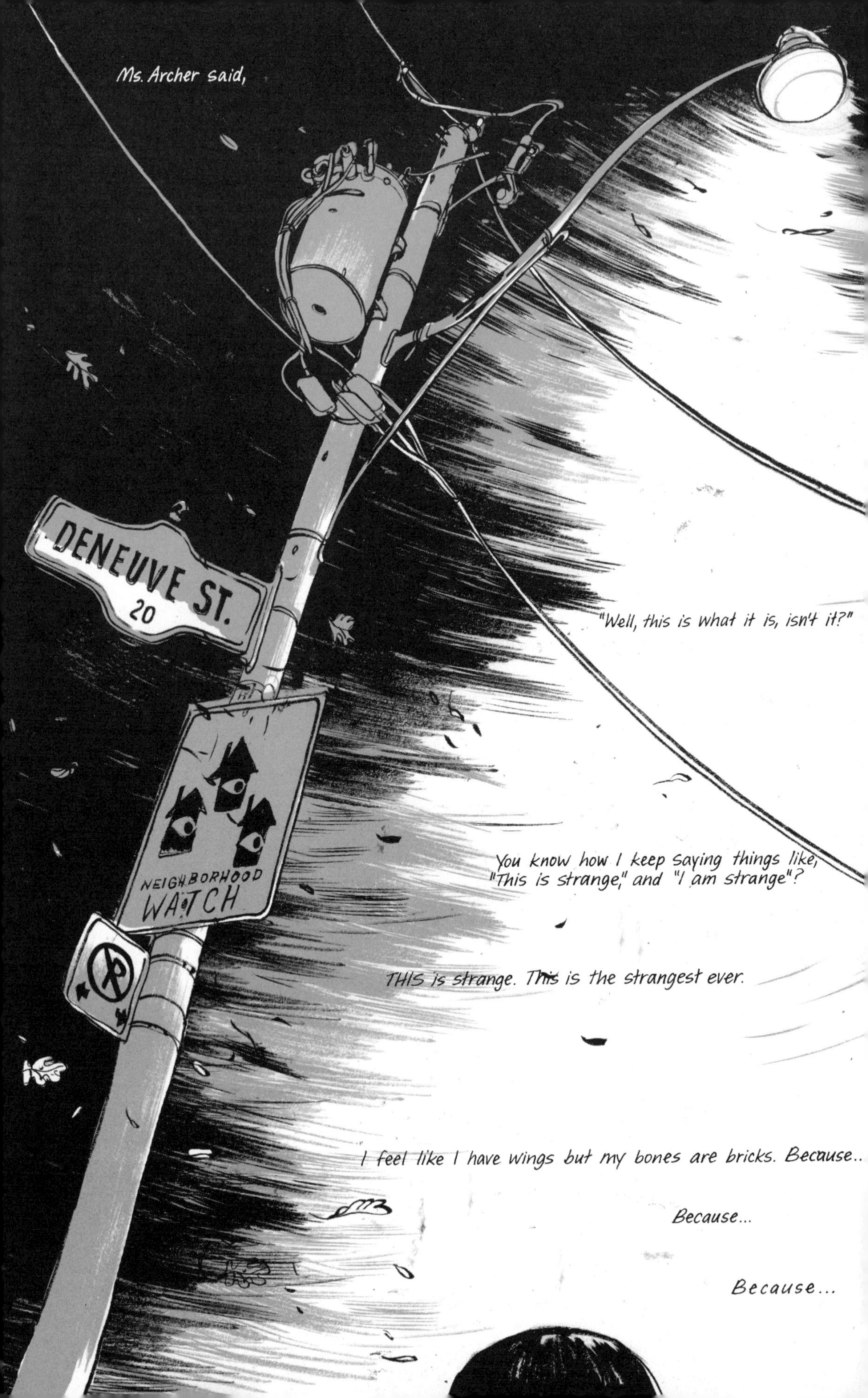

Ms. Archer said,
DENEUVE ST.
20
"Well, this is what it is, isn't it?"
NEIGHBORHOOD WATCH
You know how I keep saying things like, "This is strange," and "I am strange"?
THIS is strange. This is the strangest ever.
I feel like I have wings but my bones are bricks. Because...
Because...
Because...

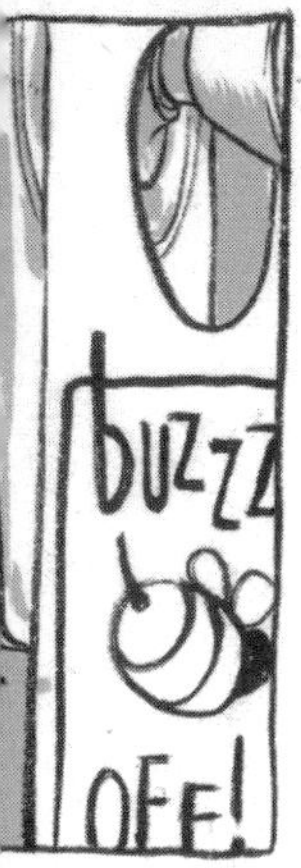
BUZZZ OFF!

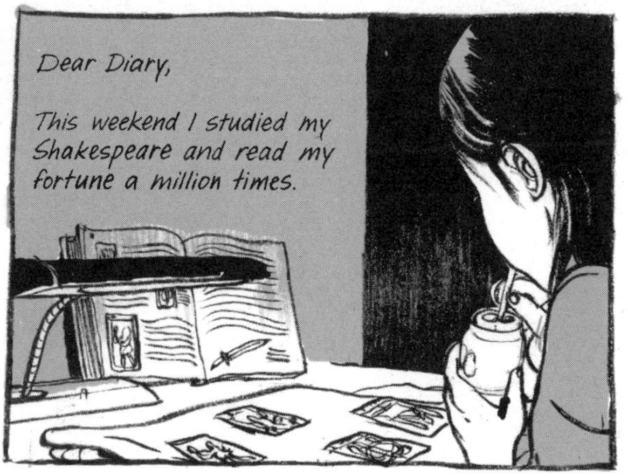
Dear Diary,
This weekend I studied my Shakespeare and read my fortune a million times.

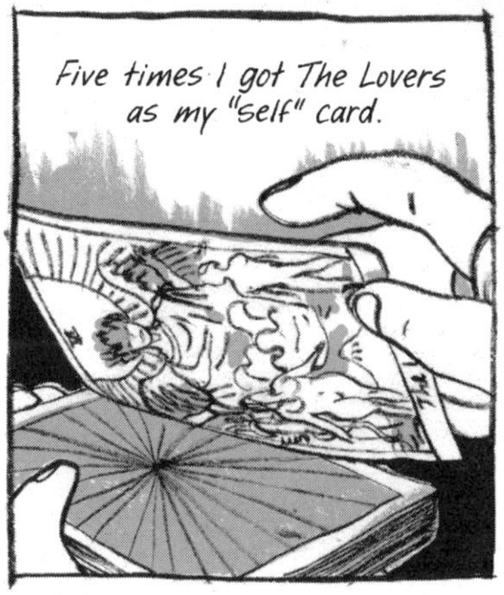
Five times I got The Lovers as my "self" card.

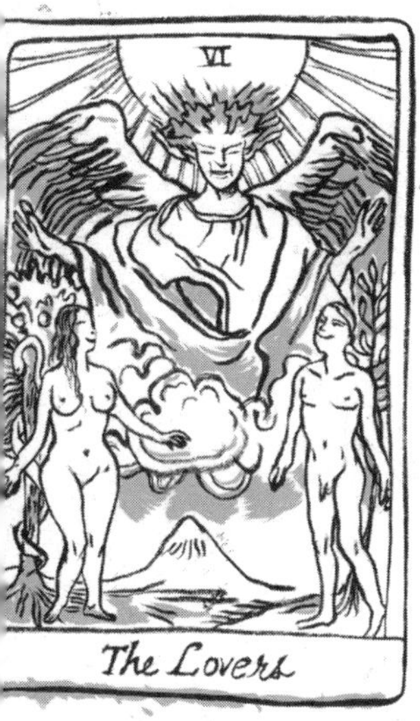
VI
The Lovers

The Lovers = love and relationships, new beginnings, new connections.

The Angel on the card = FATE. Fate is the force that makes you do things and choose things that you don't always understand. Destiny.

BUT... if you get this card reversed = upside down...

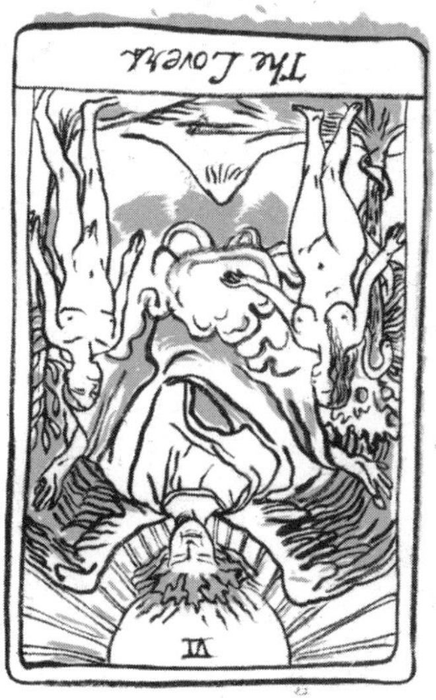
The Lovers
VI

...it means a bad decision, an untrustworthy person, a state of imbalance.

The last time I did my fortune, I got The Lovers reversed.

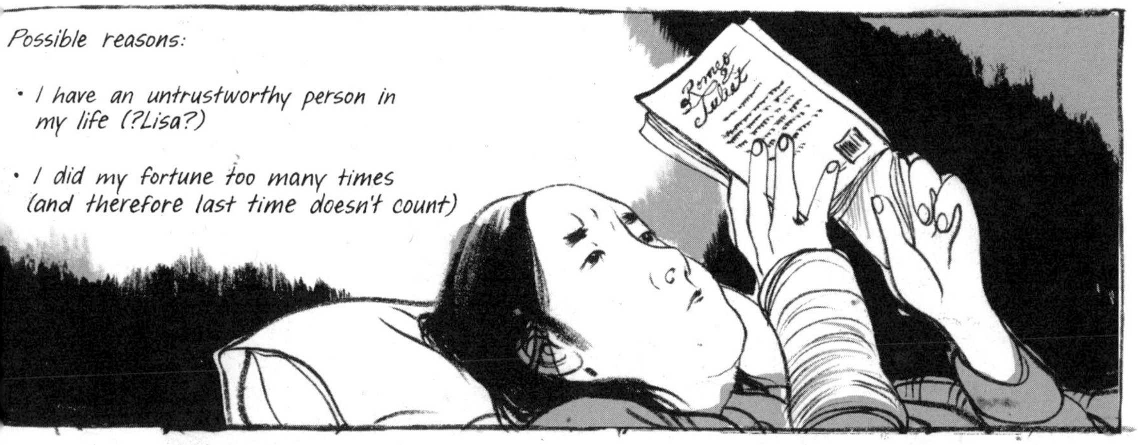
Possible reasons:
• I have an untrustworthy person in my life (?Lisa?)
• I did my fortune too many times (and therefore last time doesn't count)
Romeo & Juliet

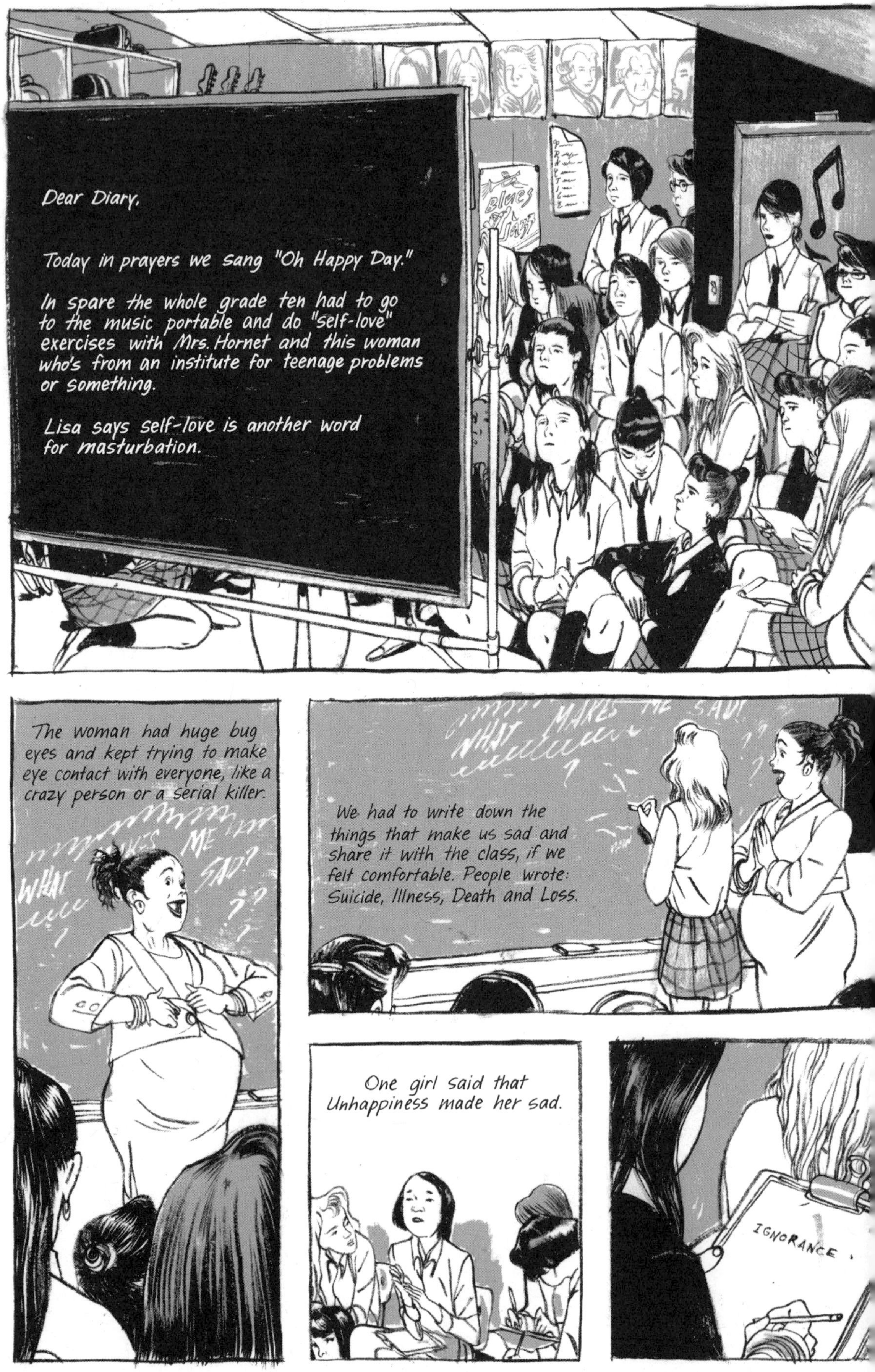
Dear Diary,
Today in prayers we sang "Oh Happy Day."
In spare the whole grade ten had to go to the music portable and do "self-love" exercises with Mrs. Hornet and this woman who's from an institute for teenage problems or something.
Lisa says self-love is another word for masturbation.
The woman had huge bug eyes and kept trying to make eye contact with everyone, like a crazy person or a serial killer.
We had to write down the things that make us sad and share it with the class, if we felt comfortable. People wrote: Suicide, Illness, Death and Loss.
One girl said that Unhappiness made her sad.
IGNORANCE.

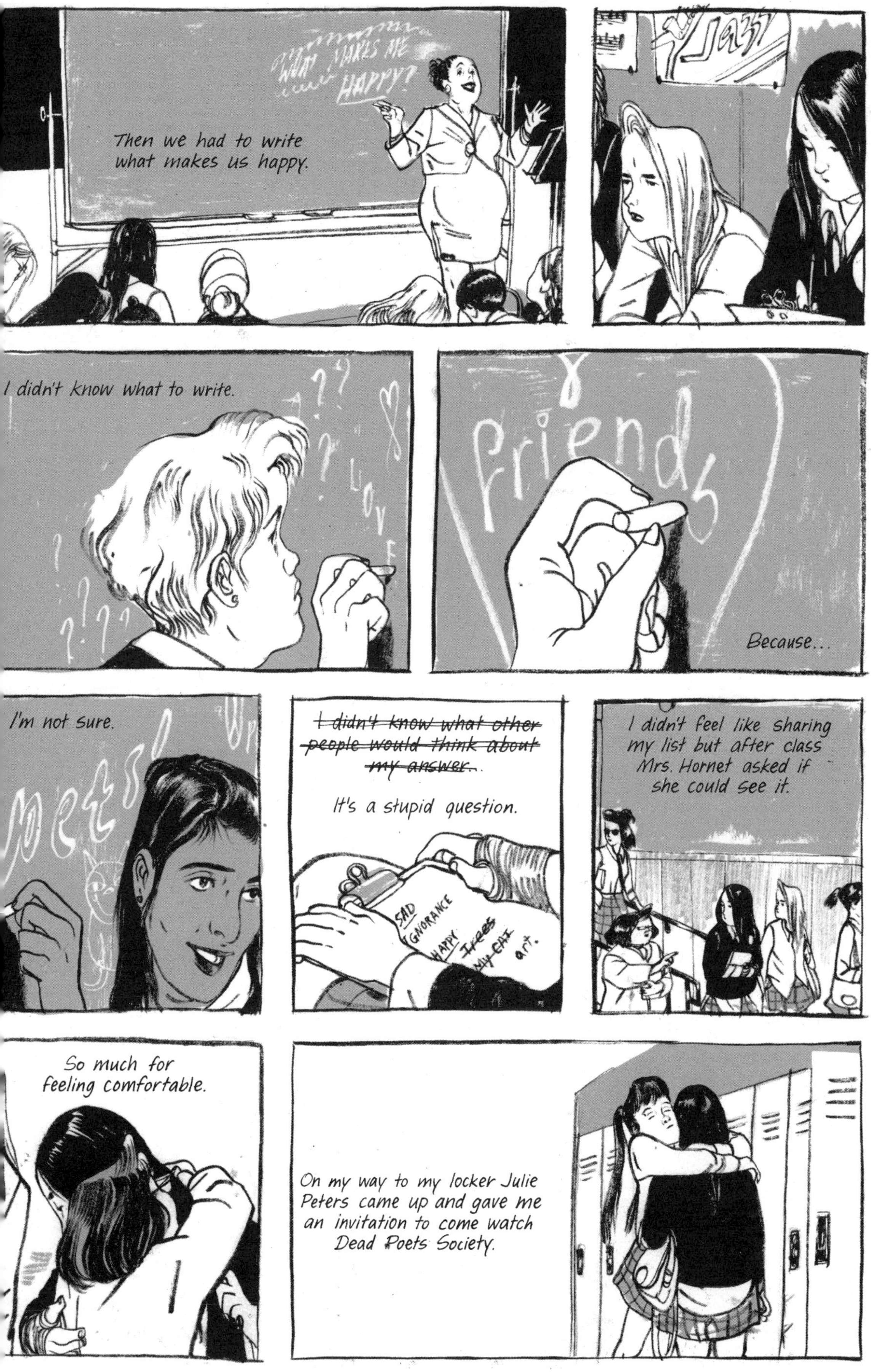
WHAT MAKES ME HAPPY?
Then we had to write what makes us happy.
I didn't know what to write.
friends
Because...
I'm not sure.
I didn't know what other people would think about my answer.
It's a stupid question.
SAD
IGNORANCE
HAPPY
art.
I didn't feel like sharing my list but after class Mrs. Hornet asked if she could see it.
So much for feeling comfortable.
On my way to my locker Julie Peters came up and gave me an invitation to come watch Dead Poets Society.

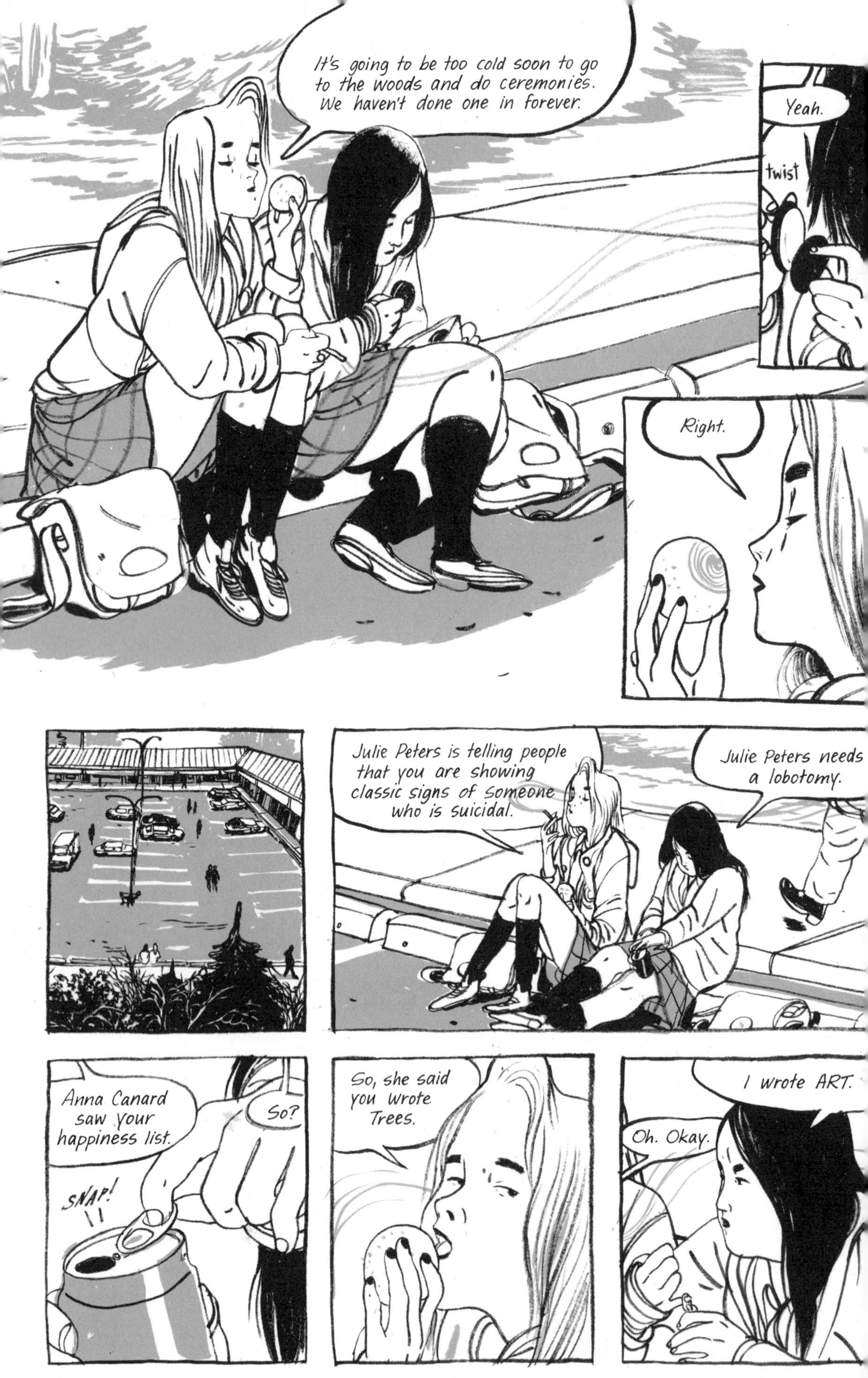
It's going to be too cold soon to go to the woods and do ceremonies. We haven't done one in forever.
Yeah.
twist
Right.
Julie Peters is telling people that you are showing classic signs of someone who is suicidal.
Julie Peters needs a lobotomy.
Anna Canard saw your happiness list.
So?
SNAP!
So, she said you wrote Trees.
I wrote ART.
Oh. Okay.

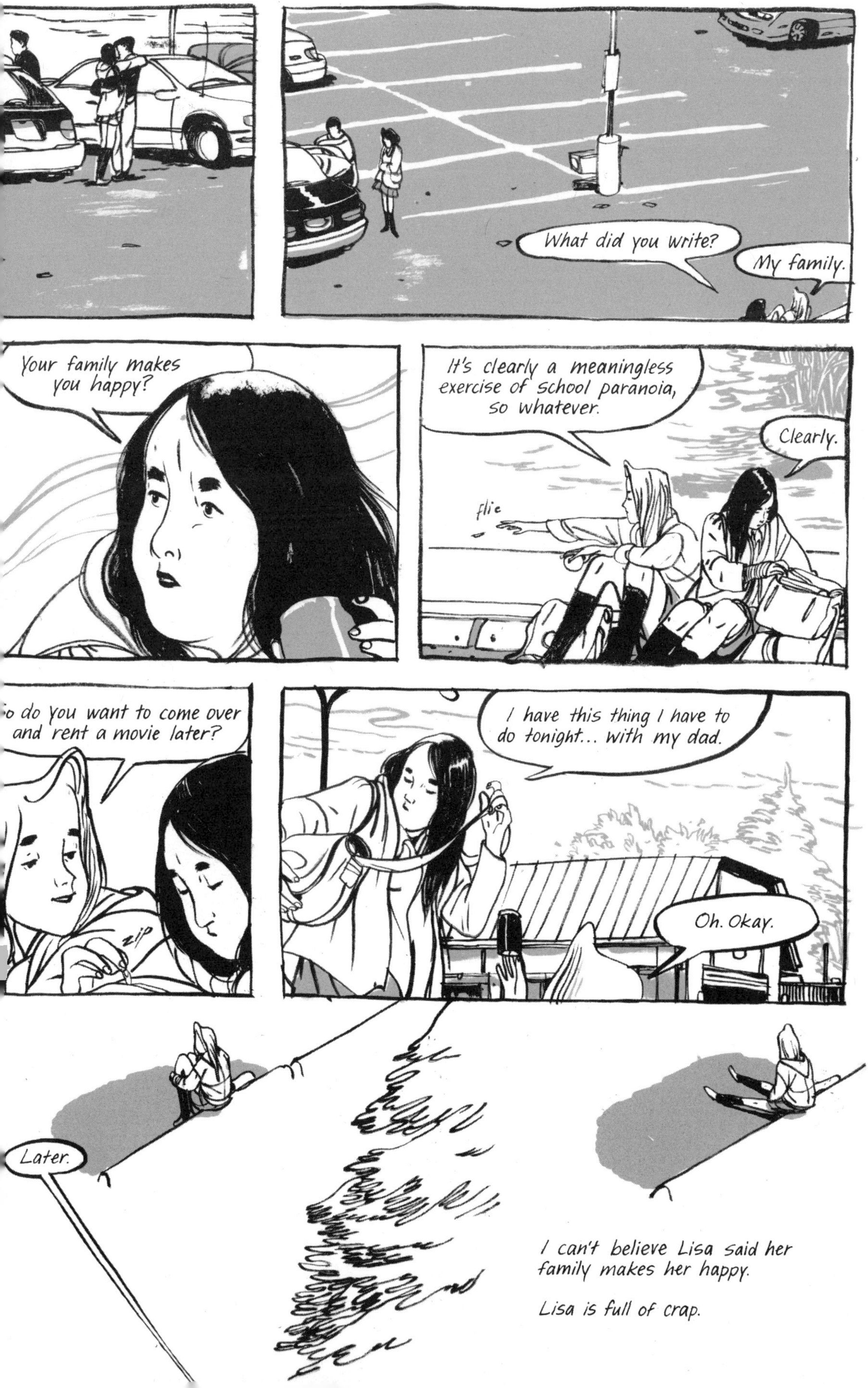
What did you write?
My family.
Your family makes you happy?
It's clearly a meaningless exercise of school paranoia, so whatever.
Clearly.
flic
o do you want to come over and rent a movie later?
zip
I have this thing I have to do tonight... with my dad.
Oh. Okay.
Later.
I can't believe Lisa said her family makes her happy.
Lisa is full of crap.

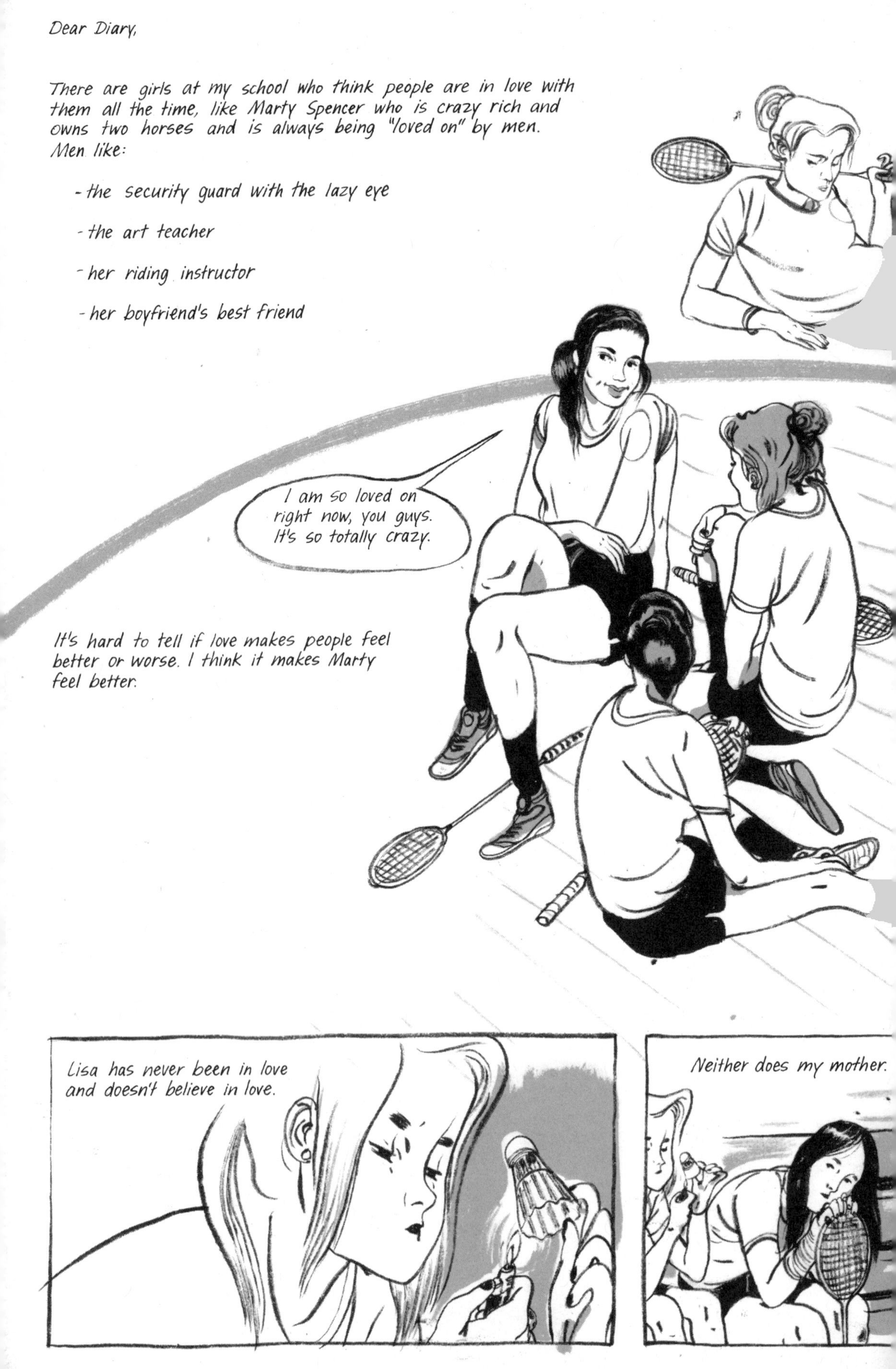
Dear Diary,
There are girls at my school who think people are in love with them all the time, like Marty Spencer who is crazy rich and owns two horses and is always being "loved on" by men. Men like:
- the security guard with the lazy eye
- the art teacher
- her riding instructor
- her boyfriend's best friend
I am so loved on right now, you guys. It's so totally crazy.
It's hard to tell if love makes people feel better or worse. I think it makes Marty feel better.
Lisa has never been in love and doesn't believe in love.
Neither does my mother.

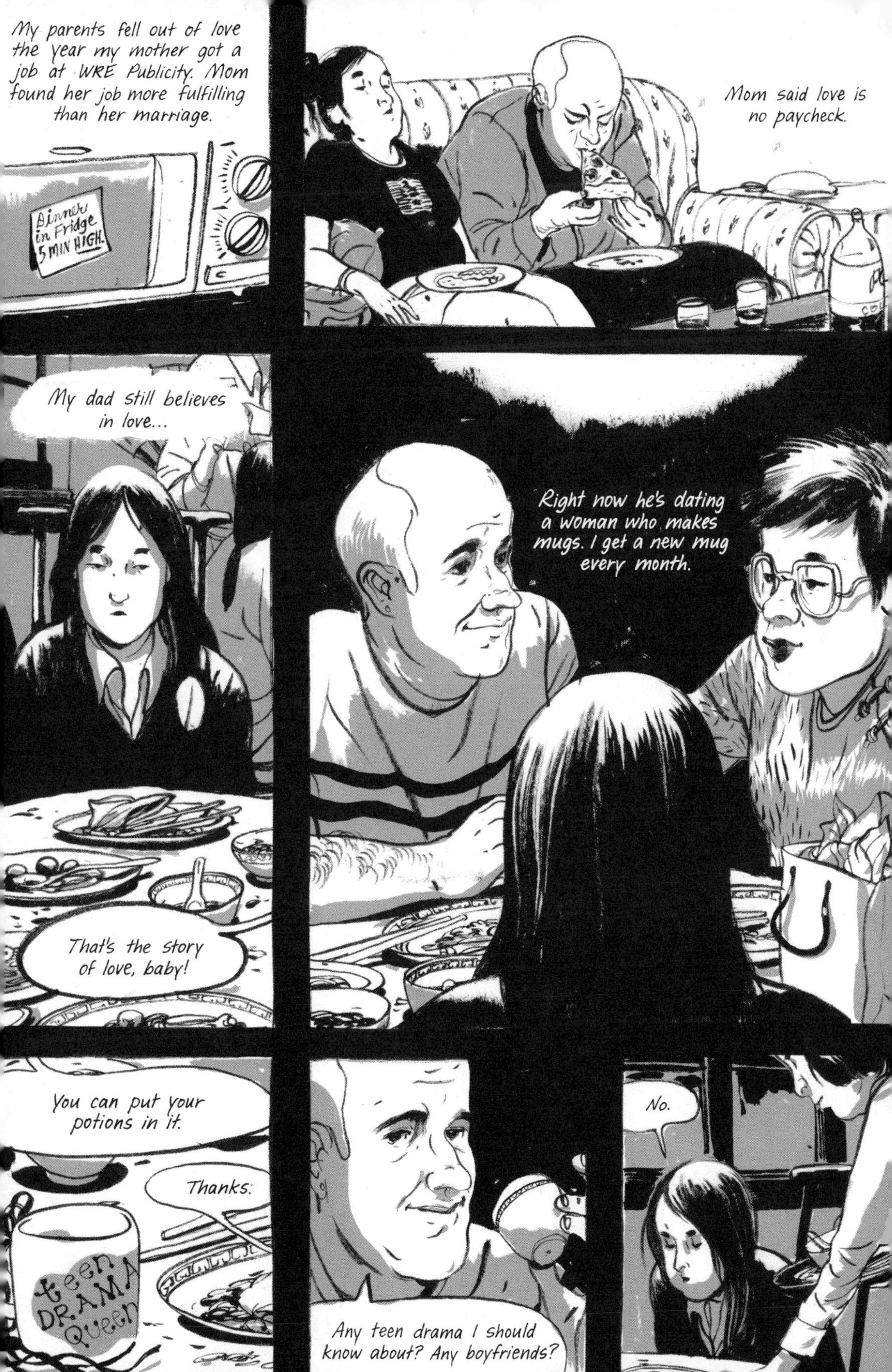
My parents fell out of love the year my mother got a job at WRE Publicity. Mom found her job more fulfilling than her marriage.
Dinner in Fridge 5 MIN HIGH.
Mom said love is no paycheck.
My dad still believes in love...
That's the story of love, baby!
Right now he's dating a woman who makes mugs. I get a new mug every month.
You can put your potions in it.
Thanks.
teen DRAMA Queen
Any teen drama I should know about? Any boyfriends?
No.

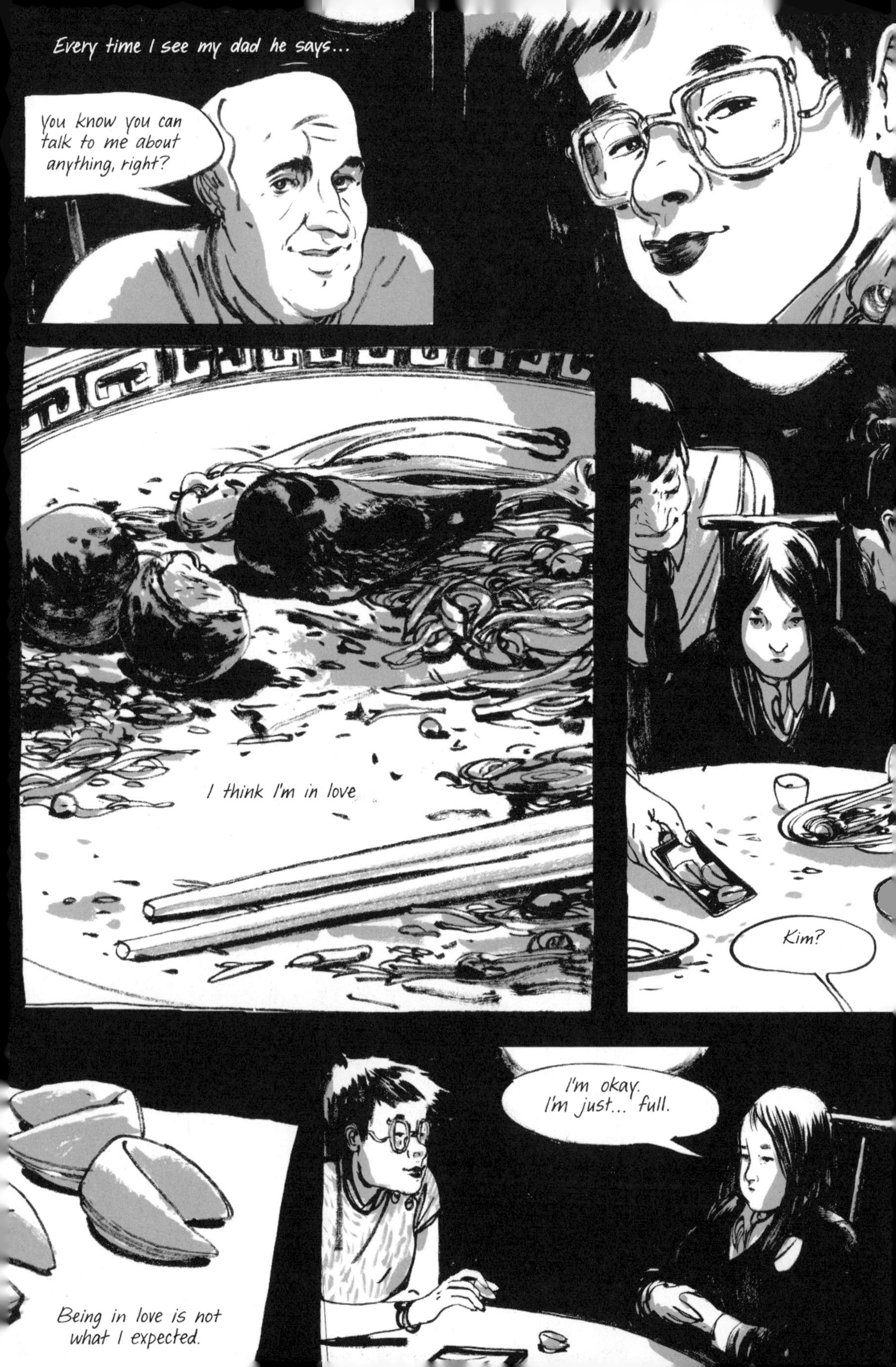
Every time I see my dad he says...
You know you can talk to me about anything, right?
I think I'm in love
Kim?
Being in love is not what I expected.
I'm okay. I'm just... full.

Dear Diary,

When I got home from dinner I called Ms. A on the phone but no one answered so I hung up. I'm not sure if I'm supposed to do that.

I put her number under my altar.

Things That Make Me Sad

Love

Things That Make Me Happy

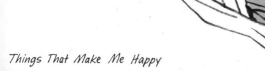

Love?

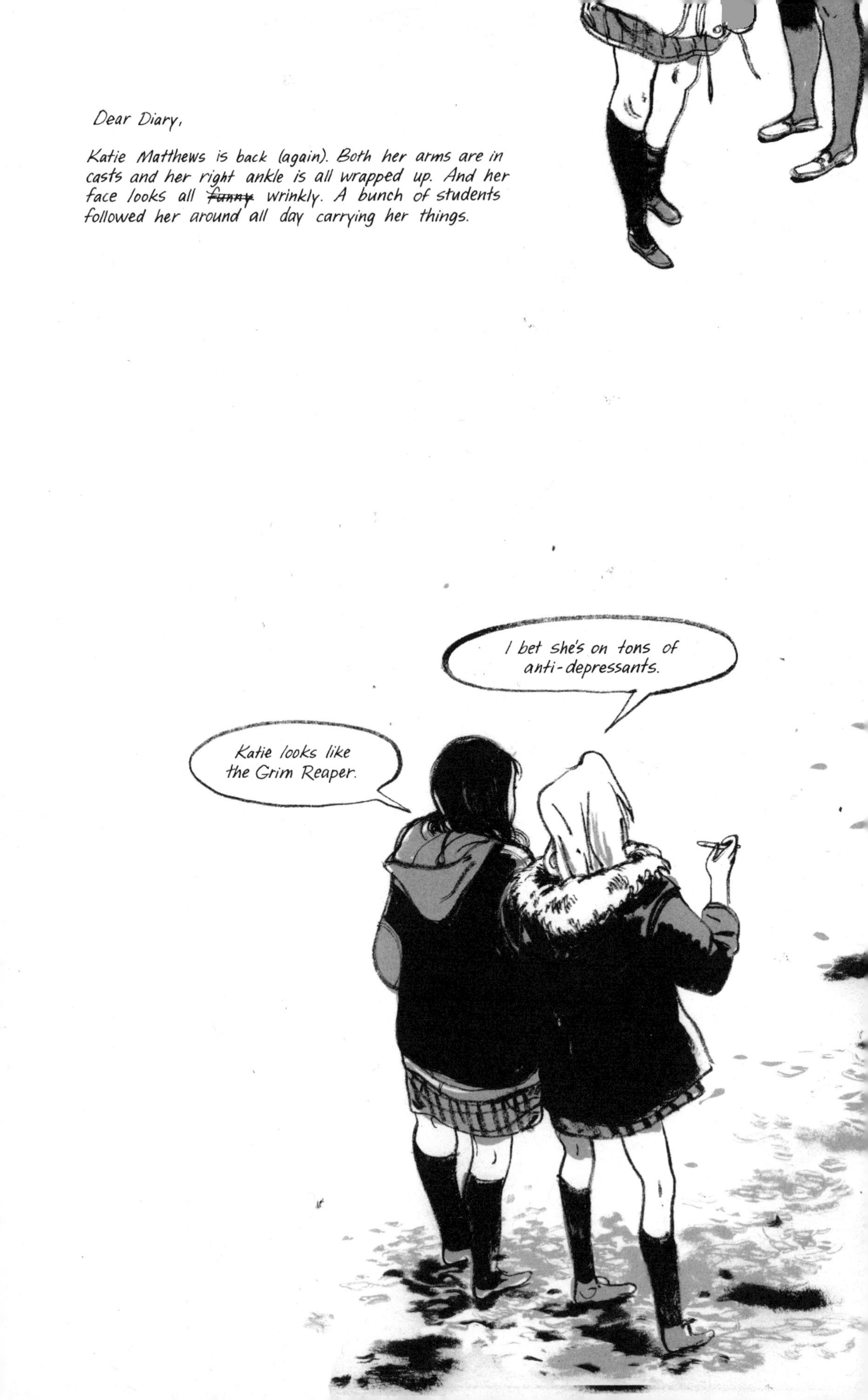
Dear Diary,
Katie Matthews is back (again). Both her arms are in casts and her right ankle is all wrapped up. And her face looks all ~~funny~~ wrinkly. A bunch of students followed her around all day carrying her things.
Katie looks like the Grim Reaper.
I bet she's on tons of anti-depressants.

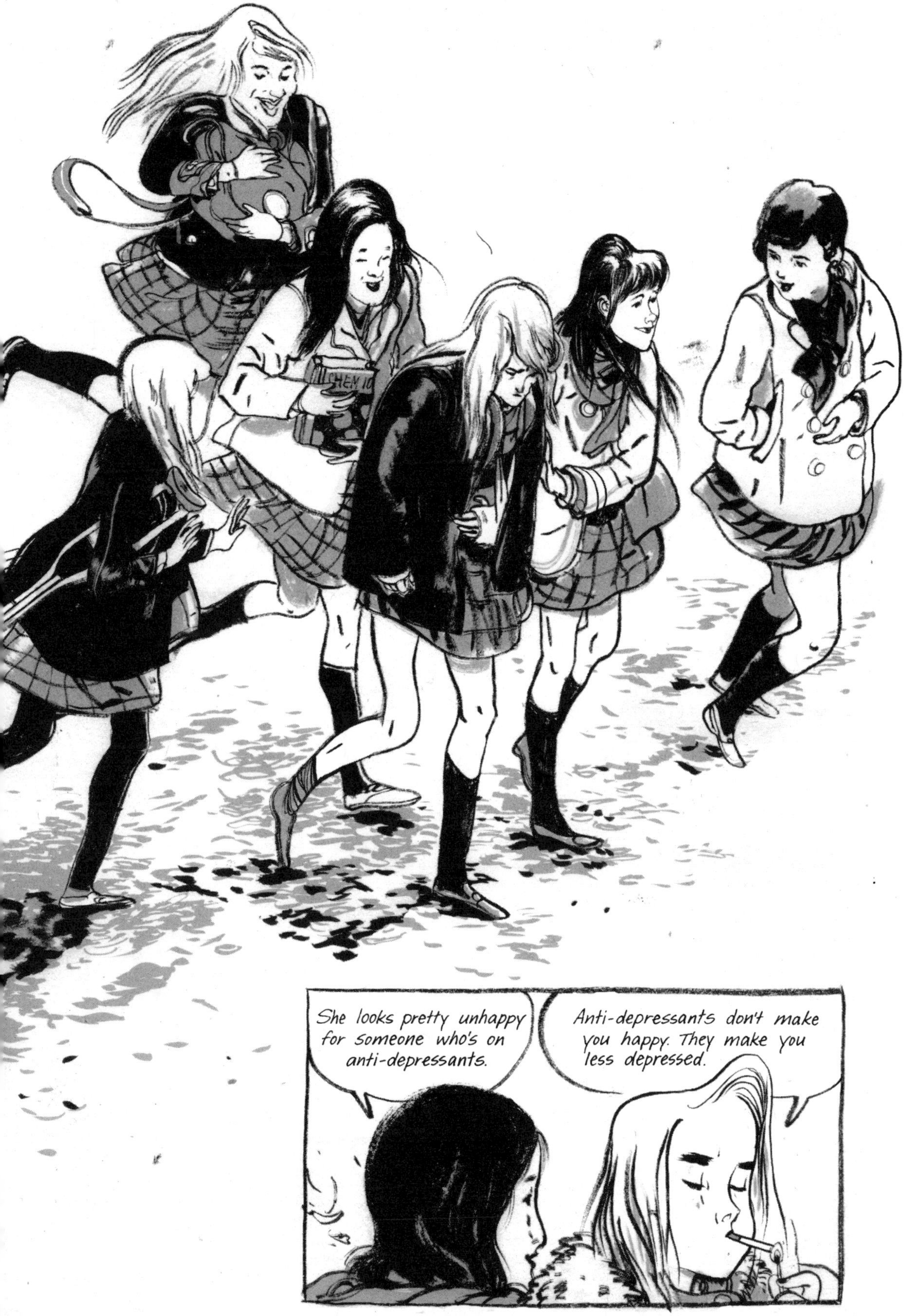
She looks pretty unhappy for someone who's on anti-depressants.
Anti-depressants don't make you happy. They make you less depressed.

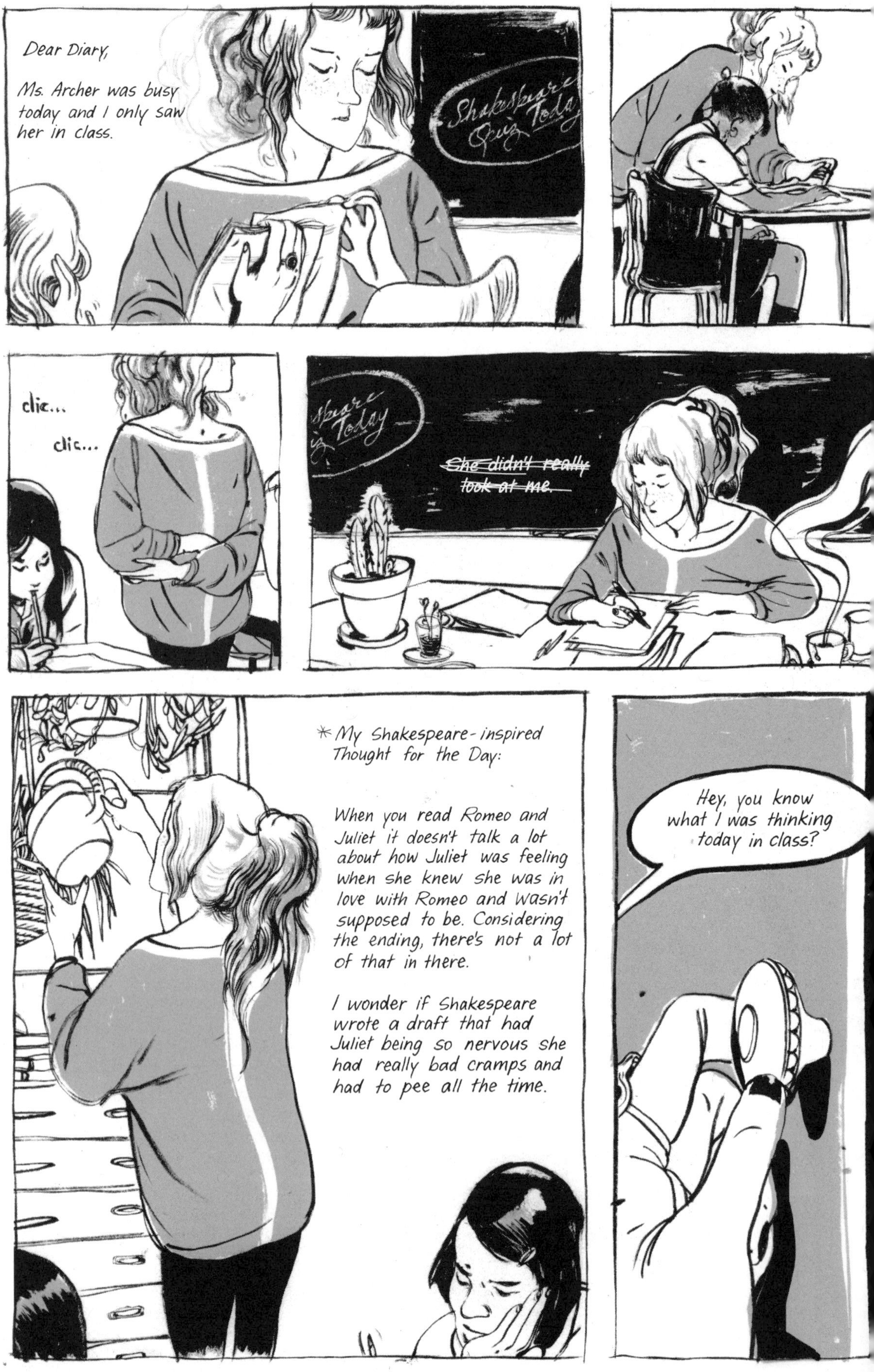
Dear Diary,
Ms. Archer was busy today and I only saw her in class.
Shakespeare Quiz Today
clic...
clic...
She didn't really look at me.
*My Shakespeare-inspired Thought for the Day:
When you read Romeo and Juliet it doesn't talk a lot about how Juliet was feeling when she knew she was in love with Romeo and wasn't supposed to be. Considering the ending, there's not a lot of that in there.
I wonder if Shakespeare wrote a draft that had Juliet being so nervous she had really bad cramps and had to pee all the time.
Hey, you know what I was thinking today in class?

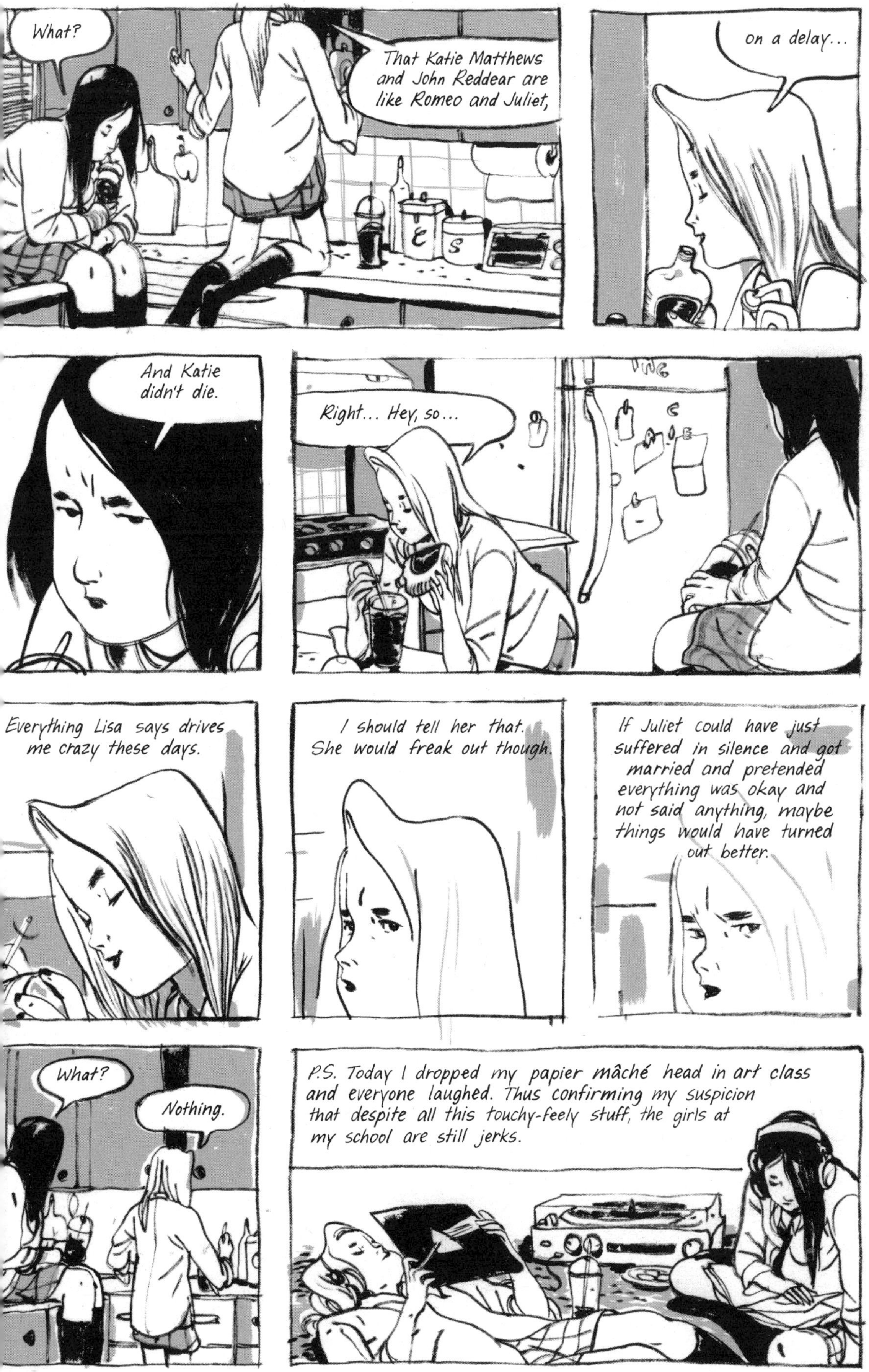
What?
That Katie Matthews and John Reddear are like Romeo and Juliet,
on a delay...
And Katie didn't die.
Right... Hey, so...
Everything Lisa says drives me crazy these days.
I should tell her that. She would freak out though.
If Juliet could have just suffered in silence and got married and pretended everything was okay and not said anything, maybe things would have turned out better.
What?
Nothing.
P.S. Today I dropped my papier mâché head in art class and everyone laughed. Thus confirming my suspicion that despite all this touchy-feely stuff, the girls at my school are still jerks.

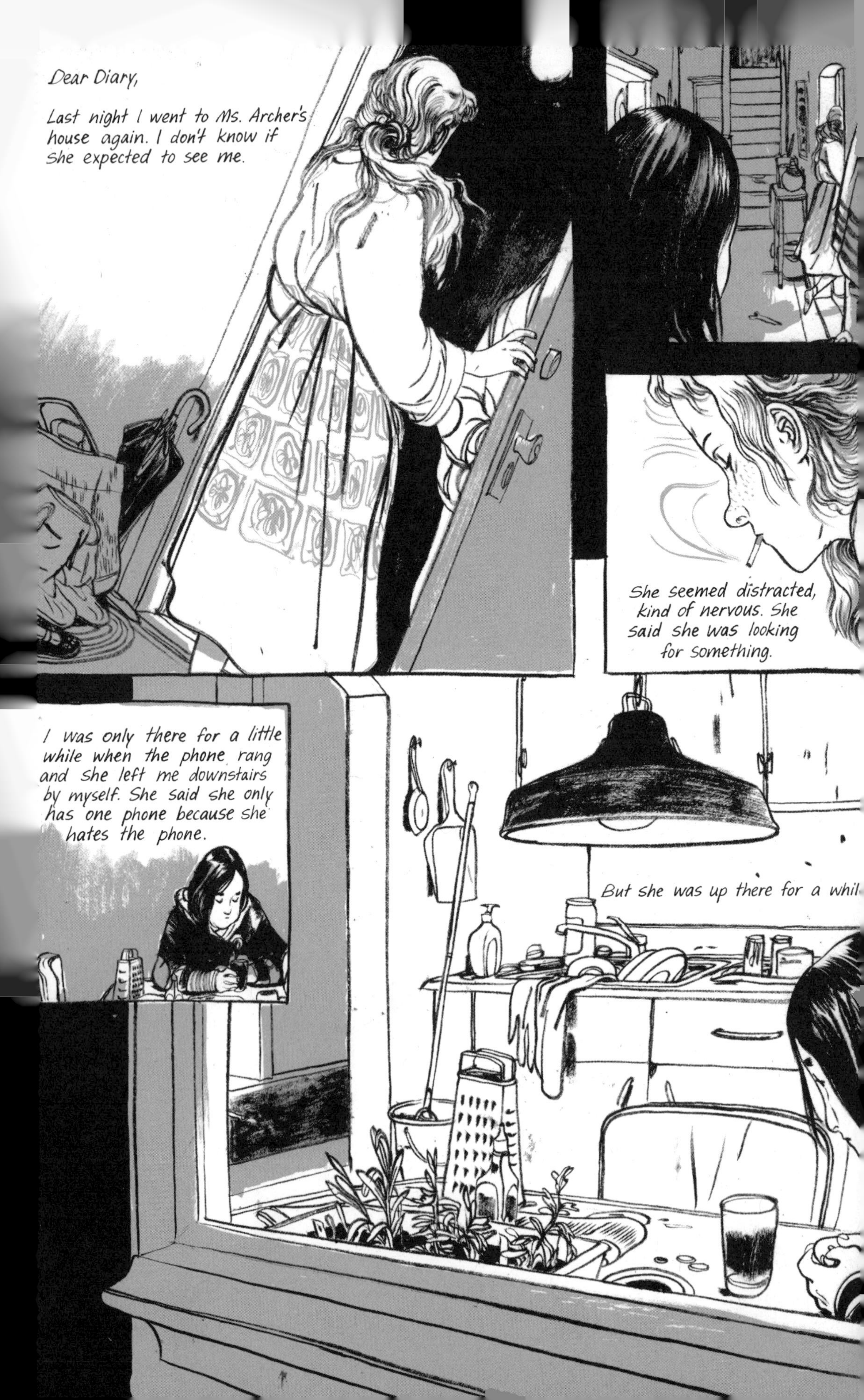
Dear Diary,
Last night I went to Ms. Archer's house again. I don't know if she expected to see me.
She seemed distracted, kind of nervous. She said she was looking for something.
I was only there for a little while when the phone rang and she left me downstairs by myself. She said she only has one phone because she hates the phone.
But she was up there for a whil

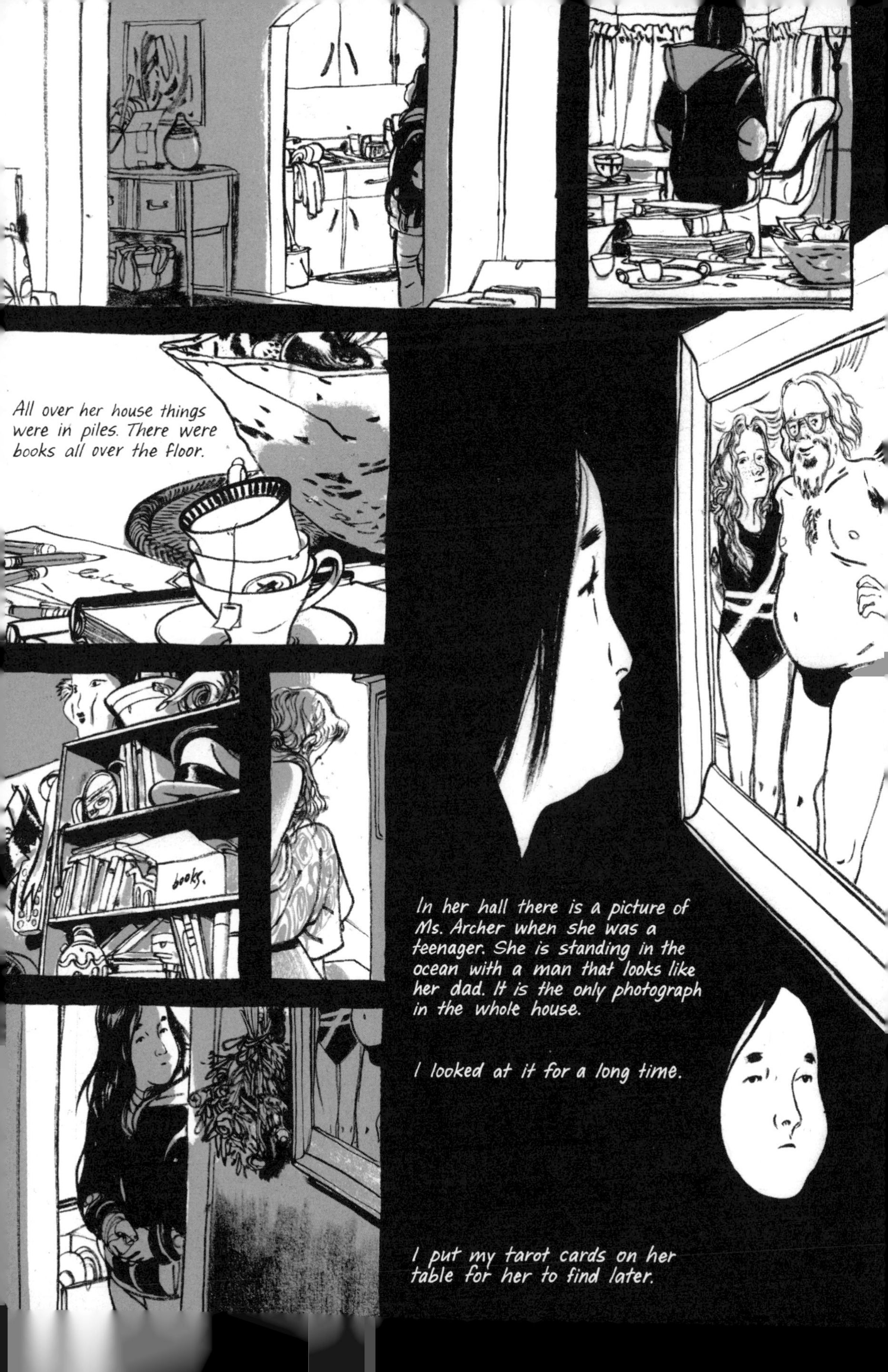
All over her house things were in piles. There were books all over the floor.
books.
In her hall there is a picture of Ms. Archer when she was a teenager. She is standing in the ocean with a man that looks like her dad. It is the only photograph in the whole house.
I looked at it for a long time.
I put my tarot cards on her table for her to find later.

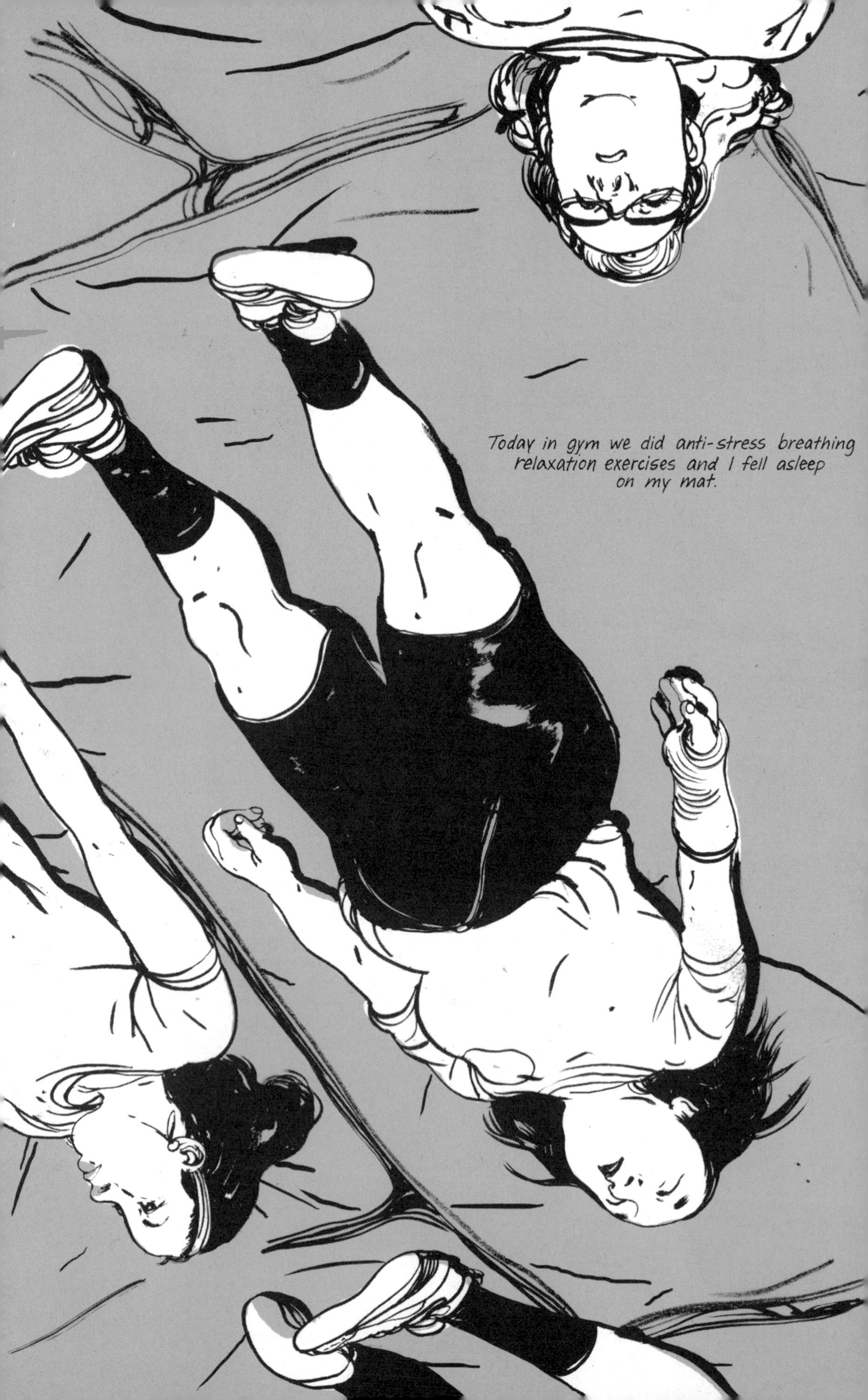
Today in gym we did anti-stress breathing relaxation exercises and I fell asleep on my mat.

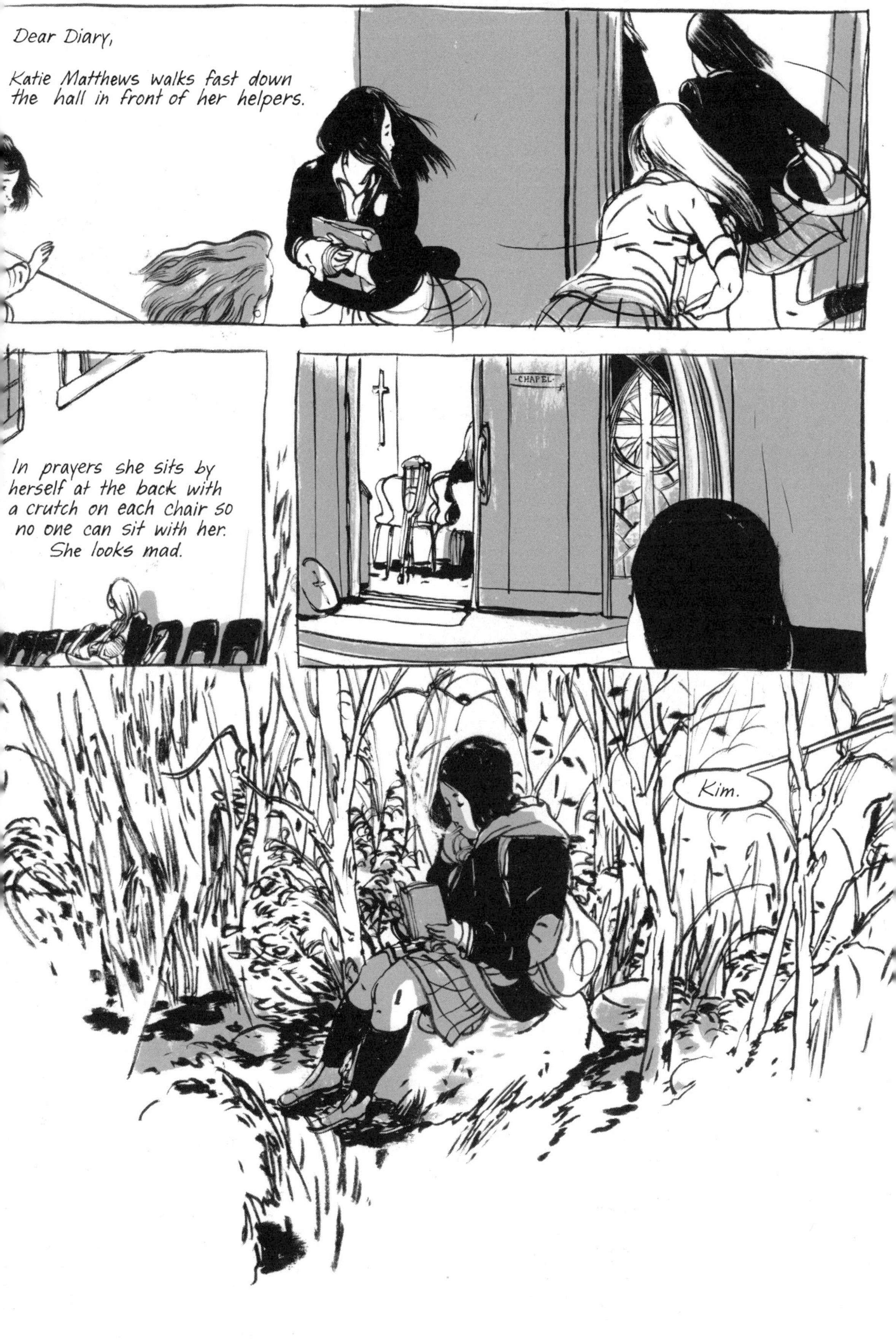
Dear Diary,
Katie Matthews walks fast down the hall in front of her helpers.
In prayers she sits by herself at the back with a crutch on each chair so no one can sit with her. She looks mad.
·CHAPEL·
Kim.

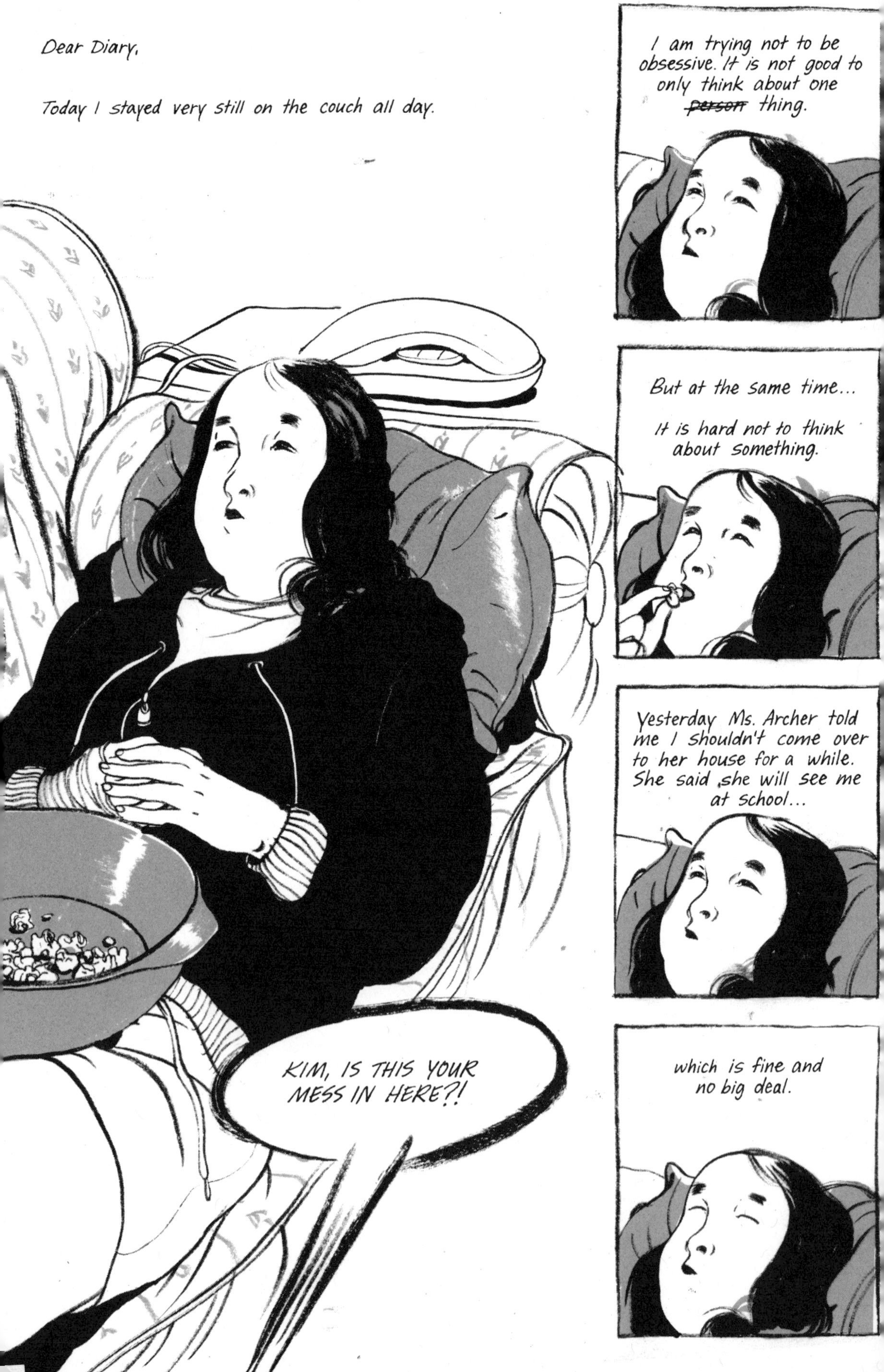
Dear Diary,
Today I stayed very still on the couch all day.
KIM, IS THIS YOUR MESS IN HERE?!
I am trying not to be obsessive. It is not good to only think about one ~~person~~ thing.
But at the same time...
It is hard not to think about something.
Yesterday Ms. Archer told me I shouldn't come over to her house for a while. She said she will see me at school...
which is fine and no big deal.

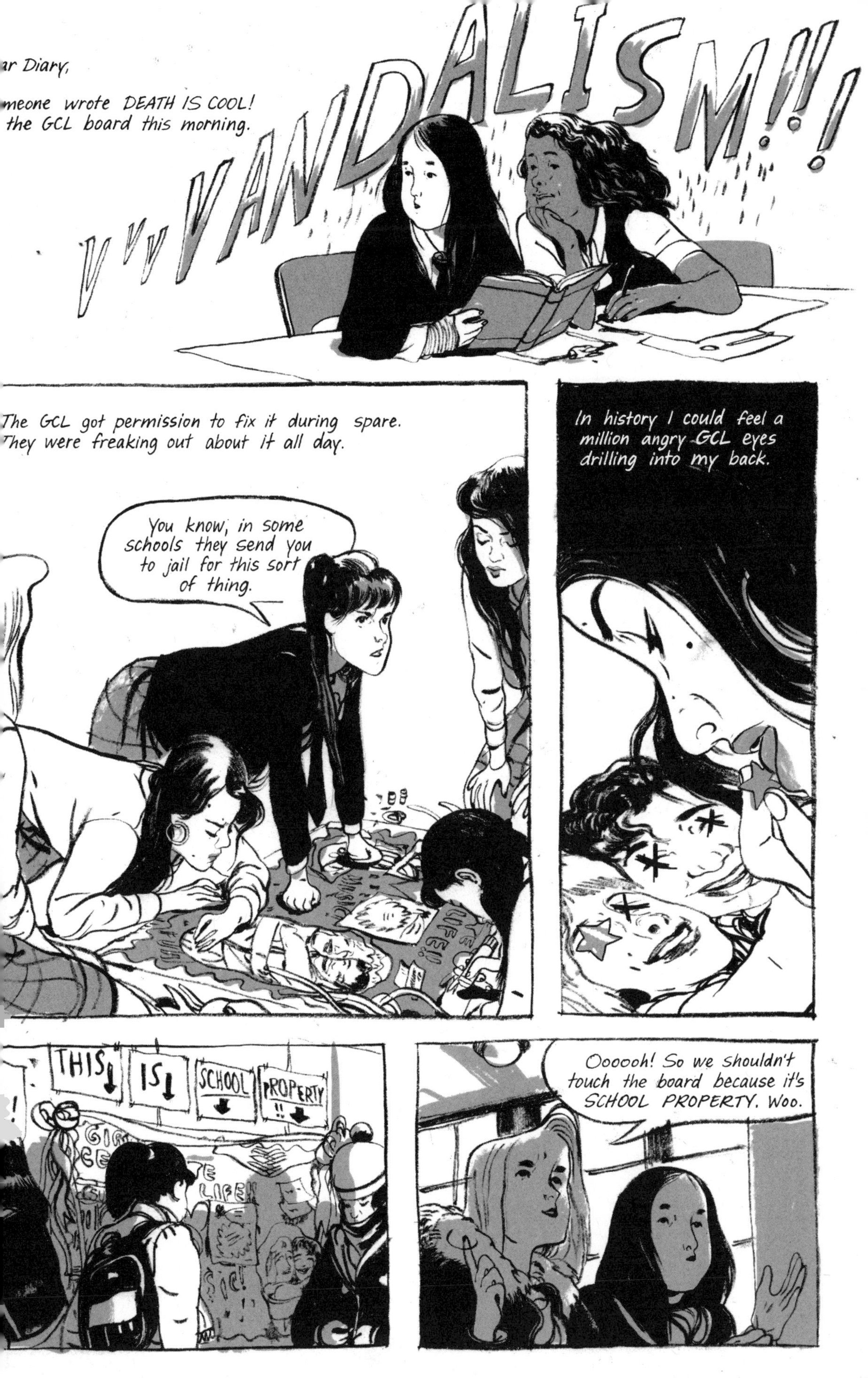

ar Diary,
meone wrote DEATH IS COOL!
the GCL board this morning.
VVVVANDALISM!!!
The GCL got permission to fix it during spare.
They were freaking out about it all day.
You know, in some schools they send you to jail for this sort of thing.
In history I could feel a million angry GCL eyes drilling into my back.
THIS IS SCHOOL PROPERTY !!
Oooooh! So we shouldn't touch the board because it's SCHOOL PROPERTY. Woo.

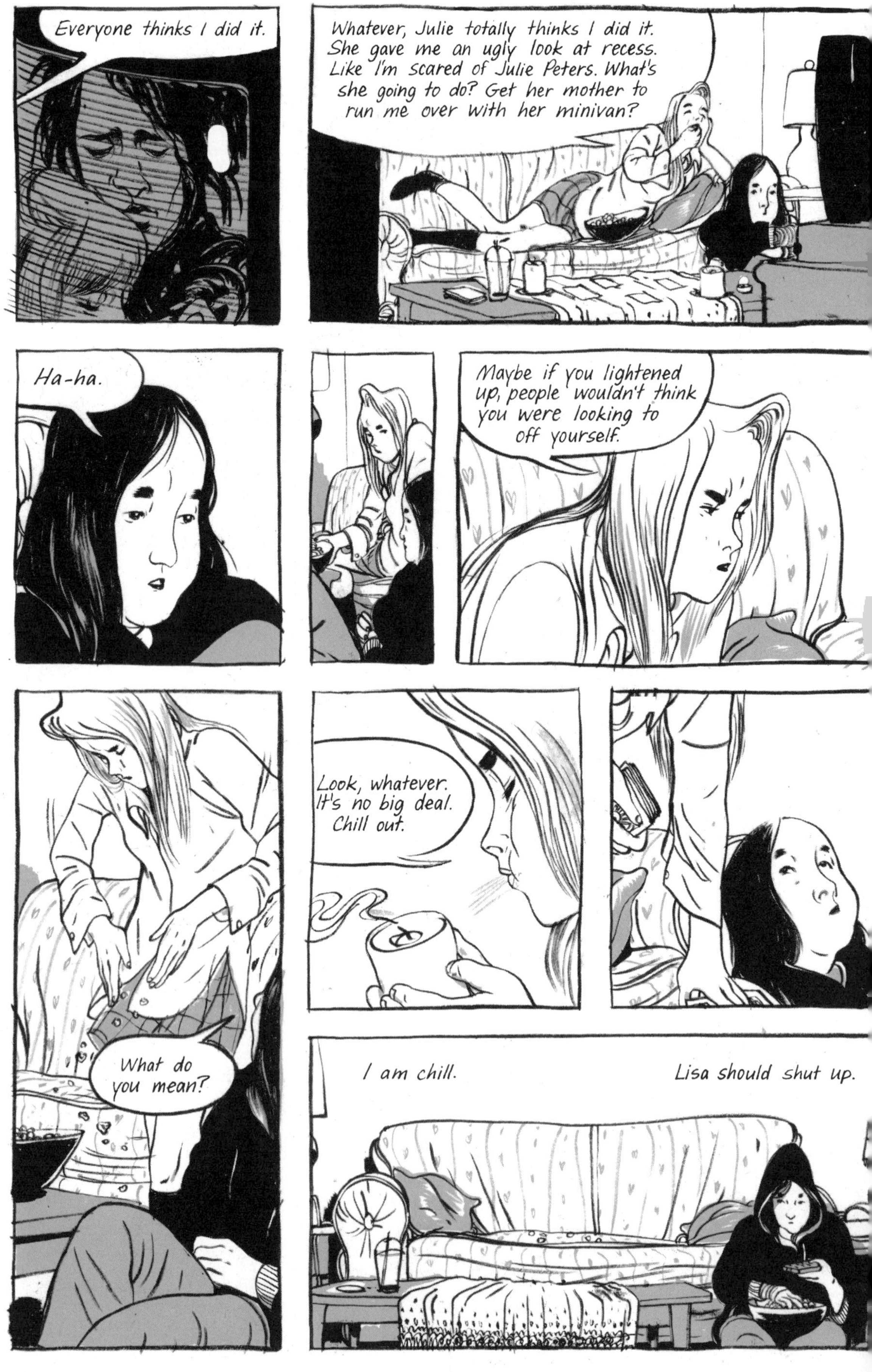
Everyone thinks I did it.
Whatever, Julie totally thinks I did it. She gave me an ugly look at recess. Like I'm scared of Julie Peters. What's she going to do? Get her mother to run me over with her minivan?
Ha-ha.
Maybe if you lightened up, people wouldn't think you were looking to off yourself.
What do you mean?
Look, whatever. It's no big deal. Chill out.
I am chill.
Lisa should shut up.

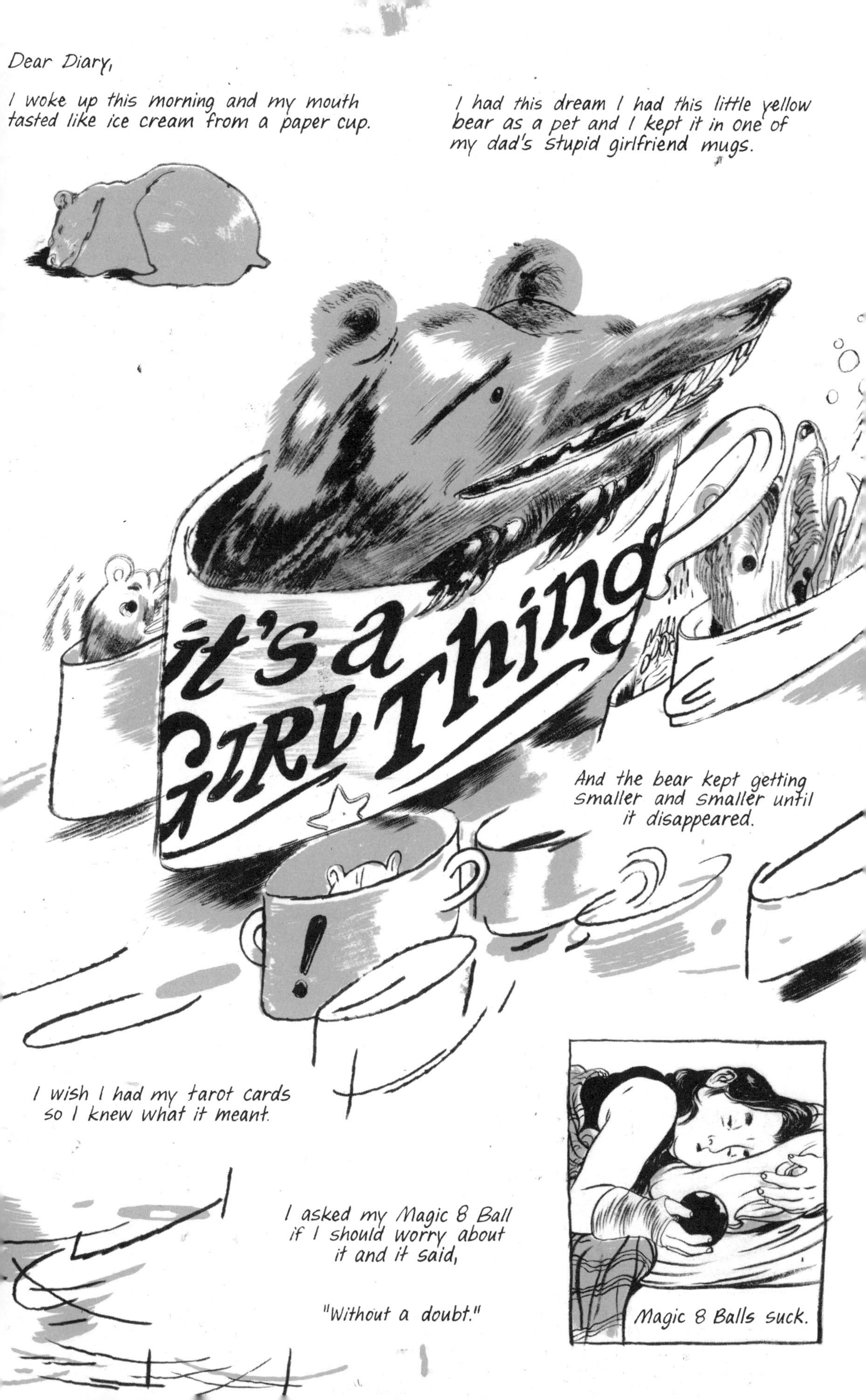
Dear Diary,
I woke up this morning and my mouth tasted like ice cream from a paper cup.
I had this dream I had this little yellow bear as a pet and I kept it in one of my dad's stupid girlfriend mugs.
it's a GIRL Thing
And the bear kept getting smaller and smaller until it disappeared.
I wish I had my tarot cards so I knew what it meant.
I asked my Magic 8 Ball if I should worry about it and it said,
"Without a doubt."
Magic 8 Balls suck.

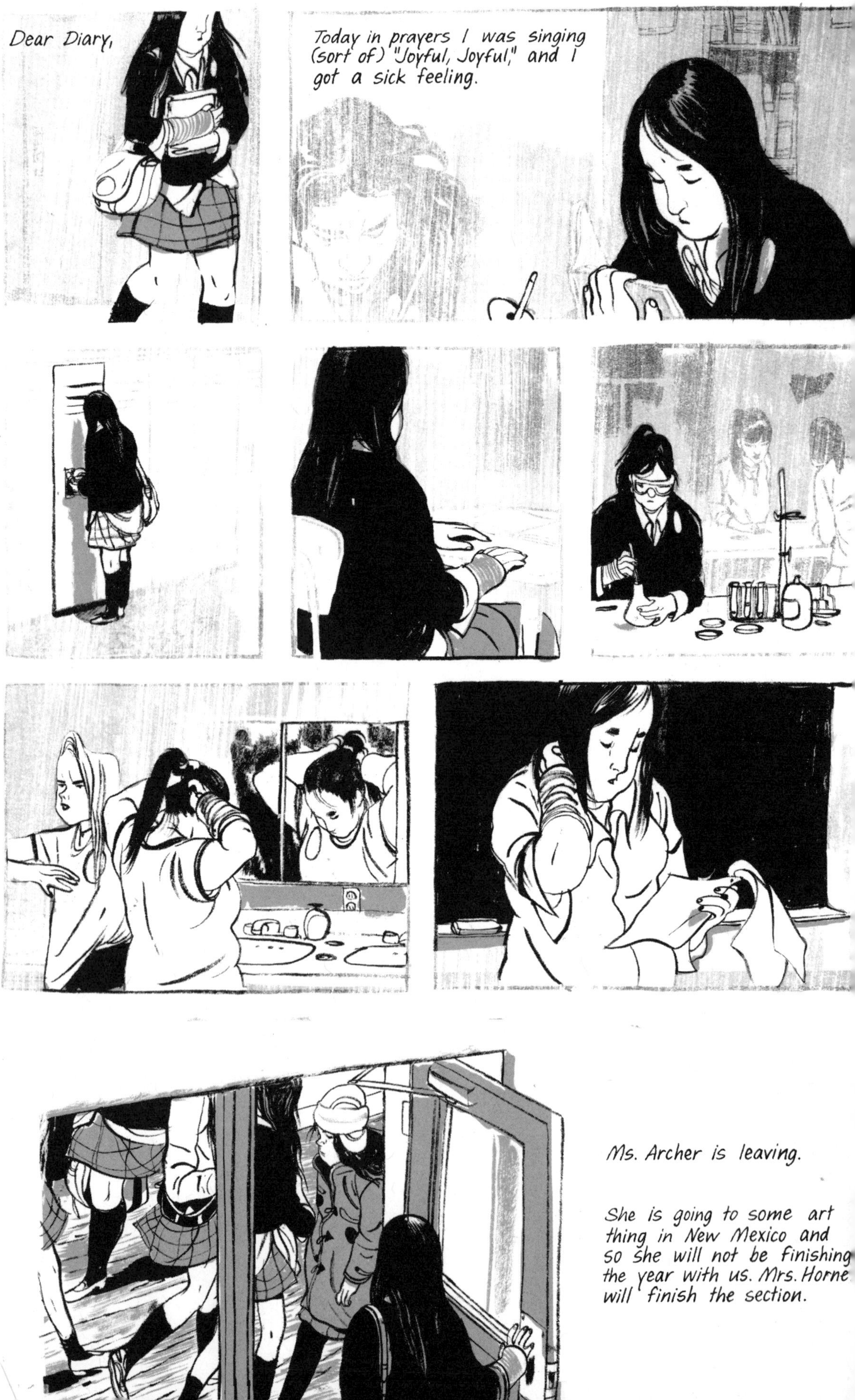
Dear Diary,
Today in prayers I was singing (sort of) "Joyful, Joyful," and I got a sick feeling.
Ms. Archer is leaving.
She is going to some art thing in New Mexico and so she will not be finishing the year with us. Mrs. Horne will finish the section.

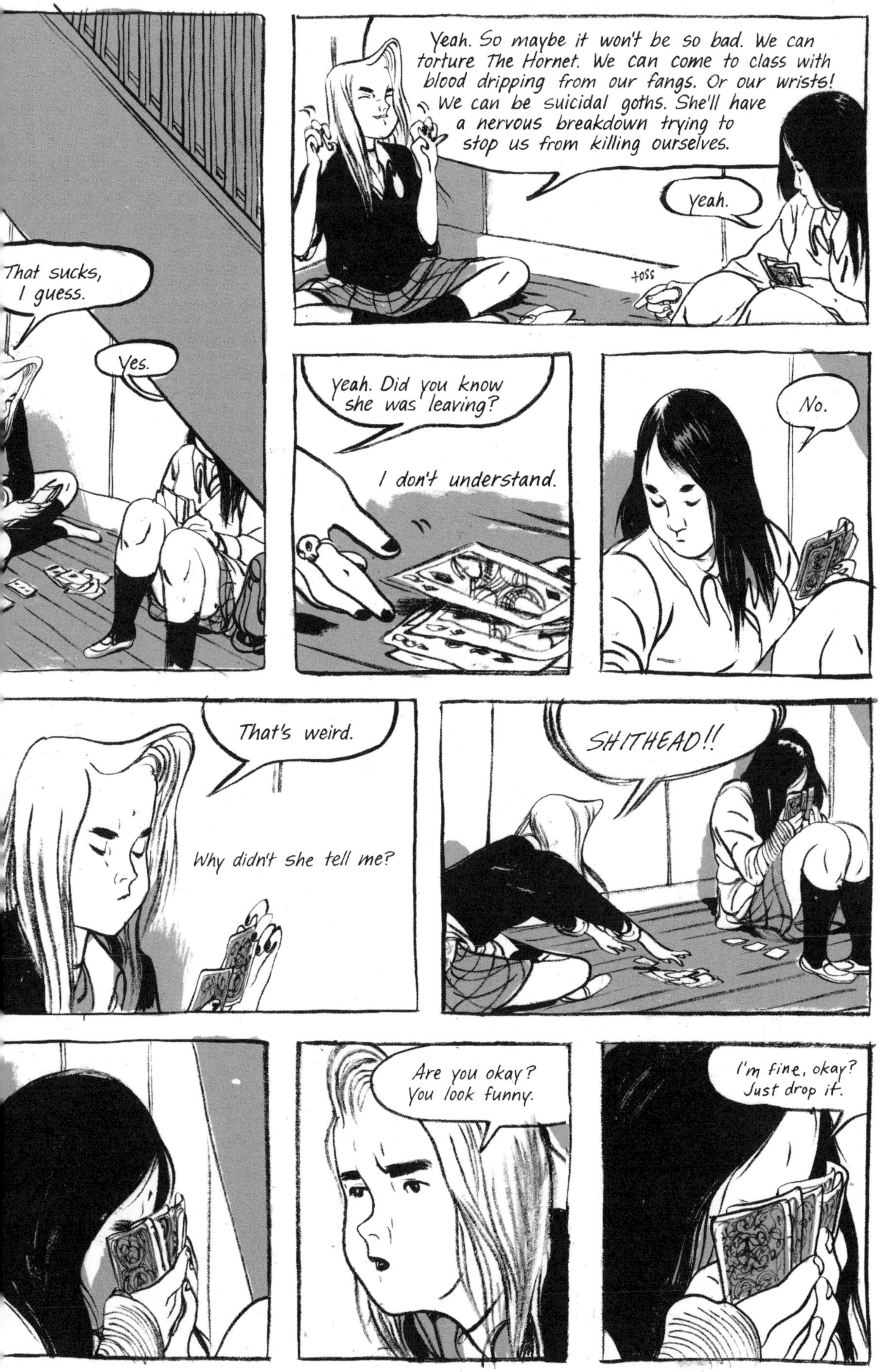
Yeah. So maybe it won't be so bad. We can torture The Hornet. We can come to class with blood dripping from our fangs. Or our wrists! We can be suicidal goths. She'll have a nervous breakdown trying to stop us from killing ourselves.
Yeah.
toss
That sucks, I guess.
Yes.
Yeah. Did you know she was leaving?
I don't understand.
No.
That's weird.
Why didn't she tell me?
SHITHEAD!!
Are you okay? You look funny.
I'm fine, okay? Just drop it.

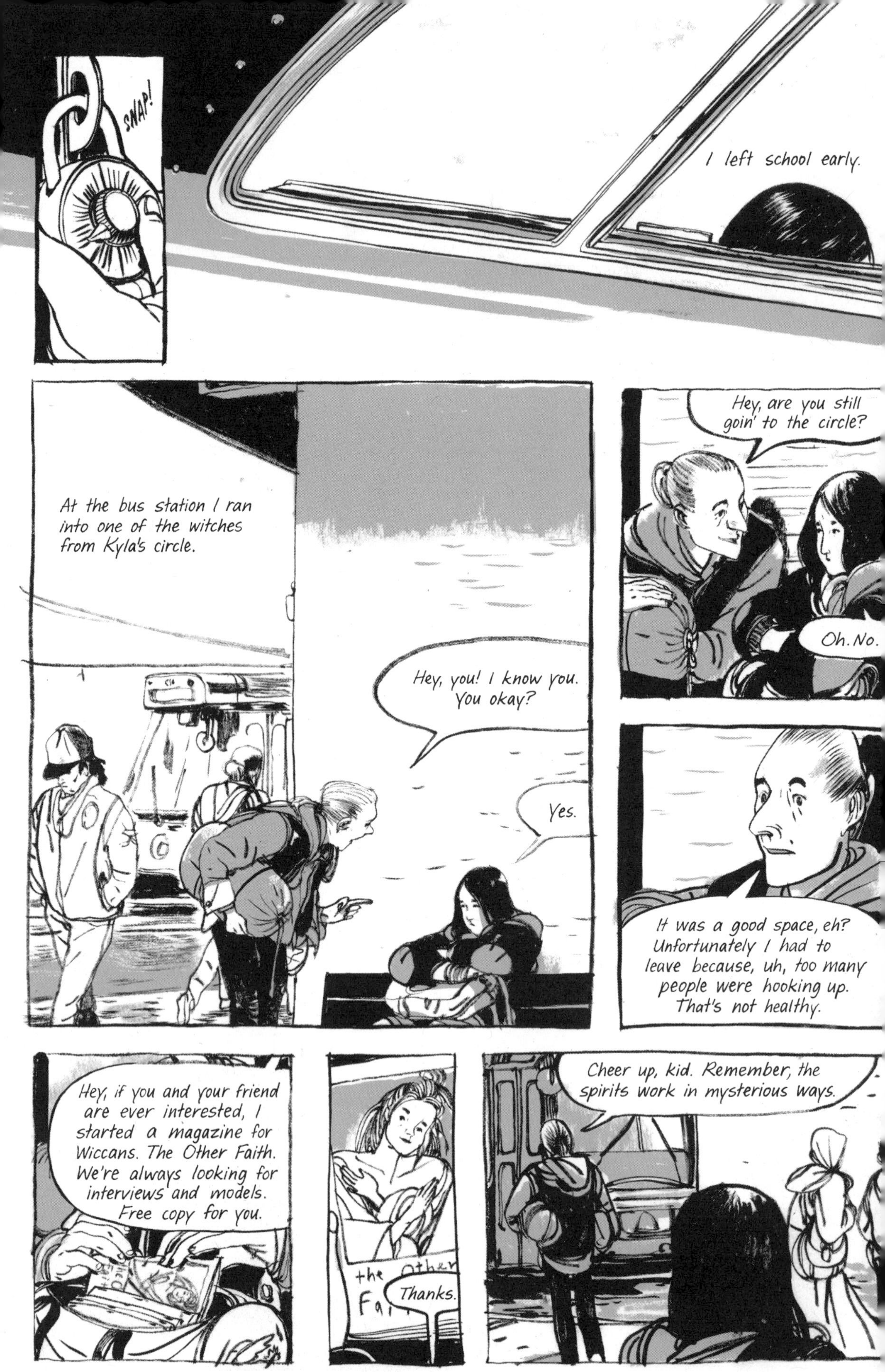
SNAP!
I left school early.
At the bus station I ran into one of the witches from Kyla's circle.
Hey, you! I know you. You okay?
Yes.
Hey, are you still goin' to the circle?
Oh. No.
It was a good space, eh? Unfortunately I had to leave because, uh, too many people were hooking up. That's not healthy.
Hey, if you and your friend are ever interested, I started a magazine for Wiccans. The Other Faith. We're always looking for interviews and models. Free copy for you.
Thanks.
Cheer up, kid. Remember, the spirits work in mysterious ways.

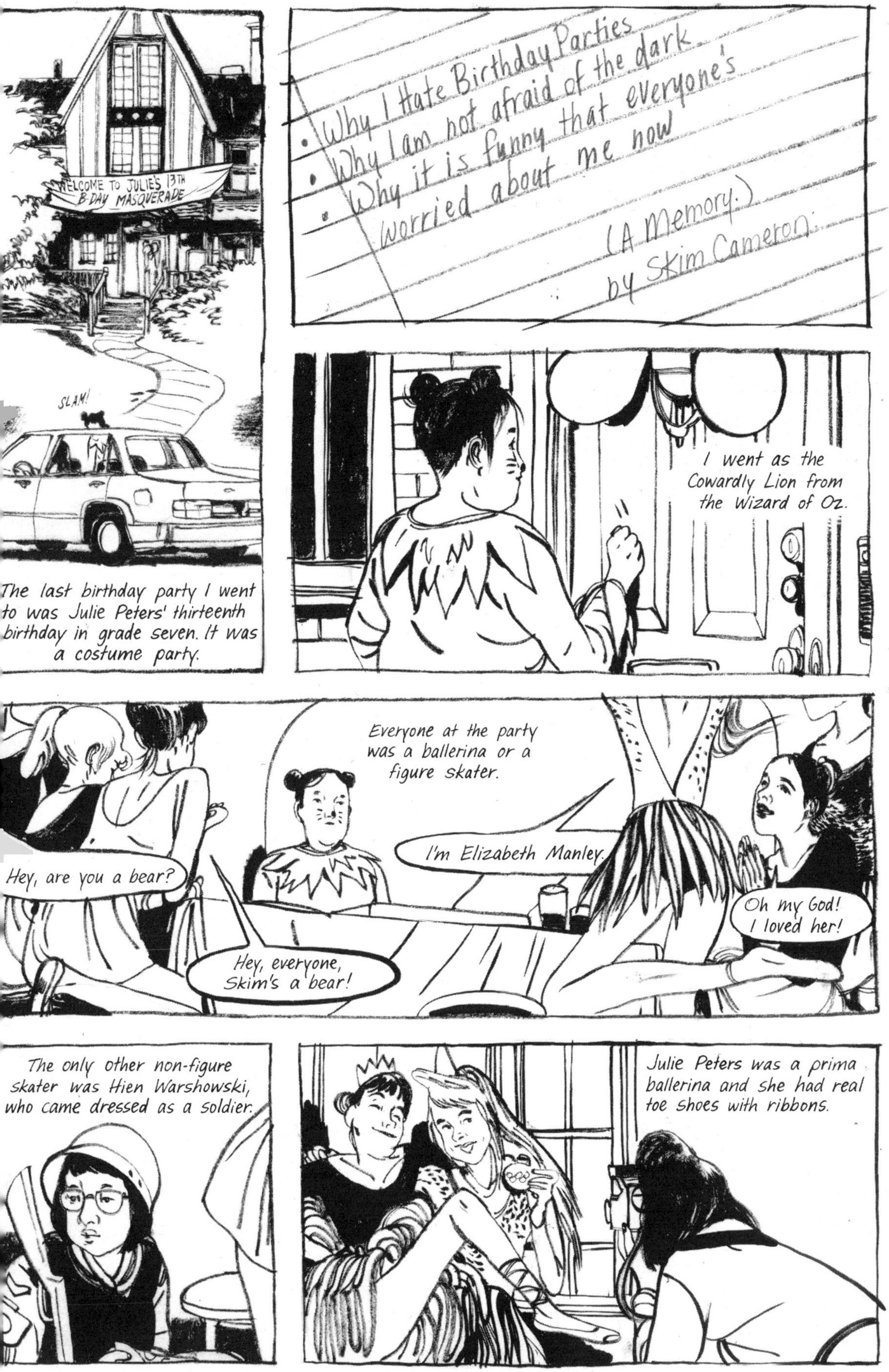
WELCOME TO JULIE'S 13TH B-DAY MASQUERADE
SLAM!
The last birthday party I went to was Julie Peters' thirteenth birthday in grade seven. It was a costume party.
• Why I Hate Birthday Parties
• Why I am not afraid of the dark
• Why it is funny that everyone's worried about me now
(A Memory.) by Skim Cameron.
I went as the Cowardly Lion from the Wizard of Oz.
Everyone at the party was a ballerina or a figure skater.
Hey, are you a bear?
I'm Elizabeth Manley.
Oh my God! I loved her!
Hey, everyone, Skim's a bear!
The only other non-figure skater was Hien Warshowski, who came dressed as a soldier.
Julie Peters was a prima ballerina and she had real toe shoes with ribbons.

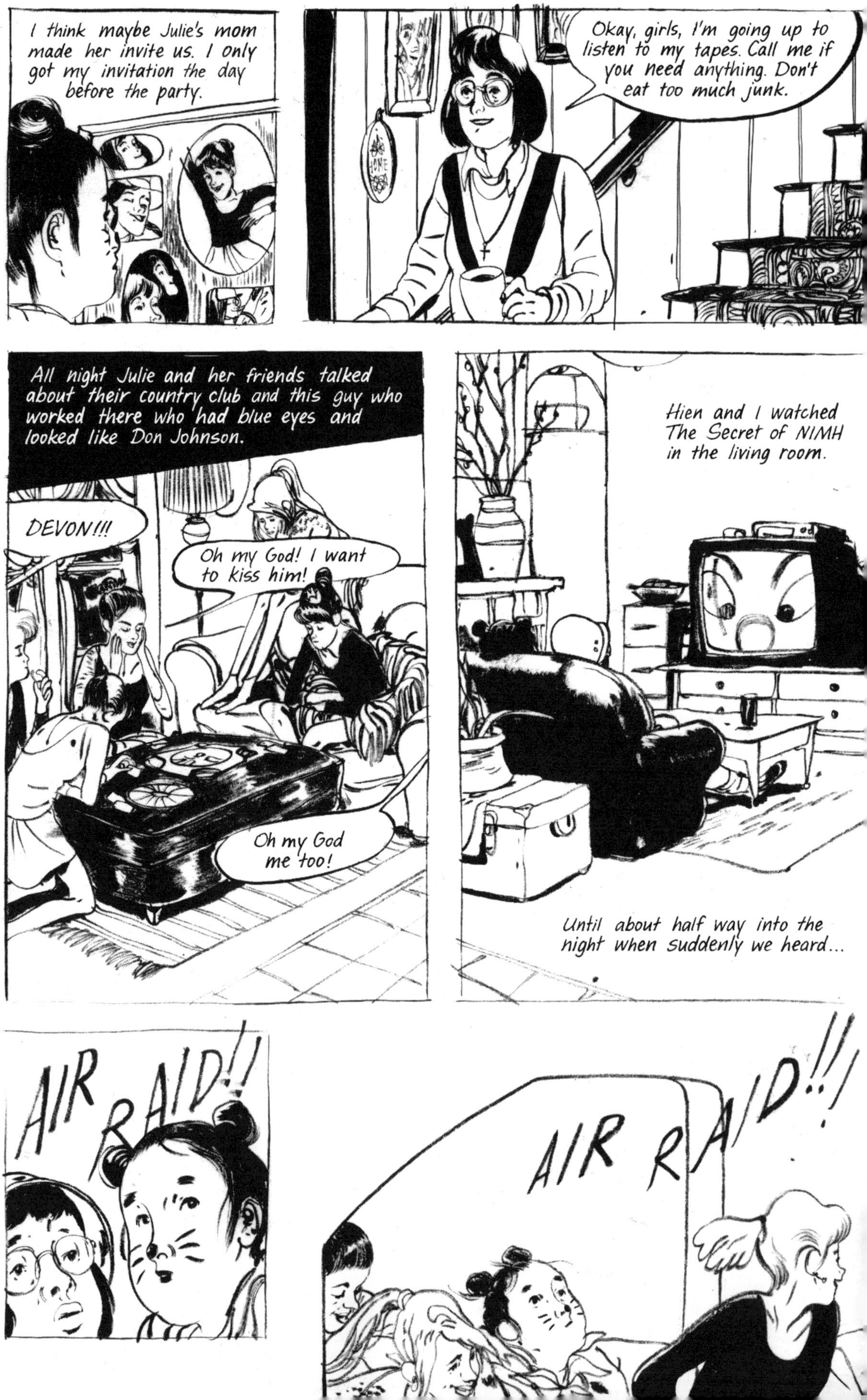
I think maybe Julie's mom made her invite us. I only got my invitation the day before the party.
Okay, girls, I'm going up to listen to my tapes. Call me if you need anything. Don't eat too much junk.
HOME
All night Julie and her friends talked about their country club and this guy who worked there who had blue eyes and looked like Don Johnson.
DEVON!!!
Oh my God! I want to kiss him!
Oh my God me too!
Hien and I watched The Secret of NIMH in the living room.
Until about half way into the night when suddenly we heard...
AIR RAID!!
AIR RAID!!

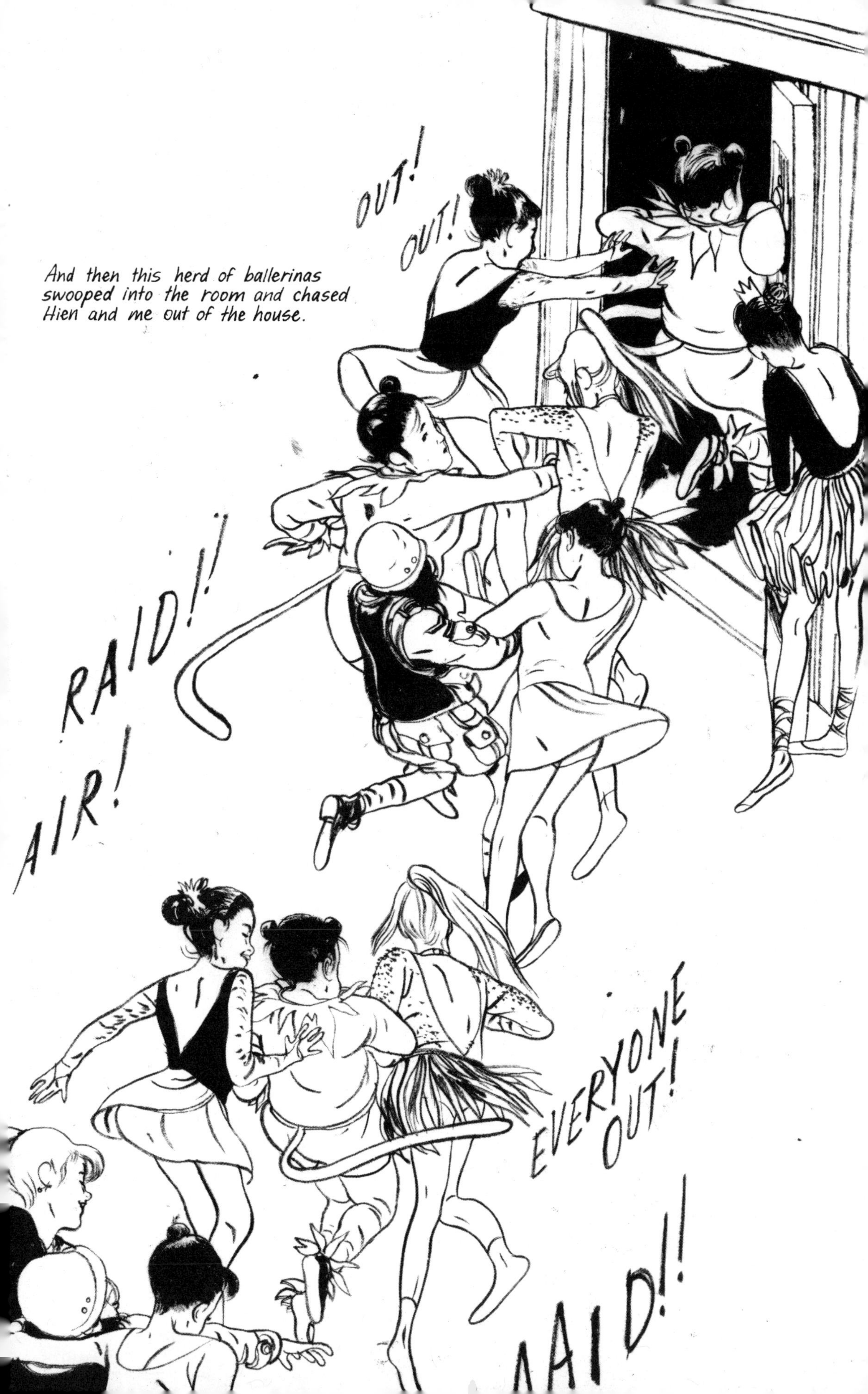

And then this herd of ballerinas swooped into the room and chased Hien and me out of the house.
OUT!
OUT!
AIR RAID!!
EVERYONE OUT!

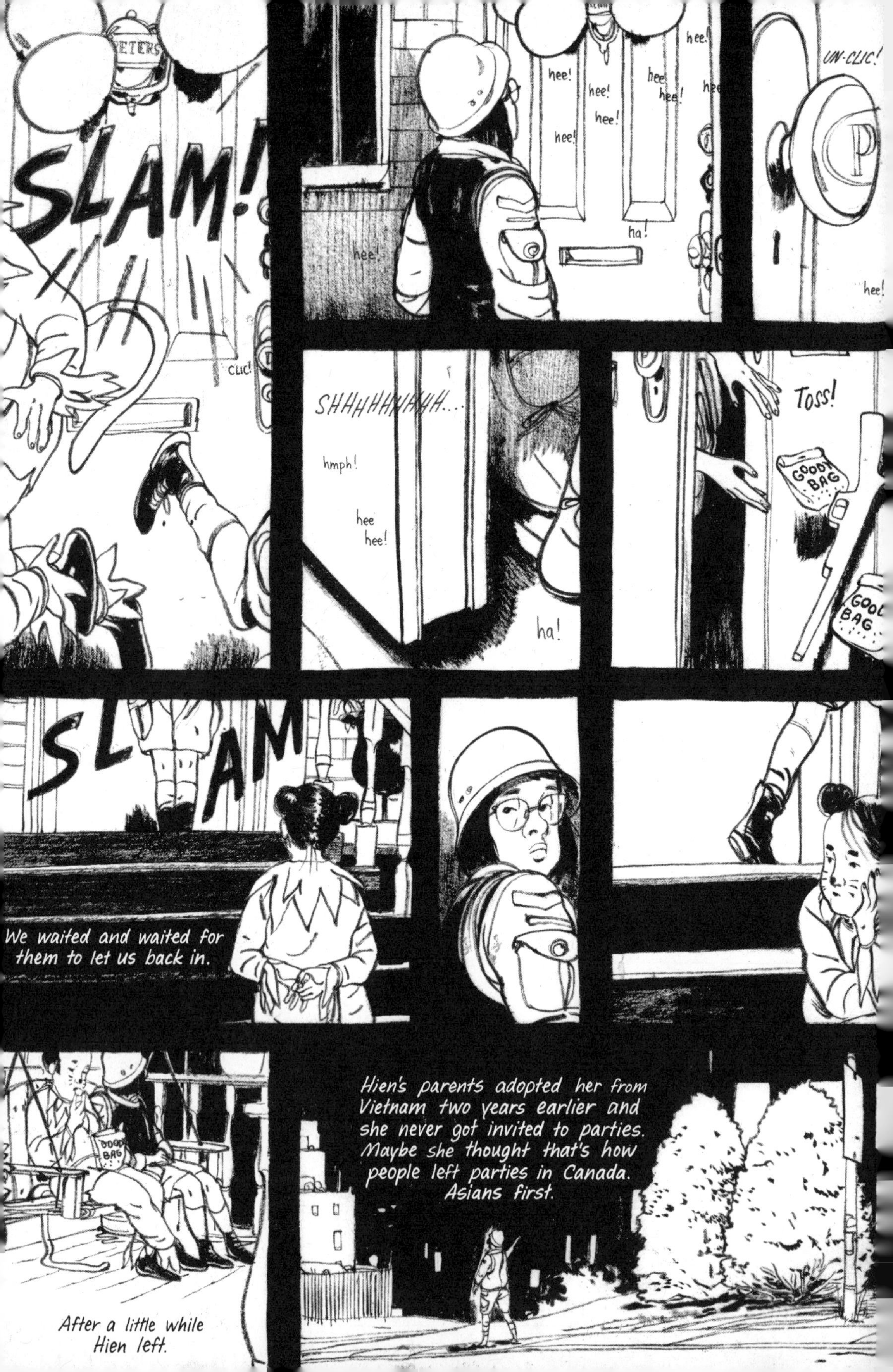
PETERS
SLAM!
CLIC!
hee!
hee!
hee!
hee!
hee!
hee!
hee!
hee!
ha!
hee!
UN-CLIC!
hee!
SHHHHHHHH...
hmph!
hee
hee!
ha!
Toss!
GOODY BAG
GOODY BAG
SLAM
We waited and waited for them to let us back in.
GOODY BAG
Hien's parents adopted her from Vietnam two years earlier and she never got invited to parties. Maybe she thought that's how people left parties in Canada. Asians first.
After a little while Hien left.

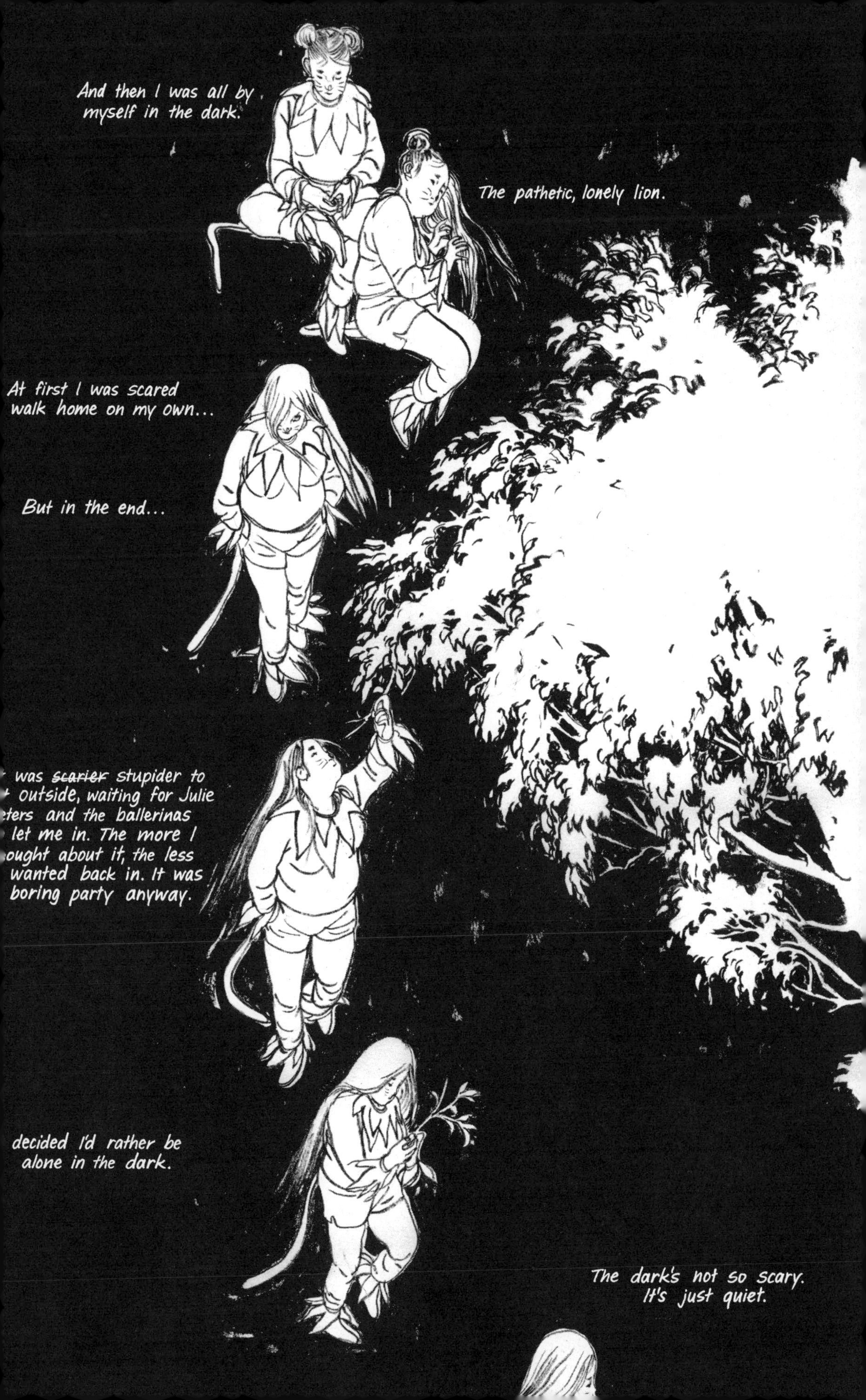

And then I was all by myself in the dark.
The pathetic, lonely lion.
At first I was scared walk home on my own...
But in the end...
was ~~scarier~~ stupider to outside, waiting for Julie eters and the ballerinas let me in. The more I ought about it, the less wanted back in. It was boring party anyway.
decided I'd rather be alone in the dark.
The dark's not so scary. It's just quiet.

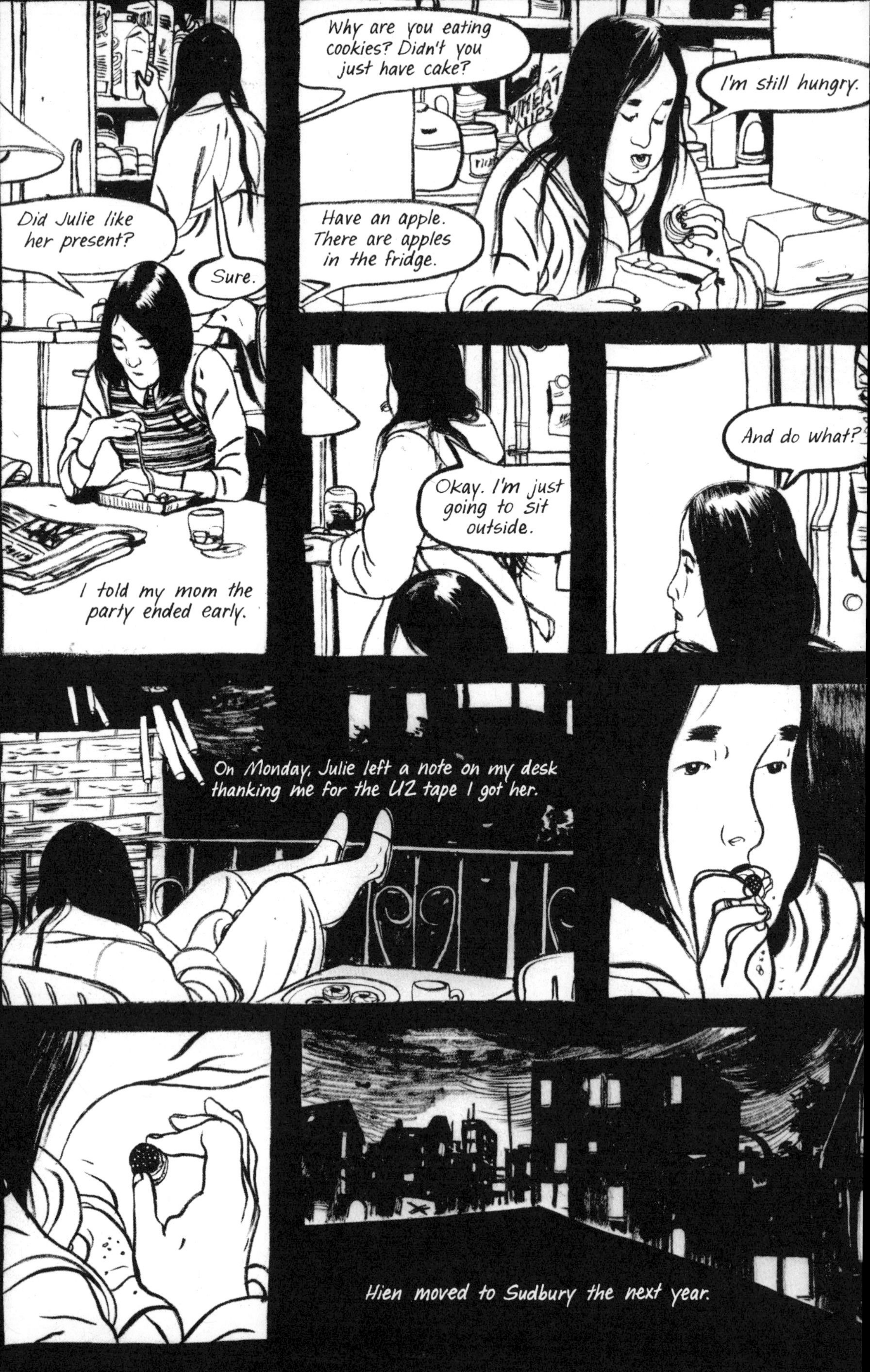
Did Julie like her present?
Sure.
I told my mom the party ended early.
Why are you eating cookies? Didn't you just have cake?
I'm still hungry.
Have an apple. There are apples in the fridge.
Okay. I'm just going to sit outside.
And do what?
On Monday, Julie left a note on my desk thanking me for the U2 tape I got her.
Hien moved to Sudbury the next year.

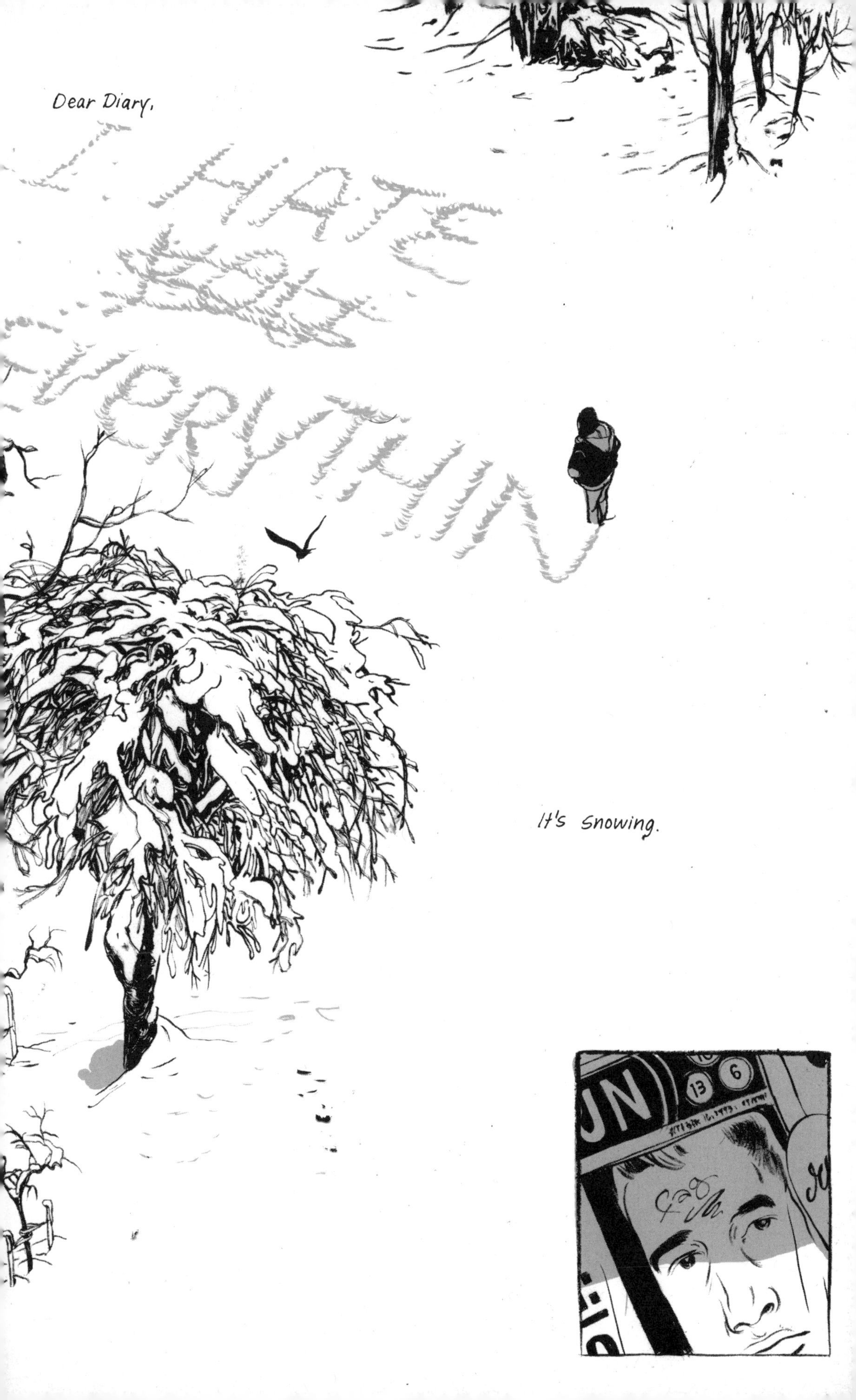
Dear Diary,
It's snowing.

Part III
Goodbye (Hello)

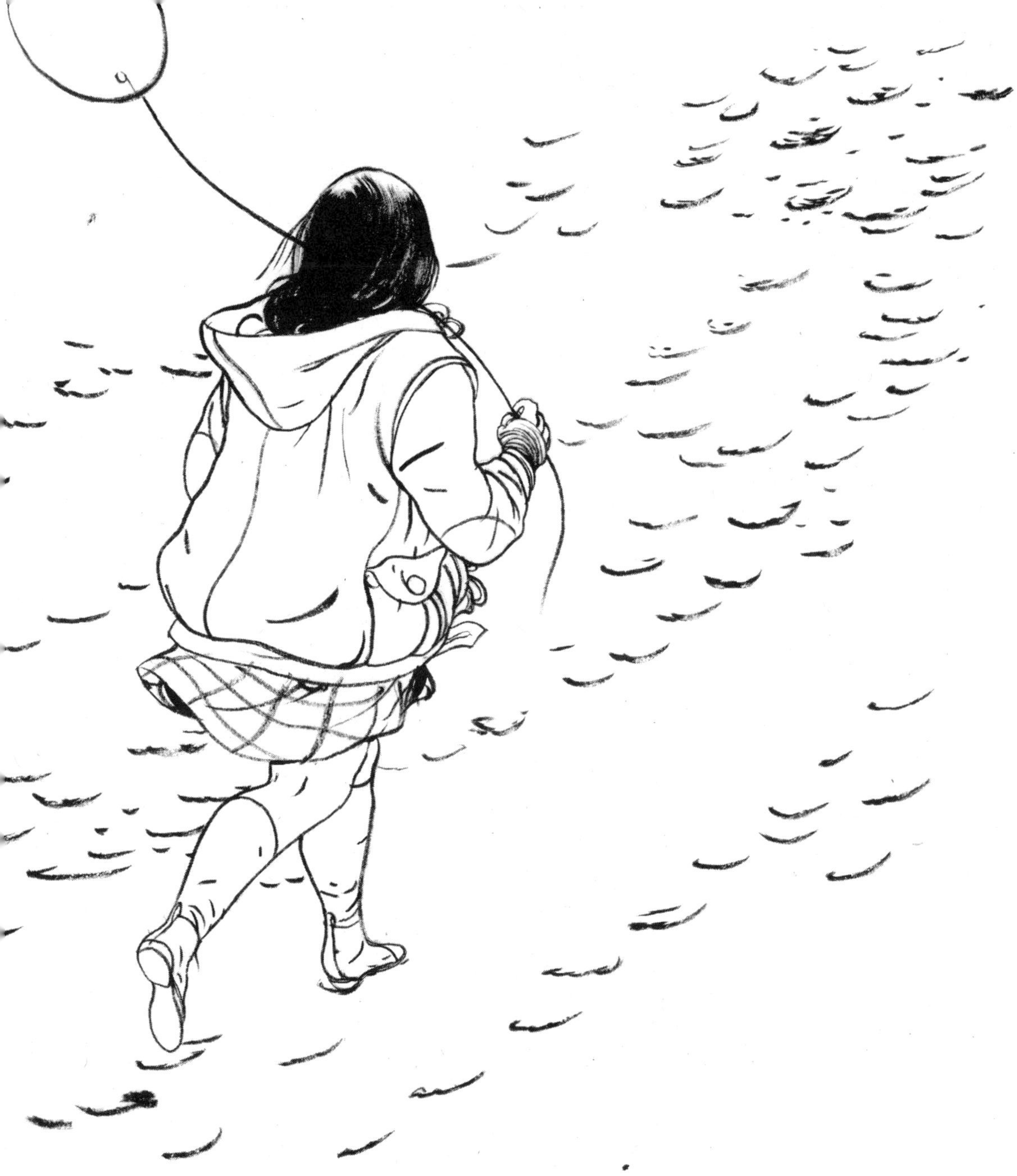

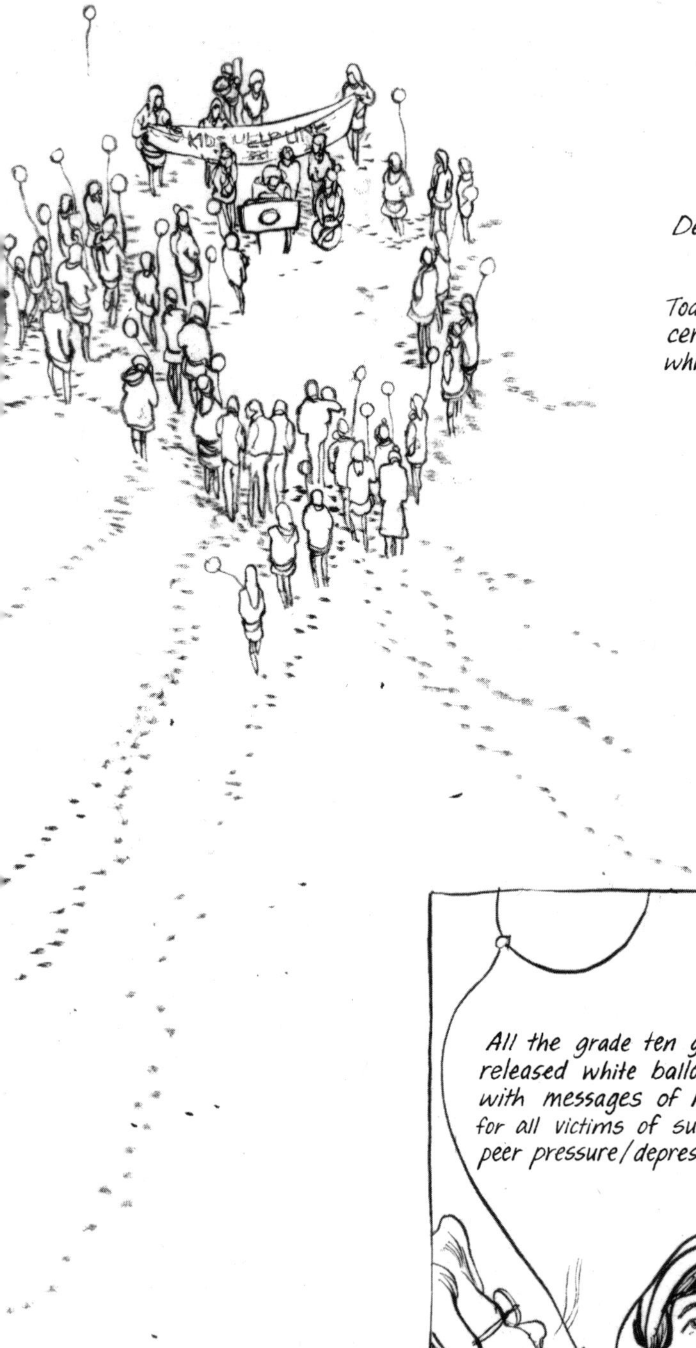

Dear Diary,

Today instead of phys ed we had a memorial ceremony on the upper athletic field, which is almost frozen.

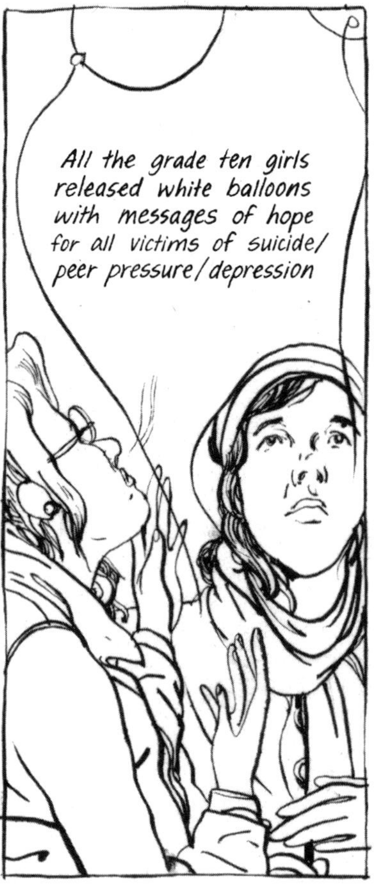
All the grade ten girls released white balloons with messages of hope for all victims of suicide/ peer pressure/ depression

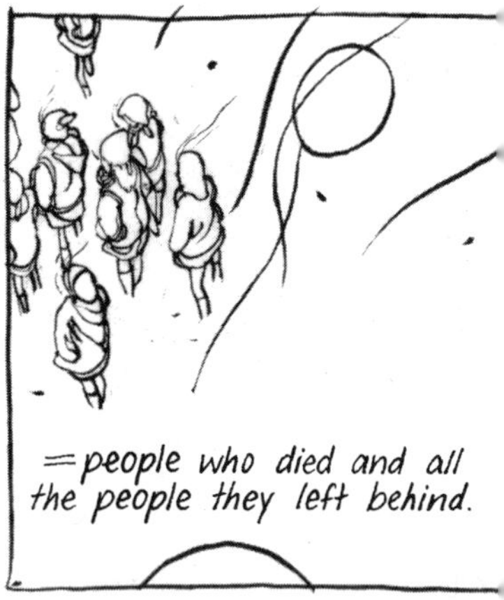
=people who died and all the people they left behind.

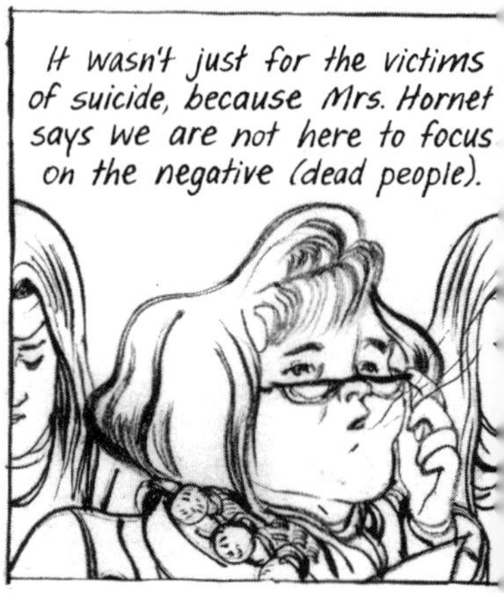
It wasn't just for the victims of suicide, because Mrs. Hornet says we are not here to focus on the negative (dead people).

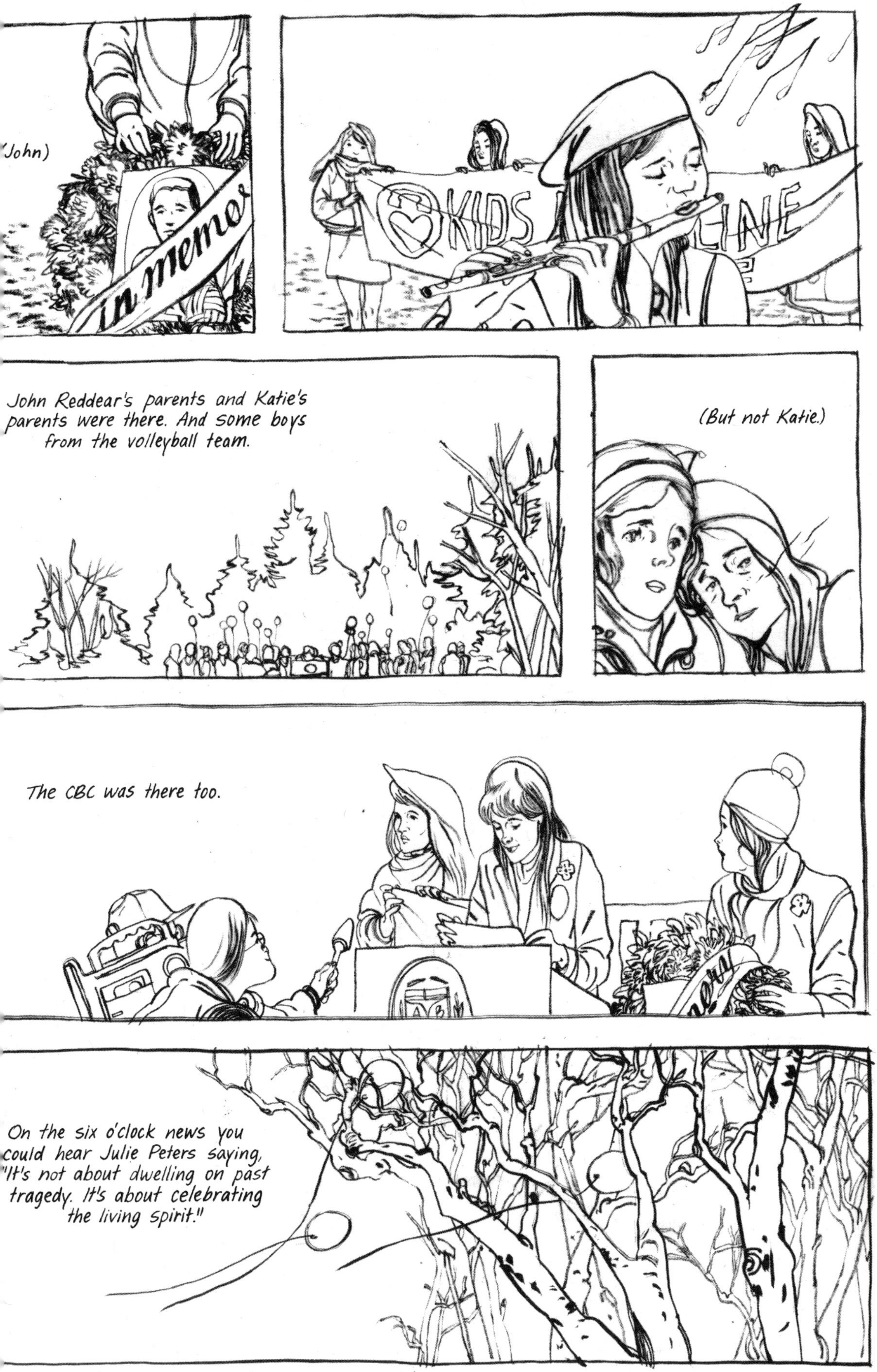

(John)
in memo
KIDS
LINE
John Reddear's parents and Katie's parents were there. And some boys from the volleyball team.
(But not Katie.)
The CBC was there too.
On the six o'clock news you could hear Julie Peters saying, "It's not about dwelling on past tragedy. It's about celebrating the living spirit."

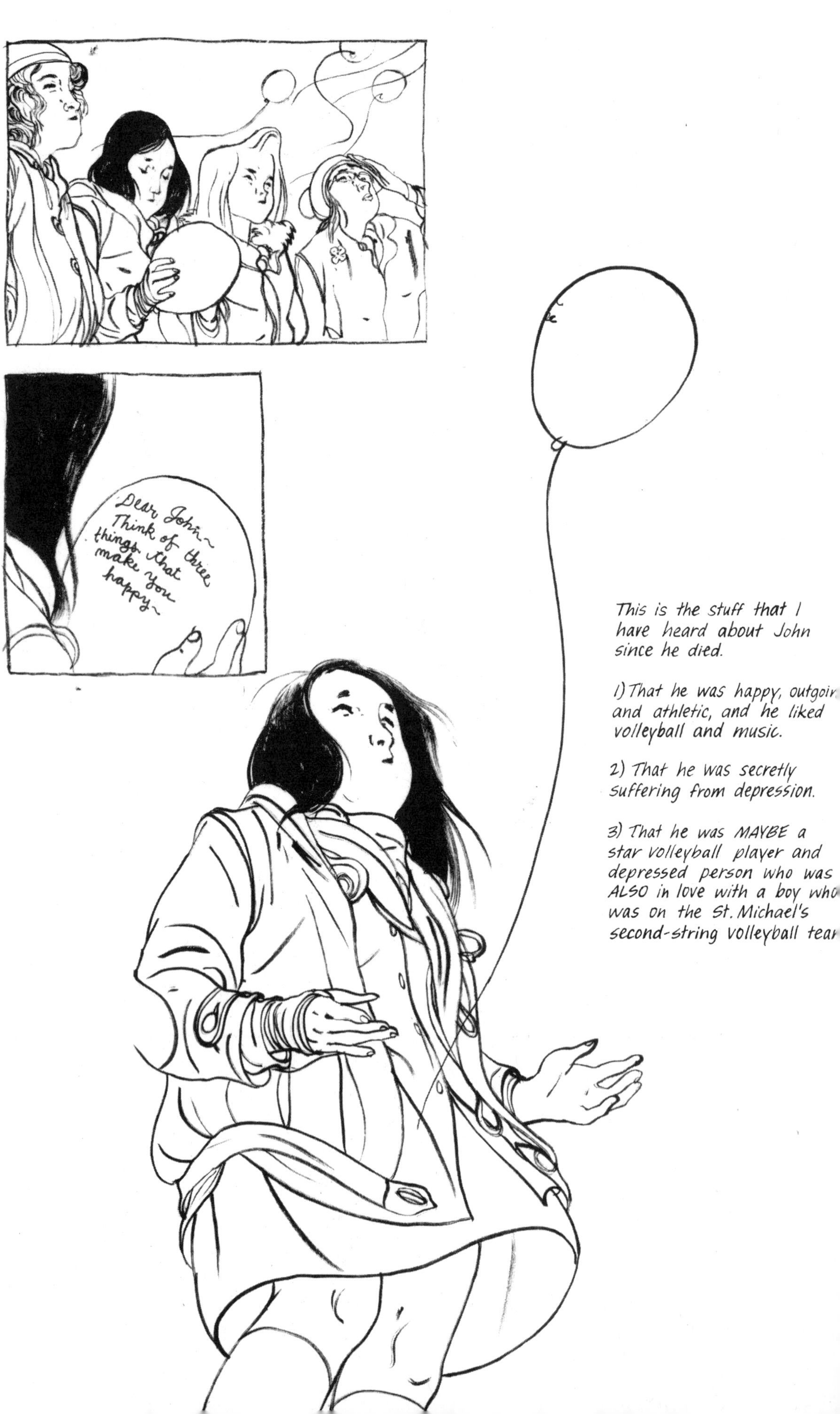
Dear John~ Think of three things that make you happy~
This is the stuff that I have heard about John since he died.
1) That he was happy, outgoin and athletic, and he liked volleyball and music.
2) That he was secretly suffering from depression.
3) That he was MAYBE a star volleyball player and depressed person who was ALSO in love with a boy who was on the St. Michael's second-string volleyball tea

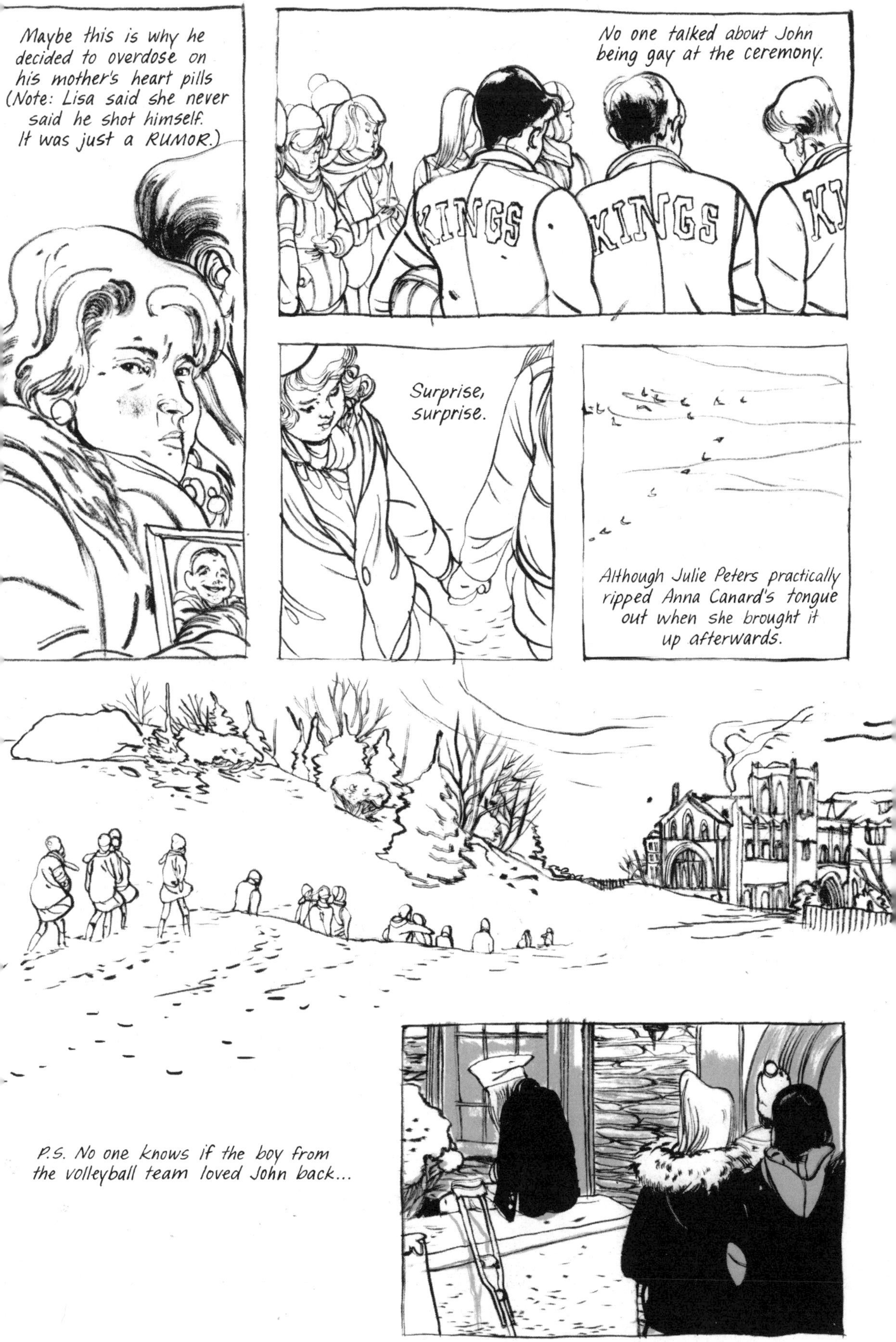
Maybe this is why he decided to overdose on his mother's heart pills
(Note: Lisa said she never said he shot himself. It was just a RUMOR.)
No one talked about John being gay at the ceremony.
KINGS
KINGS
Surprise, surprise.
Although Julie Peters practically ripped Anna Canard's tongue out when she brought it up afterwards.
P.S. No one knows if the boy from the volleyball team loved John back...

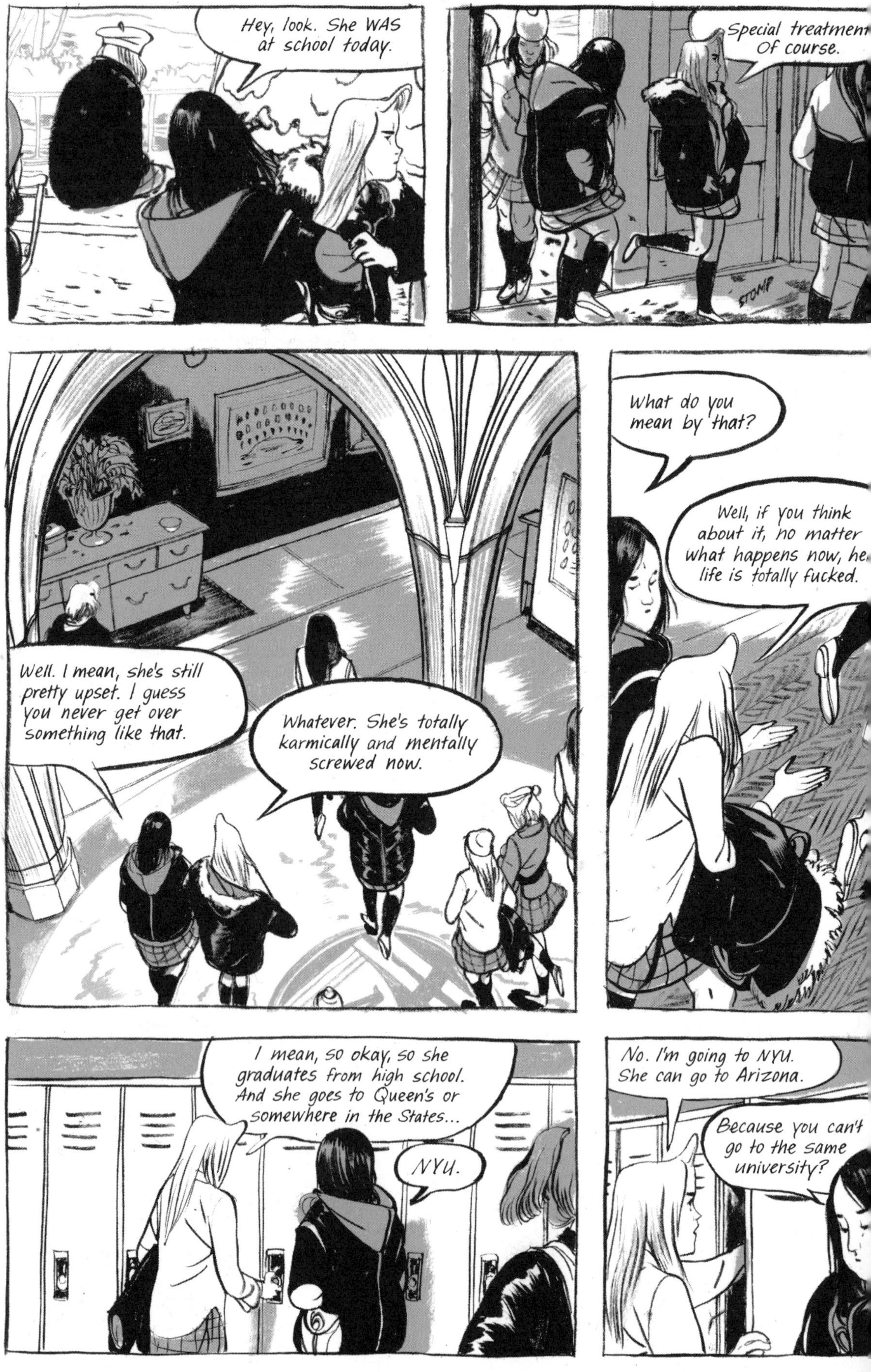
Hey, look. She WAS at school today.
Special treatment. Of course.
STOMP
What do you mean by that?
Well, if you think about it, no matter what happens now, her life is totally fucked.
Well. I mean, she's still pretty upset. I guess you never get over something like that.
Whatever. She's totally karmically and mentally screwed now.
I mean, so okay, so she graduates from high school. And she goes to Queen's or somewhere in the States...
NYU.
No. I'm going to NYU. She can go to Arizona.
Because you can't go to the same university?

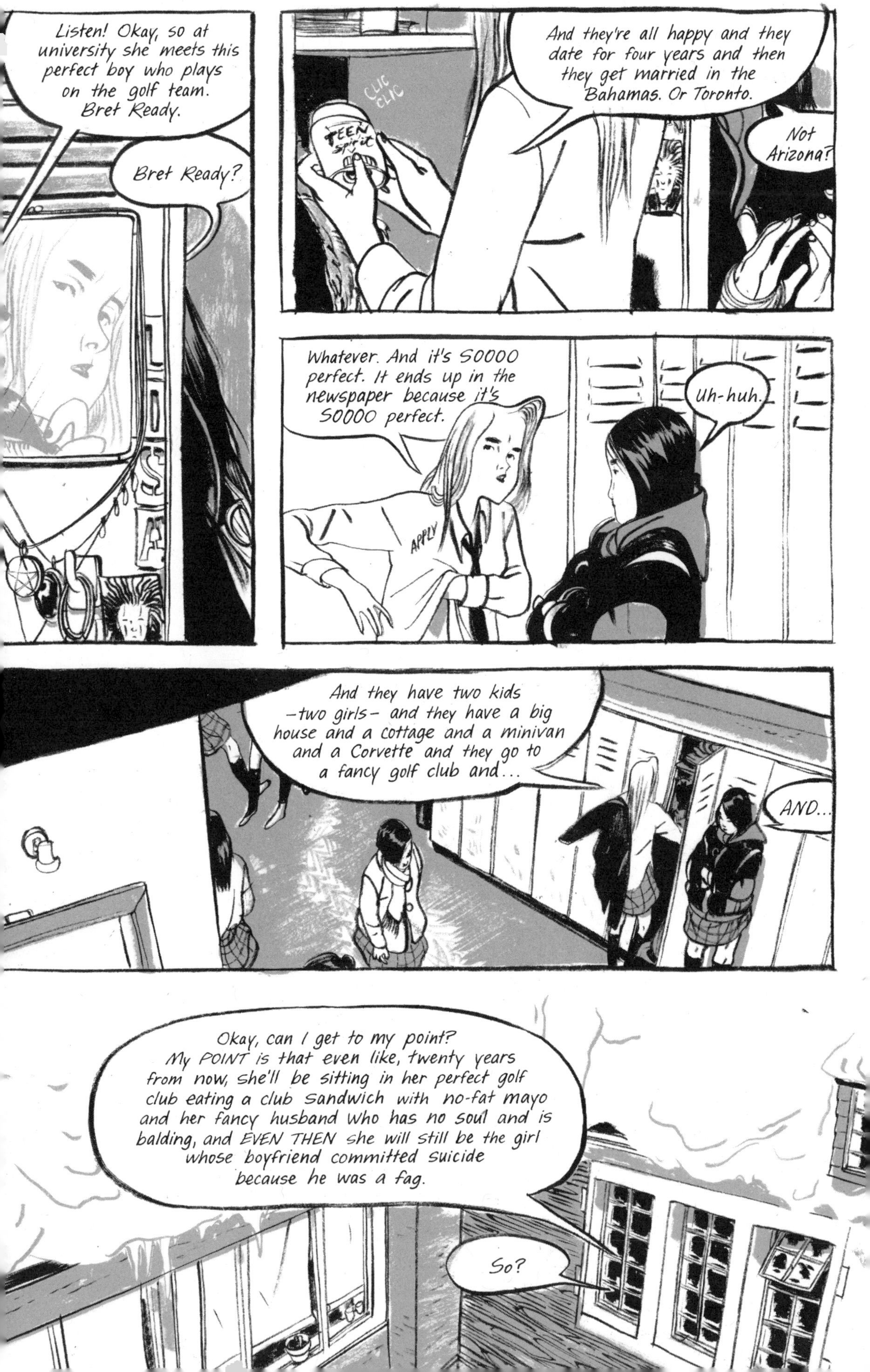
Listen! Okay, so at university she meets this perfect boy who plays on the golf team. Bret Ready.
Bret Ready?
CLIC CLIC
TEEN spirit
And they're all happy and they date for four years and then they get married in the Bahamas. Or Toronto.
Not Arizona?
Whatever. And it's SOOOO perfect. It ends up in the newspaper because it's SOOOO perfect.
Uh-huh.
APPLY
And they have two kids –two girls– and they have a big house and a cottage and a minivan and a Corvette and they go to a fancy golf club and...
AND...
Okay, can I get to my point? My POINT is that even like, twenty years from now, she'll be sitting in her perfect golf club eating a club sandwich with no-fat mayo and her fancy husband who has no soul and is balding, and EVEN THEN she will still be the girl whose boyfriend committed suicide because he was a fag.
So?

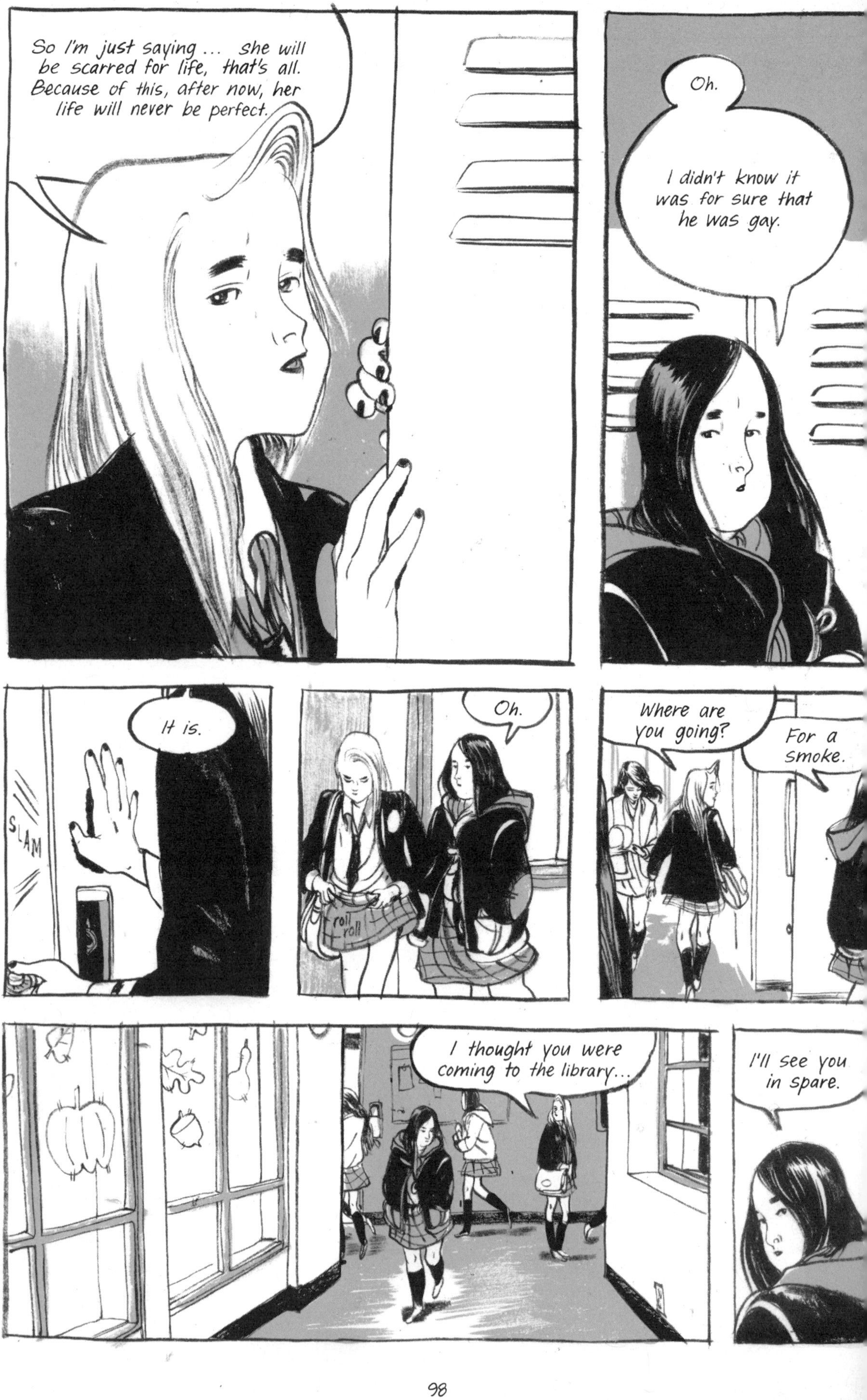

So I'm just saying ... she will be scarred for life, that's all. Because of this, after now, her life will never be perfect.
Oh.
I didn't know it was for sure that he was gay.
It is.
SLAM
Oh.
roll roll
Where are you going?
For a smoke.
I thought you were coming to the library...
I'll see you in spare.

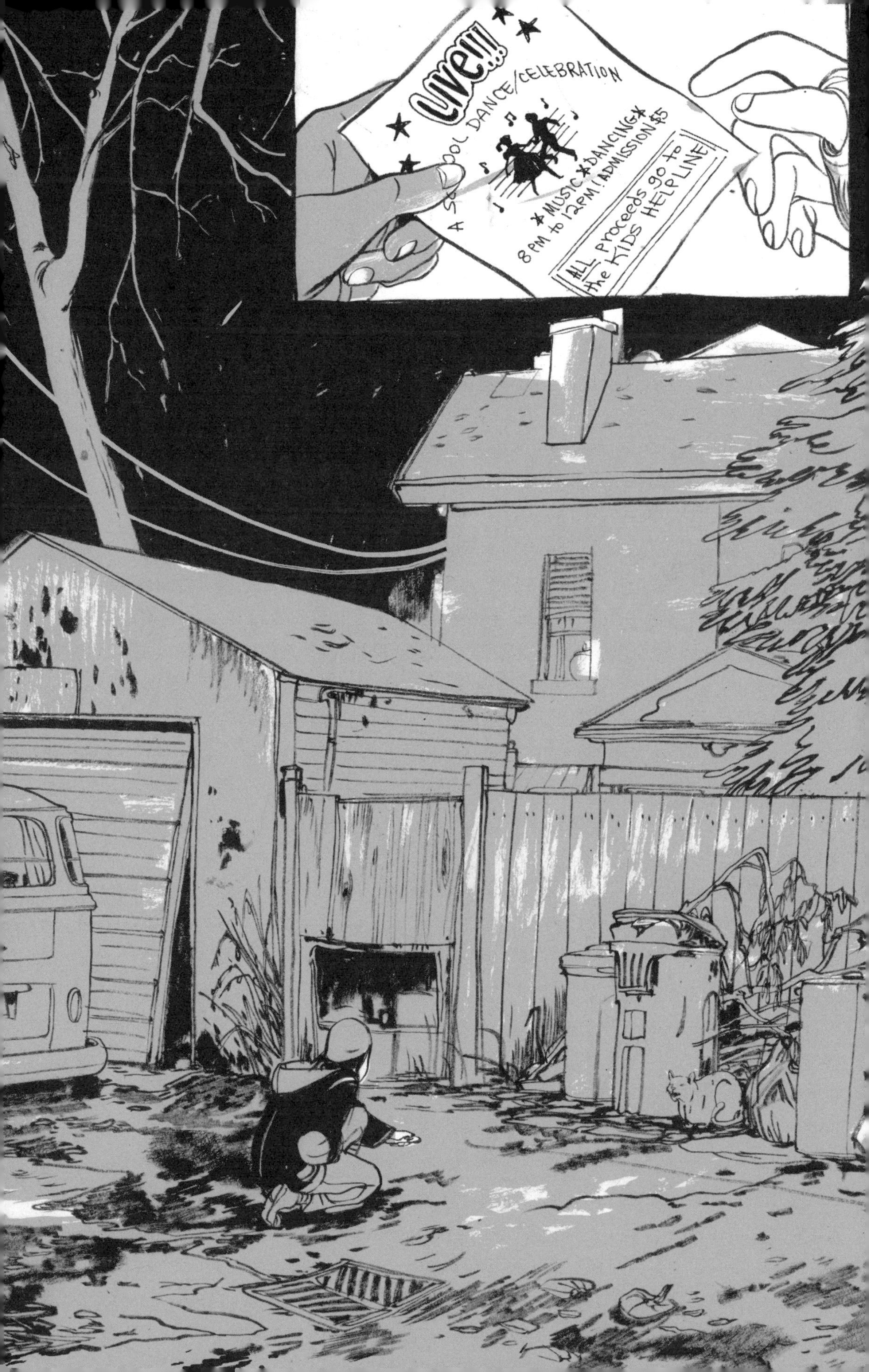
LIVE!!!
A SC OOL DANCE/CELEBRATION
*MUSIC*DANCING*
8PM to 12PM! ADMISSION $5
ALL proceeds go to the KIDS HELPLINE

Dear Diary,

I don't necessarily mean to be avoiding Lisa but I am.

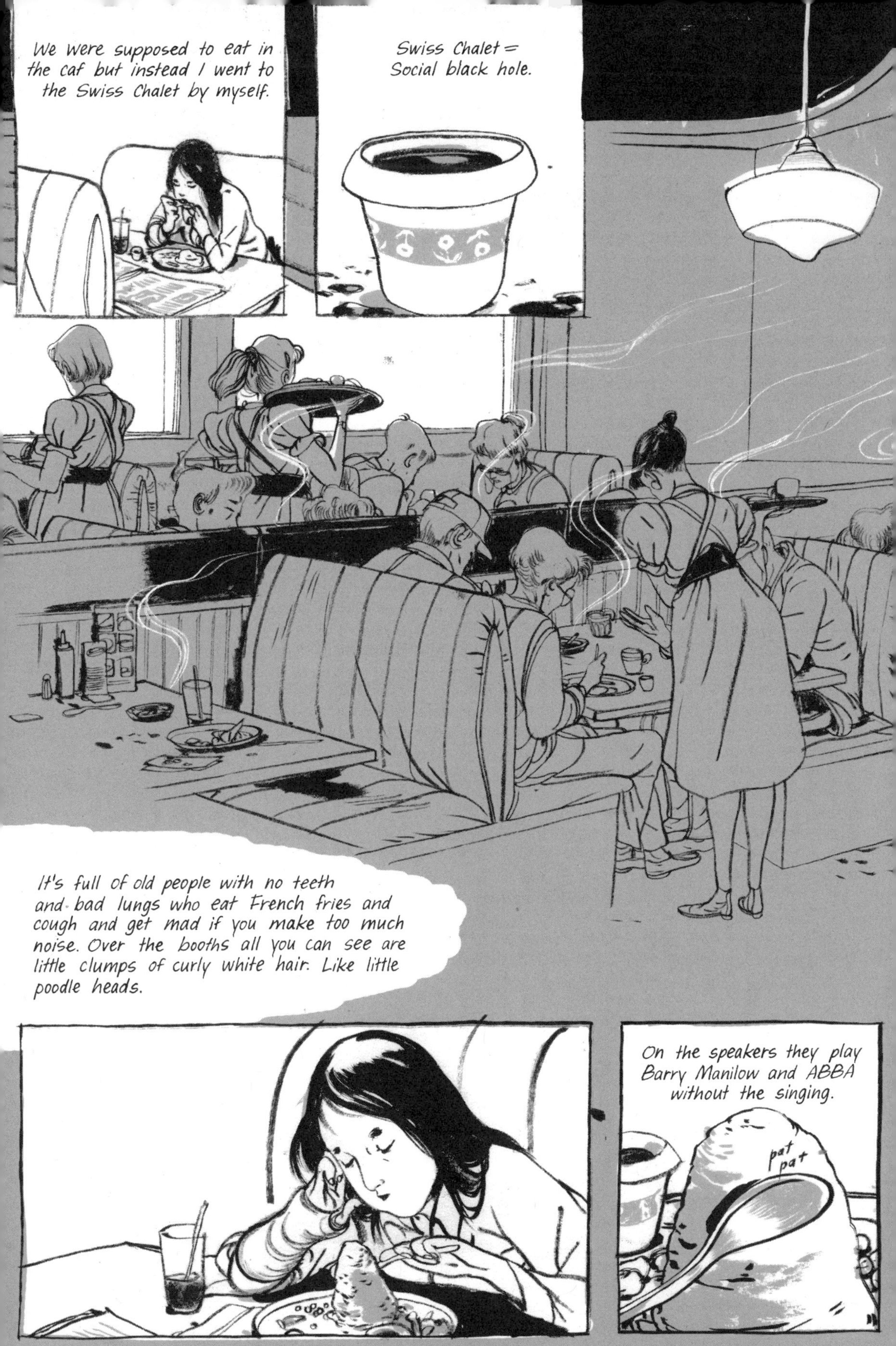
We were supposed to eat in the caf but instead I went to the Swiss Chalet by myself.
Swiss Chalet = Social black hole.
It's full of old people with no teeth and bad lungs who eat French fries and cough and get mad if you make too much noise. Over the booths all you can see are little clumps of curly white hair. Like little poodle heads.
On the speakers they play Barry Manilow and ABBA without the singing.
pat pat

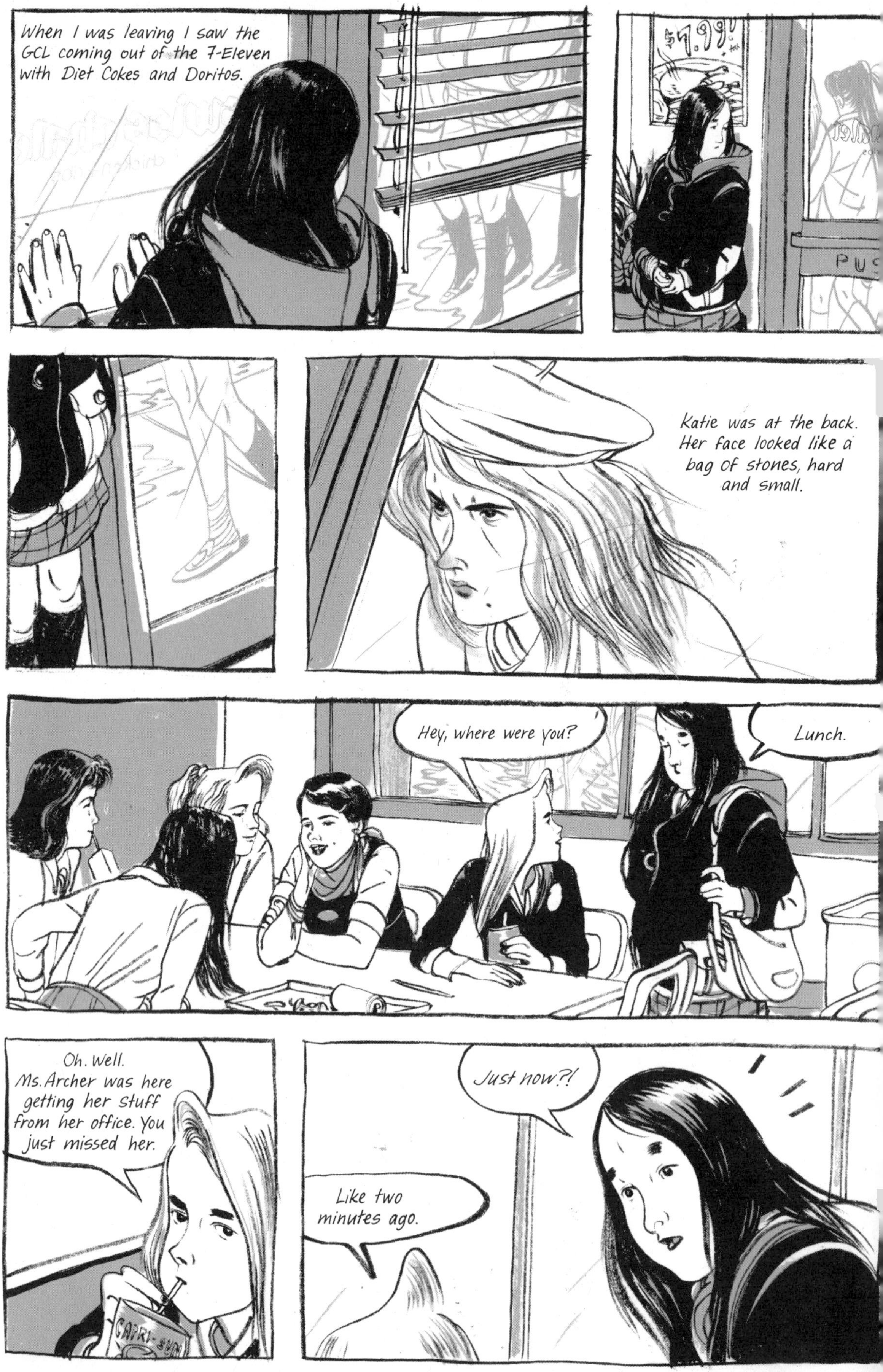
When I was leaving I saw the GCL coming out of the 7-Eleven with Diet Cokes and Doritos.
$7.99!
PUS
Katie was at the back. Her face looked like a bag of stones, hard and small.
Hey, where were you?
Lunch.
Oh. Well. Ms. Archer was here getting her stuff from her office. You just missed her.
CAPRI-SUN
Just now?!
Like two minutes ago.

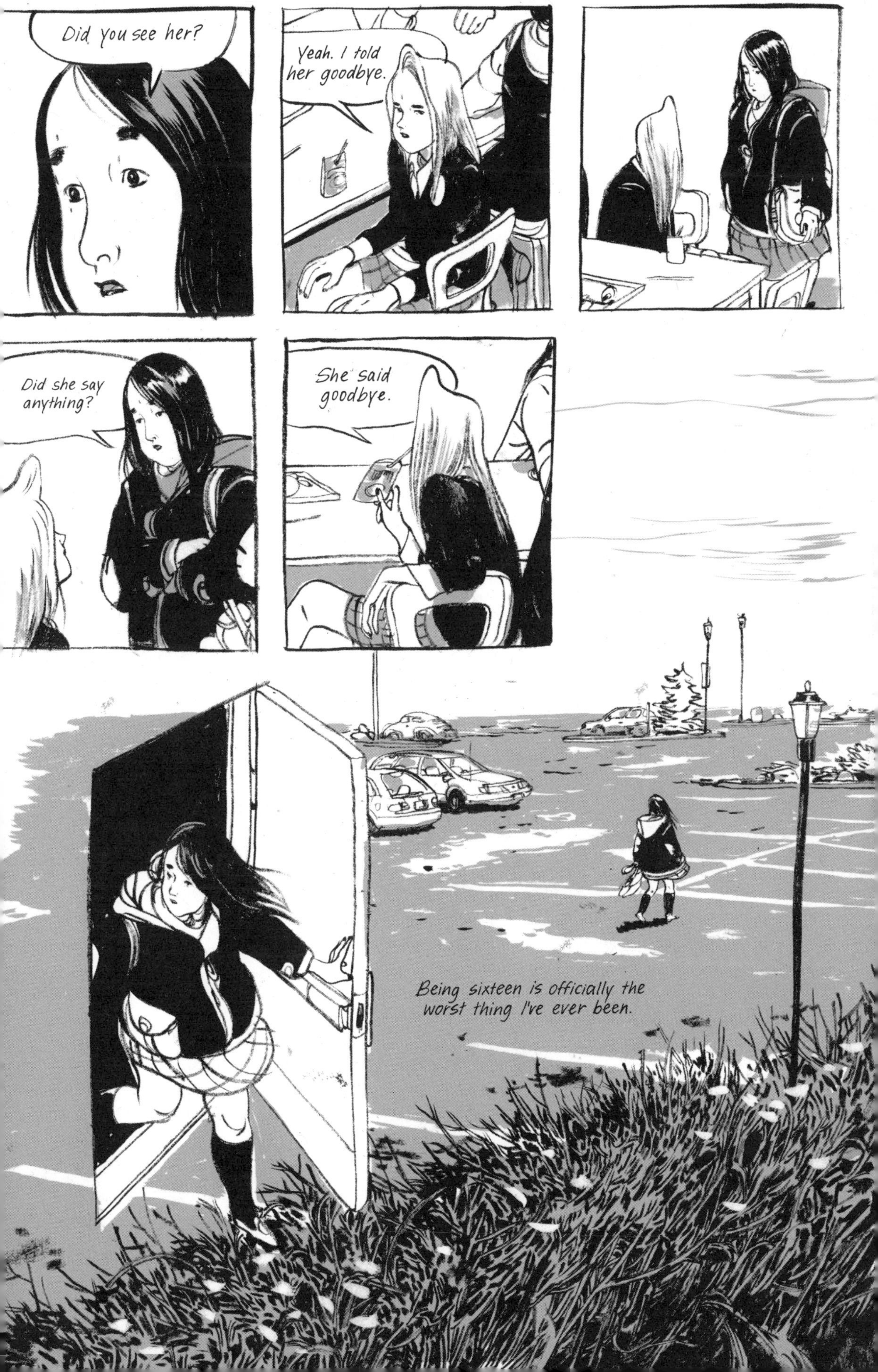
Did you see her?
Yeah. I told her goodbye.
Did she say anything?
She said goodbye.
Being sixteen is officially the worst thing I've ever been.

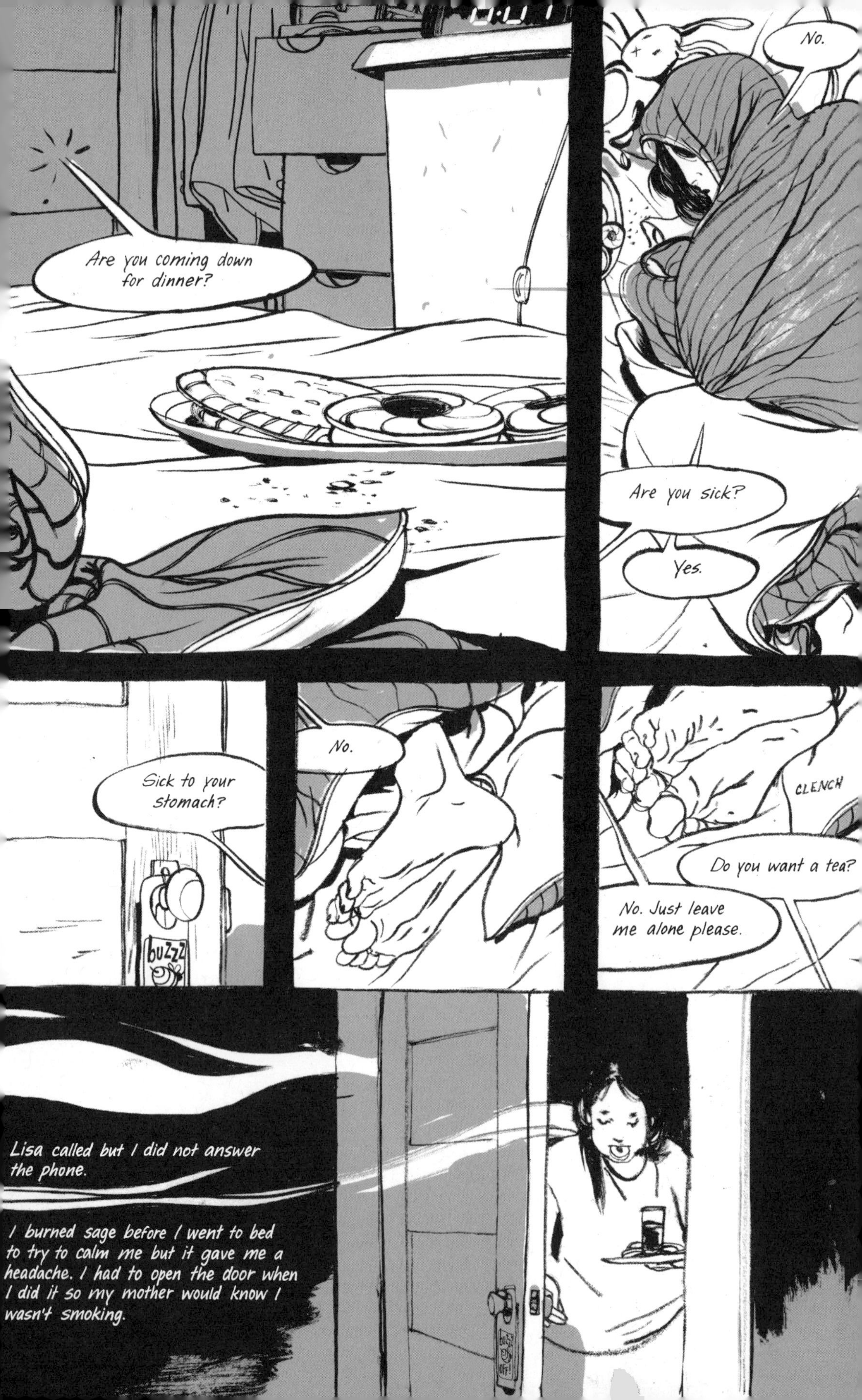
Are you coming down for dinner?
No.
Are you sick?
Yes.
Sick to your stomach?
No.
CLENCH
Do you want a tea?
No. Just leave me alone please.
Lisa called but I did not answer the phone.
I burned sage before I went to bed to try to calm me but it gave me a headache. I had to open the door when I did it so my mother would know I wasn't smoking.
buzzz
buzz off!

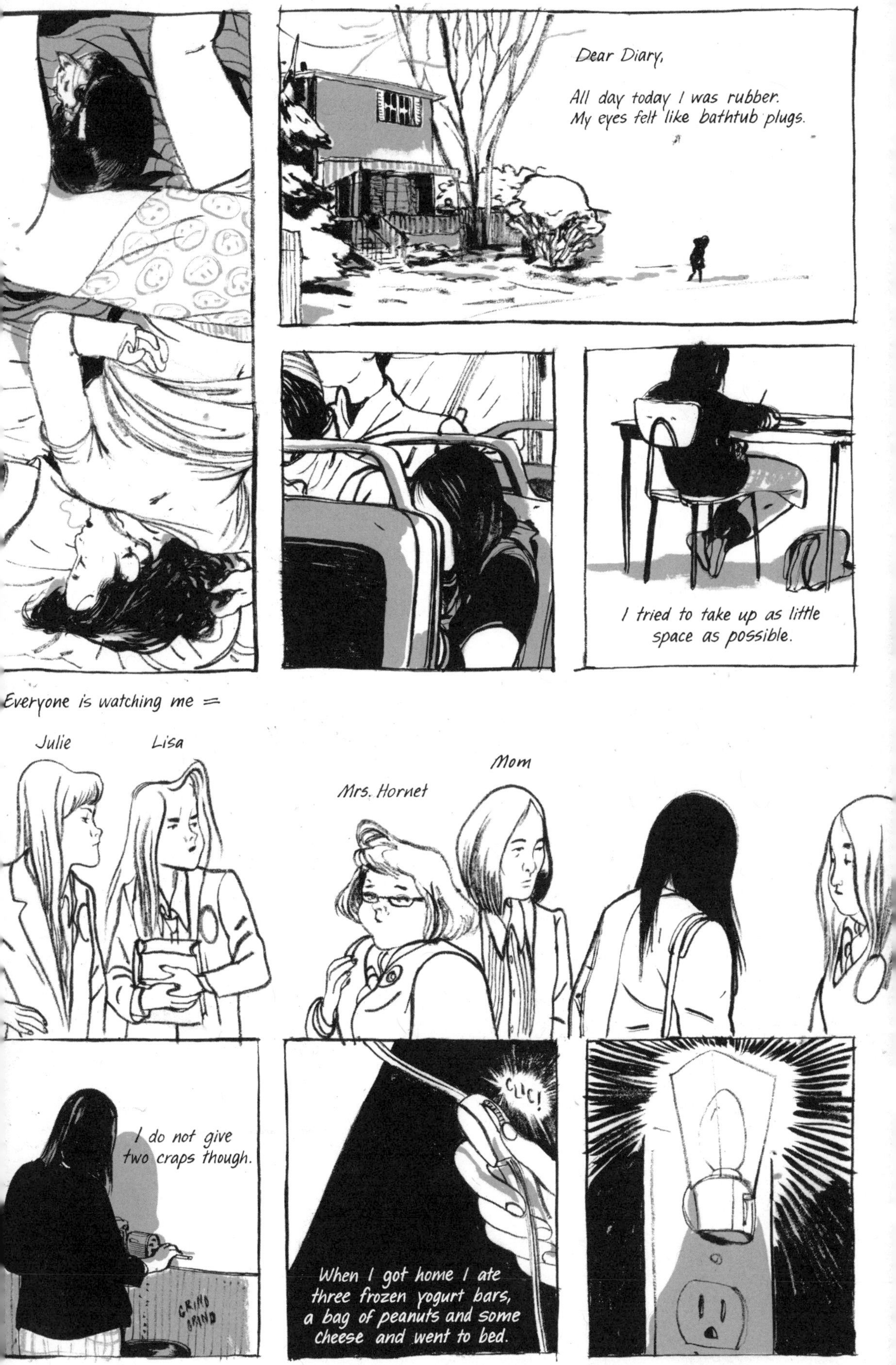

Dear Diary,
All day today I was rubber. My eyes felt like bathtub plugs.
I tried to take up as little space as possible.
Everyone is watching me =
Julie
Lisa
Mrs. Hornet
Mom
I do not give two craps though.
GRIND GRIND
CLIC!
When I got home I ate three frozen yogurt bars, a bag of peanuts and some cheese and went to bed.

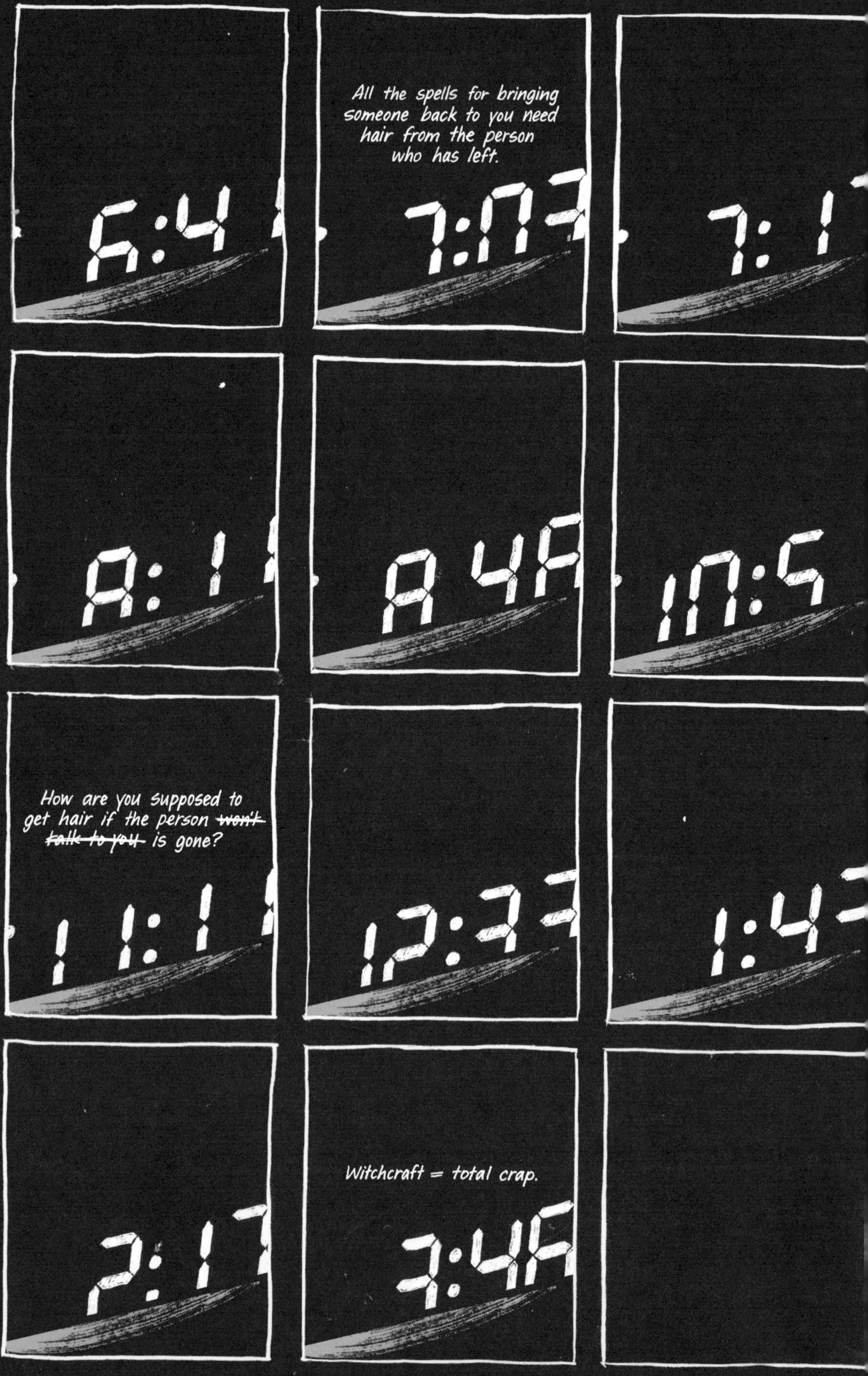
All the spells for bringing someone back to you need hair from the person who has left.
How are you supposed to get hair if the person ~~won't talk to you~~ is gone?
Witchcraft = total crap.

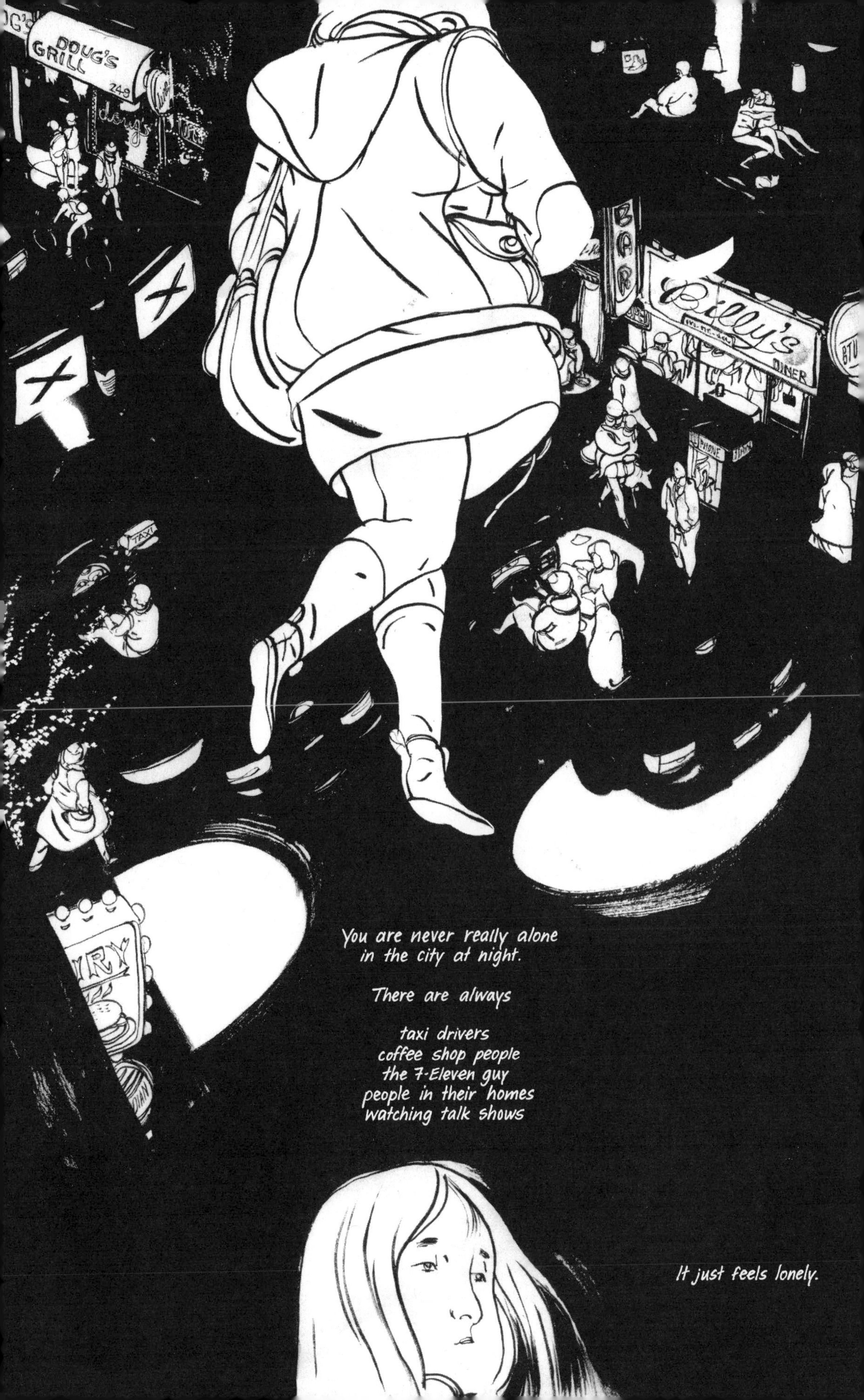
DOUG'S GRILL
249
BAR
Billy's
DINER
PHONE
TAXI
You are never really alone
in the city at night.
There are always
taxi drivers
coffee shop people
the 7-Eleven guy
people in their homes
watching talk shows
It just feels lonely.

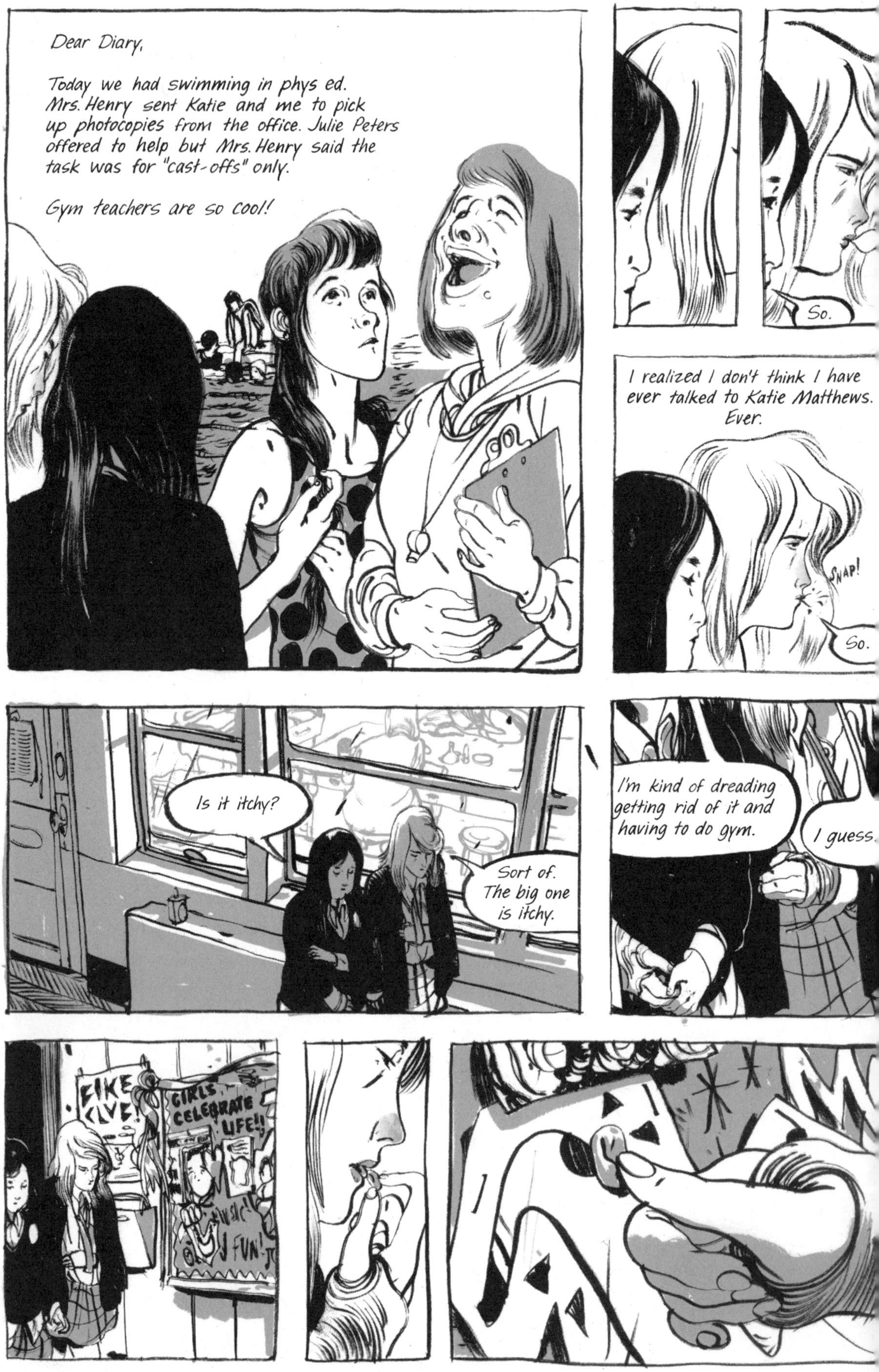

Dear Diary,
Today we had swimming in phys ed. Mrs. Henry sent Katie and me to pick up photocopies from the office. Julie Peters offered to help but Mrs. Henry said the task was for "cast-offs" only.
Gym teachers are so cool!
So.
I realized I don't think I have ever talked to Katie Matthews. Ever.
SNAP!
So.
Is it itchy?
Sort of. The big one is itchy.
I'm kind of dreading getting rid of it and having to do gym.
I guess.
BIKE CLUB!
GIRLS CELEBRATE LIFE!!
FUN!

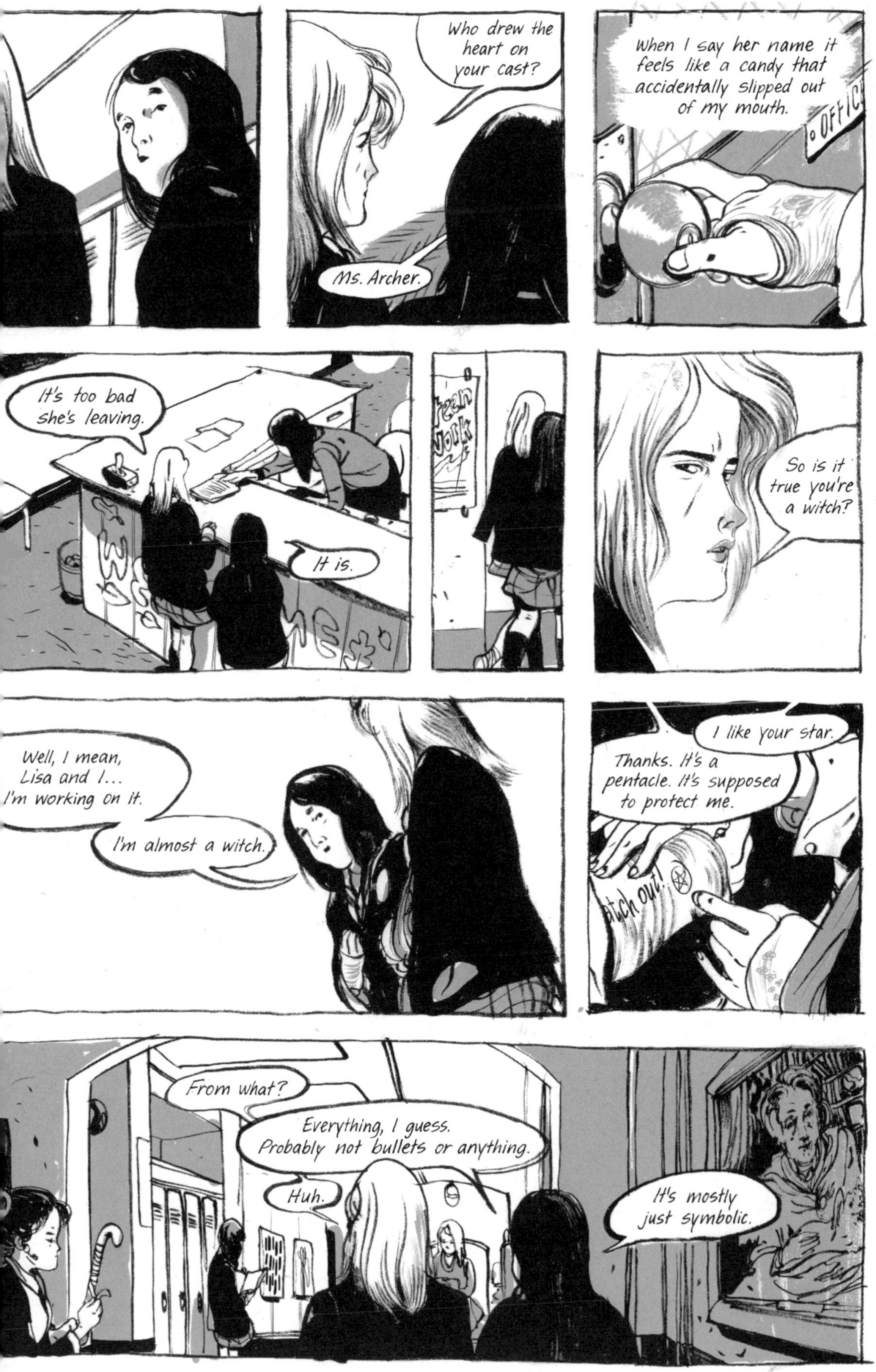
Who drew the heart on your cast?
Ms. Archer.
When I say her name it feels like a candy that accidentally slipped out of my mouth.
OFFIC
It's too bad she's leaving.
It is.
So is it true you're a witch?
Well, I mean, Lisa and I... I'm working on it.
I'm almost a witch.
I like your star.
Thanks. It's a pentacle. It's supposed to protect me.
From what?
Everything, I guess. Probably not bullets or anything.
Huh.
It's mostly just symbolic.

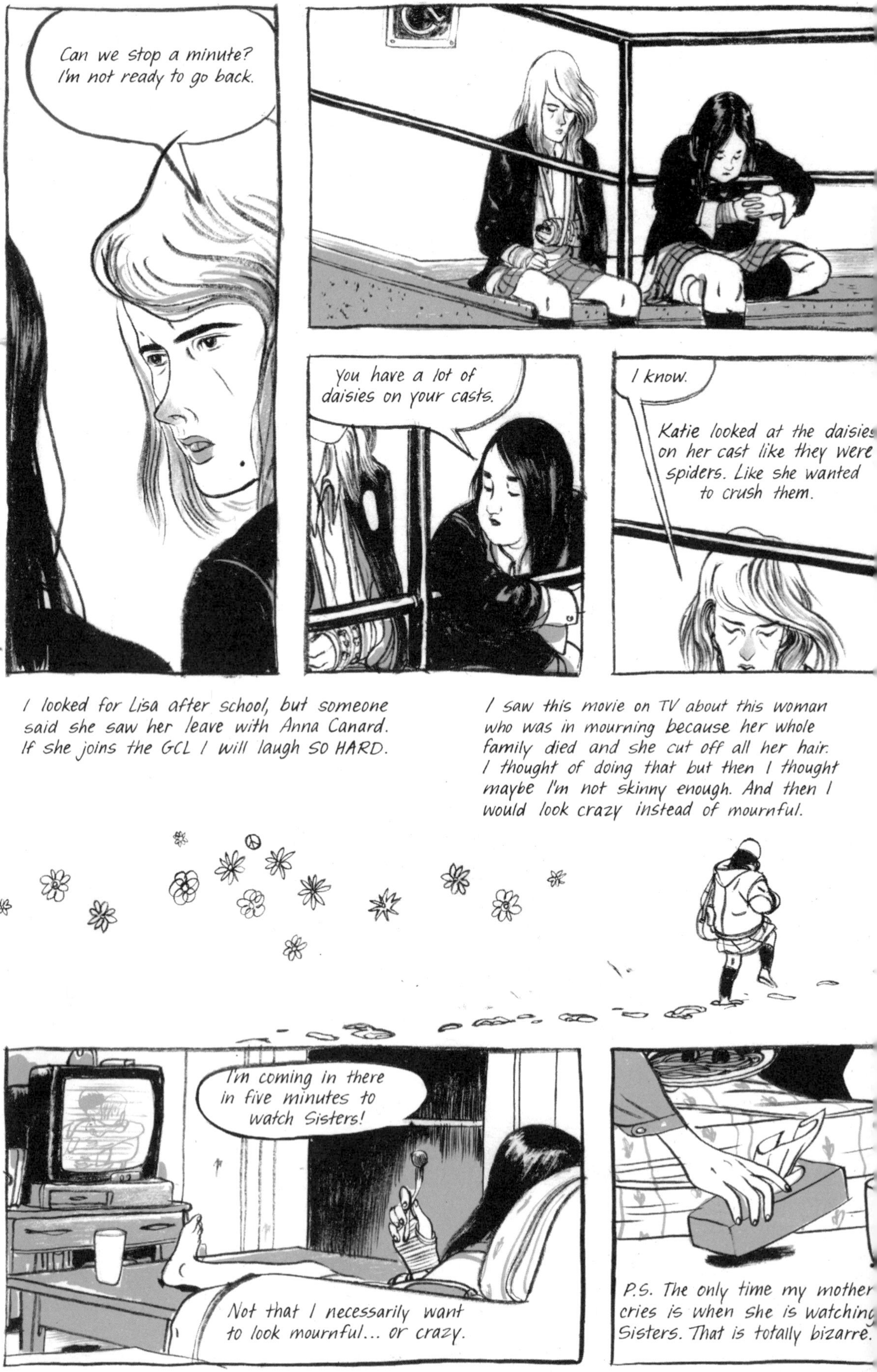
Can we stop a minute? I'm not ready to go back.
You have a lot of daisies on your casts.
I know.
Katie looked at the daisies on her cast like they were spiders. Like she wanted to crush them.
I looked for Lisa after school, but someone said she saw her leave with Anna Canard. If she joins the GCL I will laugh SO HARD.
I saw this movie on TV about this woman who was in mourning because her whole family died and she cut off all her hair. I thought of doing that but then I thought maybe I'm not skinny enough. And then I would look crazy instead of mournful.
I'm coming in there in five minutes to watch Sisters!
Not that I necessarily want to look mournful... or crazy.
P.S. The only time my mother cries is when she is watching Sisters. That is totally bizarre.

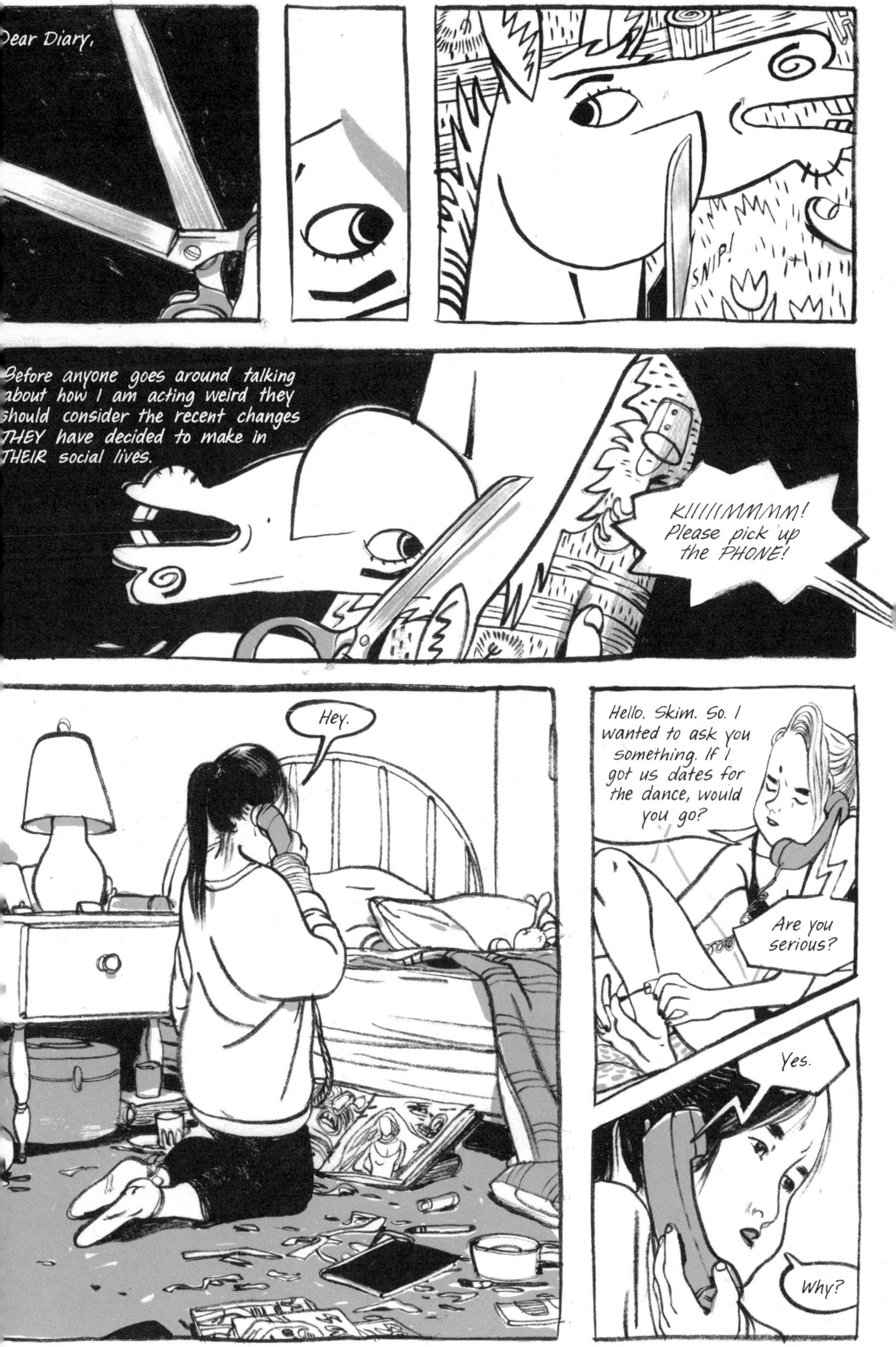
Dear Diary,
SNIP!
Before anyone goes around talking about how I am acting weird they should consider the recent changes THEY have decided to make in THEIR social lives.
KIIIIIMMMMM! Please pick up the PHONE!
Hey.
Hello. Skim. So. I wanted to ask you something. If I got us dates for the dance, would you go?
Are you serious?
Yes.
Why?

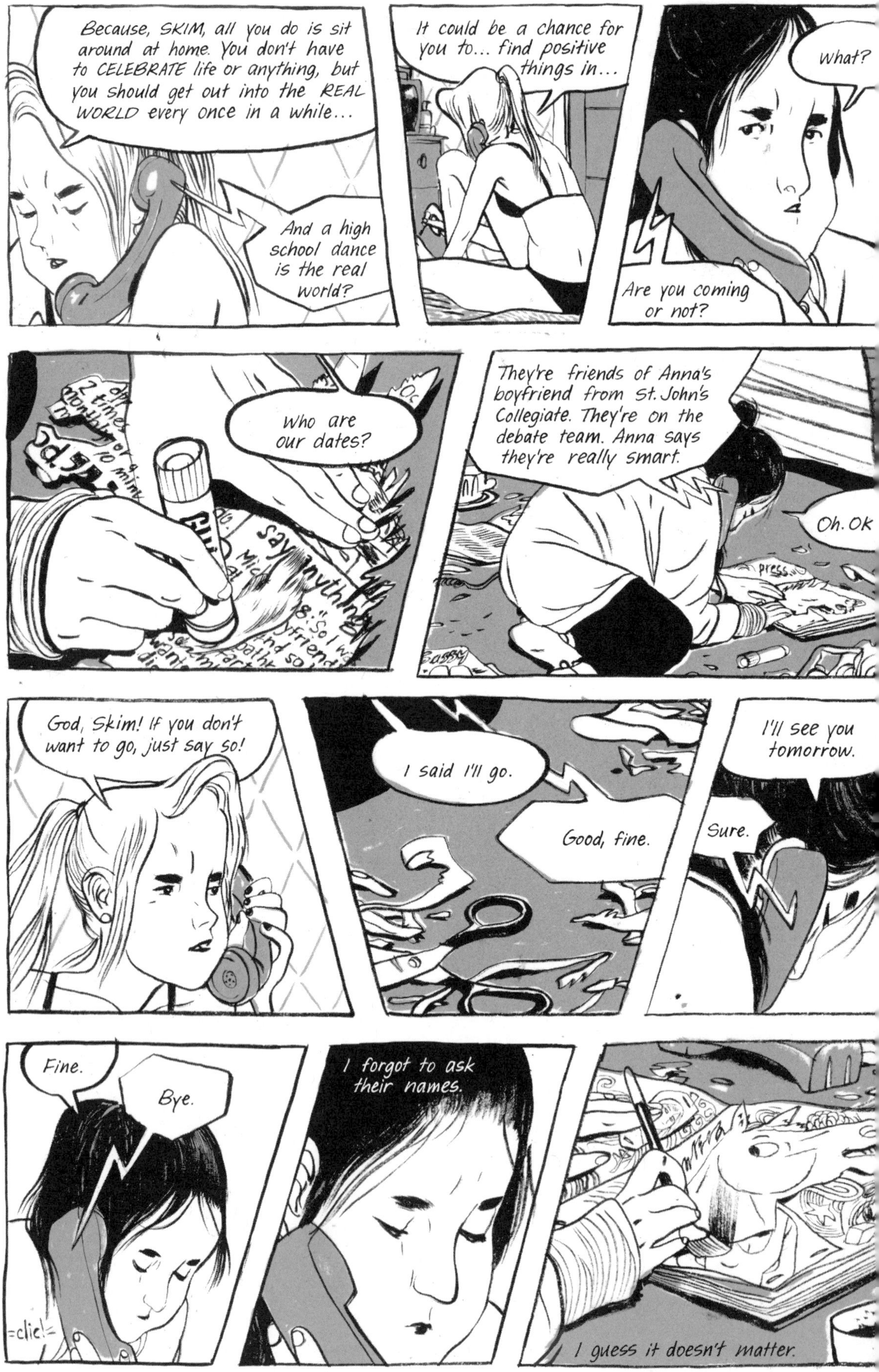
Because, SKIM, all you do is sit around at home. You don't have to CELEBRATE life or anything, but you should get out into the REAL WORLD every once in a while...
And a high school dance is the real world?
It could be a chance for you to... find positive things in...
What?
Are you coming or not?
Who are our dates?
They're friends of Anna's boyfriend from St. John's Collegiate. They're on the debate team. Anna says they're really smart.
Oh. OK
God, Skim! If you don't want to go, just say so!
I said I'll go.
Good, fine.
I'll see you tomorrow.
Sure.
Fine.
Bye.
=click!=
I forgot to ask their names.
I guess it doesn't matter.

Dear Diary,

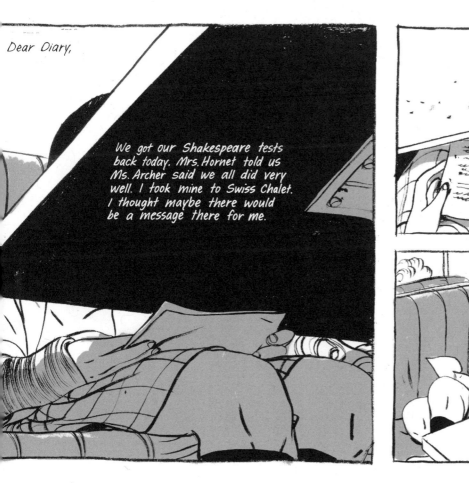

We got our Shakespeare tests back today. Mrs. Hornet told us Ms. Archer said we all did very well. I took mine to Swiss Chalet. I thought maybe there would be a message there for me.

Something.

When Ms. Archer marks, her pencil barely touches the paper. All you see are ghostly little checks and X's. At the end of the paper she wrote:

Kirie,
I'm glad to see you have developed an appreciation for Romeo and Juliet, as your work here clearly demonstrates.
Excellent work.

Ms. Archer.

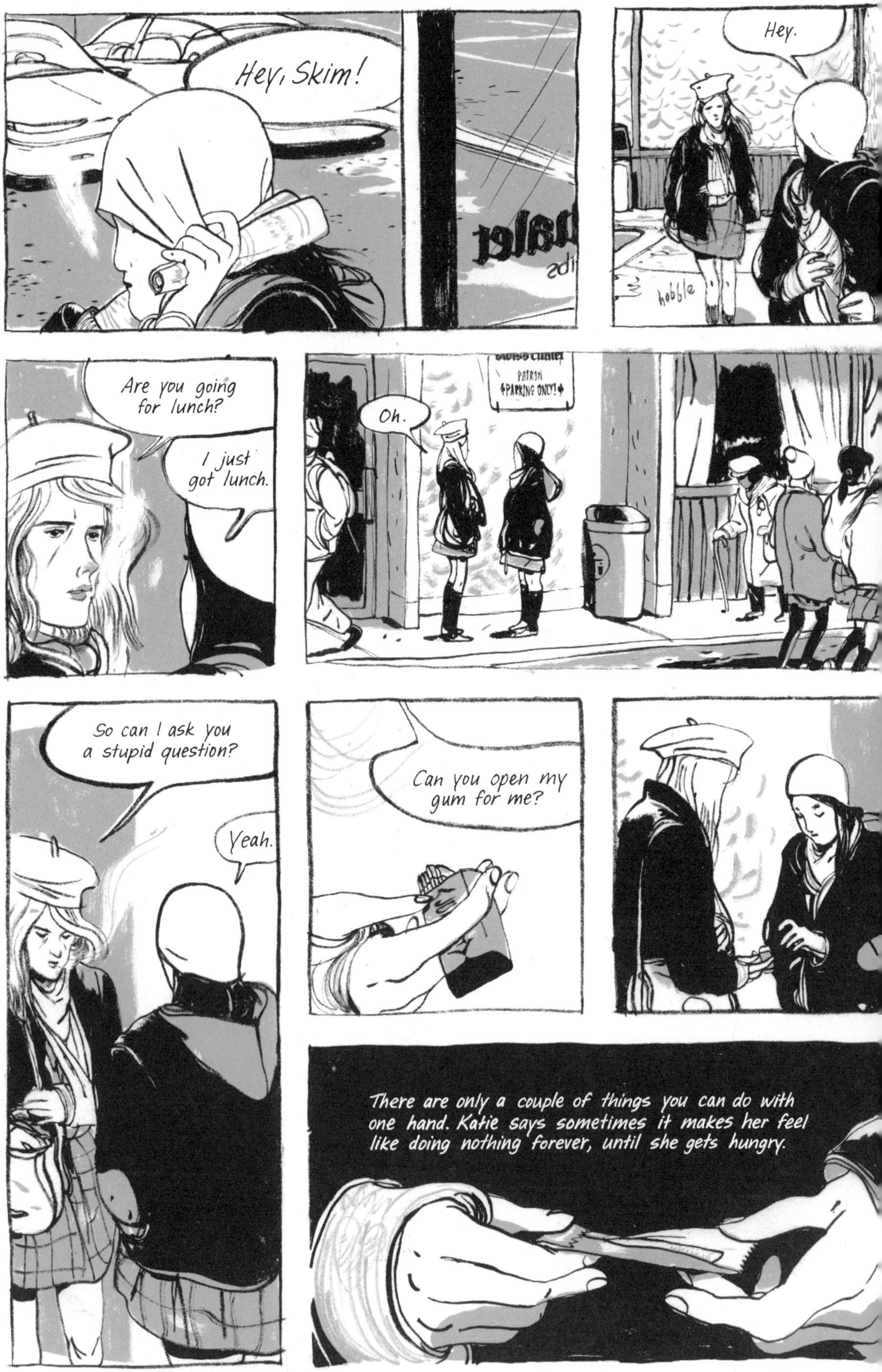
Hey, Skim!
Hey.
hobble
Are you going for lunch?
I just got lunch.
Oh.
PATRON PARKING ONLY!
So can I ask you a stupid question?
Yeah.
Can you open my gum for me?
There are only a couple of things you can do with one hand. Katie says sometimes it makes her feel like doing nothing forever, until she gets hungry.

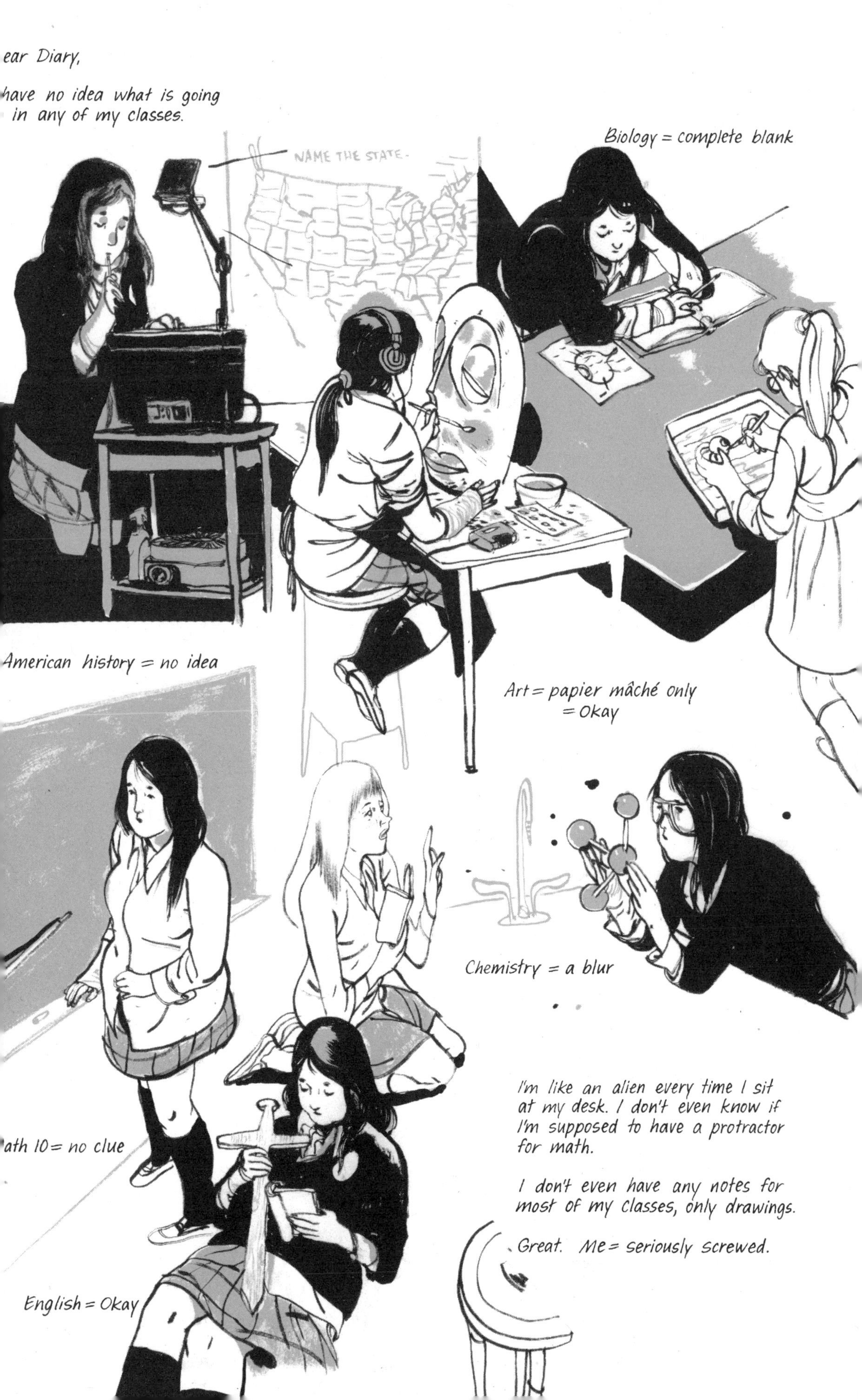
ear Diary,
have no idea what is going
in any of my classes.
NAME THE STATE
Biology = complete blank
American history = no idea
Art = papier mâché only
= Okay
Chemistry = a blur
I'm like an alien every time I sit
at my desk. I don't even know if
I'm supposed to have a protractor
for math.
I don't even have any notes for
most of my classes, only drawings.
Great. Me = seriously screwed.
ath 10 = no clue
English = Okay

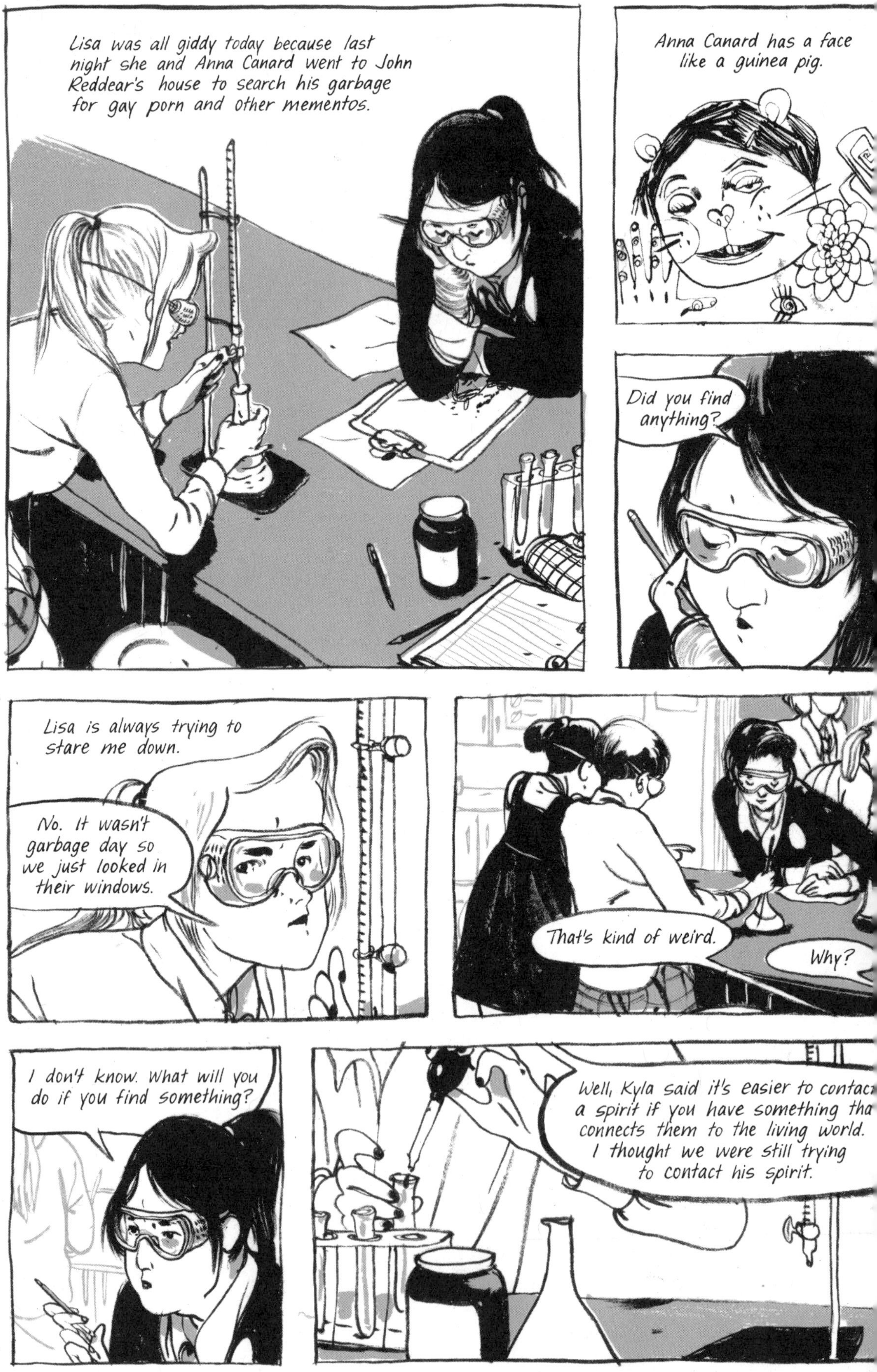
Lisa was all giddy today because last night she and Anna Canard went to John Reddear's house to search his garbage for gay porn and other mementos.
Anna Canard has a face like a guinea pig.
Did you find anything?
Lisa is always trying to stare me down.
No. It wasn't garbage day so we just looked in their windows.
That's kind of weird.
Why?
I don't know. What will you do if you find something?
Well, Kyla said it's easier to contac a spirit if you have something tha connects them to the living world. I thought we were still trying to contact his spirit.

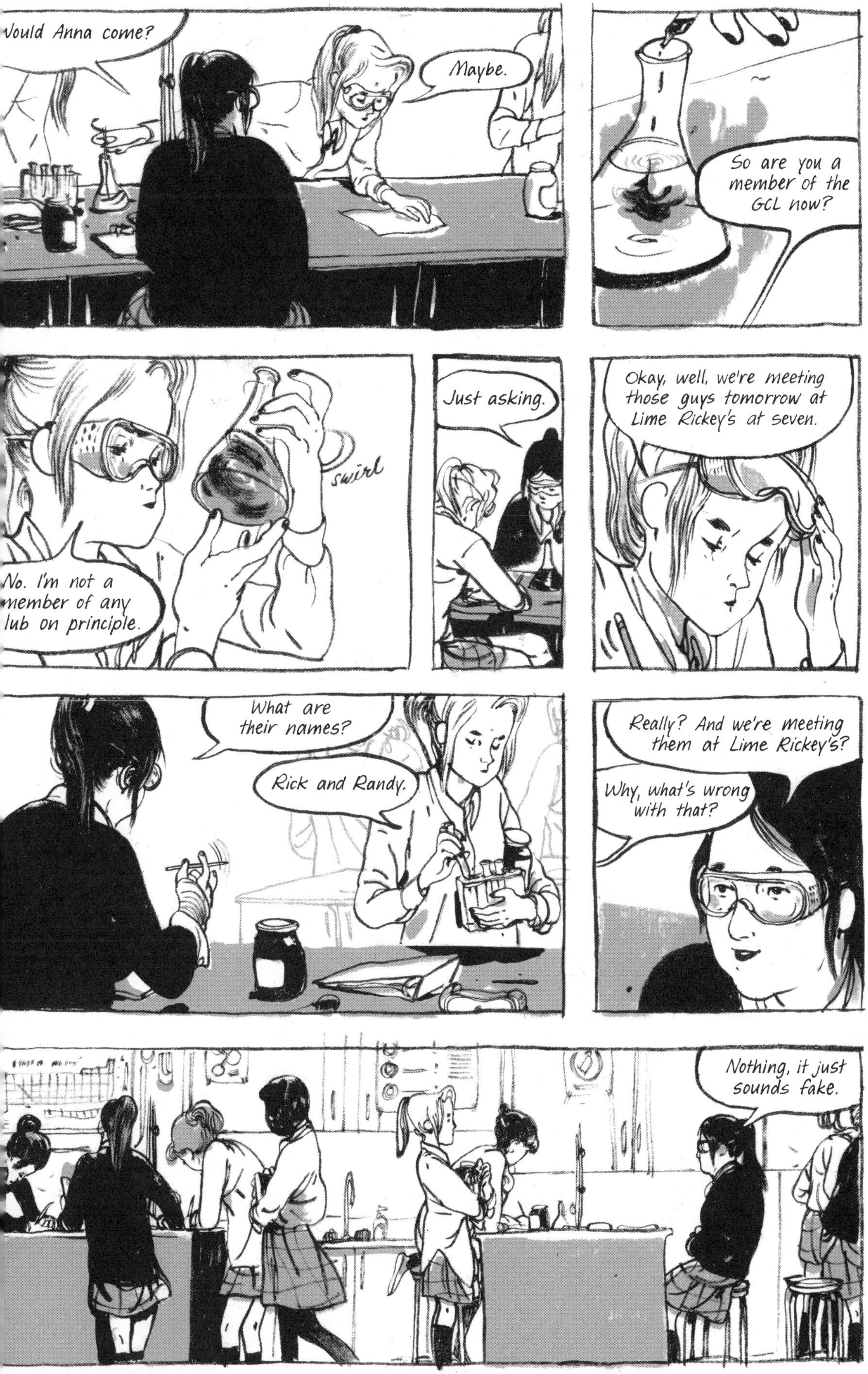
Would Anna come?
Maybe.
So are you a member of the GCL now?
No. I'm not a member of any club on principle.
swirl
Just asking.
Okay, well, we're meeting those guys tomorrow at Lime Rickey's at seven.
What are their names?
Rick and Randy.
Really? And we're meeting them at Lime Rickey's?
Why, what's wrong with that?
Nothing, it just sounds fake.

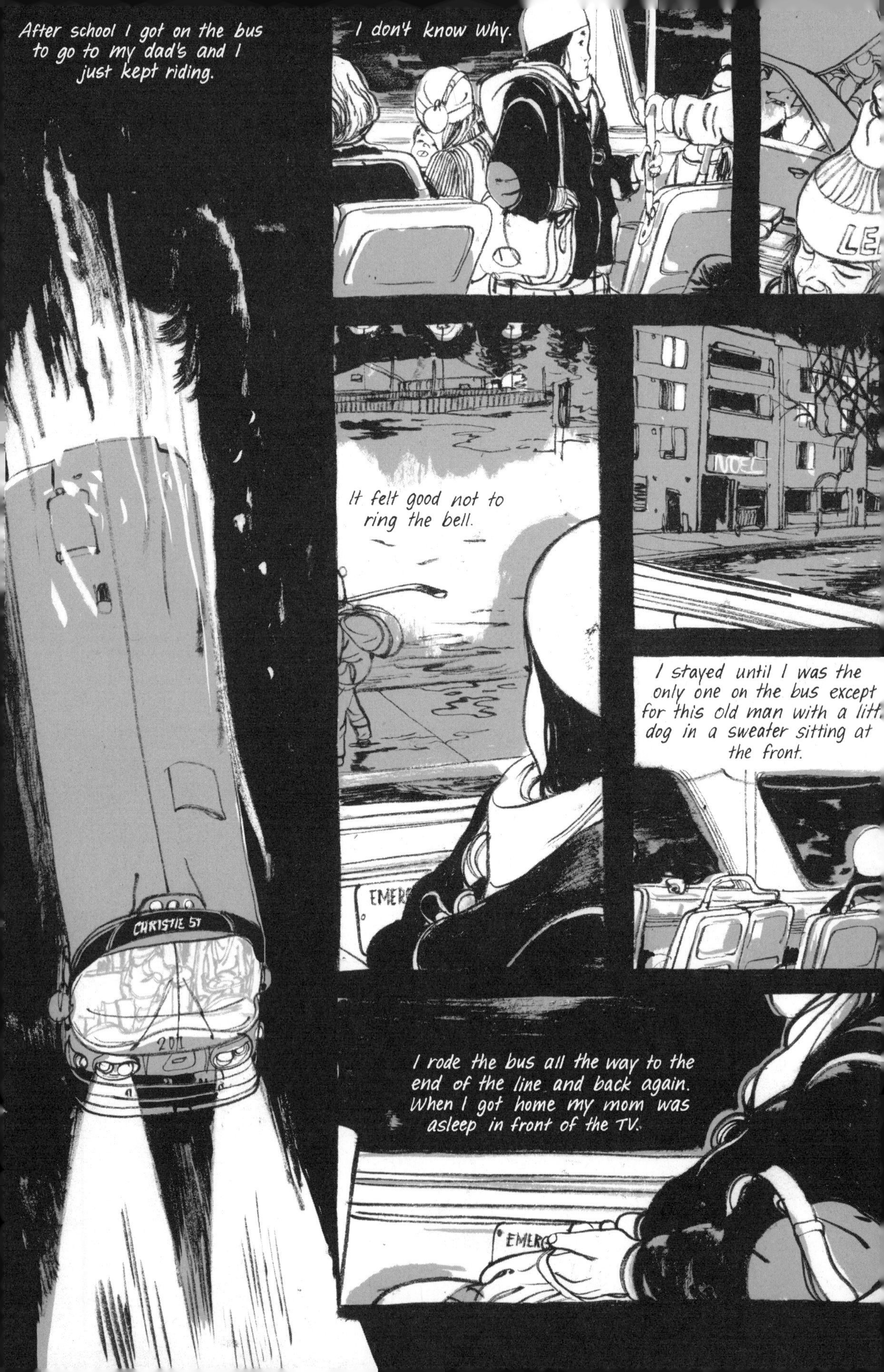
After school I got on the bus to go to my dad's and I just kept riding.
I don't know why.
LE
NOEL
It felt good not to ring the bell.
I stayed until I was the only one on the bus except for this old man with a litt dog in a sweater sitting at the front.
CHRISTIE 51
201
EMER
I rode the bus all the way to the end of the line and back again. When I got home my mom was asleep in front of the TV.
EMER

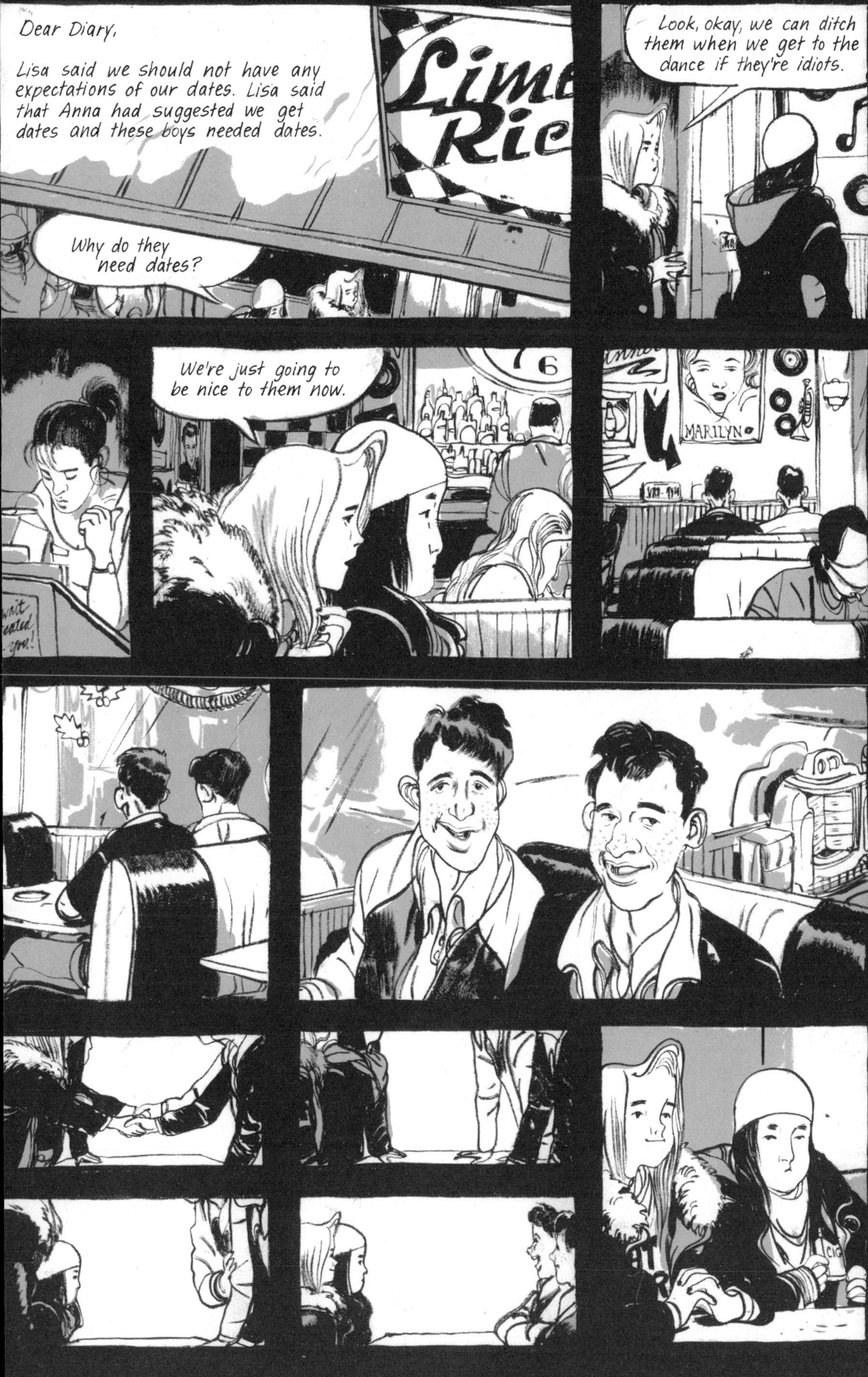
Dear Diary,
Lisa said we should not have any expectations of our dates. Lisa said that Anna had suggested we get dates and these boys needed dates.
Why do they need dates?
Look, okay, we can ditch them when we get to the dance if they're idiots.
We're just going to be nice to them now.
MARILYN

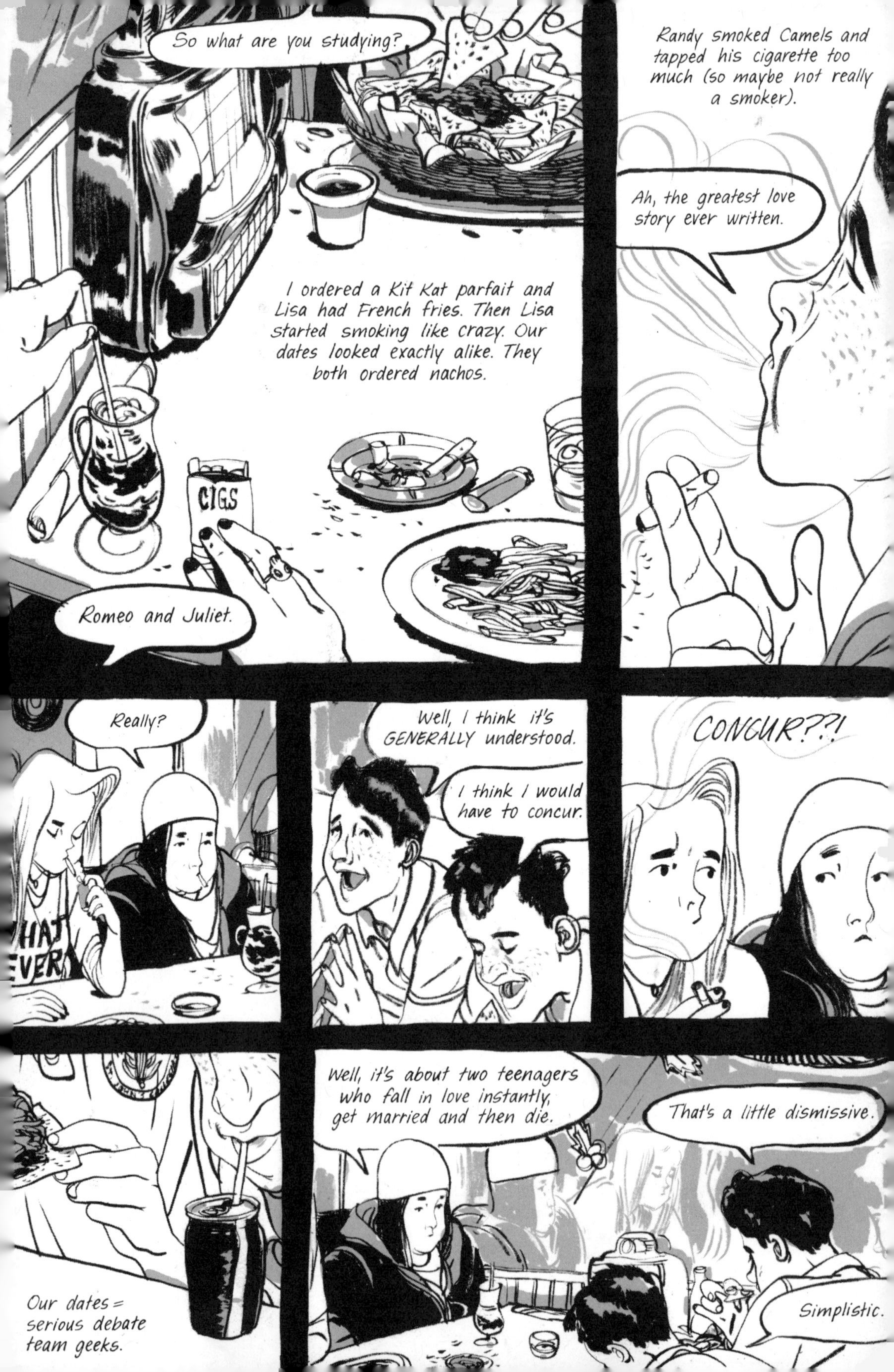
So what are you studying?
I ordered a Kit Kat parfait and Lisa had French fries. Then Lisa started smoking like crazy. Our dates looked exactly alike. They both ordered nachos.
CIGS
Romeo and Juliet.
Randy smoked Camels and tapped his cigarette too much (so maybe not really a smoker).
Ah, the greatest love story ever written.
Really?
Well, I think it's GENERALLY understood.
I think I would have to concur.
CONCUR??!
Well, it's about two teenagers who fall in love instantly, get married and then die.
That's a little dismissive.
Simplistic.
Our dates = serious debate team geeks.

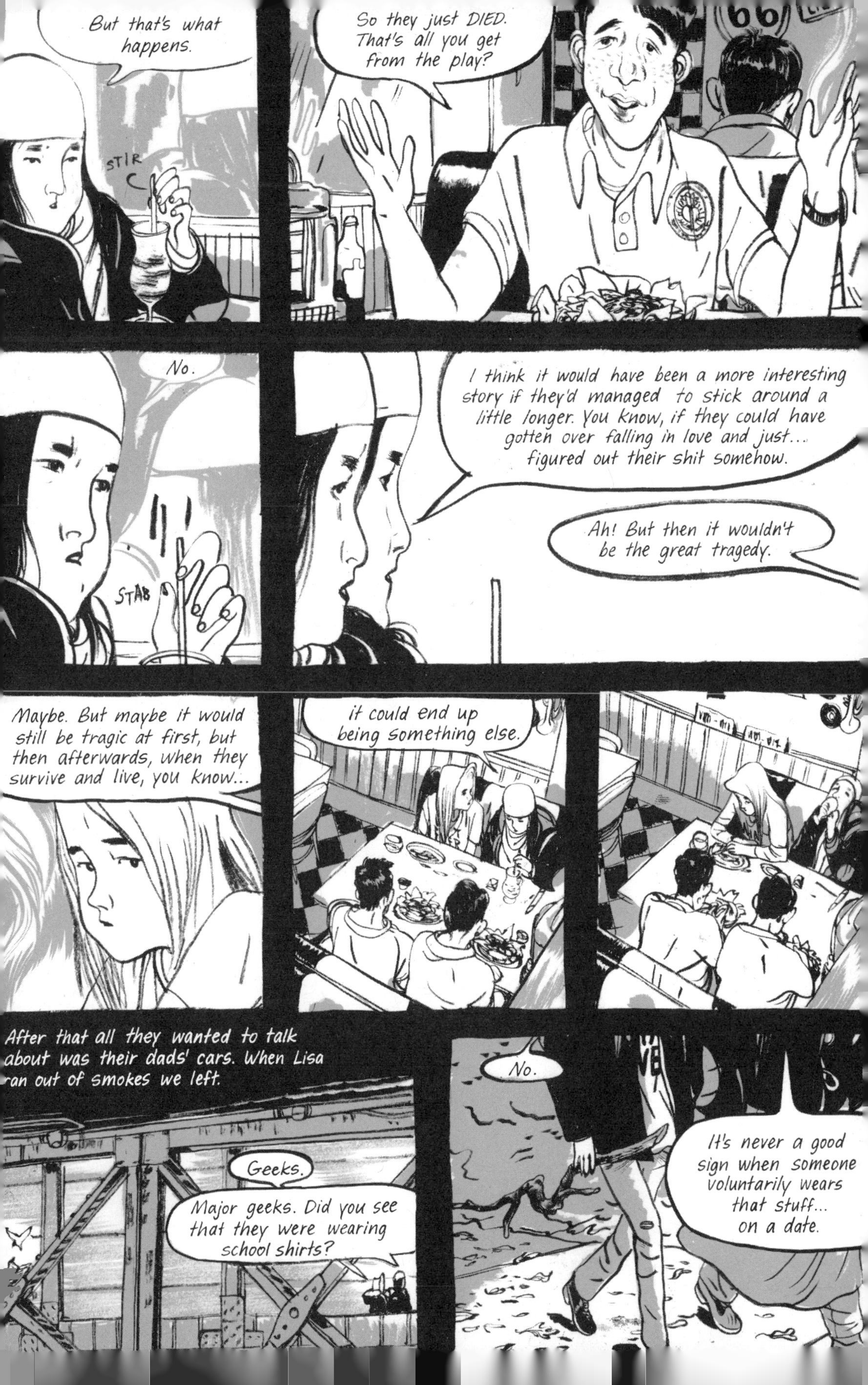
But that's what happens.
STIR
So they just DIED. That's all you get from the play?
No.
STAB
I think it would have been a more interesting story if they'd managed to stick around a little longer. You know, if they could have gotten over falling in love and just... figured out their shit somehow.
Ah! But then it wouldn't be the great tragedy.
Maybe. But maybe it would still be tragic at first, but then afterwards, when they survive and live, you know...
it could end up being something else.
After that all they wanted to talk about was their dads' cars. When Lisa ran out of smokes we left.
Geeks.
Major geeks. Did you see that they were wearing school shirts?
No.
It's never a good sign when someone voluntarily wears that stuff... on a date.

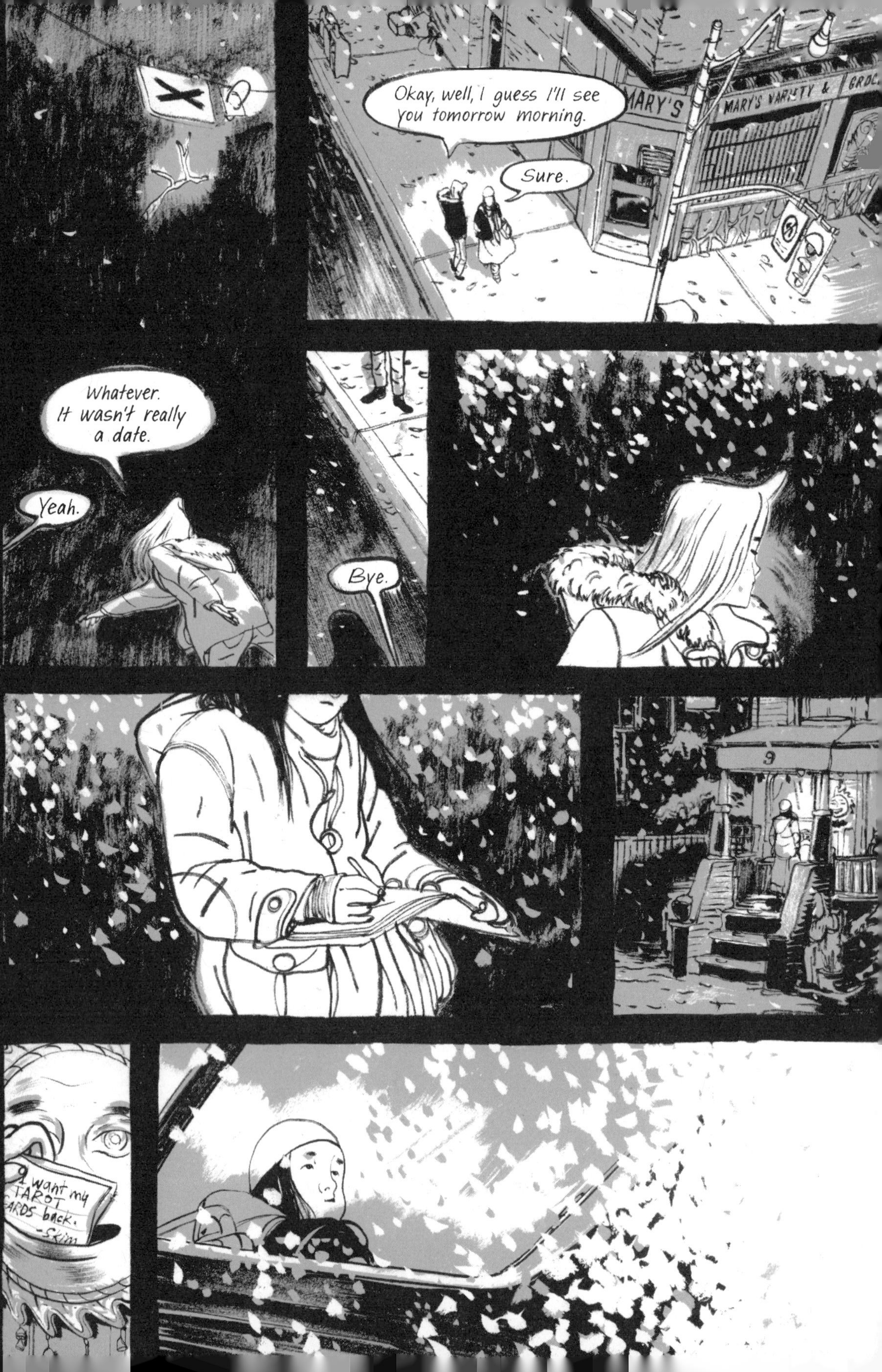
Okay, well, I guess I'll see you tomorrow morning.
Sure.
MARY'S
MARY'S VARIETY & GROC
Whatever. It wasn't really a date.
Yeah.
Bye.
I want my TAROT CARDS back. -Skim

Today I went to the hospital and the doctor sawed my cast off.

My arm looks like a dead rat.

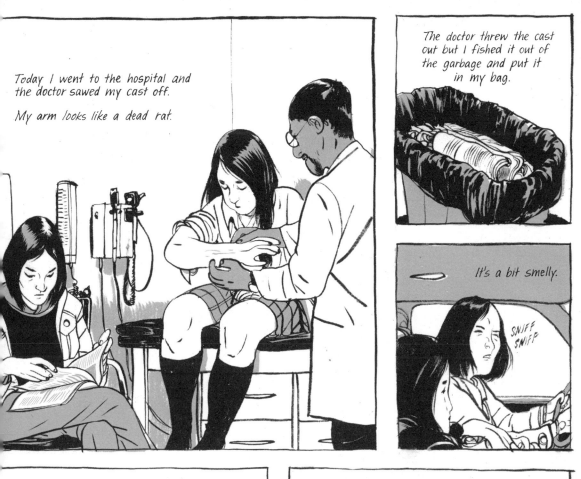

The doctor threw the cast out but I fished it out of the garbage and put it in my bag.

It's a bit smelly.

SNIFF SNIFF

At school everyone is freaking out about the dance.

There are all these useless posters up even though everyone already knows about it.

Even Katie is going, although I'm pretty sure she doesn't want to.

Mom bought me a red dress. It's velvet and heavy on the cleavage so she got me a shawl too.

Ricky called and said he couldn't get his dad's car so we would have to meet them at the school.

Car-less geeks.

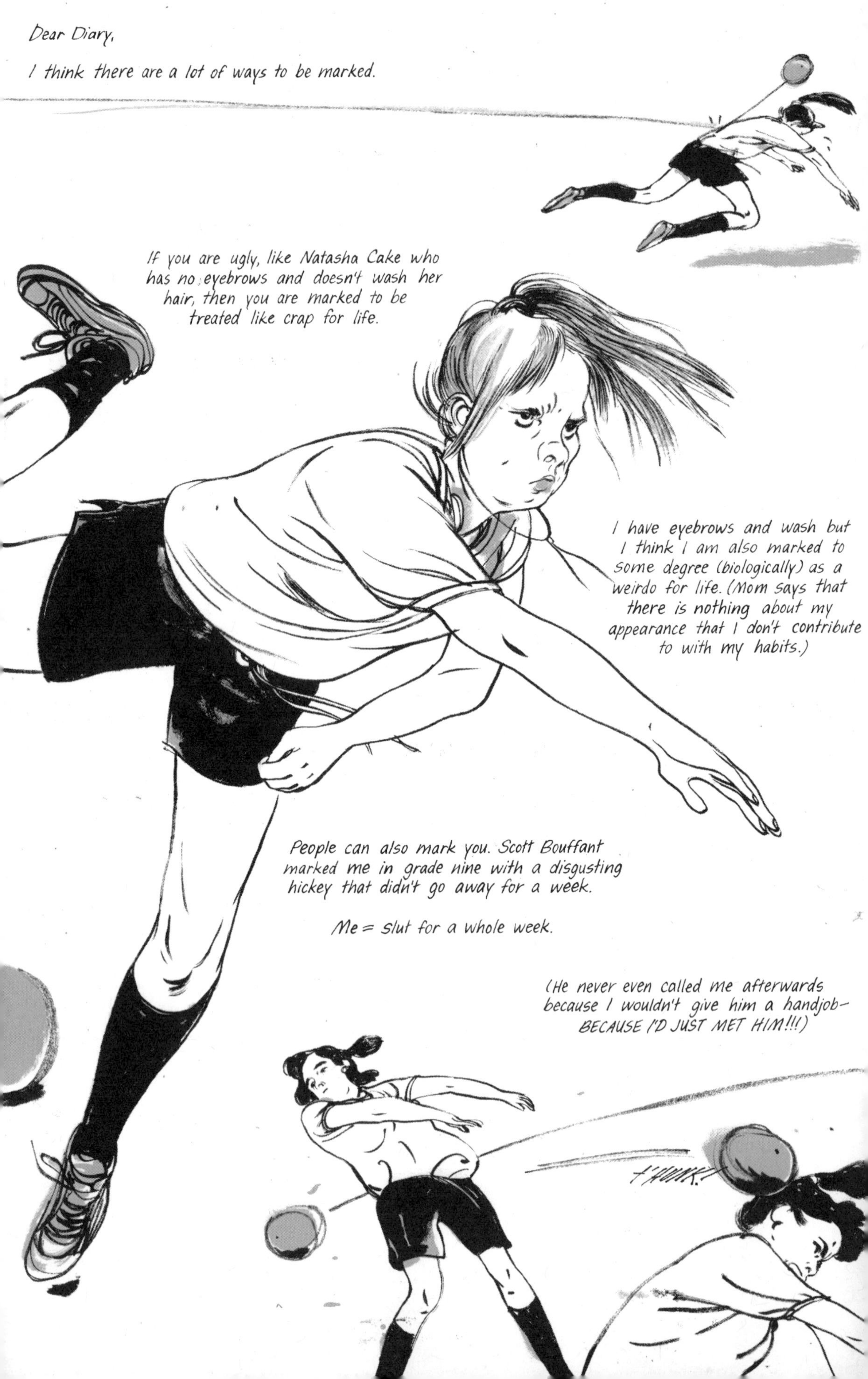
Dear Diary,
I think there are a lot of ways to be marked.
If you are ugly, like Natasha Cake who has no eyebrows and doesn't wash her hair, then you are marked to be treated like crap for life.
I have eyebrows and wash but I think I am also marked to some degree (biologically) as a weirdo for life. (Mom says that there is nothing about my appearance that I don't contribute to with my habits.)
People can also mark you. Scott Bouffant marked me in grade nine with a disgusting hickey that didn't go away for a week.
Me = slut for a whole week.
(He never even called me afterwards because I wouldn't give him a handjob—BECAUSE I'D JUST MET HIM!!!)
THUNK!

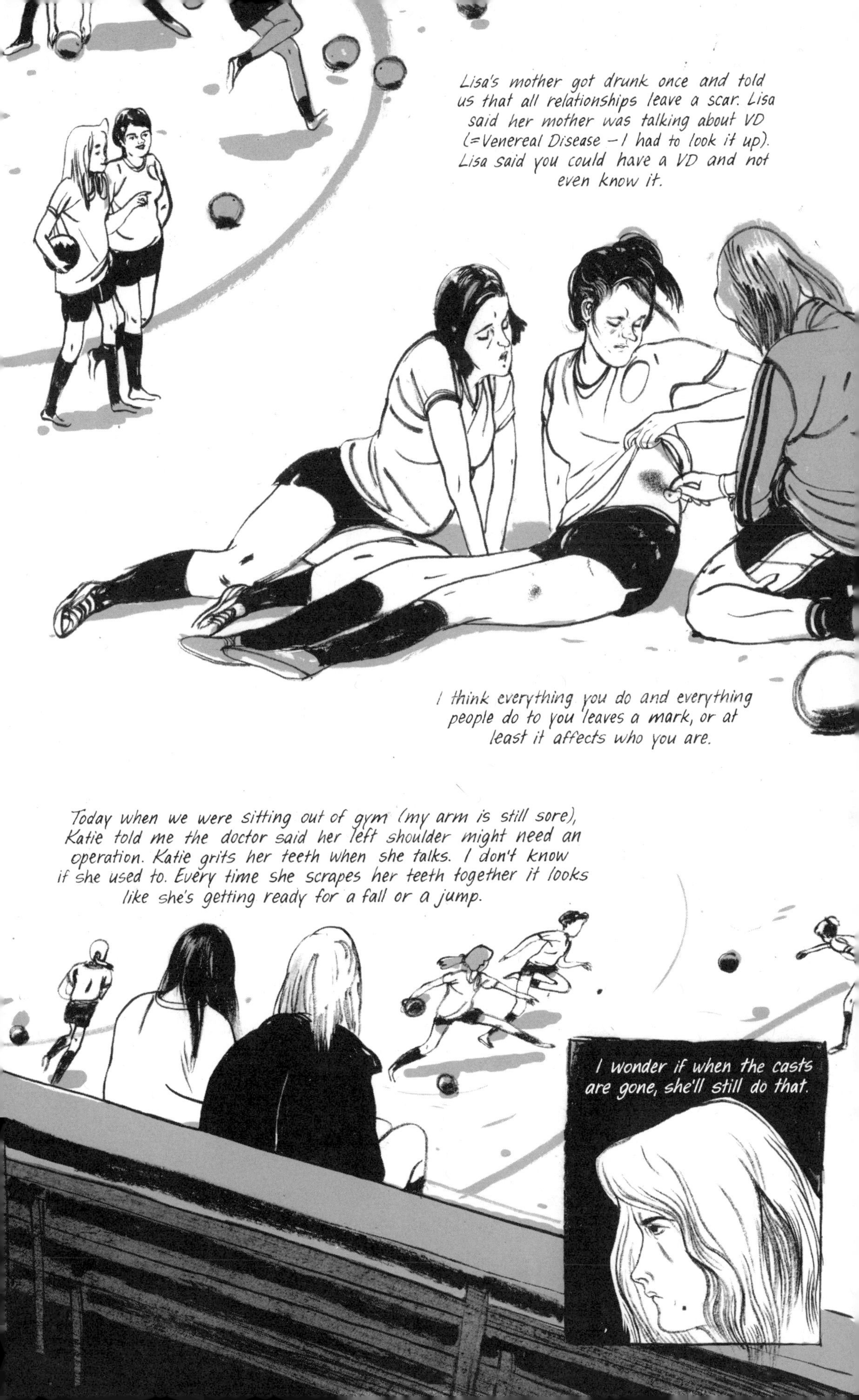
Lisa's mother got drunk once and told us that all relationships leave a scar. Lisa said her mother was talking about VD (=Venereal Disease — I had to look it up). Lisa said you could have a VD and not even know it.
I think everything you do and everything people do to you leaves a mark, or at least it affects who you are.
Today when we were sitting out of gym (my arm is still sore), Katie told me the doctor said her left shoulder might need an operation. Katie grits her teeth when she talks. I don't know if she used to. Every time she scrapes her teeth together it looks like she's getting ready for a fall or a jump.
I wonder if when the casts are gone, she'll still do that.

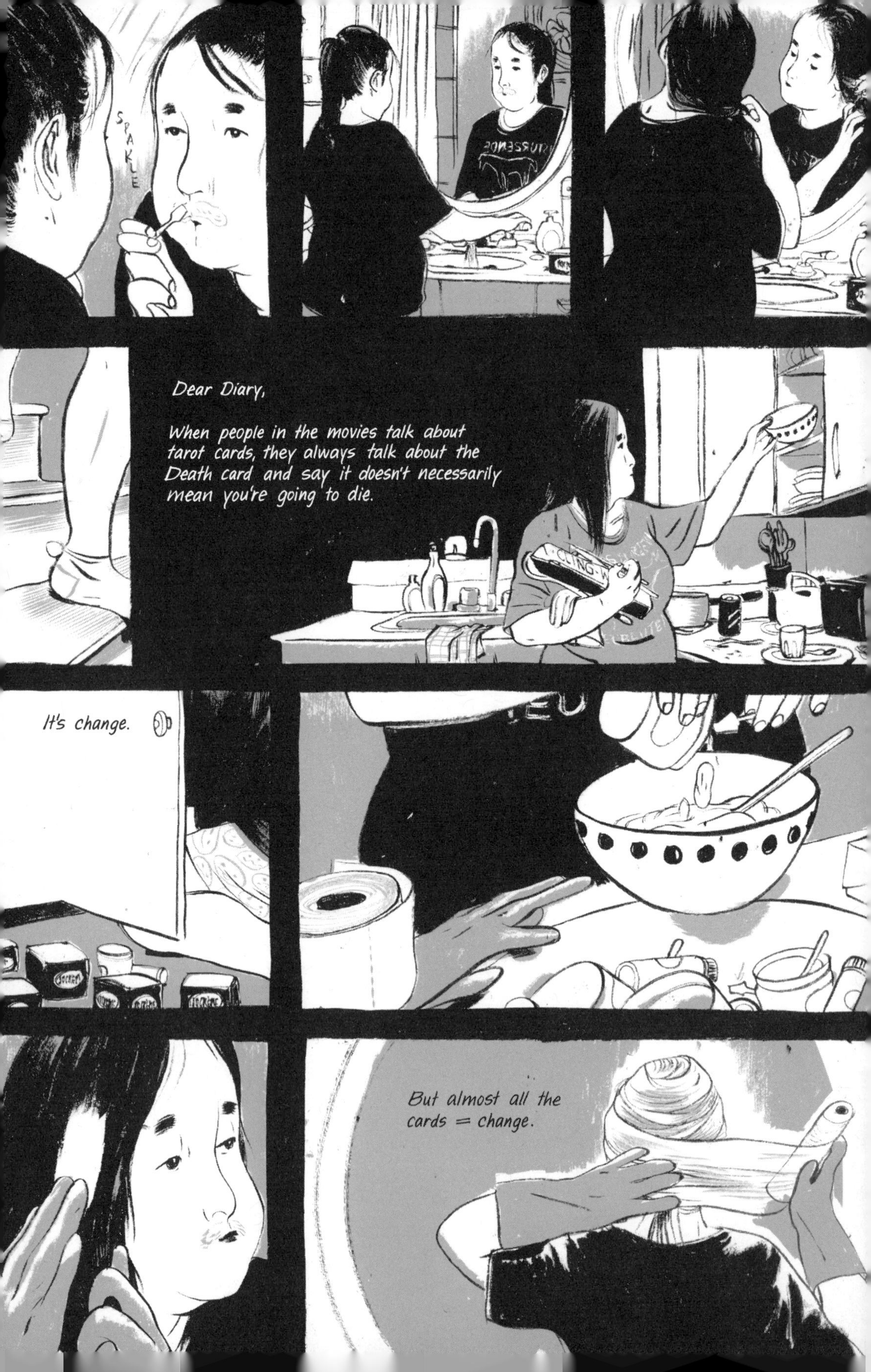
SPARKLE
Dear Diary,
When people in the movies talk about tarot cards, they always talk about the Death card and say it doesn't necessarily mean you're going to die.
It's change.
But almost all the cards = change.

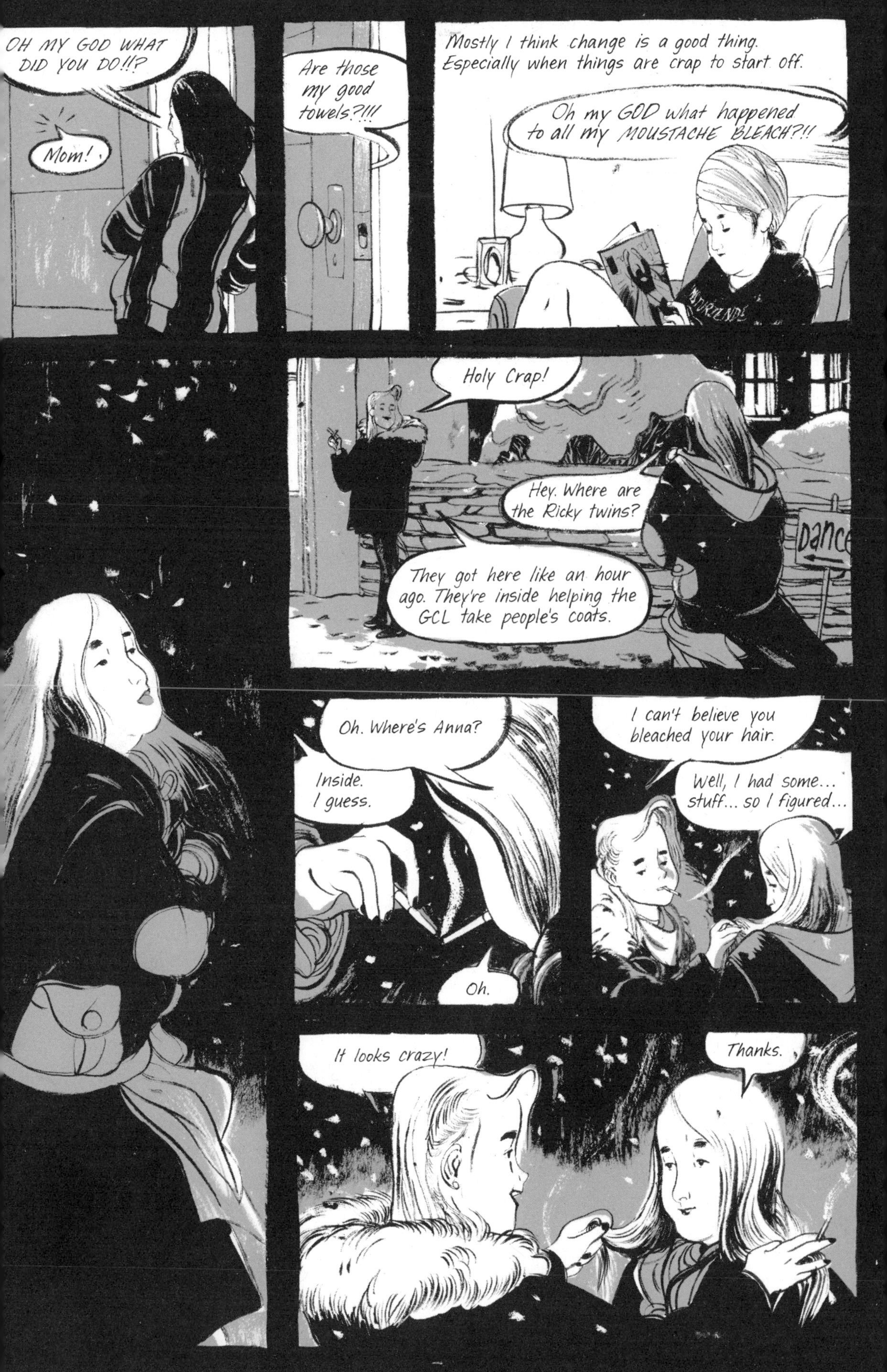
OH MY GOD WHAT DID YOU DO!!?
Mom!
Are those my good towels?!!!
Mostly I think change is a good thing. Especially when things are crap to start off.
Oh my GOD what happened to all my MOUSTACHE BLEACH?!!
Holy Crap!
Hey. Where are the Ricky twins?
They got here like an hour ago. They're inside helping the GCL take people's coats.
Dance
Oh. Where's Anna?
Inside. I guess.
Oh.
I can't believe you bleached your hair.
Well, I had some... stuff... so I figured...
It looks crazy!
Thanks.

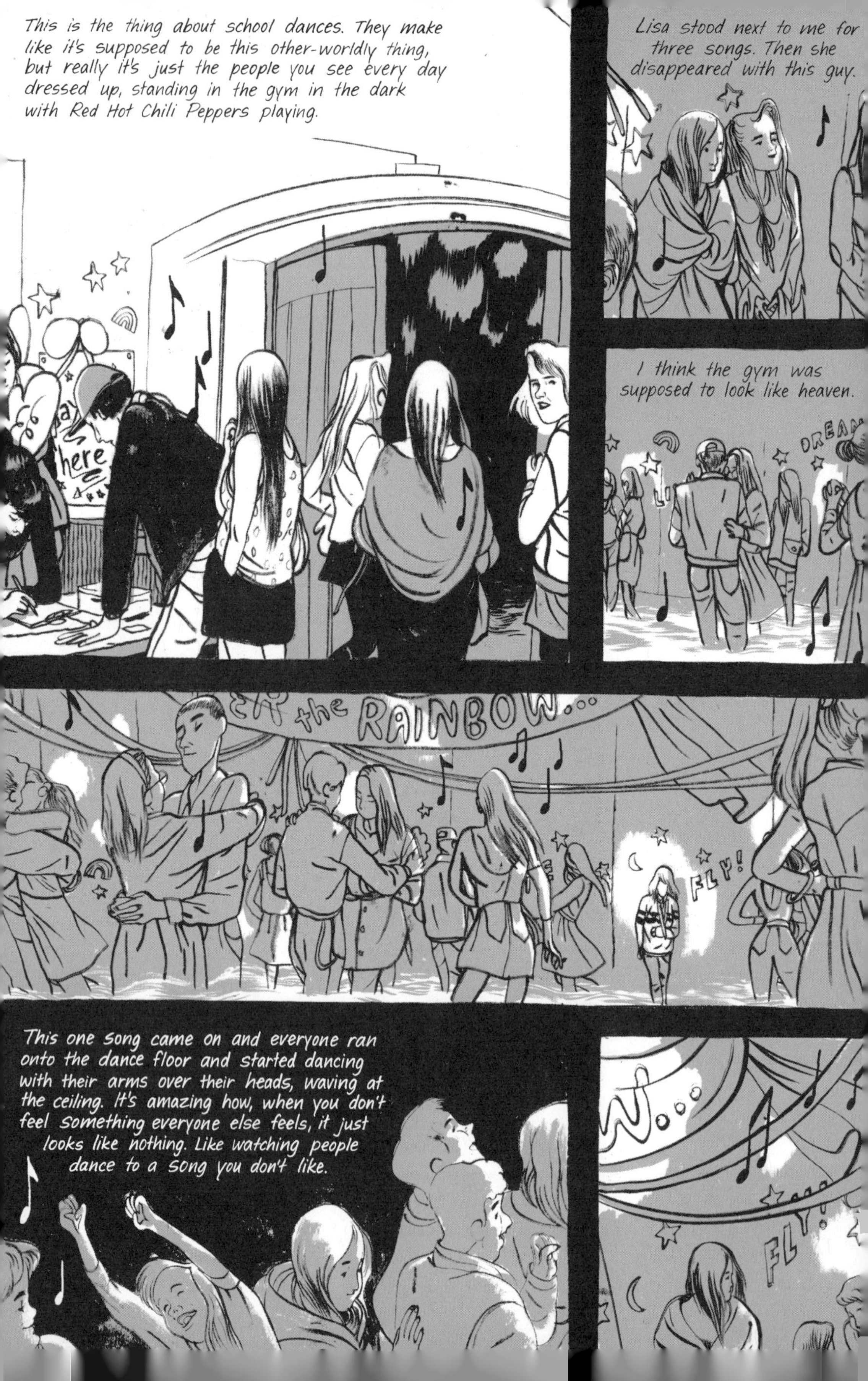
This is the thing about school dances. They make like it's supposed to be this other-worldly thing, but really it's just the people you see every day dressed up, standing in the gym in the dark with Red Hot Chili Peppers playing.
here
Lisa stood next to me for three songs. Then she disappeared with this guy.
I think the gym was supposed to look like heaven.
DREAM
the RAINBOW...
FLY!
This one song came on and everyone ran onto the dance floor and started dancing with their arms over their heads, waving at the ceiling. It's amazing how, when you don't feel something everyone else feels, it just looks like nothing. Like watching people dance to a song you don't like.

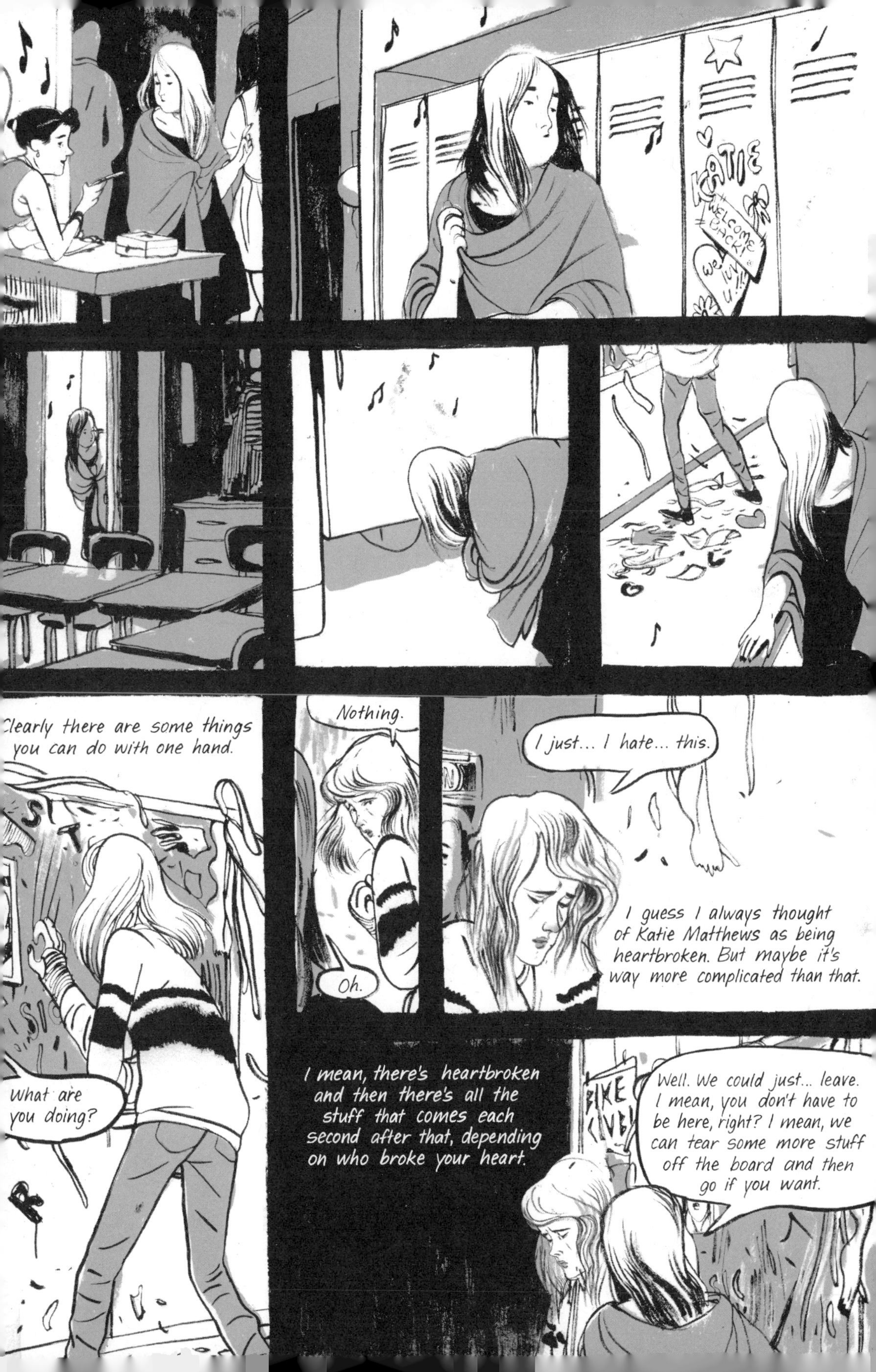
KATIE
WELCOME BACK!
we luv u!!
Clearly there are some things you can do with one hand.
What are you doing?
Nothing.
Oh.
I just... I hate... this.
I guess I always thought of Katie Matthews as being heartbroken. But maybe it's way more complicated than that.
I mean, there's heartbroken and then there's all the stuff that comes each second after that, depending on who broke your heart.
BIKE CLUB
Well. We could just... leave. I mean, you don't have to be here, right? I mean, we can tear some more stuff off the board and then go if you want.

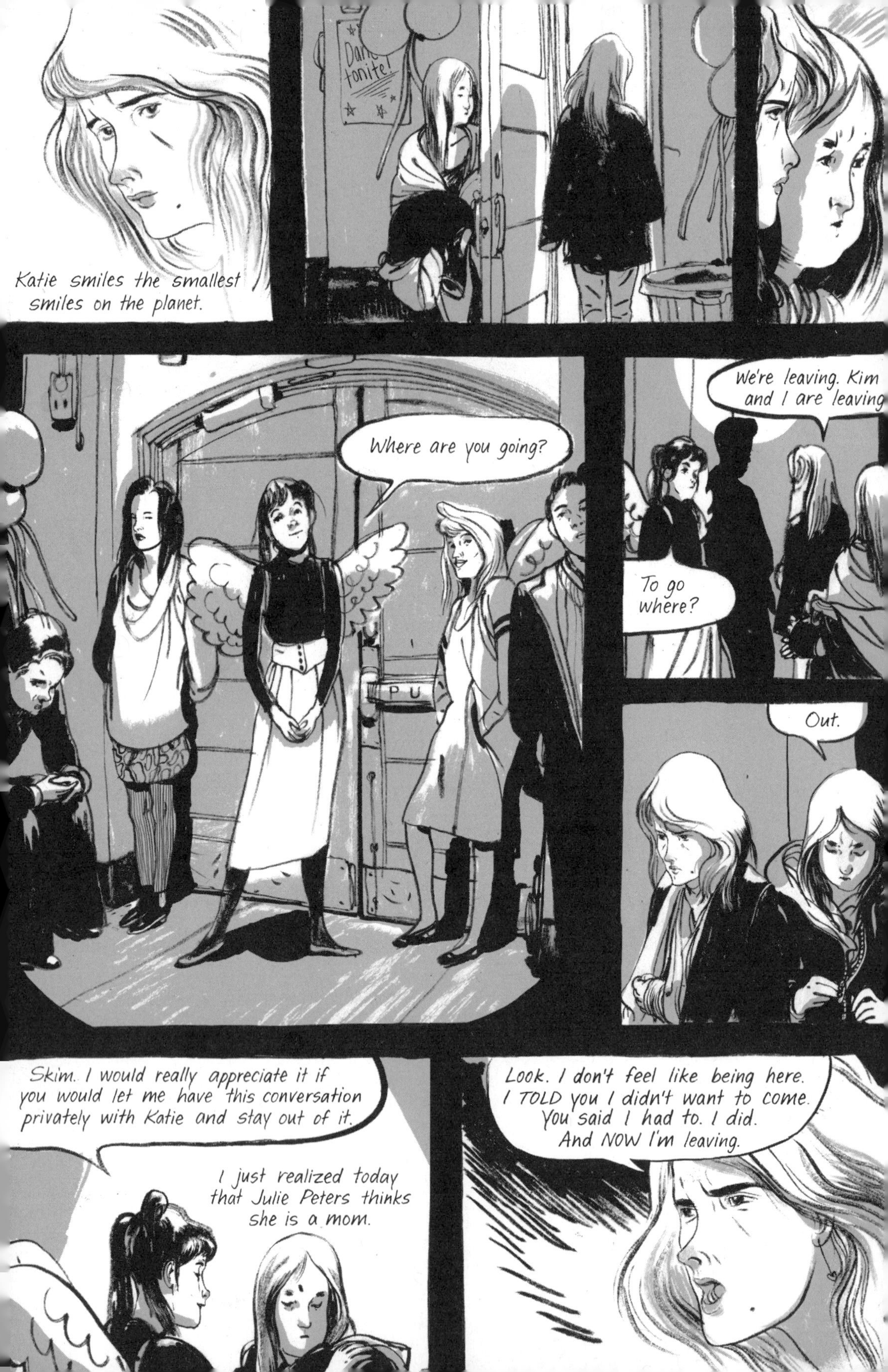
Katie smiles the smallest smiles on the planet.
tonite!
Where are you going?
We're leaving. Kim and I are leaving
To go where?
Out.
Skim. I would really appreciate it if you would let me have this conversation privately with Katie and stay out of it.
I just realized today that Julie Peters thinks she is a mom.
Look. I don't feel like being here. I TOLD you I didn't want to come. You said I had to. I did. And NOW I'm leaving.

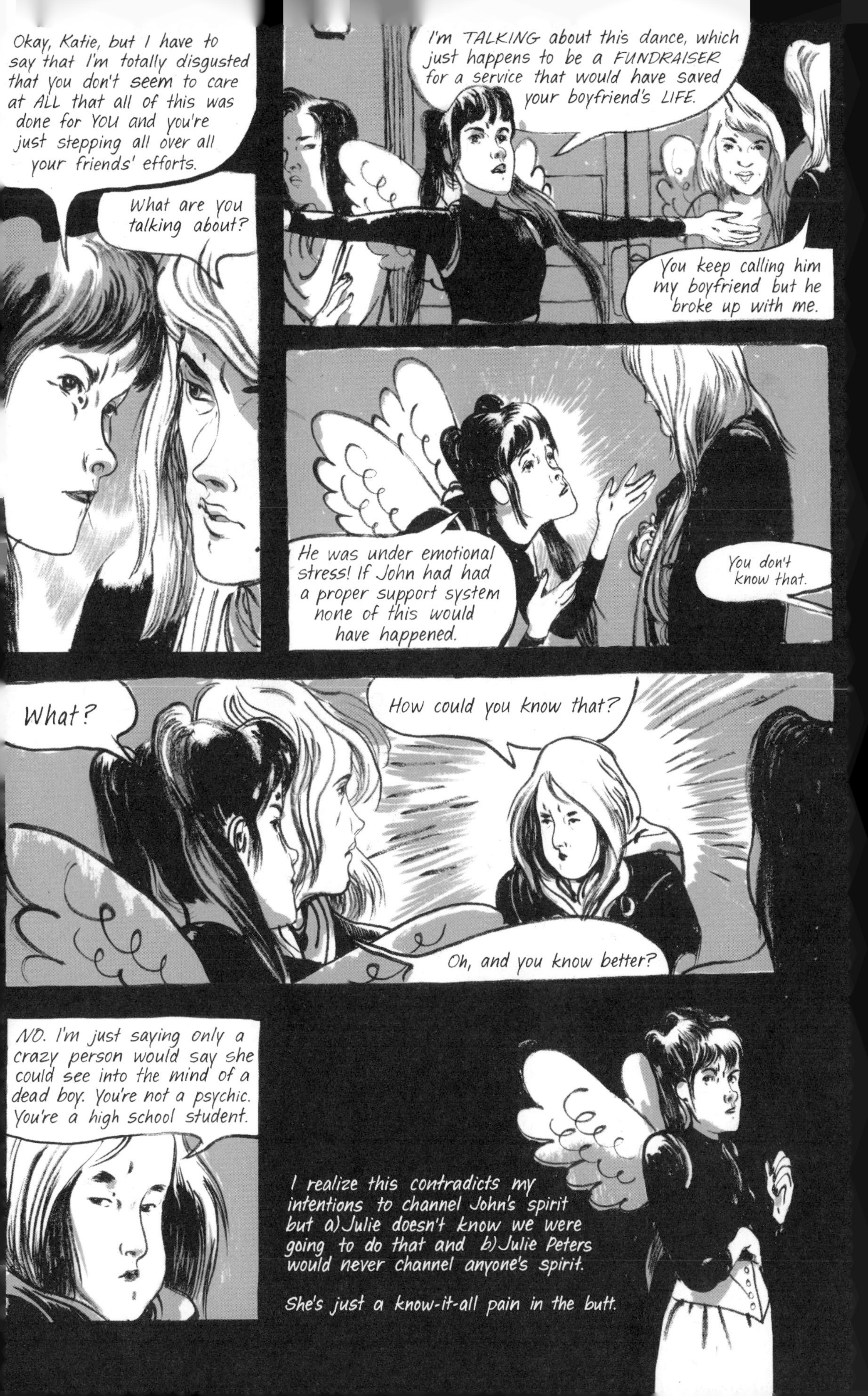
Okay, Katie, but I have to say that I'm totally disgusted that you don't seem to care at ALL that all of this was done for YOU and you're just stepping all over all your friends' efforts.
What are you talking about?
I'm TALKING about this dance, which just happens to be a FUNDRAISER for a service that would have saved your boyfriend's LIFE.
You keep calling him my boyfriend but he broke up with me.
He was under emotional stress! If John had had a proper support system none of this would have happened.
You don't know that.
What?
How could you know that?
Oh, and you know better?
NO. I'm just saying only a crazy person would say she could see into the mind of a dead boy. You're not a psychic. You're a high school student.
I realize this contradicts my intentions to channel John's spirit but a) Julie doesn't know we were going to do that and b) Julie Peters would never channel anyone's spirit.
She's just a know-it-all pain in the butt.

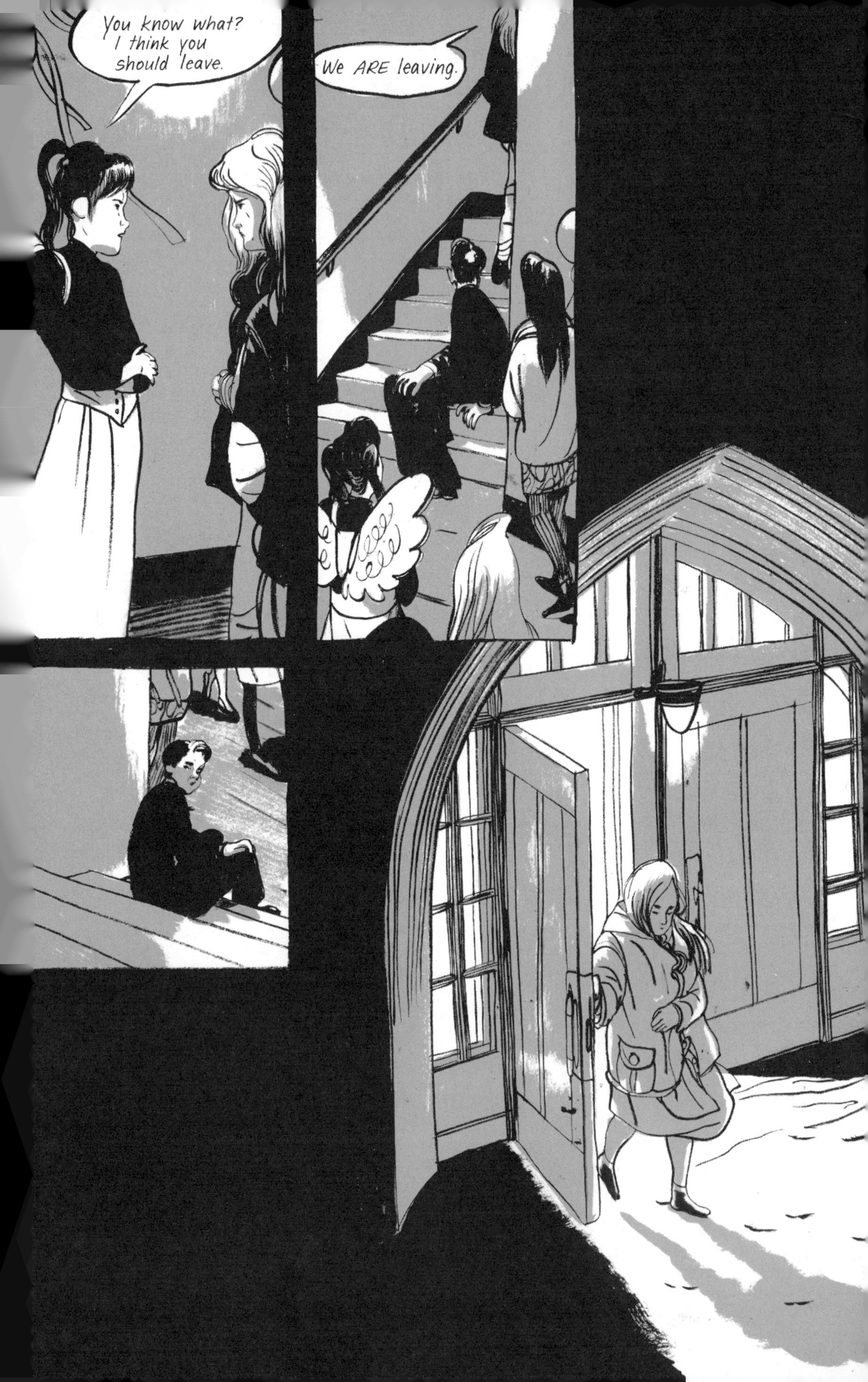
You know what? I think you should leave.
We ARE leaving.

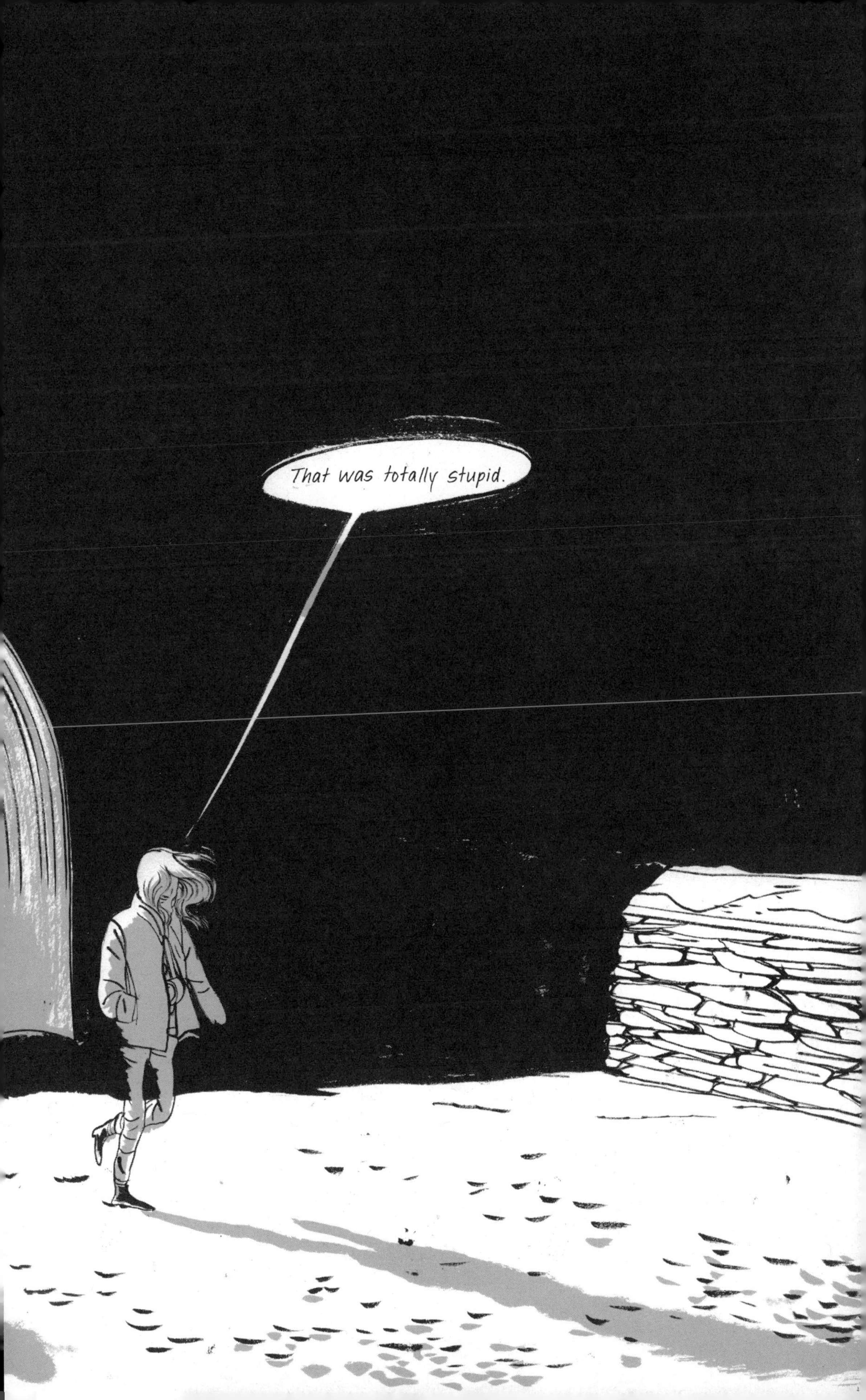
That was totally stupid.

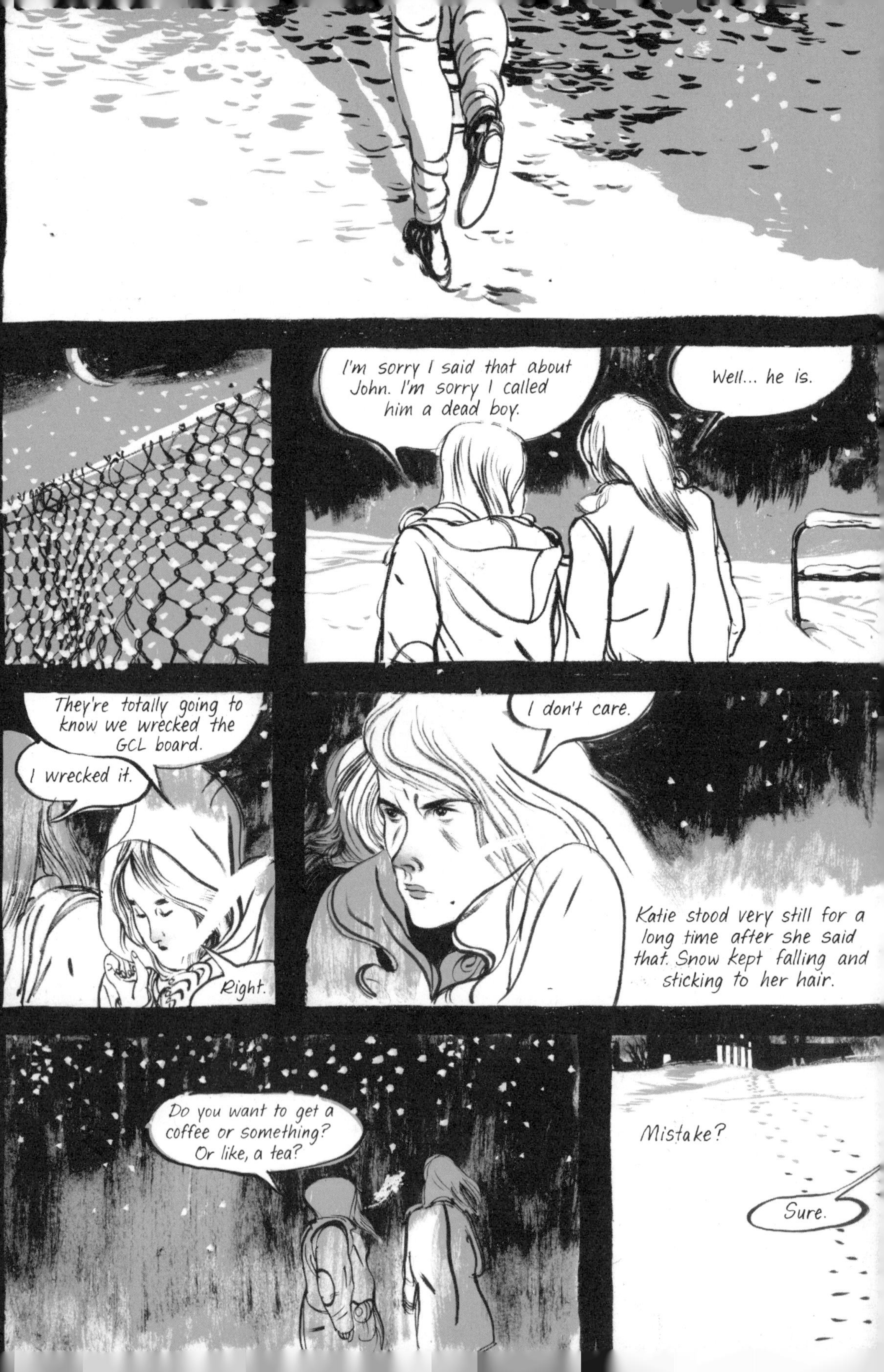

I'm sorry I said that about John. I'm sorry I called him a dead boy.
Well... he is.
They're totally going to know we wrecked the GCL board.
I wrecked it.
Right.
I don't care.
Katie stood very still for a long time after she said that. Snow kept falling and sticking to her hair.
Do you want to get a coffee or something? Or like, a tea?
Mistake?
Sure.

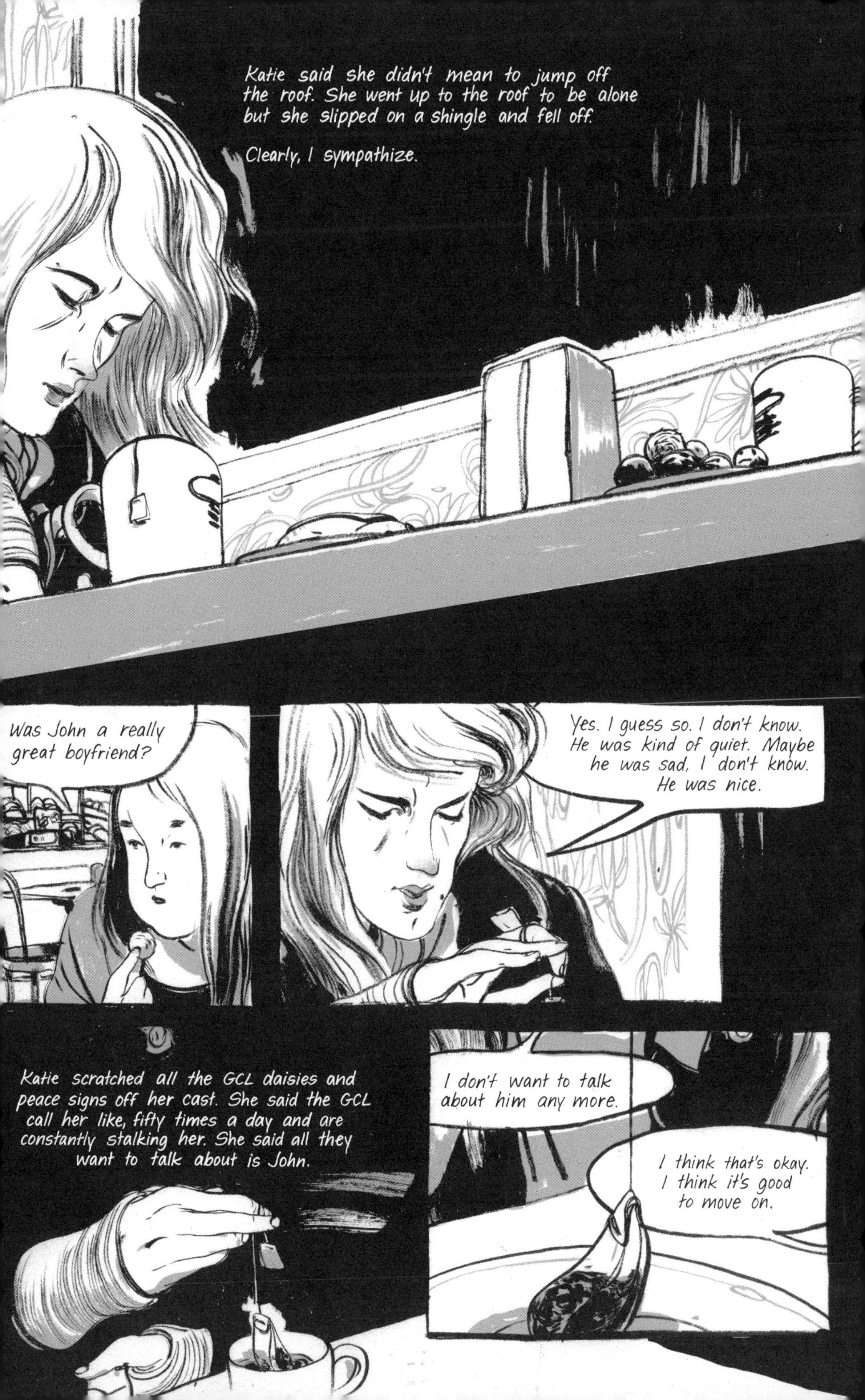
Katie said she didn't mean to jump off the roof. She went up to the roof to be alone but she slipped on a shingle and fell off.
Clearly, I sympathize.
Was John a really great boyfriend?
Yes. I guess so. I don't know. He was kind of quiet. Maybe he was sad, I don't know. He was nice.
Katie scratched all the GCL daisies and peace signs off her cast. She said the GCL call her like, fifty times a day and are constantly stalking her. She said all they want to talk about is John.
I don't want to talk about him any more.
I think that's okay. I think it's good to move on.

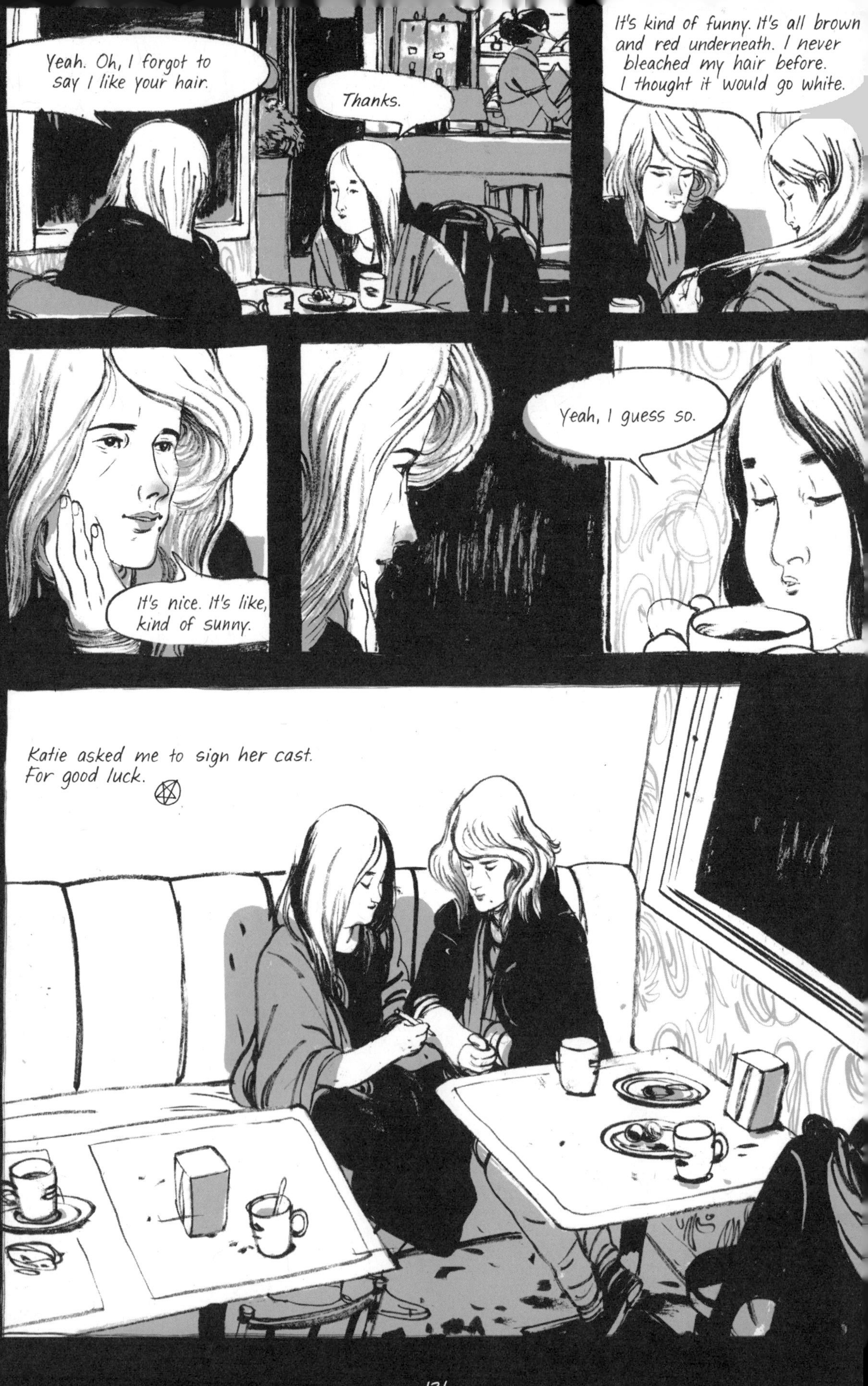
Yeah. Oh, I forgot to say I like your hair.
Thanks.
It's kind of funny. It's all brown and red underneath. I never bleached my hair before. I thought it would go white.
It's nice. It's like, kind of sunny.
Yeah, I guess so.
Katie asked me to sign her cast. For good luck.

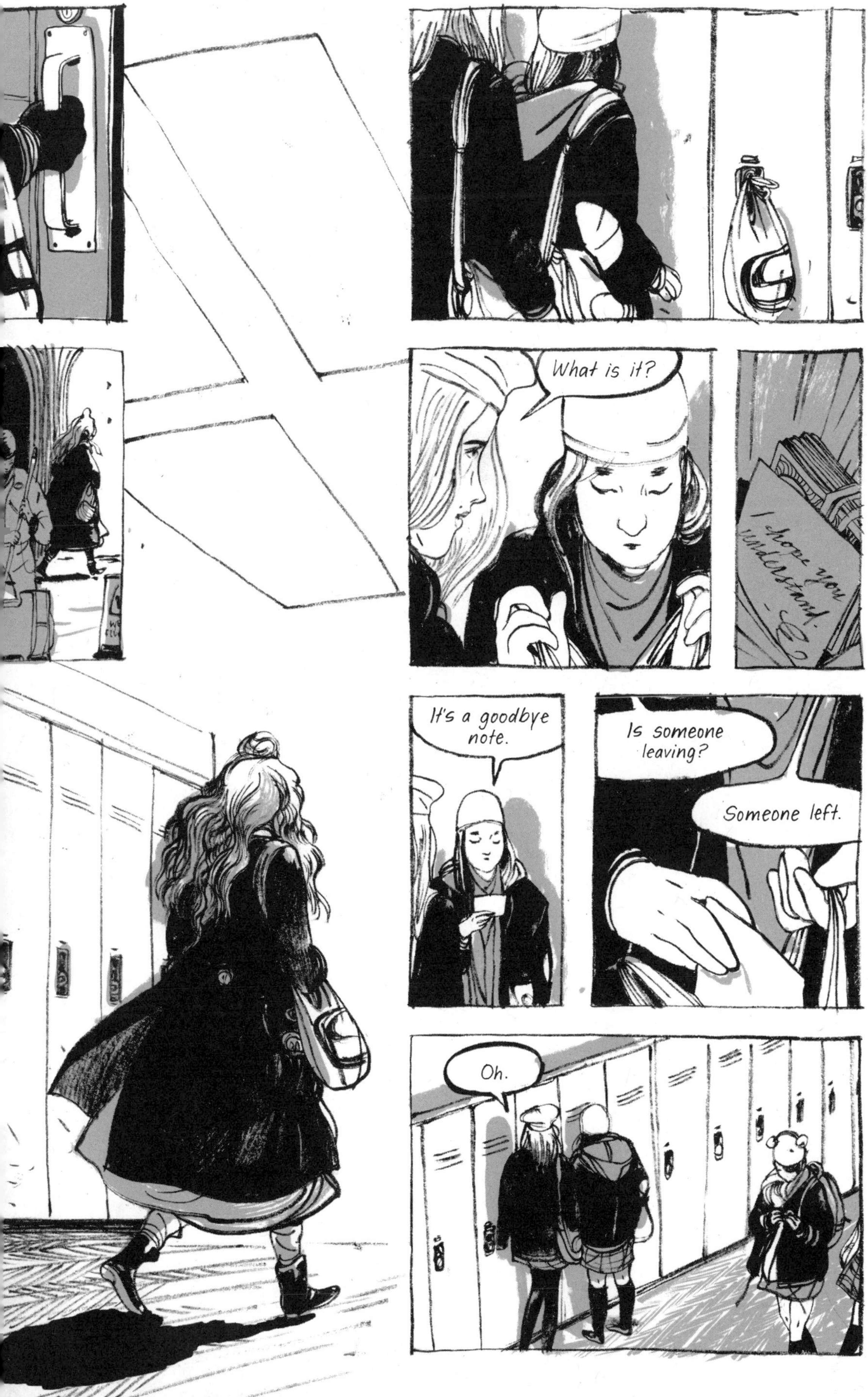
What is it?
I hope you understand.
It's a goodbye note.
Is someone leaving?
Someone left.
Oh.

Dear Diary,

Katie is always over here now. She says my house is much calmer than her house. Katie says her mother is kind of a wreck. My house is practically deserted so I guess it seems calm.

Katie is obsessed with British people and British comedies. After we study we watch Monty Python videos.

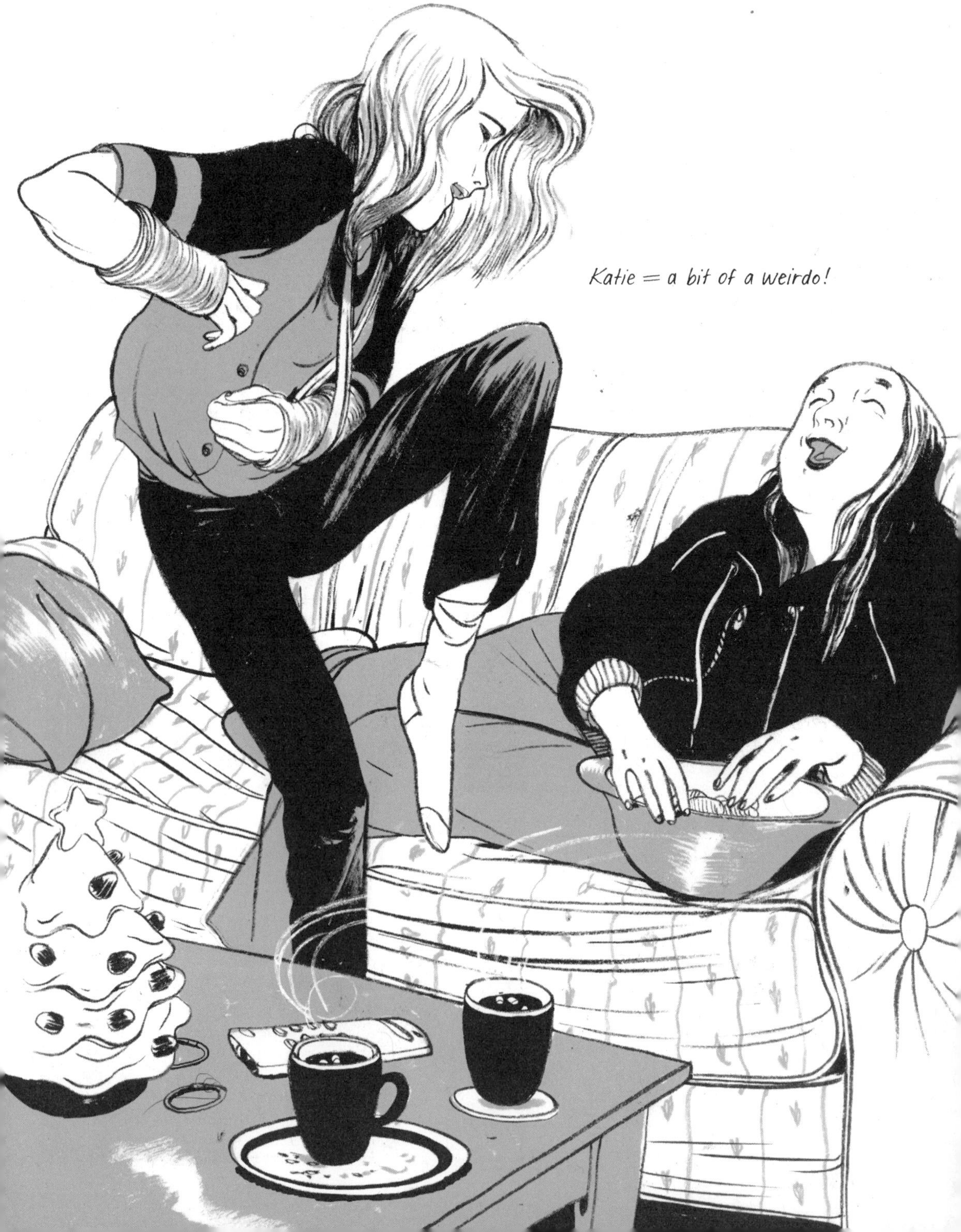
Katie = a bit of a weirdo!

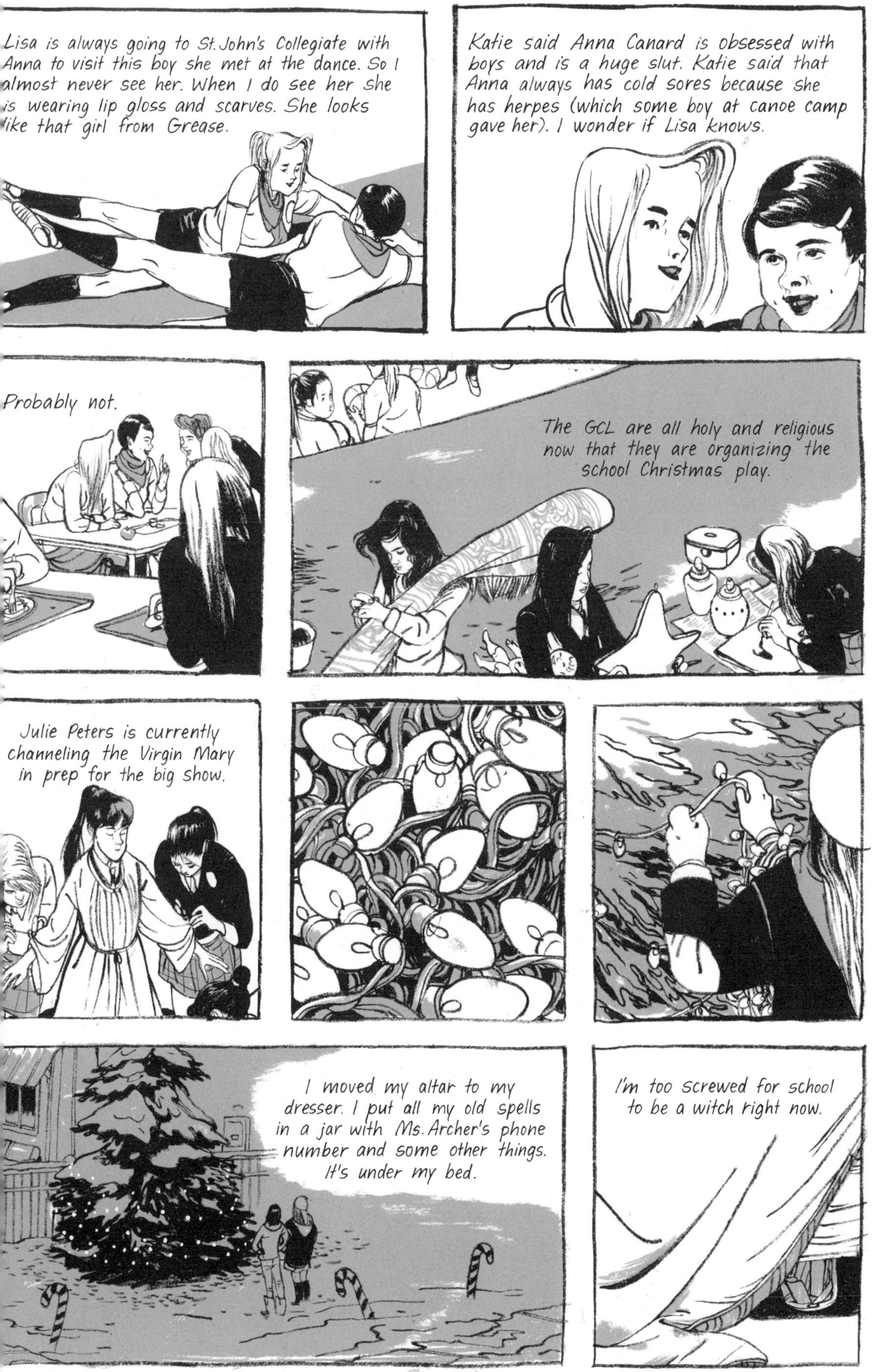
Lisa is always going to St. John's Collegiate with Anna to visit this boy she met at the dance. So I almost never see her. When I do see her she is wearing lip gloss and scarves. She looks like that girl from Grease.
Katie said Anna Canard is obsessed with boys and is a huge slut. Katie said that Anna always has cold sores because she has herpes (which some boy at canoe camp gave her). I wonder if Lisa knows.
Probably not.
The GCL are all holy and religious now that they are organizing the school Christmas play.
Julie Peters is currently channeling the Virgin Mary in prep for the big show.
I moved my altar to my dresser. I put all my old spells in a jar with Ms. Archer's phone number and some other things. It's under my bed.
I'm too screwed for school to be a witch right now.

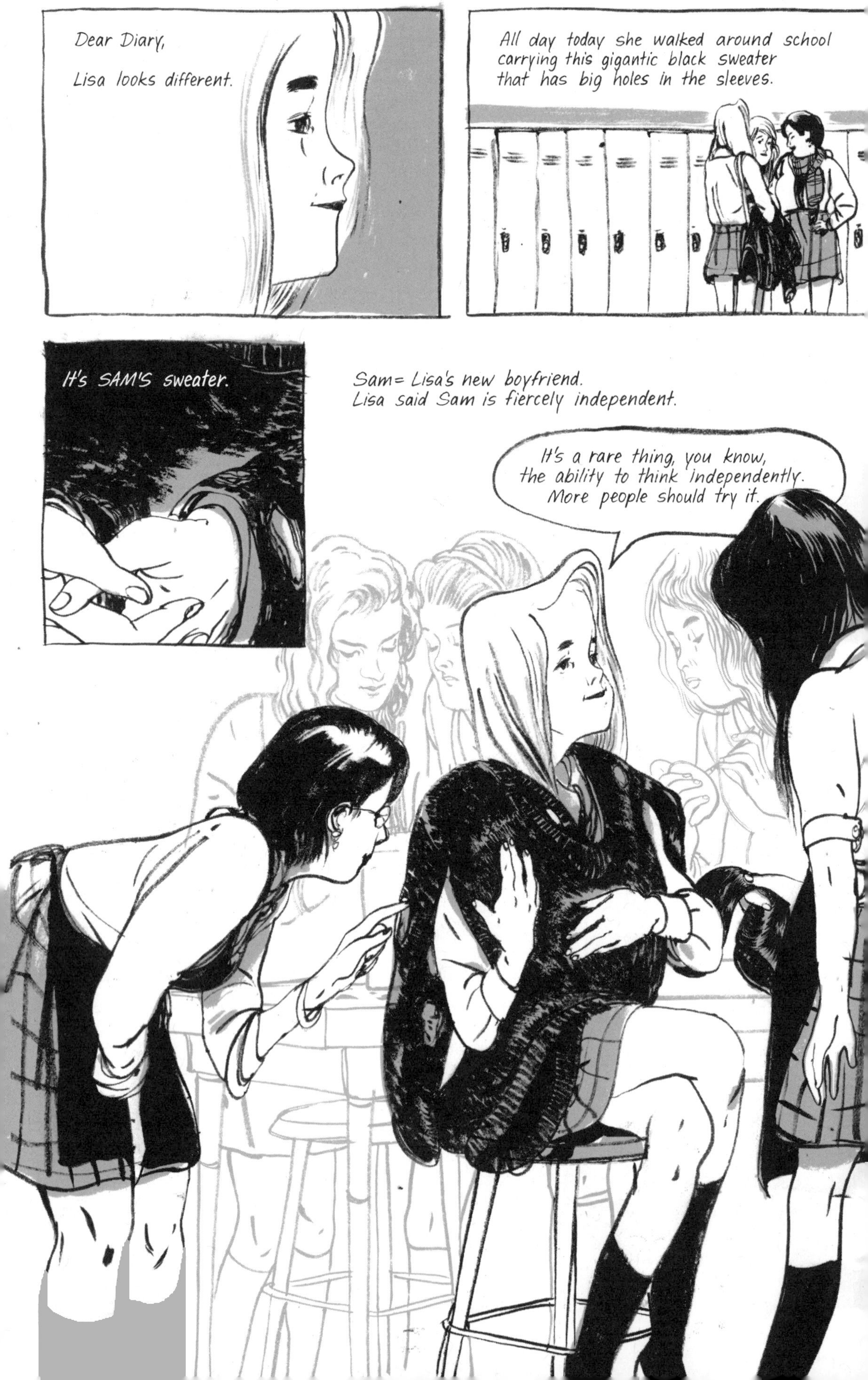

Dear Diary,
Lisa looks different.
All day today she walked around school carrying this gigantic black sweater that has big holes in the sleeves.
It's SAM'S sweater.
Sam= Lisa's new boyfriend. Lisa said Sam is fiercely independent.
It's a rare thing, you know, the ability to think independently. More people should try it.

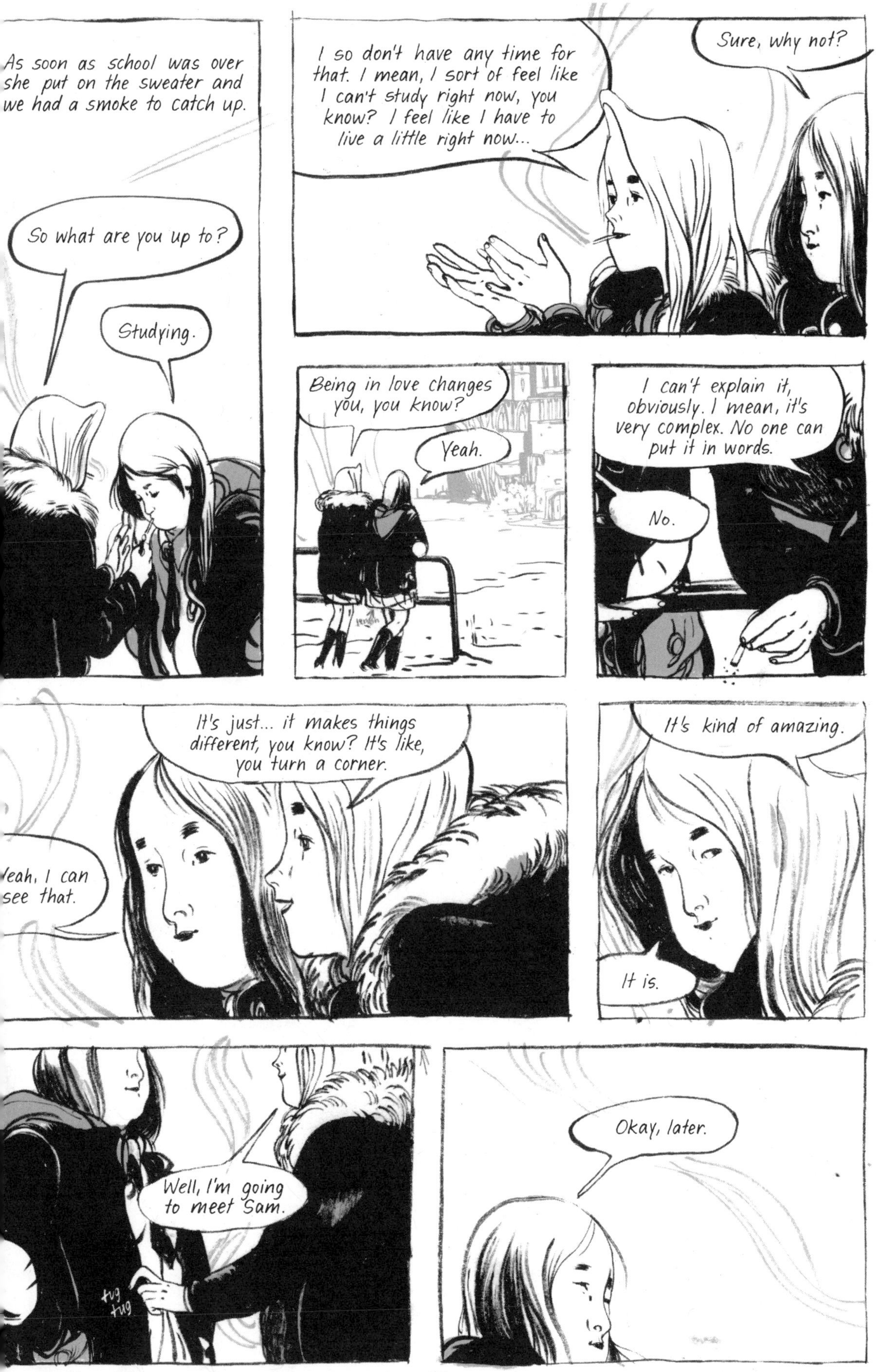

As soon as school was over she put on the sweater and we had a smoke to catch up.
So what are you up to?
Studying.
I so don't have any time for that. I mean, I sort of feel like I can't study right now, you know? I feel like I have to live a little right now...
Sure, why not?
Being in love changes you, you know?
Yeah.
I can't explain it, obviously. I mean, it's very complex. No one can put it in words.
No.
It's just... it makes things different, you know? It's like, you turn a corner.
Yeah, I can see that.
It's kind of amazing.
It is.
Well, I'm going to meet Sam.
tug tug
Okay, later.

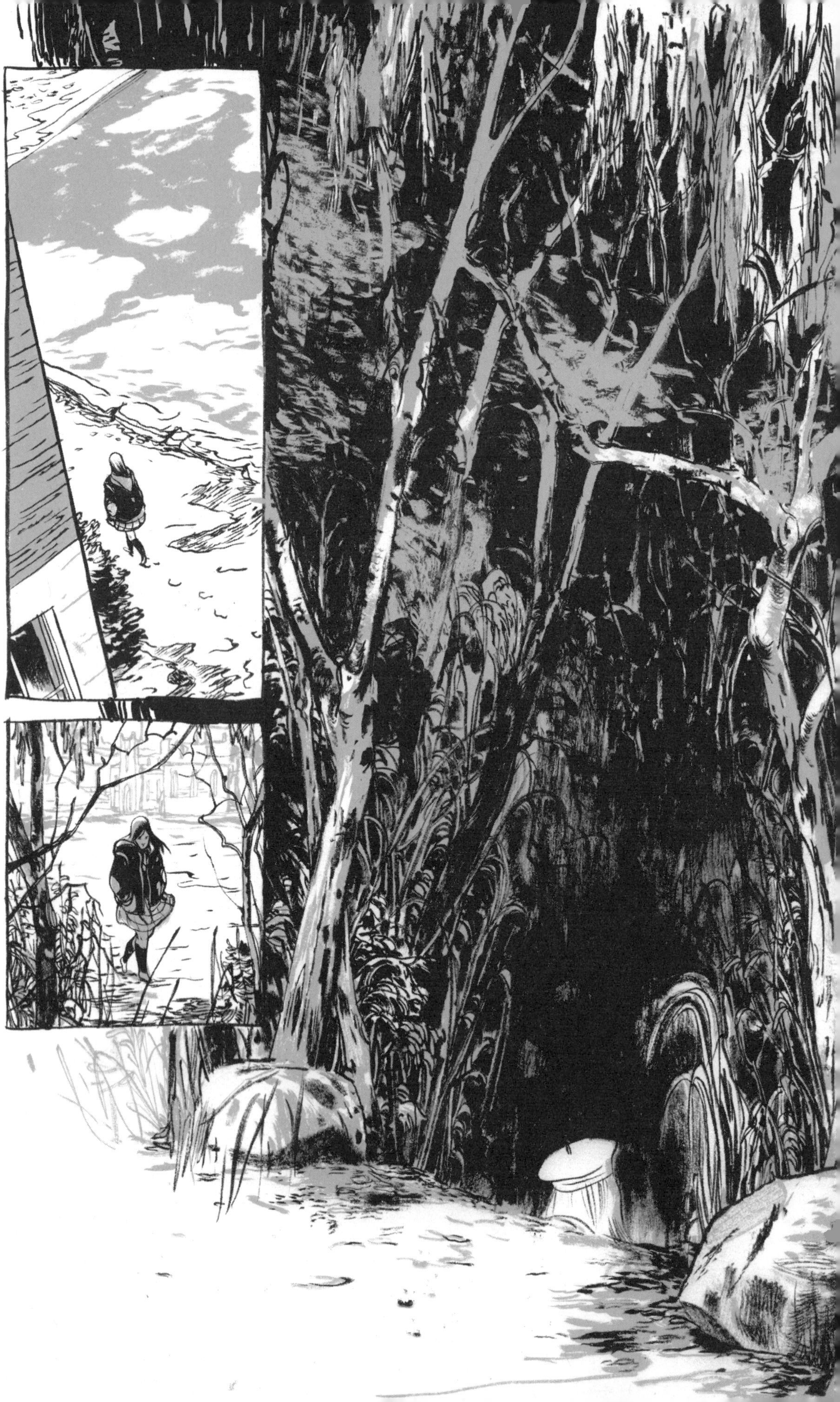

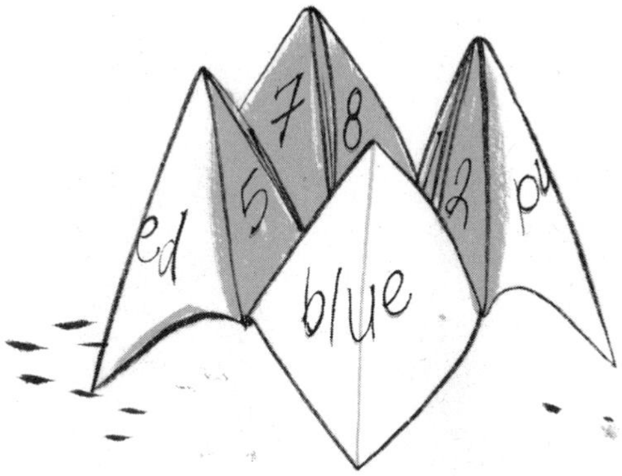
ed
5
7
8
2
pu
blue

ACKNOWLEDGMENTS

Jillian and Mariko thank (in order of appearance): Emily Pohl-Weary (who first published Part I of Skim for the comic series Kiss Machine Presents...), agent extraordinaire Sam Hiyate, and Patsy Aldana, Shelley Tanaka, Michael Solomon and everyone at Groundwood Books for all their support.